SINNER

teddekker.com

DEKKER FANTASY

BOOKS OF HISTORY CHRONICLES

THE LOST BOOKS
Chosen
Infidel
Renegade
Chaos

THE CIRCLE TRILOGY
Black
Red
White

THE PARADISE NOVELS
Showdown
Saint
Sinner

Skin
House (with Frank Peretti)

DEKKER MYSTERY

Blink of an Eye

MARTYR'S SONG SERIES
Heaven's Wager
When Heaven Weeps
Thunder of Heaven
The Martyr's Song

THE CALEB BOOKS
Blessed Child
A Man Called Blessed

DEKKER THRILLER

THR3E
Obsessed
Adam

SINNER

TED DEKKER

THOMAS NELSON
Since 1798

NASHVILLE   DALLAS   MEXICO CITY   RIO DE JANEIRO   BEIJING

Published in Nashville, Tennessee, by Thomas Nelson. Thomas Nelson is a registered trademark of Thomas Nelson, Inc.

Published in association with Thomas Nelson and Creative Trust, 5141 Virginia Way, Suite 320, Brentwood, TN 37027.

Thomas Nelson, Inc., titles may be purchased in bulk for educational, business, fund-raising, or sales promotional use. For information, please e-mail SpecialMarkets@ThomasNelson.com.

Publisher's Note: This novel is a work of fiction. Names, characters, places, and incidents are either products of the author's imagination or used fictitiously. All characters are fictional, and any similarity to people living or dead is purely coincidental.

Library of Congress Cataloging in Publication Data

Dekker, Ted, 1962–
    Sinner / Ted Dekker.
        p. cm.
    ISBN 978-1-59554-008-9
    I. Title.
PS3554.E43S565 2008
813'.54—dc22   2008024223

Printed in the United States of America

08 09 10 11 12 QW 5 4 3 2 1

AUTHOR'S NOTE

I AM often asked about the ideal reading order for the Books of History Chronicles, which include the Circle Trilogy, the Lost Books, and the Paradise Novels. Readers from all walks of life have waxed eloquent on this subject, glad to give a new reader the inside scoop on this somewhat twisted world of books I've coaxed to life.

There is an answer to the question, but it isn't what you might expect. Then again, nothing in the Books of History Chronicles is what you might expect.

I could say that the first books to read should be the Circle Trilogy—*Black, Red,* and *White*—but that isn't entirely right. They are prequels to the whole series, much like Genesis is a prequel to Matthew. Does reading Genesis before Matthew affect your appreciation for either? Not necessarily.

I could say that *Showdown* should be the first book you read, but that isn't right either. *Showdown* is a prequel to *Sinner*, much like Exodus is a prequel to the Gospel of John.

So then where is the beginning? Surely all things have a beginning and an ending. *Just quit running circles and tell me,* you're thinking.

But that's just the point. The Books of History Chronicles are unique because they are circular, not linear. You may make friends with the story at nearly any point and not feel cheated any more than making friends with your future spouse leaves you feeling cheated for not knowing him or her during grade school.

Having said that, there are some books best read in order. Read *Black* before you read *Red* and *White*, because the Circle Trilogy is one story.

Read the Lost Books—*Chosen, Infidel, Renegade,* and *Chaos*—in that order if you can.

It doesn't matter if you read the Paradise Novels (*Showdown, Saint,* and *Sinner*) before or after the Circle Trilogy, but it might be more fun to read *Sinner,* then *Saint,* then *Showdown*—the prequel about how it all began.

Each series in the Books of History Chronicles is a different experience to be engaged either on its own or with the others.

Some may take exception with me because they want everything to line up in perfect order, and that's fine for other series out there. But these are the Books of History Chronicles, and we don't like to follow the crowd here.

We like the mystery of it all. We like piecing the puzzle together. We like to take a big bite out of the middle and then work our way to either end because we get more grease and juice on our chins when we do it that way.

So go ahead, take a bite out of *Sinner,* and then decide which way you want to go. Left to *Saint.* Right to *Showdown,* or all the way around to the Circle Trilogy.

Either way, enjoy.

Ted Dekker, August 2008

I

WORDS OF PERSUASION

The apostle who saw the Light with his own two eyes said this:

I came to you in weakness
and fear, and with much trembling.

My message was not with wise
and persuasive words,
but with
power.

First-century letter written by
Paul to those in Corinth

PROLOGUE

OUR STORY began two thousand years in the future, because the Books of History came into our world from that future.

After they arrived, the Books of History lay in obscurity for many years until a Turkish dealer unwittingly sold the dusty old tomes to David Abraham, a tenured Harvard University professor and collector of antiquities. Upon discovering that the books contained the power to animate the choices of men by turning the written words of innocent children into living, breathing flesh, he swore to preserve the books in a manner consistent with their nature.

Deep in a monastery hidden from all men near a Colorado mountain town called Paradise, Father Abraham and twelve monks vowed their lives to raise thirty-seven orphans, lovingly nurturing them and teaching them all things virtuous. One day these children would use the books for the good of all mankind.

And so was born Project Showdown.

But Billy, the brightest of the students, was lured into the dungeons below the monastery, where he found the Books of History. And there, surrounded by intoxicating power, the thirteen-year-old boy wrote into existence an embodiment of his deepest fears and fantasies. And he called his creation Marsuvees Black.

Fueled by the power of evil spun from Billy's own heart, Marsuvees Black became flesh and entered the small mountain town called Paradise. There, with Marsuvees Black, Billy wreaked terrible havoc and Paradise fell.

The correction of Billy's transgression came at a terrible price, but before everything could be set right again, Marsuvees Black escaped with a book, which he used to spawn more manifestations of evil like himself.

Since that day many years ago, Black's creations have lived among us in fleshly form, determined to learn how to make all men evil as Billy was evil.

But good also came out of Paradise when it fell. Three children used the Books of History to write a great power into themselves. Their names were Johnny, Billy, and Darcy.

For twelve years, thankful only that they had survived the failed project, they forgot about what they had written in the books. But then, unknown to Billy or Darcy, the power revealed itself to Johnny, the Saint, in stunning fashion.

Now Johnny waits in the desert for his time to come, because he knows that Marsuvees Black has not been sleeping. Because he knows that the time is near.

In fact, that time has come.

CHAPTER ZERO

MARSUVEES BLACK reread the words penned on the yellow sheet of paper, intrigued by the knowledge they contained. He felt exposed, almost naked against this sheet of pulp that had come his way.

August 21, 2033

Dear Johnny,

If you're reading this letter, then my attempt to help you has failed and I've gone to meet my Maker. You are likely in hiding, so I can only hope that this letter finds you. Either way, I feel compelled to explain so that you might know my own convictions in the matter that faces us. I will be brief.

None of what's happened to you has been by accident, Johnny. I've always known this, but never with as much clarity as now, after being approached by a woman named Karas, who spoke of the Books of History with more understanding than I can express here. Not even my son, Samuel, knows what I now believe to be the whole truth.

Where to start . . . ?

The world is rushing to the brink of an abyss destined to swallow it whole. Conflict among the United States, Israel, and Iran is escalating at a frightening pace. Europe's repressing our economy. Famine is overrunning Russia, China's rattling its sabers, South America is battling the clobbering disease—all terrible issues, and I could go on.

But these challenges pale in comparison to the damage that pervasive agnosticism will cause us. The disparaging of ultimate truth is a disease worse by far than the Raison Strain.

Listen to me carefully, Johnny. I now believe that all of this was foreseen. That the Books of History came into our world for this day.

As you know, the world changed thirteen years ago when Project Showdown was shut down. I, and a dozen trusted priests, sequestered thirty-six orphans in the monastery in an attempt to raise children who were pure in heart, worthy of the ancient books hidden in the dungeons beneath the monastery. The Books of History, which came to us from another reality, contained the power to make words flesh. Whatever was written on their blank pages became real. If the world only knew what was happening!

Billy used the books to write raw evil into existence in the form of Marsuvees Black, a living, breathing man who now walks this earth, personifying Lucifer himself. He (and I cringe at calling Black anything so humane as a "he") was defeated once, but he hasn't rested since that day. There are others like him, you know that by now. At least four, maybe many more, written by Black himself from several pages he managed to escape with. I believe he's used up the pages, but he's set into motion something that he believes will undo his defeat. Something far more ominous than killers who come to steal and destroy in the dead of night. An insidious evil that walks by day, shaking our hands and offering a comforting smile before ripping our hearts out.

Billy may have repented, but his childish indiscretions will plague the world yet, as much as Adam's indiscretion has plagued the world since the Fall.

Yet all of this was foreseen! In fact, I am convinced that all of these events may have been allowed as part of a larger plan. The Books of History may have spawned raw evil in the form of Black, but those same books also exposed truth. And with that truth, your gifting. Your power!

And Billy's power. And Darcy's power. (Though they may not know of it yet.)

Do you hear me, son? The West teeters on the brink of disbelief and at the same time is infested with the very object of their disbelief. With incarnate evil! Black and the other walking dead.

But there are three who stand in his way. Johnny, Billy, Darcy.

Black is determined to obtain all the books. If he does, God help us all. Even if he fails, he escaped Paradise with a few pages and has wreaked enough havoc to plunge the world into darkness. I am convinced that only the three of you can stop him.

Find Billy. Find Darcy. Stop Black.

And pray, Johnny. Pray for your own soul. Pray for the soul of our world.

David Abraham

Marsuvees frowned. *Yes, pray, Johnny. Pray for your pathetic, wretched soul.*

He crushed the letter in his gloved hand, shoved it into the bucket of gasoline by his side, and ignited the thing with a lighter he'd withdrawn from his pocket after the first reading. Flames whooshed high, enveloping his hand along with the paper.

He could have lit the fire another way, of course, but he'd learned a number of things from his experimentation in the last decade or so. How to blend in. Be human. Humans didn't start fires by snapping their fingers.

He'd learned that subtlety could be a far more effective weapon than some of the more blatant methods they'd tried.

Black dropped the flaming page to the earth and flicked his wrist to extinguish the flame roaring about his hand. He ground the smoldering ash into the dirt with a black, silver-tipped boot and inhaled long through his nostrils.

So, the old man had known a thing or two before dying, enough to unnerve a less informed man than Black. He already knew Johnny and company were the only living souls who stood a chance of slowing him down.

But he was taking care of that. Had taken care of that.

Marsuvees spit into the black ash at his feet. Johnny's receipt of this letter would have changed nothing. It was too late for change now.

And in the end there was faith, hope, and love.

No. In the end there was Johnny, Billy, and Darcy. And the greatest of these was . . .

. . . as clueless as a brick.

CHAPTER ONE

Day One

WEDNESDAY, DAY six of a seven-day jury trial in Atlantic City, New Jersey, May 13, 2034. A thick blanket of smog hung over the city, locking in early summer's heat—ninety-five degrees at 10:05 a.m. and on its way to the forecasted one hundred and five mark, thanks to thirty years of rising global temperatures.

Billy hooked his finger over the tie knot at his collar and tugged it loose, thinking the halls of the courthouse felt like a sauna. What now? City Hall was shutting down its air-conditioning system to appease its guilt over mismanaging energy costs for the last ten years? The casinos suffered no such guilt. The air conditioners in the New Yorker would be blasting cool air, comforting those willing to make donations at its slot machines.

Billy shifted his eyes from the stares of two well-dressed attorneys passing by and headed for the large double doors that opened to Courtroom 1. His stomach turned and he had to force himself to stride on, chin held level. But there was no hiding his disheveled hair, the wrinkles in his white shirt, the hint of red in his eyes from lack of sleep. The three twelve-ounce cans of Rockstar he'd slammed for breakfast a half hour ago were just now kicking in.

He'd won his share of poker hands in the past five years—had a real streak going there last year. But at the moment he was sinking. Free-falling. Screaming in like a kamikaze pilot. Ground zero was in that courtroom and it was coming up fast. It would all end today.

The district attorney's murder case against Anthony Sacks was open and shut. Billy Rediger knew as much because he'd spent six days defending the scumbag with nothing but fast talk and pseudolitigation just to keep the jury from convicting by default.

During pretrial discovery, Billy had seen that any concrete defense was out of the question. The prosecution had an extensive amount of evidence, had subpoenaed numerous character witnesses, and retained a pair of expert witnesses to elaborate on the physical evidence. By the end of exhibition, the jury was laughing up its collective sleeve at Sacks's plea of not guilty. By the time the third witness took the stand, the jury had lost all presumption of innocence, and that was two days ago.

If left to themselves at this point, the jurors would reach a conviction in less time than it took them to reach the deliberation room. All that remained now was cross-examination and closing arguments.

Billy knew more than the court, but not much. And the jury was catching up to the facts:

Sacks was a known midlevel boss in Atlantic City's organized crime world, headed by Ricardo Muness.

Sacks ran the lower-side gambling rackets and had a long history of enforcing loans with extreme prejudice. The kind that left debtors either dead in a landfill or shopping for prosthetic limbs.

Sacks had allegedly murdered a local imam, Mohammed Ilah, for interfering with the gambling trade by speaking out against it to the Muslim community and threatening to expose Sacks personally.

The most relevant fact? Criminal defense attorney Billy Rediger, who owed just over $300,000 to Sacks, had been coerced into his defense by Ricardo Muness, the most notorious crime personality from the boardwalks to the turnpike.

It all made perfect sense to the crime boss. Sacks had loaned Billy far more than Billy could repay. Now both were in the toilet.

Solution: Billy would defend Sacks in his upcoming murder trial. If Billy got Sacks off, he would be absolved of his debt. If not, he would be relieved of his arms.

Sacks had complained bitterly. Billy might be a clever defense attorney, but at twenty-six he was only three years out of law school and already washed up, hamstrung by his addiction to gambling.

Now Sacks's life was in the hands of the man he'd unwisely extended credit to. Poetic justice, Muness had said, boots propped up on his large maple desk, grinning plastic.

A chiseled relief over the courtroom door said it all: *Permissum Justicia Exsisto Servo*, Let Justice Be Served.

Billy took a deep breath, shifted his briefcase from one sweaty palm to the other, nodded at the security guard who was watching him with one eyebrow cocked, and pushed the heavy oak door inward.

A hush fell over the packed room; every head turned, every eye focused. He was a few minutes late to his own funeral; wasn't a man allowed that much? By their reaction, *he* might as well have been on trial.

You are, Billy. You are.

The Honorable Mary Brighton was already seated behind the bench, gavel in hand, as if she *had* just, or *was* just about to issue a ruling. The prosecutor, a thin man with a long nose and sharp cheekbones, stood on the right looking smug, if looking smug was possible for a face fashioned from an ax.

"Forgive me, Your Honor." Billy dipped his head and walked briskly forward. The gallery seated one hundred, and every seat was filled. Media, well-wishers from both sides, and entertainment seekers who followed this sort of thing for a living.

"You are late, Counselor," the judge snapped. "Again."

"I am, and I regret it deeply. From the bottom of my soul. Unavoidable, I'm afraid. I called your office. Did you get my message? I was, shall we say, held up. It won't happen again."

She eyed him with the same gleam that had lit her eyes over the last six days. The Honorable Mary Brighton was known as a hard judge, but Billy thought she might have a soft spot for him. At the very least she found his methods interesting. Not that any of that mattered in this case.

"No, it won't," she said. "I expect we'll wrap up arguments today."

"Yes. I understand, Your Honor." He slipped behind the defendant's table on the left and dipped his head once more.

"This is the last of my leniency with your tardiness, Counselor. I will find you in contempt if it happens again, and I suggest you take me seriously."

"Of course. My sincere apologies, Your Honor."

Anthony Sacks sat to his left, sweating like a pig, true to form. The Greek weighed a good three hundred pounds at six feet tall and was dressed in a black pinstripe suit that failed to hide any of his bulk. He glared past bushy black brows.

"You're late!" he whispered.

"I know." Billy opened the latches to his briefcase, withdrew the Sacks file, a legal pad and pen, then eased into his seat.

"This is ridiculous!"

"I concur," Billy whispered.

"Don't screw this up."

"No, Tony, I won't screw this up."

But Billy wasn't sure he wouldn't screw *this* up. Muness had tossed them a last-minute witness . . . last night. A man who was deposed to testify in court that the victim, Imam Mohammed Ilah, had been murdered by an extremist from his own mosque. Despite the court's rigid adherence to the rules of discovery, Her Honor could allow the defense to produce the witness on the grounds that the witness was inherently material to the case, the testimony was to be given in court rather than in deposition, and the witness had volunteered to undergo vigorous cross-examination. A lucky break. A defense attorney's gift, all things considered.

But the man would be a liar. Had to be a plant. Muness couldn't produce an honest witness any more than he could join the Mormon Tabernacle Choir. His testimony would be perjury, and Billy knew it as well as he knew he still had two arms. Producing a fraudulent witness would get Billy disbarred, and he would do time for subornation of perjury. A legal term from prelaw filtered into the front of his mind: *the miscarriage of justice . . .*

And here it was, right in front of him. The miscarriage of justice.

The judge cleared her throat. "Would you like your breakfast served first, Counselor? Or are you ready to call your next witness?"

Billy stood. "Yes. No, no breakfast, Your Honor. Defense calls Musa bin Salman."

The DA was on his feet. "Objection, Your Honor. The prosecution doesn't have a Musa bin Salman listed. The defense cannot produce a witness without our knowledge unless . . ." The prosecutor, Dean Coulter, looked genuinely surprised, but trailed off. An associate attorney from his team was rifling through some papers.

"Counsel, approach the bench. *Now.*"

Billy got there first. "I sent it over last night, Your Honor. The witness is material to the case, is willing to testify before the court—"

"Please tell me you're not just posturing, Counselor," the judge said. "I am not going to take another deposition, and if you're stalling for time . . ."

"Of course he is," Coulter whispered. "Your Honor—nobody calls a material witness in the eleventh hour. We have subpoenaed every possible witness of every kind, and he just *now* finds a shake-and-bake testimony?"

"No, Your Honor. I can promise a court testimony without deposition. I believe Mr. Bin Salman is materially relevant to this trial. The prosecution is perfectly free to cross-examine him." He looked sideways at the DA, swallowed, then continued. "Discovery shouldn't preclude a material witness."

The judge nodded. "I'll allow the witness."

"His testimony will be inadmissible," the DA said. "This is unprecedented."

"Take your seats, Counsel. Both of you. Now."

Billy held his head level out, but his heart fell into his stomach. He took his seat next to Sacks and pretended to scribble some notes. He had gone out on a limb with his law license in hand, and he would most likely end the week with neither limb nor hand.

Miscarriage of justice was an understatement.

The door opened and the bailiff escorted a gray-suited man with a beard and slicked black hair to the stand.

"Please state your name for the record." He did. Musa put his hand on a copy of the United States Constitution. "Do you swear to tell the truth, the whole truth, and nothing but the truth?"

"I do."

"Please be seated."

"Your witness," Her Honor said.

Billy strolled to the podium and sized up the man on the stand for the first time. Clean-cut. Intelligent looking. A kind face, if a bit sharp. One of the millions of foreigners who'd taken up residence in this country and saved it from bankruptcy when the government's trade policies had softened a dozen years ago.

The country's socioreligious complexion had steadily changed since. So-called religious tolerance had made by far the largest gains in the West; the number of Muslims had grown to match the number of Christians. None of this mattered to Billy, but it might make for some fireworks during cross-examination, if the DA would take any bait.

"Thank you for joining us, Mr. Bin Salman. Can you tell the court what you do for a living?"

"I'm a student at the new Center for Islamic Studies."

"I see. So you are a religious man?"

"Yes."

Amazing how those words brought a deeper silence to the courtroom. Everyone was aware of religious people, saw them all the time, talked to them at work, watched sporting events with them. But for one to actually discuss a religious affiliation was frowned upon in the name of tolerance. The new cultural taboo.

"And what is your religion?"

"Islam. I am a Muslim."

The DA stood. "Objection. I don't see what a man's personal faith has to do with his testimony."

"Understood." Judge Brighton turned. "Exactly what is your point, Counselor?"

"Defense wishes to establish the relevance of the witness to alternate motives for murdering an Islamic cleric, Your Honor," Billy said. He didn't wait for her to overrule the objection and got back into questioning. Momentum was often the most critical element of persuasive litigation. He turned to the witness. "Have you ever met my client, Anthony Sacks, before today?"

"No."

"What about the victim, Imam Mohammed Ilah?" Billy hefted an enlarged photograph of the victim.

"Yes. I knew him."

"When did you meet him?"

"I met with him frequently, both as a student and at the mosque. We knew each other by name."

Billy knew where all of this was headed, of course. It made him cringe, but he pushed on, shoving aside his own objections. He shoved a hand into his pocket and slowly crossed to the jury box, eyeing each member in turn.

"How would you describe your relationship with the imam?"

"We were friends."

Alice Springs, third juror from the left, second row, doubted the witness. Billy had a knack for reading people, whether in a poker game or in a courtroom.

Billy kept his eyes on Alice. "So there was no . . . disparity between your beliefs and his teaching?"

"No."

"You both believed in tolerance?"

"Yes."

A breath from Alice signaled her acceptance of this fact, at least for the moment.

Billy put his other hand into his front pocket and faced the witness. "Musa bin Salman, do you find my client distasteful?"

Silence.

"Just be truthful. That's why we're here, to get to the truth. Do you find Anthony Sacks as disgusting a human being as I do?"

"Objection, leading the witness . . ."

Billy held up a hand. "Quite right, let me be more clear. Ignoring the fact that I think my client is a piece of human waste and should probably fry for a thousand offenses, none of which I am privy to, what is your opinion of him?"

"Your Honor, I must protest this line of argument. The witness just stated that he's never met the defendant."

"Clarification of motive, Your Honor," Billy said.

"Answer the question."

Musa looked at Sacks. "I've heard that he's a distasteful man."

"So you have no motivation to try to protect him?"

"As I said, he is a distasteful man."

"Just answer the question," Billy pushed. "Do you have any reason to protect the defendant, Anthony Sacks?"

"No."

"Good." He strolled in front of the jury, watching their eyes. Truth was always in the eyes. Not windows to the souls. Windows to a person's thoughts. At the moment, most of them were a bit lost. That would change now.

"And do you believe that Anthony Sacks murdered Mohammed Ilah as the state has accused?"

"No."

"No? You're a religious man who finds the accused distasteful, and you're presumably outraged by the murder of your friend, the imam. Yet you wouldn't want the murder pinned on this monstrous—my defendant? Why?"

"Because he didn't kill the imam."

The courtroom stilled.

"You're sure about this?"

"Yes."

"Can you tell the court why you are so sure?"

"Because I know who did kill Imam Mohammed Ilah."

The room erupted in protests and gasps, all quickly brought to an end by the judge's gavel.

"Order! Counselor, I hope you know how thin the ice beneath your feet is. I will not hear tertiary allegations—"

"He has material knowledge, Your Honor," Billy said.

"The first hint that this is a red herring and I'll have you thrown from my courtroom."

"I understand."

"Continue."

Billy pulled his hands from his pockets and walked back to the podium. He looked into the man's brown eyes. "Will you please tell the court how you came into this knowledge."

You're going to lose your arms.

The man hadn't said it, of course. Billy was thinking this himself, because although he had within his grasp the tools to free his client and save his arms, he wasn't sure he could wield those tools, knowing what he did.

Knowing that the witness was lying through his teeth, even now.

". . . the extremists last Thursday night. Seven of them."

"And what did they say?"

"That tolerance was the greatest evil in the West. That any Muslim who was afraid to stand up for the truth and convert the West was no Muslim at all, but a pretender who is worthy of death."

"Go on."

That Muness has won this case, not you. Therefore he will expect payment in full from you.

"That the imam Mohammed Ilah, in his stand for tolerance toward

Christianity and others' disbelief in God, is a stench in God's nostrils. For this reason they killed him."

Billy heard it all like a distant recording, exactly what he'd expected. And there was more to come, enough to cast doubt in any reasonable juror's mind.

But his mind was on none of it. His mind was distracted by what he was seeing in the witness's brown eyes. On what they'd said to him.

Muness has won this case, not you. Therefore he will expect payment in full from you.

Intuition was one thing, but this . . .

He stared at Salman, unable to take his eyes off the man's face. There was more there. Whispering to him. *Both arms. The punishment for stealing.*

"Counselor?"

Billy snapped out of his lapse. "Sorry." He stepped from behind the podium and regarded the judge. "I have no intention of bringing evidence that will incriminate another party, Your Honor . . ."

A thin hum erupted at the base of his skull, like a miniature buzz saw or a tiny Cox engine firing away at a million revolutions per minute. *Buzzzzzzzzzzzzzzz.*

The faint sound spread up through his head, tingling his ears as it passed. He could feel it on his skin, inside his skin, in his brain, in his eyes. Like a thousand gnats had been let in and were exploring their new home.

His eyes stared into the judge's. *Look at you, boy. Such a bright mind being wasted.*

". . . ummm . . ." he said. Had he just heard her say that? "But I do need to finish up . . ."

Billy had lost his train of thought. He wasn't sure what he was trying to say, so he just stopped.

"This whole line of questioning is outrageous!" the DA was protesting. "I object. Vigorously."

"Noted. Let's move on. Counselor?"

But Billy was staring at the witness and hearing that voice in the back of his mind again. *Just ask it, you fool. I will say it all as agreed.*

The hum in his mind faded to a distant distraction.

Ask, ask, ask!

It occurred to Billy then, staring in Musa bin Salman's eyes, that he really was picking up the man's thoughts. Hearing them, so to speak. And as stunning as this revelation was, another one was as disturbing. Namely, what the voice behind those eyes was telling him.

He was going to lose both arms. Even if he did get the Sacks of garbage off the hook. In fact, as *soon* as he got the Sacks of garbage off.

"No more questions," he said, turning, legs numb. "Your witness."

The courtroom seemed to stop breathing. He'd led them up to the edge of an acquittal and then stepped back.

A point that wasn't lost on Anthony Sacks. "What?"

Billy glanced at the man. A string of profanity flooded his mind. The contents of Tony's mind. Billy's fingertips tingled. His lungs were working harder than they should to keep his blood supplied with oxygen. The room was feeling like a sauna again.

He hurried to his table, reached for the bottle of water, and sat hard. Then he was drinking and the prosecutor was crossing to the witness, and Billy was sure that they were all staring at him.

He had just lost his mind.

CHAPTER TWO

Wednesday

THE DAY the world changed for Darcy Lange of Lewiston, Pennsylvania, was like any other day at the Hyundai assembly plant except for one bothersome detail. Today she would suffer through yet one more annual review, her seventh to be exact, return to her workstation overlooking twenty of the assembly robots, and go home a dollar or so an hour richer than when she started the day.

Honestly, she couldn't care less about the annual raise and would have gladly forgone the money if doing so meant she didn't have to endure the tedious review.

Nevertheless, here she sat, facing the slob who spilled out of his white shirt and the flat-chested rail who peered at Darcy over pencil-thin spectacles. Robert Hamblin and Ethil Ridge. Her managers, although they did nothing of the sort. She had run her station perfectly fine for the last five years without so much as a weekly nod from these two or the four sets of managers who'd preceded them.

Darcy liked it that way.

"So, you've done well," Robert said. His dark hair was shaved on either side of his head, a military cut that hardened his square face. Darcy could never quite get used to the way his upper lip came to a slight point at the center, under a sharp nose. She caught herself wondering if the vertical trough that ran between his pointed lip and his nose wasn't there by evolution's design. A facial drain for mucus were it to leak from either nostril.

"You've done your tasks as ordered," Ethil said.

Well said, Pinocchio.

Robert frowned and set the ream of production reports on the desk. He clasped his hands together, elbows bridging the papers.

"The company is changing, Ms. Lange. Progress eventually catches up to all of us. Unfortunately, today it's caught up to you as well."

They both held her in their stares, expecting a response. So she gave them one. "And?"

"And . . . we've decided that your lack of forward progression is an indication of a poor attitude. A tendency toward reclusiveness that demonstrates passivity to coworkers."

Darcy knew what he was trying to say, but the slight wag of his head as he leveled each word was enough to drive a needle into her skull. She had to clench her jaw to keep from objecting.

"Meaning?"

"Meaning," said Ethil, "that the company's needs have changed. We no longer merely need proficient workers in positions such as yours. We need employees who are both proficient and exude an enthusiasm for the workplace."

Robert took the ball. "Research tells Hyundai that the degree of enthusiasm in the workplace directly influences proficiency and turnover."

"Enthusiasm," Darcy repeated.

"Enthusiasm," Ethil said.

"You're saying you want me to punch the start button with more gusto, then," Darcy said. "Maybe use my whole fist instead of one measly finger, for example."

Robert's bottom lip twitched.

"You want me to lean forward while I watch the robots. It's not enough to make sure every weld looks right. I must make sure with a banana grin plastered on my face, is that it? Okay, sure, I get it. I'll do that. Is that all?"

"Actually, no. This is exactly the kind of misplaced enthusiasm we're talking about."

"So now you're saying I *do* have enthusiasm, but not about the right things? Things like the green buttons on high-efficiency automated assembly machines?"

"Please, Darcy. You're not making this easy."

"I wasn't aware I was supposed to make this easy for you."

"I think he meant easy for you," Ethil said. "Your hostility proves your lack of enthusiasm. Wouldn't you at least agree to that?"

Darcy sat back and crossed her legs. She wore jeans and a light sweater, as she often did. The plant was an icebox, comfortable for most maybe, but freezing for those without layers of fat to keep them warm. At the moment, however, she was sweating.

She crossed her arms, decided that her posture might come off as hostile, and set her hands on her lap. She couldn't deny that they had her pegged. Everyone knew that Darcy would just as soon be left alone to her task, keeping a watchful eye on the robotic arms as they flipped and turned and welded the automobiles on the assembly line. She'd take music or an audiobook over another person in her glass booth any day.

"I'm comfortable with myself," she said.

"Well, that's not good enough anymore," Ethil said. "You're not the nineteen-year-old girl we hired to work on the line seven years ago. You sit above the floor for the whole floor to see. We need leaders to lead by example. I'm afraid we need a change."

It wasn't until Ethil smugly uttered the last word that Darcy believed they were actually setting her up to be fired. The realization froze her solid.

She'd never even been reprimanded. Never a day late. Only three operating errors at her station in five years. She had the best record on a high-efficiency automated assembly machine in the company.

And they were going to dismiss her?

A buzz burst from the base of her neck and swarmed her mind. For a brief moment she wondered if she was suffering a stroke or something. But then she wrote off the swelling hum in her head to a panic attack. It had been awhile, but she'd had a few since her release from the monastery when she was thirteen.

"I can lead by example," she snapped. "Why sit? I'll stand up in my glass booth, pounding buttons like a drummer in a marching band. Is that what you need? Anything for the company."

"What did I tell you? Hopeless," Ethil muttered, turning away.

"No, Darcy, I'm afraid that won't do. We're going to replace you at the controls. This isn't a demotion per se. You'll still get the same wage, but we think you'd fit in better on the line among the others."

The buzz in her head grew angry. The very idea of being put back on the line was enough to send her packing immediately. She'd fought hard for the relative isolation provided by the control booth, for good reason.

"You might as well fire me," Darcy snapped, staring directly into the man's eyes.

Robert blinked. Sat back, eyes narrowed. He exchanged a glance with Ethil.

"No, no, that's not what this is about," Ethil said. "Don't think for a moment that you'll be able to run off to an attorney and file a claim for unlawful termination."

"Actually . . ." Robert looked slightly confused. "She might have a point."

Darcy felt her self-control slipping. "This is ridiculous!" she cried, leaning forward. "You have no right to demote me, and don't think that's not exactly what this is. I don't care what you say!"

She pointed at the wall to her right without removing her eyes from them. "Nobody is better suited for the control booth than I am! *Nobody!*

I like it, it likes me. We do a near perfect job together. You're idiots to think anyone would do better just because they walk around grinning like a monkey!"

Robert's jaw parted slightly. He looked like she'd slapped him in the face. Ethil stared, eyes round. Neither looked like they could quite believe she'd been so frank.

"I dare you." Darcy stood, trembling. "Tell me here and now that you have someone who could do a better job."

Neither spoke.

"You can't! Because you don't, isn't that right?"

"That's right," Robert said.

"You bet your fat—"

Darcy stopped. He'd agreed? She continued with slightly less force.

"—wallet that's right."

"Yes, you are right about that," Ethil said.

"You would be *crazy* to fire me."

"We would," Robert said. "And we didn't say we were going to fire you. In fact, we specifically said we *weren't* going to fire you."

"Or demote me. It's the same thing."

Ethil shook her head. "You're not listening to us. We aren't demoting you, we specifically—"

"I know you said that, but I'm telling you it's the same to me. You can't put me back on the line!" She walked to her right and spun back. "The line and I aren't friends. Do you hear me? You can't do that to me."

Robert looked at Ethil. For a moment Darcy thought he was actually reconsidering. But it wasn't Robert who changed the tone.

"She's right," Ethil said, walking behind Robert, eyes shifting to Darcy. "We can't put her on the line. It would be tantamount to firing her. The lawyers would have a field day."

A barely perceptible nod from Robert. "They would."

She had no intention of hiring a lawyer, but if the threat helped her position, let them tremble in their boots.

"I can't believe you actually threatened to do this to me," she snapped. "If you had any sense at all, you'd be offering me a raise rather than tearing down your most productive operator. Excellence needs to be rewarded, not chastised."

"She does have a point," Robert said. "And we were considering that."

"We were." Ethil took her seat, folded one leg over the other, and looked into Darcy's eyes. "How much?"

"Excuse me?"

"How much of a raise do you think you deserve?"

Darcy felt her blood rush through her face with renewed anger. They were mocking her. Maybe an attorney wouldn't be such a bad idea after all.

"You guys don't know how to quit, do you?" she snapped. "I'm worth twice what you pay me!"

"Double?" Robert said. "That's a lot of money for an automated assembly machine operator."

"And that's another thing. Titles don't mean squat. Call me whatever you want, but don't try to cover up an unlawful termination by throwing around titles. Let me do the job I do well and leave it at that."

The room went quiet. Both of them looked at her as if she'd lost her mind.

"A new title," Robert said. "Makes sense."

"She's earned it, after all."

"Assembly machines supervisor. Joseph mentioned the idea once."

Ethil frowned. "I think it could work."

"And we passed her by at the five-year mark. She's due."

They fell silent.

Darcy wasn't sure what was happening or why, but it occurred to her that they weren't mocking her as she'd assumed. They had actually seen some sense in her comments.

"You're serious?"

Ethil forced a grin. "Should we be?"

"Yes. Of course you should be."

The grin softened. "There you are, then."

"Congratulations," Robert said. "We've just doubled your salary and given you a new title. Assembly machines supervisor."

CHAPTER THREE

BILLY REDIGER knew a few things with particular clarity as he sat and focused on the papers spread across the defendant's table.

He'd just committed an unpardonable sin by walking away from a defense that undoubtedly would have improved his client's fate.

He'd done so because he'd also come into certain and disturbing information about his own fate, namely that he was about to lose both arms for failing to come through on his own, with or without this witness, whom Muness so conveniently dropped in his lap at the last moment.

And he'd come into such disturbing information by . . .

This was where everything became a bit trickier. Unnerving. Troubling on its own face, wholly apart from the prospect of amputation.

He'd gained it by hearing, as clear as day, the thoughts of Musa bin Salman, who seemed to have no doubts as to the accuracy of said information.

Furthermore, Billy had heard the judge's thoughts. *Such a bright mind being wasted.*

The prosecutor had risen and was subjecting the witness to a brutal cross-examination that all but associated the man with maggots worming though week-old garbage. But Billy wasn't listening.

He was busy avoiding his client's glare. And plotting his next move, which would directly involve said client.

Tony's hot breath filled his ear. "You get your useless butt back up there and ask what you were told to ask. I go down for this and you'll spend the rest of your life in a wheelchair. You hear me?"

Billy looked in the man's eyes and heard it all, again, this time with more detail than he needed. A flood of thoughts rushed him, some abstract, some very clear. Like the one involving chainsaws and machetes and his legs.

"I do." He shifted his sight from the man and the thoughts were silenced.

The sounds of the courtroom faded completely, this time because Billy's consciousness was thoroughly focused on the phenomenon afflicting him.

So it was real? He was actually hearing the thoughts of whomever he made eye contact with? An image of the monastery he'd grown up in flashed through his mind. Was it possible?

Marsuvees Black.

Sweat seeped from his pores. He shut the name out of his thoughts and opened his eyes.

"So what you're telling us," the prosecutor was saying, "is that you didn't actually see any of this with your own eyes."

"No, but—"

"That however compelled you were by what you *think* you heard, all you really know is hearsay. Isn't that right? Sir?"

The prosecutor was leading the witness while arguing his case. There were several clear objections Billy could have voiced and had upheld by the judge, but a new thought was drowning out the usefulness of continuing with Musa bin Salman.

"No. That is not what I said."

"Thank you, no further questions."

Dean Coulter took a seat, picked up a pen, and began tapping his notepad, eyes dead ahead. He'd stemmed the tide for the moment, but Billy could blow it all open easily enough with a redirect.

The judge looked at Billy. *I don't know what trick you think you're pulling, but honestly, I can't wait to hear this one.*

"Counselor?" she said

Billy remained seated. "No further questions."

Anthony Sacks clambered to his feet. "I object!"

"Sit down!" the judge snapped.

The defendant glared from the judge to Billy, then slowly sat.

"One more outburst like that and I'll have you removed. There's a reason why we have order in a court, Mr. Sacks. Your counsel speaks for your defense. Unless you have an entire legal firm in your back pocket, don't sabotage your own case."

The man muttered a curse under his breath.

"The witness is excused."

Musa stood, having been refused his chance to spill the lies he was either being forced or paid to tell. Billy wondered how long the man had to live. Muness would be fuming already.

"Any more witnesses?"

Billy leaned over to Sacks. "You go along with me here or you spend the rest of your natural life in prison. *Capisce?*"

Without waiting for a response, he stood and stepped behind the podium, knowing that what he was about to do would change his life forever. But as he saw it, he had no good alternatives.

He pushed his sweating hands into his pockets. "Your Honor, I would like to call the defendant, Anthony Sacks, to the stand to testify on his own behalf."

The barely audible gasp behind him betrayed his client's surprise. Billy turned, drilled him with a stare, and winked.

All he got from the man was a mental flood of obscenities, so he cut it off by glancing at the jury. Their thoughts came to him quickly and with amazing clarity as he scanned their eyes.

He's trying to sabotage his own client?

What if the towel-head was on to something?

Flat out guilty, doesn't matter what anybody says at this point.

I'm going to ask Nancy for her hand in marriage and she's going to agree. Just because her friends have put the fear of God in her doesn't mean she's stopped loving me.

Reddish-brown hair, green eyes, the cutest face . . . Gasp, he's looking at me! Man, he's sexy.

That last thought from Candice, juror number nine, a forty-nine-year-old banker who'd gone out of her way to tell him that she tended bar at the New Yorker on weekends for extra money.

"I'll allow the witness," Judge Brighton said. "Mr. Sacks, you have been called. Please take the stand."

Sacks did, trying his best to put on a good face, but it was red and hid none of his agitation. He stated his name and was sworn in.

"Proceed."

Billy lifted his eyes to the jury and fired off his first question to Sacks. "Anthony Sacks, I want you to state clearly for the court your true beliefs in this case. Are you guilty of murder as charged, or are you innocent?"

A quick look at the man settled the matter for Billy. *I cut the rat's throat, and you know that, you fool.*

"Innocent. Totally, completely innocent."

But Billy was more interested in the jury's reaction.

Guilty.

Guilty.

This guy was born guilty.

Only three had any doubts at all, that Billy could tell. So, as of now he had only one objective. He left the podium and casually approached the witness stand, hands still in his pockets.

"Innocent," he said, careful to prevent his eyes from making contact with anyone for the moment. "Mr. Sacks, do you consider yourself an upstanding citizen?"

"Yes."

But the man was fuming inside, spewing filth.

"A family man?"

"Of course."

"Of course," Billy repeated. "Do you find this charge of murder offensive?"

"Deeply."

"How many daughters do you have?"

"Three."

"And sons?"

Anthony hesitated. "None."

"None? Did you ever want a son?"

"Yes. My . . . we lost one at childbirth."

"I'm sorry."

Billy ran through the questions staring at the man's forehead rather than his eyes.

"What do you know, the monster's got a soft spot in his heart for the son he always wanted."

The prosecutor stood. "Objection, Your Honor. This grandstanding is a transparent attempt to illicit sympathy. It has no bearing on the facts of the case."

"I'm establishing character as allowed," Billy said, withdrawing his hands from his pockets.

The judge dipped her head. "Don't belabor character that has no relation to the charges. Insults constitute contempt, Counselor. I suggest you weigh your words. Continue."

"Thank you." To the accused, looking at the wall over the man's shoulder: "I'm going to run down a series of questions, and I want you to answer them as quickly and as frankly as you can, okay?"

"Okay."

"What is your age?"

"Forty-nine."

"What is your height?"

"Six foot."

"How much do you weigh?"

"Two hundred ten."

"Good. Are you on a diet?"

"Depends who you ask."

"I'm asking you."

"Then no. I always eat healthy."

"You never indulge?"

"Not lately, no."

Billy glanced at him. Evidently Sacks considered Double Stuf Oreo cookies healthy, because they were filling his mind at the moment.

"Waist size?"

"Forty-two."

"Shoe size?"

"Fourteen."

Another plea from the prosecution. "Please, Your Honor."

"Hurry it up, Counselor," the judge warned.

"Do you ever cheat on your wife, Anthony?"

"No."

Billy didn't bother looking.

"Cheat on your taxes?"

"No."

"Never? Not even a little bit? Fail to report that tip money you receive at the tables now and then?"

"Never."

Wrong answer, Billy thought. The man had just thrown out his credibility.

"Good." Billy looked at his client. "Tell the court how much money you reported on your return last year. Roughly."

Sacks looked at the judge.

"Answer the question."

"A hundred ninety thousand."

"And that was all the income that passed through your hands from all sources? No more cash?"

Now the numbers started to come, streaming into Billy's mind as if fired from a machine gun.

Seven million, cash, gambling only.

Twenty-nine million if you count the trades.

The gravy though, only two million five.

What the heck is he doing?

"Cash? Less cash actually. That was my total income."

"Have you ever had the opportunity to steal, Mr. Sacks?"

He stared the man down and let the answers flow.

I make my living stealing. If they only knew how much I skimmed . . .

"Sure."

"And have you ever stolen from your employer?"

Of course. Everyone steals.

Billy pushed on before the man could answer. "Let me rephrase the question. How much did you steal from your employer?"

Which time? Half a mil. What are you doing? The man's right cheek twitched.

Billy rescued him. "I realize this line of questioning seems strange. I mean, I'm your attorney, right? I have no business even bringing up the possibility that you might steal money from your employer. But I do because I know what you know, Mr. Sacks. That you wouldn't dare steal from your employer. Isn't that right?"

"Objection, leading the witness."

None of what Billy was saying could mean anything, and that was part of the point. He had to get Sacks off his center quickly, before the judge stepped in.

Billy held up his hand to accept the objection. "My point is, Mr. Sacks is a family man who has his daughters' well-being on his mind. Even if he did steal a dime here or a dime there, he wouldn't dare confess it here, in court, any more than he would tell us where he put that dime. Or if he still had that dime." He paused. "Or how to get to that dime. The account numbers . . ." Another pause. "The PIN numbers . . ."

Billy let the numbers flow into his mind.

". . . all of it buried in his mind. It'll go with him to his grave."

"Counselor! " Now the judge was beyond herself. "Approach the bench."

"I'm coming in for a landing, Your Honor. I promise, I have a point. Please don't stop this midstream."

Billy took the courtroom's absolute silence as an invitation to proceed, and he did so quickly, spinning to the jury.

"My point is this: every one of you on the jury has stolen at some point in your lives. Cheated your employer, misreported to the IRS, lied to your husband—"

"Objection! The jury is not on trial here. Your Honor?" the DA squealed, face red.

Billy continued. The jurists looked at him, and he threw their answers back at them without using names.

"A hundred dollars from the teacher's lunch fund, fifty thousand in charity donations you never made, your secretary, Barbara, Pete, Joe, Susan. Those tips are income, all twenty thousand of them. Those SAT scores that got you into Harvard . . ."

Their eyes widened ever so slightly as he named their sins.

"If you've done that and yet refuse to confess, can you really blame my client for doing the same as you?"

"Counselor, this is *enough*!" The judge slammed her gavel down.

Time for an exit. His argument was convoluted. Butchered. Meaningless. But he didn't care. Nothing mattered except for the numbers that already ran circles in his head.

Anthony Sacks's numbers were his only means of salvation now.

Billy raised his voice and made his final impassioned plea. "Just because a man is a liar and a cheat doesn't mean he's a murderer. You may not like

Anthony Sacks any more than I do, but don't hold his lying against him—you're as guilty as he."

He faced the courtroom and spread his hands. "We all are. No more questions."

CHAPTER FOUR

THERE WAS a God after all, Darcy thought, pouring boiling water over a mint tea bag. Then she immediately pushed the thought from her mind.

At the very least it was a good day to be alive. She dropped in two cubes of sugar, stirred the tea with a teaspoon, and stepped lightly across the tile floor toward the living room, warming her hands with the steaming porcelain cup.

Eight p.m. She could either watch the latest episode of *The Thirty*, which she recorded weekly, or settle for a bit of Net surfing before curling up in bed with the latest Frakes novel, *Birthright*, which had to be the best of the vampire series so far.

Thinking of the book, she stopped halfway to the love seat in the middle of her living room. Maybe she should just skip the Net and head to bed. Nothing was worse than reading too late and falling asleep two or three pages into a novel. It had taken her a month to read a novel in fits and starts last year—some vampire-romance book that wasn't very interesting, but that was beside the point. She vowed never to read in such short spurts again.

No, she would surf first and see if anyone had left her any messages while she was at it. She eased into the large leather seat and tapped the built-in controller on the right arm. A five-foot screen on the wall brightened.

Loading . . .

Her mind tripped back to the review at the plant. She still wasn't entirely sure what had happened. The world was running scared from lawsuits, and her employers had seen her aggressive reaction as a sure sign of her intent.

Had they really doubled her salary? Or had she misunderstood that part? Either way, she hardly cared as long as they left her alone, which they were. For now.

She had a near perfect job.

She had her sweet mint tea.

She had the Net.

It was indeed good to be alive.

Truth be told, she couldn't remember ever feeling so content as she did now. It had taken years of hard work and hundreds of hours of counseling, but she was finally coming to grips with her demons. So to speak.

She'd repressed large chunks of her memory in an effort to survive a tortured past in a monastery, her therapist had concluded. Dissociative amnesia resulting from traumatic events. This was why she'd withdrawn from normal living in favor of the protected environment she'd built for herself.

Billy.

A smile tempted her lips. She did remember her first love. More of a crush, maybe.

The screen waited, homepage loaded. Square windows into her customized on-demand world displayed slots for *Entertainment*, *News*, *Friends*, *Services*, and *Other*.

She quickly checked to see if any messages had come from Susan, a Net friend whom she'd met only once in person but a thousand times on the screen. The only person other than her therapist who knew everything about Darcy. No messages.

The only noteworthy news was a story about a lynching in Kansas City, the third such lynching in three states. Race related. You'd think the world would have learned by now that race had nothing to do with anything. She had no patience for such stories.

No need to order groceries. She spun through the menus, running through a mental checklist of loose ends and options. This screen was her world in a box. A nice, easy world that accommodated her love of vampires and heroes and saber-toothed villains capped in black. Fictional bad guys, mythical monsters. *Safe* fantasy.

Finding nothing that drew her attention, Darcy got stuck on a half-hour comedy show that she found only vaguely humorous, *Three's Company,* a new show that made fun of one Hindu, one Muslim, and one Christian who shared an apartment in Manhattan.

She found anything religious unsettling; anything to do with priests deeply disturbing. But the writers of this show leveled some of the most audacious religious slurs imaginable with a humorous boldness that she found at times irresistible, if a bit embarrassing. Particularly when it came to Christians, or, as the show sometimes characterized them using the most offensive of all religious slurs, *blood*—

Darcy cut the thought short. However wounded she might be over her own run-in with the church, she wouldn't stoop to such bigoted name-calling. Society at large had turned against Christianity with a vengeance over the past decade, and for good reason, Darcy thought. But poking fun at those who still embraced the faith was mean-spirited.

She changed the feed and began to surf. News? No, not news. Reality game shows? She didn't have enough patience to watch others make a spectacle of themselves tonight. She should just head to bed with the Frakes novel.

She rotated into the Discovery feed. Tonight's documentary examined events that led to the two assassination attempts on President Robert Stenton last year—the second of which succeeded. Numerous theories were still argued, but the one that dominated suggested that Stenton had been hit by Muslim extremists in retaliation for the Iranian prime minister's death—while on U.S. soil.

If there was a silver lining to the upheaval last year, it was the West's final awaking to the volatility of religion, or more rightly, faith. The last twenty years were replete with examples of violence carried out in the name of God or Allah or whatever the fundamental extremists worshipped with their raging hearts and bloody swords.

Tolerance had become the watchword of the day. A modest but important bit of progress in world history. Or at least American history. It was a step in the right direction, to be sure, but only a step. What the world needed was a thousand more steps in the same direction.

Darcy sipped her tea and lingered on the feed. The commentator switched to an interview with an expert on the subject. The peace in Darcy's small, protected bubble was shattered with a single image.

A priest in a black robe.

She set her cup down, felt it tip as she scrambled for the controls. Hot tea burned her thumb, but her mind was more interested in changing channels.

Not until she'd successfully done so did she manage a curse. That was it; she was done with the screen tonight.

She cleaned up the mess with a towel, went through what she called her retiring ritual—pink flannel pajamas, face wash, face cream, tall glass of iced water, covers back, book in hand—and slipped between her sheets with a sigh.

That night Darcy read two chapters of *Birthright* before setting the book on the nightstand, turning the lights off, and snuggling three pillows tight against her body as her mind drifted into the land of flying black beasts seducing young maidens with promises of immortality and power.

She was asleep before she had time to wonder if she would fall asleep quickly.

The sounds began at one that morning. At first in her dreams, a

steady thumping knocked about the edges of the tale she was construct-
ing deep in REM sleep.

Knock, knock, knock.

An innocent construction of a healthy imagination.

I'm a-knockin', knockin', knockin' at your back door, baby.

She felt herself smile at the sound of that voice. She knew it, of course.
It was Billy.

*Wanna take a look, Darcy? Just one look, one taste, one tiny spike in their
minds. Wanna trip, baby?*

I don't know, should I, Billy?

One look, baby. Only one.

Thunk, thunk, thunk.

Darcy's eyes snapped open. The clock read 1:23 in bold red letters.
She'd had a nightmare. They came and went every few months, not like
they used to.

She flipped her pillow over so the cool side would rest against her
cheek. Wouldn't really call them nightmares anymore. Just recurring
dreams. They hardly bothered—

Thunk. Thunk. Thunk.

Darcy gasped and pushed herself up. Had she actually *heard* that?

Rat-a-tat-tat. Thunk, thunk.

Her heart slammed into her throat. Someone was beating on the house.
The front door?

Thunk, thunk . . . crash.

Darcy threw the sheets off and slid her feet to the floor. Someone
or something was beating on the front door. She lived in a small two-
bedroom house surrounded by three acres just outside of Lewiston. She'd
chosen the place because it was affordable and private. Animals were
known to come in now and then, but this sounded too . . . regular . . .

Bang, bang, bang, bang, bang!

The sound was now loud enough to wake the dead. Like a hammer.

She jumped from the bed and whirled, looking for . . . unsure of what to look for. A weapon, but she had no gun. A knife.

Slow down, Darcy. It's a deer or a raccoon. Just go out and take a look.

Thunk, thunk, thunk.

The sound had shifted. Darcy reached a trembling hand for the bedroom doorknob, turned it slowly, and eased the door open.

She crouched and hurried into the dark living room on the balls of her feet, eyes peeled and pointed toward the front door.

Bang.

Just one, but it was loud and it was most definitely the sound of something hitting the front door. Right there, not ten feet from where Darcy stood in the dark. Then another one.

Bang!

Move, move, go, *go*. Go where? She stood fixed to the floor with fear. Should she call out? What? *Hey you? What do you want?* No.

Should she call the police? Yes. Yes, the police. And tell them what? The thoughts crashing through her mind were chased off by another loud *bang*.

There was a window that looked out onto the front door from the breakfast nook on her left. Without allowing herself any more delay, Darcy crept to the window, carefully spread two of the blinds, and peered out into the night.

There was a large man at her door dressed in a black trench coat. He held a hammer the length of his arm and was sealing her in with planks and long nails through the door. *Thunk, thunk.*

Had sealed her doorway.

The man stood back, lowered the huge hammer. Slowly, as if it were controlled by small electric motors, his head turned and looked in her direction.

Darcy's blood turned to ice.

CHAPTER FIVE

NOT EVERYONE knew where in Atlantic City Ricardo Muness could be found, but Billy did. He knew because he'd been in the office at the back of the Lady Luck Hotel and Casino twice before. Once with Anthony Sacks, making a desperate and successful plea to double his credit from $150,000, and again three months later to be told that he would be defending that same scumbag, Anthony Sacks, who had vouched for his credit worthiness.

Tonight he went alone, knowing that his chances of leaving the Lady Luck with all four limbs intact were smaller than a blind throw of the dice at the craps table.

He hadn't changed his shirt or the black slacks since leaving the courtroom. Personal hygiene, dress, food—none of these rated high on his list of priorities today.

Survival went straight to the top spot. Self-preservation was the only thing on his mind, gnawing the edges of his brain into frayed pasta.

He walked down a dingy hall behind the casino, ducked into a stairwell, and descended to the underground level.

After a series of motions and objections thrown about by his own client and the prosecution, the judge had dismissed the jury and demanded counsel meet her in her chambers immediately.

She was curious as to Billy's tactics in the courtroom, even wondered if he hadn't pulled off a brilliant defense in what she thought had been a foregone trial. The jury would have seen through the last witness, she thought.

You could go places, Counselor. Get a grip on your life. And put on a clean shirt the next time you stand before a judge.

But she didn't say any of it. She only expressed her dismay at his antics in her courtroom and demanded that prosecution and defense present closing arguments next. No more motions, no more surprise witnesses, this case was going to the jury room first thing Monday.

So agreed.

It no longer mattered. Billy wasn't going to be around Monday morning or any morning, for that matter.

"Can I help you?" A hand on his chest stopped him.

"Yes, counselor of Anthony Sacks. I have to see Ricardo Muness immediately."

"He knows you're coming?" The man was dressed in a blue pinstripe suit that looked completely out of place in the dingy hall.

"If he's as smart as I think he is, he does."

"Wait here." He stepped back in the shadows, spoke softly into a cell phone, then emerged.

"No."

"No? What do you mean, no?"

"It means you have about ten seconds before I break your face. Leave."

"Tell Muness that I have $526,000 dollars for him. If he refuses it, I will assume he intends for me to have it. The choice is his."

"You don't understand the word *no*, I take it."

"And I take it that you're about as stupid as a sack of air. Have it your way." Billy spun and headed back up the stairs.

He made it all the way into the main casino before the suited muscle caught him by the arm from behind.

"This way."

A single look in the man's eyes told him that the guy's head really was about as empty as a sack of air.

Ricardo Muness sat behind the pale desk that had become synonymous with Billy's image of the man. Bleached maple. Like bone. Otherwise everything about the man was dark. Boots, goatee, slicked hair, tanned skin. Even the dark glasses that covered his eyes.

"Sit," he said softly.

Billy sat in one of two black leather chairs and stared at Atlantic City's wealthiest underground financier.

Nothing. Not a whisper of the man's thoughts.

Glasses.

Okay, well, that was new. So he needed to actually see a person's eyeballs to hear their thoughts. Billy crossed his legs and nonchalantly dried his palms on his thighs. Over the last six hours his focus had been split between the keys into cyberspace that Sacks had given him, and the phenomenon that was opening his mind to the world's thoughts.

Between the two he'd discovered just how badly one could sweat when truly freaked out.

"I understand you have a death wish," Muness said.

"Is that what you heard? No, sir. I did what I knew you would want me to do given the information I was able to obtain."

"Never assume to know my mind."

The order struck Billy as a little too direct. Muness knew about his new talent?

"Then maybe I was mistaken," he said. "I could leave now if you wish."

"Or?"

"Or I could tell you about the money Anthony Sacks stole from you."

"And?"

"And show you how to retrieve it."

"How much?"

"Five hundred twenty-six thousand. And change."

"You missed some."

Billy felt his face flush. "What do you mean?"

"He's taken five hundred and thirty-seven thousand from me in the last twelve months. Eleven thousand of that was a loan he never paid back. The rest is in a bank in Belize, under my watch."

The fact that Sacks probably didn't consider the eleven thousand as stolen accounted for the disparity. But Muness knew about the money anyway.

"So you've come all this way to return money that is already in my hands?" the man said.

"Evidently."

The man stared at him through the dark glasses. It was almost as if he really did know about Billy's gift and was playing him.

"We have a problem, my friend."

"We? Or me?"

"For the moment, we. There are those in my organization that know about our little arrangement. Which means I am obligated to follow through with the promises I made to you. If Tony goes down, so do you, it's that simple."

"That's my problem," Billy said. "What's yours?"

"The fact that you know about the money. I need to know how you found out."

Leverage. But not much.

"And you expect me to tell you when? After you remove my left arm?"

The man smiled. "The thought had occurred to me. If you don't tell me, I'll assume Sacks told you, in which case I'll have to kill both of you. The choice is yours. So much power in your hands, Billy boy. To give or take a man's life. Power."

"I tell you, you let me live but take my arms."

"Correct."

"I think I'd rather take a bullet in the head."

The man's hand came up, snugged around a stainless nine-millimeter pistol. "If you insist."

"You have to ask yourself, Ricardo, what else I might know about your organization. And whom I've told."

It was hard to tell in the dim light, but Billy thought the man's cheek had twitched, so he pressed on with the slight advantage.

"Do you really think I would be stupid enough to hang your man out to dry and then waltz into this gamble without an ace up my sleeve? You kill me and you'll be taken down within the week, my friend."

The fact that his voice held a slight tremor didn't help his cause, but he wasn't accustomed to looking death in the face.

"I think you're bluffing."

"I may be a gambling addict, but I'm not a complete idiot." He stood. "The real question is, are you willing to gamble your life on a hunch that I'm bluffing?"

Muness seemed at a loss for words.

Billy knew he had the man on his heels, if only for a moment. He moved then, forcing himself to ignore the black hole of the pistol.

"What I'm about to tell you will determine if you live out the week, Mr. Muness."

He slowly leaned forward, reached out his hand, and removed the man's glasses.

The room remained quiet. No gunshot.

He stared into Muness's eyes and let the man's thoughts stream into his mind.

"I hope you don't mind. It's important that we see things . . . eye to eye as it were." He set the glasses down. "You wonder whom I've told about the nine million dollars you've socked away in the Dominican Republic, don't you? Or if I've left instructions with my attorney to mail a letter to your wife in the event of my death, explaining why Angela has accompanied you on so many business trips."

He let the information settle in. Muness hadn't been wondering anything quite so detailed, naturally, but Billy had lifted enough information to make it clear he knew about both Angela and the money in the West Indies.

"Should I go on?"

"You've just sealed your fate."

"And now your fate is directly tied to mine. If I go, you go. If I get hurt, you get hurt."

Muness slammed a fist on the desk. "You have the audacity to even *think* you can blackmail me?"

"I do."

For a long time, the man just stared at him. And in that time, Billy learned precisely how a man as filthy rich as Ricardo Muness got to be so filthy rich.

A grin slowly split the man's mouth. "Well, well, well, I guess I underestimated you, didn't I?"

"So it seems. All I want is a week to prove to you that I will never use this information against you unless you exploit me. Just give me time."

"Time. Yes, of course. Isn't that what we all want? More time. But you're not the only one who knows things they have no business knowing, Billy."

Darcy.

The man's thoughts wrapped around the name with disturbing images that stopped Billy cold. He knew about Darcy? What possible connection could a loan secured in New Jersey have to Darcy, wherever she was?

Apart from scattered details, *Billy* didn't even know about Darcy. But now he did, because Muness knew where she lived, what she did for a living, other details that streamed into Billy's mind.

Clearly, Muness assumed that Billy cared.

"Only a fool loans a man three hundred thousand dollars without doing some homework," Muness said. "Insurance. Not everyone is as concerned about their own arms as they are someone else's arms."

"And you think that's me."

"Does the name Darcy ring a bell?"

Billy searched the man's thoughts for a few seconds, finding nothing useful.

"You've dug deep," he said.

Muness dipped his head. "You do anything I don't like, she pays."

"Fine."

"And your debt?"

Billy withdrew a slip of paper with the information he'd assembled on Sacks's theft and handed it to Muness. "My debt was three hundred thousand dollars. Now we're even."

Muness hesitated, then took the paper. His mind was running through ways to eliminate Billy along with the threat as efficiently as a college graduate might run through single-digit addition tables.

"I don't like to be blackmailed, Mr. Rediger. I can't live with the pressure hanging over my head, you understand. You want a week; I'll give you three days. Then we settle this, one way or another."

Billy took a deep breath, nodded once, and turned for the door. "Agreed."

But nothing could be further from the truth. Muness had already settled on his decision, one that made liberal use of force and torture within the hour of closing arguments in the case against Anthony Sacks.

Muness had no intention of allowing blackmail to rule his life. And Billy had no intention of allowing Muness to rule his.

He was going on the run. Tonight.

CHAPTER SIX

WATCHING A cloaked stranger nail her door shut in the middle of the night was enough to stop her lungs from inhaling. Staring into the stranger's shadowed eyes was enough to freeze her heart.

Darcy didn't know if he could see her eyeballs through the gap in the slats, but if he saw movement, he would know she was awake and watching him.

She had to get to the phone!

The man abruptly turned and walked along the wall, then disappeared around the corner. Going where? To seal the back door too?

Darcy released the blinds and ran toward the kitchen. White venetian blinds covered all of the windows in the family room adjacent to the kitchen. From her vantage point, the back door looked undisturbed.

She considered making a run for it now, into the garage, into her Chevy, into the night. But she hesitated—surely there was an explanation for all of this. Who'd ever heard of a woman being sealed in her own home by a man with a hammer? If he wanted in, he would have just shattered the door, not nailed it shut.

Run, Darcy! Get out now while you still can.

She ran for the garage door, thinking she should grab a knife just in case. But her urgency to escape, to get out now while she still could, overpowered the desire for a weapon. And she didn't want to alert the intruder by clattering through a drawer full of knives.

She slid her keys off the hook on the back wall and tried the door leading to the garage. Locked. She eased the dead bolt back and shoved again.

No. *Locked.*

She checked the dead bolt again, thinking she'd turned it the wrong way, but the bolt was open. And the door handle twisted in her palm. The door was jammed from the outside.

Gooseflesh rippled on her arms. He'd gotten to the garage door?

Darcy spun around, breathing hard. Her mind was blank. She turned and slammed into the door, grunting, ignoring the pain in her shoulder.

It refused to budge.

The back door! She whirled, took one step, and slipped on the rug in front of the sink. Her arm caught her fall, but not without slapping into the metal sink. Loud.

She scrambled to her feet. The delay in her progress to the back door gave her time to recall her first impulse to call for help. Moving with less concern about stealth, she crossed the kitchen, snatched the phone off the counter, and pressed it to her ear.

It was programmed to engage upon contact with her fingers. But the familiar dial tone was gone. Instead, static.

Darcy punched the manual power button, tried again, and heard the same static.

Now, true panic collided with her mind. He'd cut her phone line! "Darcy..."

His voice came from the direction of her bedroom. Low and long, then again, tasting each syllable.

"Darcy..."

He was inside!

She ran for the back door, fumbled with the locks, and discovered exactly what she'd expected to find. A door that would not open. Which left only the windows and the attic.

All that banging from her dreams filled her ears. How long had he been building her house into a prison?

She tore for the nearest window, yanked the blinds up, and saw nothing but black. Black boards. He'd boarded up the windows too.

Darcy whispered frantically under her breath. "No, no, no, no, no!"

"Darcy, Darcy . . . Wanna play?"

She clamped a trembling hand over her mouth.

"There's no way out, honey. I know how to fix a house."

Access to the attic was in the master bath, and from the sound of it the intruder was between her and the bedroom. She had to let him enter the kitchen area and sneak past him if she hoped to make it.

The attic had a round vent she might be able to squeeze through if she could dislodge it before he found her. She knew this because she'd been up there with a cable repairman, tracking down a cable that a mouse had chewed through. The vent would put her on the roof, but from there she might stand a chance.

She eased to her knees and crawled toward the couch.

"You have to ask yourself if after going to all that trouble . . ."

He was in the kitchen already and she hadn't even heard him move.

". . . I would be stupid enough to give you a way out. Hmmm?"

Darcy lay flat, shivering. How had he come in? If there was a way in, there had to be a way out.

"You're wondering about the attic?"

Darcy inched forward on her knees again.

"Forget the attic, honey."

She went then, while the sound of his voice came from the garage area.

Sprinting through the doorway that led to the living room with her five-foot media screen. Scanning the walls for a window he'd left open.

None.

She spun into the master bedroom and saw the opened miniblind beyond her bed. He'd crawled in through the window and shut it behind him. But he hadn't had the time to nail it, right?

"You want out so soon?" His voice was behind her, only feet, it seemed. She'd never make it!

Darcy dived forward, rolled across her bed, and came up airborne.

Behind her the lights came on.

She crashed against the wall next to the open window and fumbled with the latch. Opened it. Pulled the window open.

"Shh, shh, shh . . ." A hand grabbed her collar and jerked her back against his body. "Please, I just want to talk." Hot breath.

Darcy screamed, but his hand smothered her mouth. She bit into his flesh, felt warm blood rush between her teeth.

He withdrew his hand and slapped something else in its place. Around her head. Tape.

Her muffled cry filled her taped mouth, powerless now. She struggled hopelessly against his steel grip. Like a man who'd won his share of hog-tying contests, he secured her wrists behind her back, spun her around, and shoved her to the ground.

The black-clad man strode for the window, shut the blinds, and faced her. His hand was bleeding where she'd bitten him, but he didn't seem to notice.

"Well, well, well. So you would be Darcy, or, as you are so affectionately referred to back in the group, number thirty-five."

Her assailant stood over six feet, dressed in dark brown slacks and a black collared shirt, a day's stubble lining his jaw. Sweat glistened on his face, but otherwise he looked clean for a man who'd spent the night sealing her in her house.

"Now, just take a deep breath, Thirty-five. I've done this more times than I care to remember—gets old after a while. We'll be here for a while, a day, maybe more, depending on you."

He eyed her from head to toe. Grunted. "I really hope you're not the stubborn kind."

She told him what she thought of him in no uncertain terms, but it came out in a long "Uhummmmmmm!"

"This doesn't have to be difficult," he said. "You're brimming with questions, and I don't blame you. We'll get to them. Where do you keep the bandages?"

She stared him in the eyes, refusing to clue him in.

"The bathroom, naturally. Just seeing if you were warming up." He walked to her, grabbed her by her hair, and tugged her to her feet. She stumbled beside him into the living room, where he shoved her onto the love seat.

Producing a pair of cuffs, he cinched one end to her ankle and the other to the sofa leg.

"Be right back. Can I get you anything? Coffee, lemonade, mint tea?"

The man left, banged about in the bathroom for a minute, then returned, hand bandaged in a strip of sterile cotton.

"Problem with giving you a drink," he said, "is drinking it. If everything they tell me about your yapper is correct, I don't think I'll be taking the tape off any time soon."

He disappeared into the kitchen and returned with one of her wooden chairs. Spun it around and straddled it.

"You can call me Agent Smith. Not my real name, but it has a ring to it. You like old movies?" He pointed at her. "You, we'll call Darcy. Number thirty-five sounds a bit too clinical. Fair enough?"

She stared at him.

"Good. Now, the first thing you have to understand is that whether I kill you or not depends on how cooperative you are. If it were up to me, I would let you live. You're dangerous, I'm sure, but I think the world needs a bit of danger to make it interesting, and I'm not about to be the only one providing it. Follow?"

She didn't. She was about as dangerous as a mouse. He was mistaking her for someone else. This whole thing was a mistake! Which gave her some hope. If she could make him understand, he might let her go.

"But," he continued, "they disagree and they call the shots." He stared at the tape around her mouth. "If you really can do all they say you can, maybe it's best for everyone."

What was he talking about? She shook her head hard.

Agent Smith slowly smiled. "You really don't know, do you?"

"Hmmmm!" she shouted. *No!*

"We'll start with me and then move on to you. You're the prize here, after all."

Smith stood, withdrew a toothpick from his breast pocket, and began to pick his teeth. "I work for Rome. The Roman Catholic Church. Not as a priest, obviously, but I'm on the payroll. Evidently you have a history they aren't crazy about. A certain monastery in which you and thirty-six other children were sequestered for the first thirteen years of your lives. You remember?"

Long fingers of horror reached around Darcy's throat. Smith had the right girl, then. The nightmare she'd fled all these years had caught up to her. And this time it would finally kill her. Darcy felt hot tears leak down her cheek and drop onto her lap.

"One year ago, one of those children, a man now named Johnny Drake, demonstrated a rather remarkable set of powers that could ultimately embarrass the Catholic Church. Evidently, Johnny wasn't the only one who came into the possession of such powers."

Not me! You have the wrong person! But the words refused to form in her frozen throat.

"My mission is a simple one: find the grown children, find out what they really know, and then decide whether they should die."

She felt herself shiver with a deep-seated rage. Not only against this emissary but also at the institution that had reduced her to a shell of what most people were.

Smith drawled on. "The church is in a bit of a spot as you probably know. Everyone seems to hate her these days. Not without reason, mind you, but there it is. The only group of people more despised than Catholics are Protestants. Used to be Muslims and Hindus and all the Eastern freaks took the cake. Well that's all changed, and as a good Christian solider I feel compelled to do my part in cleaning things up."

He winked.

"Which brings me here. So then, let's begin. I need to know what you know." Agent Smith got off the wooden kitchen chair, settled into the leather recliner to the right of the sofa, crossed his legs, lay his head back, and closed his eyes.

"Go ahead, take some time. I'm in no hurry."

CHAPTER SEVEN

Day Two

BILLY REDIGER left his apartment at two in the morning, climbed into the old cobalt-blue Porsche 911 he'd won in a poker game a few months ago, ignited the engine, and left 2917 Atlantic Street behind for the last time.

At least that was the plan.

He'd made an emergency call to the judge and explained that, however inconvenient it might be for the court, health issues were forcing him to remove himself from the defense of Anthony Sacks. Unless, of course, she was willing to let him present his closing arguments *in absentia*, to be read by the clerk.

After five minutes of chastisement, she agreed to let the clerk read his closing arguments, only because the case against Sacks was so airtight that closing arguments were futile anyway, she claimed.

So much for Anthony Sacks's day in court.

Billy had typed up his closing argument—which took one last stab at confusing the jury by reminding them of their own sins—sent it to the judge via the Net, packed up his few belongings, and cleared out.

The night was cool and the traffic nearly nonexistent at such an early hour, so he lowered the top, turned up the stereo, and pretended that all was as fine as a sunny Sunday in June.

Truth was, he'd just hit bottom. And even now, the bottom felt like it was about to give way. Muness had long arms, and it would only take him a day at most to figure out that Billy had fled the city and done the only thing that made any sense.

Gone after Darcy. Which in Billy's mind didn't make much sense at all.

According to the online digital map index, Lewistown, Pennsylvania, was two hundred thirty miles from Atlantic City, up the 42 to the 76 to the 22. A good four hours without traffic. With any luck he'd beat the morning rush and arrive before she headed out for the Hyundai plant where she worked, information according to the thoughts of Ricardo Muness.

Billy tried to tap his hand to the beat crackling through the old speakers but couldn't get it right in such a ragged state of mind. He settled for chewing on his fingernail.

Darcy. He wasn't sure how he'd feel seeing her again. Depended if she attempted to bite his head off or not.

Butterflies fluttered in his belly. He'd sworn her off and gone his own way when they were still fourteen, but she'd been his first true love, if indeed love could be found in hell, which was the only way he could succinctly characterize the monastery they'd grown up in. But their experience had forged a bond between them that he could never deny. A part of Darcy had remained with him to this day. Though which part, he wasn't sure.

The thought made him swallow. What did she look like? Was she large, skinny? Had she become a socialite or retreated into a cocoon? Was she married, dating, an ax murderer, into sports? Did she think about him?

And above all, what would she say about what was happening? This new gift he'd suddenly found, out of thin air it seemed. It had to do with the monastery, didn't it? Strange things like this had occurred in the monastery, but not since, not till now.

The thought had drummed through his mind all day. Whatever was happening to him was tied directly to his childhood. Darcy had stood by his side then, and the fact that he was being driven to her side now felt more than a little ironic.

Muness said he'd dug into Billy's past and found out about Darcy, but how? The whole project had been buried, literally, if he'd heard it right. As far as the world was concerned, Project Showdown had never existed.

Most of the time *he* wasn't even sure it had all occurred. They'd only been thirteen, for Pete's sake. But it had happened, hadn't it?

He had conspired to do terrible evil.

He had persuaded Darcy to join him, then fallen in love with her.

He had opened a window into hell.

He now loathed all forms of religion, anything that reminded him of his abject failure as a child, because it wasn't really a failure at all. It was only doing what all thirteen-year-old boys do if given the chance.

And he now had this . . . he didn't even know what to call it . . . this gift. The ability to know thoughts.

Billy glanced at the speedometer, saw he was doing only seventy, and accelerated with renewed urgency to reach Darcy. Muness had threatened her, and that was reason enough to go to her after all these years.

But it wasn't really the threat that was driving him, was it? No, it was Darcy herself. The feisty girl who might very well be his only true friend now.

Assuming she didn't bite his head off.

DARCY SAT in near darkness, taped and bound as the minutes stretched into ten, at which time the man who'd boarded up her house stood and walked into the master bedroom.

The sound of his hammer pounding nails home fleshed out her fears of his intentions. Having rested from his work, Smith was putting the finishing touches on the job. He clearly had no intention of leaving any time soon.

Smith could have more easily broken into her house, tied her up, and threatened her. The fact that he'd gone to such trouble to seal her in could only mean he was the kind who preferred the weapon of terror and enjoyed taking the time to watch it work.

And it *was* working.

Par for the course, she thought. Religion had always used terror to wield power. Fear of hell, fear of getting your head blown off, your towers blown down, or just plain old fear for fear's sake. Thou shalt not, thou shalt not, thou shalt not. The church that Smith worked for had perfected terror.

She still wasn't sure she understood exactly what he intended her to confess, or how she should confess with her mouth sealed as tightly as her house. But his threat had accomplished what she assumed was his purpose: to throw her mind back into the monastery.

Problem was, she really couldn't remember. The names of a few, yes.

Billy. And she did know a few things about Billy.

Johnny.

Samuel.

The overseers. Paul. They were all orphans. And that was it. She'd spent thirteen years wiping her mind free of the experience. Going back now was digging around in the sewer to salvage a few coins.

Sewer. There was something about the sewers at the monastery that filled her throat with an urge to throw up. The worms from her nightmares.

He'd stopped hammering. His feet moved softly across the carpet behind her. Darcy stared at the dark screen on the wall and blinked away tears that had filled her eyes.

"Darcy . . ." His voice came breathy and low. He walked past her, picking his teeth again. "Thirty-five of thirty-six. I've found thirty-four of you. All dead now. The fact that most of you were given new surnames didn't help. I got your name from a pigheaded reporter named Paul Strang."

He turned to her.

"Ring any bells?"

Paul. The overseer? She shook her head anyway.

"Too bad. It usually takes them a few hours to start remembering. And then I start with the nails. Amazing what a few nails in one's thigh will do to jolt the memory."

Darcy glared at him, furious. At this Agent Smith. At the parents who'd abandoned her in the first place. At Billy, for clinging to her mind. At the monastery and the powers that had allowed such a careless project to be conducted in the first place. And if there was a God, at God. Above everything else she was *furious* at God.

"Take your time, Darcy. It's been a long night for both of us. And I have a feeling tomorrow will be even longer."

Agent Smith crossed to the recliner, eased his large body into the leather seat, and lay his head back again.

"I'm a light sleeper—anything more than breathing will wake me. Please don't try anything stupid. I suggest you get some sleep, you'll need it."

And that was it.

Darcy sat with her hands tied behind her back and her foot chained to the couch, expecting something, anything, to move the night forward.

But nothing happened. Smith looked like he'd fallen asleep within minutes of suggesting she do the same.

Her shoulders ached and her mind spun and her heart pumped hot blood through her veins—all reminders that she was definitely alive. But no other memories surfaced.

So she sat still, sweating and waiting and hating Smith and all those who pulled his strings. Terror frayed her nerves, numbed her mind. Fear, more fear than she'd ever felt, wore her thin, and in that thinness came exhaustion.

Darcy didn't know what time she slipped into a deep, peaceful sleep.

CHAPTER EIGHT

THE WARMTH of thick worms sliding over her face woke her.

She jerked upright and stared at the dark wall screen. She'd fallen asleep watching the Net in her pajamas and put an awful cramp in her shoulder from sleeping on her . . .

Agent Smith.

She turned her head to the leather chair on her left. No sign of the intruder. But a single tug from her arms confirmed her memory of being bound. And taped.

The harrowing events of the night flooded her mind. She craned her neck left, then right, searching for his form in the dim light. Gray seeped past the boards—it must be dawn or near dawn outside.

Darcy bolted from the sofa, caught her right foot on something and fell flat on her face, remembering too late that he'd cuffed her ankle to the furniture.

Unable to use her arms to push herself up, she lay still with her cheek pressed into the shaggy maroon area rug she'd bought online to brighten up the beige carpet. The whole thing had to be a bad nightmare.

It was then, as she recalled the name of the town where the monastery had been located, that she first heard the creaking from the direction of the kitchen.

Darcy lifted her head off the carpet and listened, eyes wide.

Creeeeaaaak . . .

She knew that sound. A nail, not going into wood, but coming out of it. Someone was prying a plank from a window or the back door! The police had been called, perhaps. Should she call out?

If she heard it, than he'd hear it. Unless he was too far from the source of the sound to make sense of it.

It came again, and this time Darcy began to scream into her tape to cover the sound as much as to attract attention.

She half expected a boot to her side, but none came, so she screamed, muted by the tape.

A dark shape filled the doorway into the kitchen. Her scream caught in her throat. She could tell immediately that this wasn't Smith. Not large enough.

The form held a knife out. No gun, no flashlight. Not police? The thought embedded instantly.

This wasn't the police! Some idiot had stumbled upon the boarded up house and ventured in wielding only a knife. Which meant that they were both dead.

Darcy cried her warning too late. The visitor had already seen her and rushed to her side. Slid to his knees, whispering loud and harsh.

"Shh, shh, quiet, quiet!"

He snapped only two words, but they awakened such a conflict of emotion in her consciousness that she went rigid.

"It's Billy," he whispered. "I'm here. Oh man! Oh man! What have they done? Are you okay?"

His name triggered unwelcome emotions in her mind. She forced them aside and violently shook her head.

Still no reaction from Smith. He was there, though. He had to have heard!

Billy's fingers searched her face, found the edge of the tape, and pulled it from her mouth. She was whispering frantically before it was fully removed.

"He's here," she whispered, "be quiet, *quiet* . . ."

Breath.

"Get my wrists!"

Breath.

"I'm chained to the sofa! Hurry, hurry!"

Billy reached, found her wrists, elbows at her back, and sawed through the tape with his knife.

"My foot!" she whispered. "It's chained, get them off."

He shouldered the couch and tried to slip the cuffs off, but they were latched to a metal bar that ran perpendicular to the frame.

So close, they were so close to freedom! Darcy grabbed Billy by the collar with both hands and pulled him near so she could talk quietly. Came face-to-face with him.

"Billy." Her voice sounded panicked. She tried to calm herself. "Don't leave me, Billy! Don't let him do this to me! I need you, I'm sorry, I . . ."

His eyes stared wide, six inches from hers. Whether it was the panic speaking or some deep-seated bond, she didn't know, she didn't care. But she'd never been so grateful to see, to touch, to have another human so close.

"Promise me you'll never leave me, Billy, please, please . . ."

Her hands trembled on his collar.

"I won't leave you."

And then he went to work on the handcuffs.

"He's in here," Darcy whispered.

Billy spun back. "Where?"

"I don't know . . ." She looked around. "He boarded up the house and he's inside!"

"Who? Muness? From Atlantic City—"

"No, no, from the Vatican! He's after the survivors of the project

back in Paradise. You have to get us out, Billy! He's planning to kill
me—*us*."

Billy looked into her eyes, frozen by her words. *Survivors of Paradise.*
But there was more than fear behind his eyes, she thought.

"I'm going to get you out of here, Darcy." His voice was strung tight.
He took her head in one arm and pulled her close. "I promise, I swear,
I'm not going to let you go."

Something more than fear was driving them together, Darcy thought.
She clung to him. And all she could think to say was, "Thank you."

"Yes, thank you, Billy."

They both spun to Smith's deep voice. Lights blazed to life.

The bulky man from the Vatican stood by her bedroom door, legs
spread, right arm cocked by his ear. In his left hand, he held a pistol and
on his face he wore dark reflective glasses. Like desert goggles.

"What took you so long?"

Darcy screamed. She closed her eyes and screamed at the top of her
lungs. A grunt from Billy stopped her.

When she opened her eyes, he was slumped to his side and Smith
stood over him, big hand balled into a fist like a brick. The man withdrew a roll of gray tape, ripped off a two-foot piece, and held it up to her.

She tried to scramble out of the way, but his powerful grip pinned her
to the floor. Agent Smith secured her hands behind her back again, then
plastered another strip of tape over her lips.

She managed to squirm into a half-seated position against the couch,
and she watched him work; he bound Billy—tape and chain—and
shackled his ankle to the sofa like hers.

The boy she'd fallen in love with when she was barely a teen had
grown into a man, but his hair still had the same red tones and his face
didn't look a day older. Perhaps she was reacting out of sheer relief to
have company in her misery, but she'd never felt such a powerful affin-
ity with Billy as she did in this moment.

Why or how he'd found her and come at this precise moment was beyond her. But he had risked his life for her. He'd held her and sworn to save her.

When Smith was done securing Billy, he slapped him, hard. Billy groaned and struggled into a sitting position next to her on the floor.

Smith spun his pistol in his fingers and then shoved it into his belt. "That's better." He withdrew earplugs from both ears with his free hand and paced before them.

"Like two peas in the pod. Darcy and Billy. Rome is going to be pleased. Absolutely *ecstatic*. Two at one time? I'm outdoing myself, and that . . . that is hard to do. Now let's start from the top, shall we?

"The last two, thirty-five and thirty-six in the same shot. Two birds, one stone. You're going to tell what you know. Who else knows."

"You can tell Muness that my promise still stands," Billy said. "I'm going to burn him."

"Muness doesn't concern me," Smith said. "You think that your being here is a stroke of fortune, boy?" He chuckled. "What's the matter? You don't know what I'm thinking? Really?" His lips flattened. "Then let me tell you what: I'm thinking that your days of traipsing through the daisies are over. For both of you. You can help us by telling me what you know about Johnny Drake and Samuel Abraham, or you can lose your fingers and toes, tongues and eyes, eventually your lives. That's what I'm thinking."

Darcy's first thought was a simple one. *Do it, Billy! We'll do it! Make something up if you have to.*

But one look at Billy's twisted face and she doubted he was on the same page. And neither was she, not really. She might be panicked now, predisposed by her nightmares to turn against anyone who had anything to do with Paradise; but in truth, she couldn't betray another human to this beast.

"Go to hell," Billy said.

"I see we're not making progress here. Let me help." Smith knelt beside him, grabbed his hands behind his back, and reached around with a cigar cutter he'd withdrawn from his pocket.

Clink . . .

Billy started to scream. Blood squirted from his finger, now missing just the very tip.

"Shut *up!*"

Billy clamped his mouth shut and shook. Sweat vibrated from his forehead.

The man from the Vatican stepped over him, grabbed Darcy's foot, and clamped it under his arm. She felt his fingers spreading her toes and she cried out in horror. The tape muffled her voice. She kicked out.

Phffft! Phffft!

Agent Smith's head snapped back. His glasses exploded into shards of crimson glass. He dropped the cigar cutter and collapsed with one lip twitching and one finger squeezing a trigger that wasn't there anymore. After a moment, he didn't move at all.

"Billy Rediger and Darcy Lange?"

The man who'd killed Smith had appeared in similar fashion to Billy's entrance. With one exception.

He held a gun and he held it like he knew how to use it. And he, like Smith, wore dark glasses.

"Yes," Billy panted.

"Are there any more of them?"

"No."

"Thank goodness I made it in time."

CHAPTER NINE

BILLY SAT next to Darcy, nursing his bandaged finger. The man who saved them had cut them both free and suggested that Darcy tend to Billy's hand. When they emerged from the bathroom, the man had already hauled Smith's body into the garage.

He stood in front of them, sunglasses fixed in place, hands on hips like a platoon sergeant looking at two new recruits.

"Okay . . ." Darcy glanced from one to the other. "Will someone please tell me what's happening here?"

"More than meets the eyes," the man said. He removed one hand from his hip and tapped his chest. "My name is Brian Kinnard. A good guy, okay? The man I killed?" He jabbed at the garage doorway behind him. "Definitely a very bad guy."

"And what would that make us?" Billy asked.

"You two are the prize. Everyone wants you. Some prefer dead, some alive, but then you've probably already figured that out."

"No," Darcy said. "I haven't figured anything out. I was sleeping and this maniac boarded up my house and he . . ." She swallowed and faced Billy, eyes wide.

Thank you, Billy. You're like an angel. I could kiss you right now!

He felt heat in his face and looked back at Kinnard, whose mind he could not read, thanks to the glasses.

"Obviously you know more than we do," Billy said. "Tell us."

"How much do you know?"

"Just tell us everything," Billy said. "We need to know what you know."

Kinnard nodded and walked to his right. "Fair enough. You were both part of an experiment that went all wrong thirteen years ago. I'm sure you remember that much."

"I'm not sure I want to hear this," Darcy said, eyes misted with tears.

Billy nodded. "Like I said, tell us what you know. All of it."

"What I know was told to me by David Abraham, the director of the monastery, but then you both know that. What you may not know is that he's no longer with us."

"Dead?" Billy blinked.

"Long story I won't go into now. He told me about Project Showdown." Kinnard paced, face toward them. "An incredible story about a project sanctioned by the Roman Catholic Church that left Paradise, Colorado, in shambles and thirty-six orphans homeless. Damaged for life. The project was designed to study the effects of isolation and indoctrination on children. An attempt to create 'noble savages' destined to live lives pure enough to change the world. Three of you—you two and a boy from Paradise named Johnny Drake—came away not only damaged but gifted. Of course, I believed none of it. Until I met Johnny Drake."

"So you know him?" Darcy said. "If he's still alive, how could Billy and I be the last two?" She glanced at the carpet stain left by the assassin's head wound.

"Johnny wasn't technically from the monastery," Billy said. "We're the last two orphans from the monastery."

"Correct," Kinnard said. "And if Johnny is right, you're the only other two who have . . ." He left it there.

"This crazy power," Billy finished.

Kinnard's jaw flexed. "So it's real, then. The three of you received inhuman powers from the books you wrote in as children." He lifted a hand and ran it through his hair. "Your powers are the same as his?"

"You're wearing glasses," Billy said.

"I learned that from Johnny. The effectiveness of the power has something to do with eye contact. Johnny never subjected me to his . . . his gift, but I've seen it work."

"What in the world are you talking about?" Darcy demanded. "I don't know anything about Johnny or gifts. How did you happen to find me—us—anyway?"

"I made a vow to David Abraham. No contact until you came out, so to speak, but the minute I heard what happened to Billy in Atlantic City I left Washington."

"How did you know to come here?" Billy pushed.

"I've had a team keeping close tabs on both of you ever since my last meeting with Johnny, nearly a year ago. Your car is tagged with an electronic signal."

Kinnard turned to Darcy. "You think that the executive board at your plant doubles employees' salaries every day?"

She stared at him, confused.

"Just an educated guess at this point, but I think David was right. I think your powers have to do with your voices and ears and eyes. Johnny can make a man see; Billy can hear thoughts, can't you, Billy?"

So he did know. Billy's mind flashed back to the courtroom. A person who knew what to look for might easily suspect what Kinnard had just suggested.

"So it seems," he said.

Kinnard nodded. "And I doubt your voice is normal, Darcy. I suspect that you can be *very* persuasive."

"I *can?*"

"You can. And Smith somehow suspected it, which is why he taped your mouth shut before you had the opportunity to persuade him to kill himself or something." The intruder again, hammers and nails and duct tape and earplugs. Smith had been trying to *contain* Darcy?

Darcy arched an eyebrow at Billy. "You can't be serious. You can read thoughts?"

"Think something and look at me."

She stared into Billy's eyes.

"You're pleasantly surprised at how handsome I've turned out," he said. "You don't trust me because you don't trust anyone. But you *want* to trust me. And you just thought I might have been able to guess all of that so you switched your thinking to a candied apple being eaten by . . ." *Really? How odd.* ". . . by a vampire." Now it was his turn to cock an eyebrow.

"There you have it," Kinnard said. "A candied apple eaten by a vampire."

She looked at Billy, horrified.

"You don't remember?" he asked. "The ancient book we wrote in—you, me, Johnny Drake?"

"No. I don't remember much."

Billy faced Kinnard. "How did David Abraham know this?"

"Like I said, he didn't exactly know. The point is, he was right."

It was all incredible, but Billy found some comfort in any explanation. "Where's Johnny?"

"He's been allowed to remain in hiding. He was very adamant about that."

"So you don't know where he is."

"Like I said, he's been allowed to remain in hiding."

Which probably meant Kinnard knew more than he would admit.

"And what do you want from us?"

Kinnard took a deep breath. "To let me fulfill my obligation to David Abraham. To let me keep you alive." Kinnard looked at the bloodstained carpet. "There are others who will stop at nothing to see you both dead."

"Marsuvees Black?" Billy said.

Kinnard slowly nodded. "I hope you will agree."

"Agree to what?"

"To go with me to Washington, D.C. Under our full protection, naturally."

"Hold on . . ." Darcy stood. "Just slow down! You're saying all of this dates back to that experiment in Paradise . . ." She clenched her jaw, and Billy knew with a single glance into her eyes that she was fighting a flood.

It occurred to him again that he wouldn't leave her. And now he thought he understood why. She'd spoken to him, begged him to never leave her. Her words had cut deep into his heart, jerking long lost emotions to the surface. And this was her *gift*?

"I have a house here," she snapped. "I can't leave."

And she had a point, Billy thought. A very good one.

"You stay here and you die," Kinnard said. "It's as simple as that. Sure, you'll be able to work some of your magic and hold them off for a while, but eventually one of them will get in, tape your mouth shut, and slit your throat—I'm sorry to be so straightforward."

And he, too, had an excellent point.

"What about Muness?" Billy asked.

"And Muness too," Kinnard said. He glanced at the door. "For all we know, Muness is with them."

"He was wearing glasses," Billy said.

"Stop it!" Darcy looked at him.

"Glasses," Billy said, surprised that he was so unruffled about Kinnard's revelations. "He's right. I have to be able to see people in the eye to know what they're thinking. Muness was wearing glasses the last time I saw him. At night. It was almost as if he knew. And when I removed his glasses, he was thinking about you, Darcy. As if he wanted me to come after you."

"Smith . . ." she said.

Billy finished her thoughts. "Was expecting *me*. Exactly. A trap, set and baited."

"Which is why you need to make your decision," Kinnard said. "If you know anything about the Agent Smiths of the world, you know that they aren't the soft-and-sensitive type."

"So you're saying that there are more. How many?"

"Don't know. Only that they are efficient and experienced killers. Which brings us back to the question."

"You want us to go to D.C. and do what?" Billy asked.

"Help us."

"With what, your laundry?" Darcy snapped.

"Us?" Billy said. "Who else knows about this?"

"No one. Not really. Last year a small group of powerful leaders agreed to meet with me, should this day ever arrive. I will give you full protection, comfortable living quarters, transportation, and a healthy stipend."

"In exchange for?"

"Your agreement to meet with this council I'm pulling together and help us figure out how to best deal with your . . . with this situation. We may end up being the only friends you now have. I strongly suggest you take the offer."

"Please tell me it's not a religious group," Darcy said.

"No. If there are men or women of faith among us, they are fully tolerant and keep it to themselves."

"You?"

"Does it matter?" Kinnard said. "The man I killed worked for the Catholic Church; that should be enough."

Billy was at a loss for argument. Having just fled Atlantic City, the offer seemed perfectly reasonable to him. A godsend, in fact. He looked at Darcy, absorbed her with his eyes.

She had the same medium-length brunette hair, the same high cheekbones, same flashing eyes and aggressive spirit, same pouting lips. A woman now, roughly twenty-six, but how much had she really changed from the thirteen-year-old he'd fallen for at the monastery?

"Give us a moment," he said to Kinnard.

"We don't have a moment."

"Then leave and tell us where to find you."

Kinnard hesitated, then turned for the kitchen. "Please hurry."

For a moment neither of them spoke. Circumstances beyond their control had thrown them together, but a history of their own making weighed as heavily in Billy's mind as the predicament they now found themselves in.

She turned away and crossed her arms.

"Darcy . . ."

"You have no right to pry around my mind," she snapped.

"You're right. And I didn't ask to."

"This whole business is crazy."

"You don't think I know that? But we aren't exactly full of alternatives."

She turned, eyeing him. "I don't even know how you found me. Or what you do for a living. Or if you have a wife or children. I know nothing about you. And he wants me to leave my life here to run off with you?"

"No wife, no children. Hello, I'm an attorney. Now you know more than I know about you."

"No, you know my every thought. That's a disadvantage."

"I may know some of your thoughts, but by the sounds of it, you can create mine. Sounds to me like you're the one with the advantage."

She stared at him, wondering how this power she supposedly had actually worked. Wondering if she could get him to do what she suggested he do.

She was going to try it, he realized.

"Darcy—"

"Please be quiet, Billy. You're saying too much."

The suggestion was perfectly logical. There were a hundred things he could say, but none of them was necessary at the moment. He really had no reason to speak. In fact, speaking now would only make him look like a fool.

So he didn't.

She was wondering if she'd made him quiet. For several long seconds they faced each other in silence. And then the assailant named Agent Smith filled her thoughts and she blinked.

She glanced at the kitchen door, then back, thinking now that she needed Billy, wanted him to stay with her. Afraid of what might happen if they became separated. She'd forgotten that he could read her mind.

And in that moment she exposed her true feelings. *Please, Billy.*

Tears filled her eyes.

Please don't leave me. Promise me.

He felt his heart rise into his throat. She was a wounded child, caught up in a predicament that was far beyond the small world she'd constructed to protect herself here in Pennsylvania. But her world had collapsed around her today and she was afraid.

Finally she said it. "I'm afraid, Billy."

It was an invitation to speak. "I know. So am I."

There was a tremor in her voice. "What should we do?"

"I think we should go with him. I know it's all so sudden, but he's right. If you stay here . . ."

"Don't say it."

So he didn't.

Her fear was so great that Billy felt he would cry. But he refused. Someone had to be strong for Darcy.

"Come with me," he said and reached for her hand.

She hesitated, looked at his hand, then up into his eyes, taking his hand. *Please don't betray me, Billy. Please don't leave me.*

"I won't," he said.

CHAPTER TEN

ACCORDING TO the latest census, 89,213 people lived in Boulder City, Nevada, a scant twenty-nine miles south of Las Vegas, City of Sin. What was particularly interesting to the older residents was that much of the growth in the last two decades was within the Islamic community, a group that had been so vocal about the decadence of the Western world.

But the world had discovered a few things in the last twenty years, and chief among them was the realization that radical elements could tinge any group's image and trigger conflict where conflict could be easily avoided.

Most Muslims, like most Christians, like most Hindus, were moderate people who observed their faith as they might observe a high-school dance. The festivities could continue as long as there were no problems. And if a problem did surface, the adults would simply step in and either change it or cancel it.

In the realm of culture, religion in particular, the West had long ago embraced an all-inclusive disposition and called it *tolerance*. If a person did have a conviction of faith, which accounted for roughly 50 percent of the American populace, they learned to keep it to themselves in the name of tolerance. Common sense.

It was estimated that a full 30 percent of Boulder City residents were Muslims. Twenty-five percent Christian. Another 15 percent Hindu. Five percent miscellaneous, a blend of Buddhists and mystics. Only 25 percent were avowed atheists, which by national standards meant that this small city, nestled up against Las Vegas, was a hotbed of religious diversity.

Katrina Kivi, or Kat, as her friends and family called her, was a witch. Not the black-suited, spell-casting type that rode a broom or, for that matter, the Satan-worshipping die-hard type who believed that Lucifer would give them power if they cut themselves enough times or drank blood at one of the séances down by the river.

Kat was a witch because she wanted to be one, a choice that was as much a statement to herself as to the rest of the school. And the statement was unmistakable. *I am me, not any of you. Your rules and regulations are meaningless to me. And if I want to express my religion, I will; you can go to hell for all I care.*

A significant statement for a sixteen-year-old to make in the sea of adolescents who attended Boulder City High School, she thought.

Particularly an African American witch in a city that was mostly Anglo-Saxon Christian and Middle Eastern Muslim. Although she was not purely African American. Her grandfather had come from India and married an African American model from Los Angeles. They'd given birth to her father, who had married a Caucasian European, Helena, Kat's mother, then divorced her five years later. So what did that make Kat?

She wasn't sure, but she preferred to think of herself as African American. It had a desirable feel to it.

The negative consequences for such an admirable stand against the status quo came with the territory. Which was why she was on the city bus now, headed downtown to serve the first two of a hundred community service hours ordered by the judge for breaking Leila's jaw.

Leila, one of the Muslims who had overrun the school, had spit on the floor by Kat's feet and muttered something about burning in hell, and Kat had responded with a fist to the cheek.

Needless to say, Kat had never gotten along with the Muslims. Or the Christians. Or, for that matter, the Hindus. And she found those who walked around professing no faith to be the worst of the cattle, cowing to trends of the day to avoid disrupting the peace.

The school board put her before a local judge within the week, her second such appearance in the last two years. Among other things, the judge had made it painstakingly clear that this was the court's final expression of leniency. The next offense, and Kat would be subject to Nevada's adult criminal code. Any act of aggression or violence, regardless of the circumstance, would constitute a third strike and land her in jail for up to a year. No questions, no consideration.

The judge had then given Kat a choice—forty hours of anger-management classes, or a hundred hours of community service at one of the shelters. She'd taken anger classes twice before. At least the shelter would give her an opportunity to hang out downtown. The consensus between her friends Jay and Carla was that choosing a hundred hours over forty hours was stupid, but then they didn't *really* know Kat. They dressed the same, talked the same, dated the same types now and then, but deep down, Kat wasn't like any of them. Not the Christians, not the Muslims, not the Jews, not even the other witches.

The bus rocked down Adams Boulevard and slowed to a stop in front of the shelter. Kat walked to the rear door, watched an older man with pale blue eyes look her over. And what did he see? A dark-skinned teenager with long straight hair who looked part Indian, part Anglo, part black, all attitude. Jeans. Black flip-flops. If he looked closer he might see the scars on her arm from the period she and her friends had taken to cutting themselves before deciding it was a pointless expression of angst.

An object, not a person, that's what he saw.

His gaze shifted from hers when he saw that she was staring back at him. Same thing every time in this town. They looked because they disapproved, but they didn't have the guts to hold a stare. No one in this world did. How could they expect anyone to follow a certain path if they weren't willing to hold eyes while giving directions? The world had lost its willpower, she thought.

She swung onto the steps and exited the bus. Boulder City had grown from the small-town tourist-trap at the entrance to Lake Mead. The homeless and less fortunate had spread south from Las Vegas. Now it was nothing more than a gray city without the bright lights that Vegas offered at night.

Kat walked into Our Lady of the Desert Community Shelter and looked around. No religious icons suggested it was run by the Catholics, naturally; not if they accepted any government funding. Five or six brown couches faced the walls. A television hung in one corner, playing a twenty-four-hour news feed. Small groups of ragged-looking poor— or scammers, as her friends called them—loitered.

Signs hung over several doors: Dining Room, Recreation Hall, Boarding, Office.

Kat entered the office, signed in after speaking to a Miss Barbara Collins (the Manager on Duty according to her badge), a large woman with red hair who processed her court orders and handed her a blue volunteer badge.

"So what am I supposed to do?"

"You can start by mopping the bathroom floor. You think you can handle that?"

"Do I have a choice?"

"You always got a choice. Next time you might want to wear sneakers. Them flip-flops is liable to get wet working around here."

"I thought I was going to work in the kitchen."

"Cleaning up in the kitchen goes two hours past chowtime and commences an hour prior. When that time comes, if you're here, you can do all the work you want in the kitchen. We feed fifty hungry mouths every night. Right now, you need to clean the bathroom. Mop's in the closet next to the women's stalls."

The whole notion of completing a hundred hours of service in this building weighed like a mountain on her shoulders. But then she'd known it would be like this even as she took the swing that cracked Leila's jaw. *This is gonna hurt me more than it is you, and I already hate you for it.*

"We good?"

"Not really, no," Kat said. She turned without another word and left the office.

"I'm leaving, so check in with the kitchen when you have the floor clean," the MOD called after her. "And don't forget to put up them wet-floor cones."

It took her less than half an hour to do the floors, because from the moment water splashed on her flip-flops she began slipping like a fish. There was no way she could do a decent job, so she slapped the mop around enough to wet the floor and then put the bucket away.

When she poked her head into the office, she saw that Miss Barbara was gone, as promised. In fact, this whole end of the shelter looked vacant. The scammers had probably gone off for some handout or other. She decided to give the premises a quick once-over before reporting to the kitchen.

Kat walked through bunkrooms, wondering what it would be like to spend a night under one of the army-green blankets next to some stranger. She headed for the recreation hall.

Her father had long ago split, leaving her mother with an only child. Amazing they hadn't ended up in one of these places. Her mother, Helena, seemed to do well dealing nights at the casino tables at the new casino in Henderson. They shared a two-bedroom apartment on the north side of Boulder City and saw each other several times a week. It wasn't the lifestyle of the rich or famous, but at least they weren't forced to beg on the streets.

Kat entered the recreation hall—a gym actually, with a basketball court and a stage. These didn't concern her. The seven meatheads who stood in a line facing her, however, did.

They were from her school. Several from her grade, a few juniors and seniors, standing there like they were lined up for a game, staring her down.

"Hello, witch."

She turned around, surprised by the voice. The student standing in the doorway she'd entered through was an older student she'd seen around school—a Muslim who wore a black bandana over slicked hair, signifying his loyalty to his faith. Any such religious symbol was prohibited on school grounds, naturally, but it was still a free country off school property.

He grinned. "You know who I am?"

"A Muslim who knows I'm a witch," she said. "Why, are you lost?"

"Very funny, lady." The boy stepped a few steps closer. "Are all witches so funny?"

She'd walked into an ambush. These were friends of Leila, whose jaw she'd broken. They'd come to teach her a lesson.

One of the boys who stood abreast spoke in Arabic, thinking she didn't understand. But she'd learned enough around school to make out that he was saying they should do it quickly, whatever *it* was.

Kat backed onto the wood floor and scanned the walls for exits. Only two: one beyond the boys, and the door she'd entered.

"Asad," the boy said. "Asad bin Fadil. So that you will remember who has done this to you."

"Katrina Kivi," Kat said. "So that when you wake up blind, you'll know who took your eyes."

He wasn't sure what to do with her response; she knew by the way his eyes narrowed ever so slightly. *Easy, Kat, remember the judge's terms.* She should be running already.

But running felt like suicide to her, not because it was dangerous but because it was cowardly. There were some things she couldn't bring herself to do. Running from a person she hated was one of them.

And Katrina hated Asad. She knew this having only just made his acquaintance.

"You struck a Muslim," the older boy said.

"No, actually, I struck an idiot. The fact that she was also a Muslim was coincidental."

"She was also a very close friend of mine."

"I thought Muslim men kept their women in order. So why did you allow her to insult me?"

Asad let his grin fade. "Don't make the mistake of thinking that all Muslims are as tolerant as the millions of pretenders who call themselves Muslims. I would as soon insult any Muslim who mocks God by refusing to follow the Koran as insult an infidel who worships Satan."

"Then we have more in common than you think," she said. "I hate pretenders as well."

He stopped. "We have nothing in common but the ground we walk on, and I promise you that it will soon be covered with your blood."

"Or the fluid from your eyes."

One of the others chuckled, coaxing a smile from Asad. "A feisty one. You'd make a good wife for the cold nights."

"I think I'd probably throw up all over you," she said. The familiar calm before the storm settled over her.

Asad dipped his head. "And for that I would kill you."

"Didn't Muhammad preach peace?"

"Peace for the peaceful. Death to those who refuse to convert. How can you worship Satan? It's an abomination!"

"I'm not a Satanist. I'm a witch, for the fun of it. My way of protesting all world religions. Christianity, Islam, Judaism, and for that matter, Satanism. I find them all absurd. So I converted to my own religion. Witchery."

"Then you worship only yourself. Disgusting." Asad cast a glance at the others, who closed in slowly. He spit to one side. "Don't be fooled by the weak. God is great."

"Really? He's no longer willing to defend the helpless in this godforsaken place. I assumed it was because he is dead."

Asad's hands balled into fists.

She continued to goad him, seeking an advantage. "Your God, this so-called God of Abraham, Isaac, and Jesus that you Muslims live and kill for, is no more real than the God Christians have been killing for since the dawn of time. Muhammad was no more a prophet than Jesus was."

Asad's eyes flashed in the face of all of the terrible insults to his sacred faith.

"Muslims are as deluded as Christians. You're all a bunch of—"

"Stop!" he screamed. And Kat threw herself at him then, while his eyes were momentarily shut, midscream.

She reached his face before he could knock her away, cutting his jaw with two of her black nails.

Asad flailed with both arms, but the abruptness of her attack had taken him off guard. He swiped thin air as she ducked under and away.

She brought her knee up into his gut and shoved him toward his friends, who were diving in for the kill.

Run, Katrina!

Running from seven boys who had blood in their faces was no act of cowardice. But this realization came too late. She should have tried to outrun them instead of trying to infuriate their leader—a strategy that offered no advantage over the others.

She clawed at Asad's back, ripping his shirt and the skin beneath. And then she sprinted for the rear door.

A hand slammed into her back, shoving her forward. The flip-flops had dried, but they weren't made for running. She tripped over her own feet as she tried to catch herself, slammed to the floor, and rolled to avoid a vicious kick.

One of the boys fell on her—his mistake, because he could have just as easily kept her down with his boots. But Kat was best close in, where her claws and teeth became effective weapons.

Screaming, she grabbed the boy by his hair and jerked his head closer. She got her teeth on his chin and bit hard.

He howled and rolled off, leaving a chunk of his skin behind. Kat spat it out and rolled to her feet, energized by her small victory.

"Is that all the power your God gave you?" she cried. "You can't lick one stinking witch!"

Five of them descended on her at once, and she knew that she was in real trouble now. A fist smashed into her back. Another struck the side of her head.

She kicked hard, felt her heel connect with a bone. Heard it snap.

"Enough!"

The voice rang through the rafters from behind her attackers. As one, the Muslims spun to face it. In the doorway stood a white-collared priest dressed in jeans, black boots, and jacket. Tall, blond, and at first glance Kat could see that he was well built under his loose-fitting clothes. He wore dark sunglasses despite the dim light.

"Get away from the girl."

Asad clearly wasn't ready to release the woman who'd bloodied him, bitten off one friend's chin, and broken the bone of another, who was cradling his left arm.

"Trust me, son, you don't want me to tell you again. Get your hands off the girl and leave this building before I lose my patience."

Asad released her shoulder.

"Leave," the man said.

The boy nodded at his friends, then looked at Kat. "Hide behind his collar today. Tomorrow is a new day, witch."

They left reluctantly out the back door, wearing scowls.

Kat walked toward him, mind swelling with the judge's words. "I'm sorry, Father, I swear I didn't start that. We can keep this to ourselves. Right?"

The man pulled off his white collar, turned, and left the room. What kind of priest would do such thing? She'd just been assaulted, for heaven's sake! Kat walked after him.

"Hey! Did you see what happened in there? You saw it, right?"

He walked down the hall.

"Listen to me!" she shouted.

The man reached for the door that led into the main atrium and turned back. "The whole world is listening, Katrina Kivi."

Only then did she see the camera mounted in the corner above him. Of course, for legal reasons, every move in this publicly funded facility was captured on film. Including the violence she'd leveled at the Muslims, regardless of how justified.

"Then help me," she said. "You're a priest, please help me."

"I'm not a priest. But I do know your case, and I know that help is the last thing you want. A few months in prison might adjust your attitude."

Kat stood trembling with rage. She had the right to defend herself from extremists like Asad. For that matter she'd had the right to break Leila's jaw. She would be completely within her rights to slap this fellow for his arrogance.

Her anger was pointless, she realized, and as soon as she did, it was replaced by thoughts of prison.

"Then why did you save me?"

"Because you need saving. But the judge will see the video feed and she will stay true to her word."

"I had no choice!"

"You could have run."

"I don't run."

"No. You fight." The man stared at her through his dark glasses, hand still on the door handle. "It's a pity."

"You pity me standing up to them?"

"I pity you for standing up for your pitiful self." He opened the door and started to step through.

"Wait. What's your name?"

The man in dark glasses turned his head back to her and hesitated like a man trying to decide if he should answer.

"Johnny," he said.

"Then listen to me, Johnny, whoever you are. I'm begging you, I'll do anything. Please don't tell the judge."

"I don't think you understand. This institution is managed by the church, but it's state owned. We have protocol. I've read the file. The court has ordered your service monitored."

"Then you're saying that there's nothing you can do. Absolutely nothing, so help you God?"

He stared at her for a long moment.

"Please, Johnny. It's not like me to beg, surely you've gathered that much. But I'm begging you. Just give me one more chance. I'll do anything. Legal, that is."

He hadn't moved for over a minute now. Finally he pulled a pen and slip of paper from his shirt pocket, scribbled something on it, and offered it to her. She hurried forward and plucked it from his hand.

"Be at this address at six o'clock tonight. We'll talk to you."

She glanced at the address. "We?"

"Kelly and I."

"Talk to me about what?"

"About if there's any hope for you."

CHAPTER ELEVEN

WASHINGTON, D.C. Darcy rode in the back of the black Lexus sport utility vehicle, trying to adjust herself after five hours of dead sleep. Billy sat to her right, still sacked out. Prior to leaving, Brian Kinnard had given her fifteen minutes to pull together what belongings she needed and promised that his people would secure the house until she returned. Someone would come for the body he'd laid out on a tarp in the garage.

How long until she returned, Kinnard refused to speculate. But he insisted there was no need to take any personal belongings that could be replaced. Money would not be an issue.

She'd gathered the clothes she felt most comfortable wearing—mostly jeans and cotton dresses often pegging her as a hippie—her vampire novels, journal, more novels, iPod containing her entire collection of audiobooks and over a thousand albums. Her stuffed bunny, which she'd hugged every night for the last ten years, affectionately named . . . Bunny.

The rest of her life fit on one twenty-terabyte jump drive—large enough to fit a backup of her main drive and her entire HD3D movie collection.

When all was said and done, Darcy felt humbled by the fact that her whole world fit so easily inside two rolling duffel bags.

Kinnard had made Billy park the Porsche next to the electric Chevy in Darcy's garage. She watched him quickly transfer his possessions into the back of the Lexus, taking some comfort in the realization that his whole world fit into one duffel bag.

He shrugged. "I'm not big on things."

"Yeah," she said. "Me either."

They'd left Lewistown and headed south through Maryland toward Washington, the District of Columbia.

Kinnard spent the trip on the phone, setting up a meeting of what he was calling the council. It was clear that none of this so-called council was eager to drop whatever they had going tonight to meet about "something they couldn't afford to miss," as Kinnard was putting it. Not even "something that could change the landscape of American politics."

Darcy didn't share his conviction. She had no intention of changing anything but the current situation, which was dragging her away from a good life, thank you very much.

"Welcome to the Beltway," Kinnard said as they neared their destination. "The home of politics. Abandon all hope, ye who enter."

They drove along I-495, eighteen lanes of expressway that formed a loop around D.C., twenty miles across. "Falls Church is that way." Kinnard jabbed a thumb over his shoulder. "Bethesda is down south, and once we hit the Woodrow Wilson Bridge, you'll be over the Potomac and inside the Beltway proper. Make sure your soul is attached at all times—this town will steal it in a second, given the chance."

"God help us all," Billy said. Darcy turned to see that he was awake and staring at her. She had her glasses on, something she would be more careful about now.

"You're an attorney, I would think this town would sit well with you."

"Don't mistake the profession for the person," he said. "You mind clarifying a few things for me?" he asked Kinnard.

"Not at all. You're alive. Breathing. Is that clear enough?"

"Don't patronize us," Darcy said.

"Look around. Tell me what you see."

Darcy let her eyes wander over the traffic, the Potomac River ahead, the sea of towering office buildings in the skyline.

"A city," she said.

"A city of almost a million by the 2017 census. We're finally ahead of Wyoming. There's a lot more, though. D.C. isn't just a city. It's a *culture.* You're looking at the seat of the nation, a political representation of us all. What happens here affects every living person in the world. Each policy decision made here echoes into the jungles of Indonesia. You know what we call that?"

"Power," Billy said. "Absolute power."

The man adjusted his shades as if he suspected Billy had read his mind. "Power. This small piece of real estate is home to all three branches of government—not to mention the World Bank and the International Monetary Fund. Enough political power to flatten the earth again. Definitely a war zone too; a political battlefield mined with special interest groups, think tanks, some of the nation's most . . . um . . . *ambitious* minds."

"A good reason to stay away," Billy said.

"Also a good reason to come, apparently. There are as many paid consultants and lobbyists in Washington as there are homeless people on its streets. Almost as though they attract each other."

He merged onto George Washington Memorial Parkway, parallel to the Potomac.

"Here you can be homeless, and I mean hooked and doped, but you're never far from the political version of the same: a suit, a briefcase, and a congressional proposal. You can't politic if you can't beg. Washington is a collection of representatives who have learned to close the blinds and take the phone off the hook. Politically, the United States is bipolar. But then that's just my opinion."

"So how does any of this help Billy and me understand what we're doing here?" Darcy asked.

"I asked you what you saw outside, you said a city. What I see is a world of cutthroats, more than a few of whom are determined to cut yours. Patronizing or not, my observation that you're alive is recognizing a rather astonishing fact. I don't think you can see just how fortunate you are to be breathing any more than you can truly see just how dangerous Washington is, not without surviving it yourself."

Darcy glanced at Billy, who was trying to suppress a grin. Kinnard came across more like a seasoned litigator than a hired henchman.

Then again, he was from Washington. He was obviously more than he let on.

"Assuming, that is, you do survive it," Kinnard said. "They won't stop coming for you."

"But you can protect us," Darcy said. "Right?"

"If you play ball."

He was speaking in circles and Darcy was running out of patience. "And who exactly are you?"

"Me? I'm your best friend in the making, ma'am. I can be anything you need, anytime, for any reason. And that's a promise." He paused. "Or you can just think of me as one of those highly paid consultants I mentioned."

"And what does that make us?" Billy asked.

"Besides alive?"

"I think you've made your point."

"For now just think of yourselves as two more highly paid consultants." And then he added, "Unless this all works out."

"In which case?"

"In which case you just might change the world."

IT TOOK them another half hour to pull up to the secure glass-paneled building on Wilson Boulevard that housed dignitaries visiting the capitol. Kinnard had saved them, brought them to Washington in one piece as promised, and by all accounts Billy knew he should be relieved.

But it wasn't until he looked into Kinnard's eyes for the first time that he gained confidence in the man. Kinnard exited the car, spoke into a radiophone, and exchanged quiet words with two plain guards who stood by the door.

Billy caught one of the guard's eyes through the tinted window and heard his thoughts. The man's concern lay in his rules of engagement. No secrets on the surface.

Kinnard removed his glasses absently. Rubbed the bridge of his nose. Glanced at the car's tinted window. And for the first time, Billy knew what he was thinking. Which was nothing more than how best to facilitate their safety.

Kinnard replaced his glasses.

"Do you trust him?" Darcy had seen the connection.

"Crazy, huh?" He shook his head.

"You do trust him, or you don't?"

"I do, I think. But this reading thoughts . . ."

"Yeah," she said. "Crazy."

Kinnard hurried them from the car into a small atrium featuring a waterfall and two large brass sculptures that could be considered flowers with a little imagination. A security station stood between the front rotating doors and a bank of elevators. Three guards dressed in maroon and gray watched them from their stations behind the counter.

No threatening thoughts.

Kinnard checked them in, ushered them into one of the elevators. A bellboy lugging their duffel bags stepped in last. The doors slid shut.

"You'll need elevator keys to get to the fortieth floor flat," Kinnard said and slid his card through a slot that read Penthouse Access. The elevator rose with enough acceleration to shove Billy's throat into his gut. He glanced at Darcy and saw that she'd kept her glasses on.

Double doors led to their flat. They spread open with a chirp, revealing an expansive glass room overlooking the city. Billy stood next to Darcy at the threshold, stunned by the view.

"Wow." Darcy took a step into the apartment. "This is where we're staying?"

"All yours." Kinnard stepped past them and paid the bellboy. "Thank you."

The bellboy nodded and left.

Billy entered the flat and looked at the white sofas, the ten-foot square Persian rug, the liquor decanter on the built-in bar by the door, the wall screen now showing ocean waves breaking.

But it was the outer wall that arrested his attention. Glass from floor to ceiling, side to side, forty feet of it. Beyond, Washington, D.C., in all of its glory.

"No kidding. Wow."

"The glass will stop anything short of a nuclear blast," Kinnard said. "Nice view, but our primary objective is to keep you safe." He handed them data cards.

"These will get you in and out. You need to go anywhere, you call the security desk and they contact me. A secure car will take you. Unfortunately, your access to the city will be limited due to safety concerns. The flat will have to do for now."

Darcy gazed about the room. "This place is incredible."

"Not bad," Kinnard agreed. He walked to the wall and hit a switch. Lights illuminated a kitchen that had been hidden by a dark wall until now. "Virtual wall," Kinnard said. "Lot of the upscale homes use them now. You'll find the refrigerator fully stocked with food and drinks. Call for anything you want. Anything."

Darcy ran her hands along the back of one of two white sofas facing a hand-carved, resin-coated coffee table inlaid with rivers of brass or gold. The large purple orchids in the vase were fresh, perfectly arranged except for one petal that was broken and browning along the break.

"Is this real?" Darcy asked, eyes on the sofa.

"No. That would be illegal, wouldn't it? Imitation lynx, bleached. Costs more than the real thing, but it's nice."

Billy walked past the couch, running his hand on the silken fabric. *Nice* was an understatement. Everything about the flat was extravagant. This was the kind of place that visiting heads of state paid dearly for.

He stood before the glass, where Darcy joined him, overlooking Washington. The Potomac River's gray-green waters were spanned by a bridge directly below them. Across the river, a wide swath of green parks, memorials, and pools ran a few miles or so, ending in the large domed Capitol. Stunning.

"I assume you know what you're looking at," Kinnard said.

Neither answered. Billy knew some, but not all.

Kinnard pointed with two fingers and dictated, working from the Potomac east. "Below us is West Potomac Park. Not actually part of the National Mall, but connected to it. Directly ahead and across the river is the Lincoln Memorial, and moving on to the reflecting pool, the Ulysses S. Grant Memorial, the Washington Monument, and the National Mall, all ending at the Capitol. In all, it's about three hundred acres of memorials, statues, and other reliquaries of American history."

He indicated a building to their left, which Billy recognized as the White House, and started clicking off buildings in rapid order. "Draw a line from the Jefferson directly northwest along Pennsylvania Avenue and you end up at the White House. Within ten minutes you can walk from the State Department to the Supreme Court. It's all here, Department of the Treasury, the World Bank, the IMF . . . all of it."

"That's it?" Darcy asked. "Somehow I was expecting it to be larger than life."

Kinnard chuckled. "No. Place hasn't been modified much since Congress restricted expansion in 2003." He turned from the window. "Bedrooms are on either side. I trust you'll find them satisfactory. I have more work to do. I'll pick you up at six. Get some rest."

They watched him close the door behind himself. For a long moment Billy stood still, unsure how they should proceed.

Twenty-four hours ago he'd been in the courtroom, facing a bitter end to his life. Now here he stood, forty floors above Washington, next to the girl he'd played God with when they were thirteen. It was all too fast. Too easy.

He walked to the bedroom on the right, peeked into a large room with a huge four-poster bed covered in white linens, and pulled his head back out.

"I don't like it," he said, turning.

Darcy was looking in the other bedroom. She closed the door. "Mine looks nice enough."

"Not the bed. The whole thing. It's way too fast." He crossed to the glass wall and paced in front of it. "Too easy."

"Maybe." She walked into the kitchen and began to inspect the appliances. "Do you have a theory to suggest?"

"Come on, Darcy. A few hours ago you were reluctant to leave your house. Don't tell me you're swallowing all of this like a good little baby."

She faced him, jaw firm. "Don't call me that."

Baby. Wanna trip, baby?

A shiver passed through his shoulders. "You remember writing in the books?"

"No." But her curiosity of the appliance had stalled. "And if I did, I wouldn't want to talk about it."

"We have to!" he said. "The fact is, we're here because of the monastery. Because we both embraced Black's ways. We wrote evil into this world and—"

"Evil existed long before we wrote!" she snapped. "Don't you saddle me with that."

"I'm not. But you have to admit that we're here because of those books we found in the monastery. The Books of History."

"I'm not willing to accept that!" She crossed her arms and walked to the window. "Please, don't do this. You of all people, Billy, should understand."

He nodded. Sat on the arm of the couch. "I know you're hurt, God only knows how much you're hurt. And I know that it was my fault. I practically forced you into the dungeons . . ."

"Please, Billy . . ."

"You have no idea how destroyed I felt when it was all over. I've gone to any lengths to stay clear of anyone even loosely tied to Project Showdown."

"Billy." A tear ran past her dark lenses. "Please."

"Fine." He stood and half lifted his right hand, turning away. The notion that they could continue pretending that none of it happened felt both ridiculous and obscene.

"Fine, we can pretend," he said, facing her again. "None of that really happened. I wasn't responsible for Marsuvees Black or the showdown he forced on Paradise. No one died, no damage done, and Black vanished forever. None of the books, not even a single page from the books, survived when they buried the monastery."

Emotion boiled to the surface, enough to make Billy's throat feel swollen.

"You weren't scarred for life, were you? No, life's been a rose garden. I haven't been looking over my shoulder for the last thirteen years, wondering what might come out of the night to cut me down. I haven't washed out my life with bourbon and poker."

"Stop it!"

But he'd smothered the words for too many years to hold them back now. "Black hasn't spawned any more monsters like himself. You didn't spend the night taped up by a man who sealed you into your own house. He didn't cut off my fingertip. I can't read minds and you can't speak into them! It's all a farce!"

"Okay!" she screamed. "Just stop it!"

She stood trembling in her jeans, on the verge of breaking. Her arms were white and frail, a homebody who rarely saw the sun, if ever. She'd lived in her bubble of protection, peering out at a world she hated. Retreating into those vampire novels of hers for comfort.

But she was strong, and she refused to turn away.

"Just because it happened doesn't mean you have to swim in it."

"I've run from it my whole life. Forgive the observation, but it seems to have caught *us*. I really don't think running's in the cards anymore."

She didn't have an answer to that.

Billy crossed to the window beside her and stared out at the city that hadn't changed in thirty years.

"I'm sorry. I'm afraid too, but I don't think I can run anymore, I just don't. We have these abilities because we defied the rules, found the ancient books, and wrote in them. We can't change that."

She had one elbow propped against her arm now, with her face in her hand. On one hand her reaction was understandable, on the other she was suffering far more than he had. Why? Six hours earlier she'd begged him never to leave her, and thinking about the words now, she knew he wouldn't dare.

"Why are you so afraid of the past?" he asked.

"Because," she said, "it's not the past. I feel like it's here, inside of me, waiting to raise its ugly head." She swallowed hard. "You ever feel like that? I think I have a snake inside."

Made sense.

"Then I need you to believe something," he said, reaching for her hand. "Look at me."

She lifted her face and looked at him through the dark glasses.

"I need you to believe that I'm not that snake. Can you do that?"

Darcy just looked at him.

"We're together again, Darcy; you and I. We're not in a dungeon, but for all we know it could be worse. Something tells me we're going to need each other. That means we have to trust each other."

She wiped her nose and nodded.

"Can you trust me?"

"Should I?"

"Yes," Billy said.

"How?"

"Take off your glasses," he said.

A soft smile played across her mouth. "Is that fair?"

"It's quid pro quo. When your eyes are covered, your own power isn't effective. Glasses blind us both, so to speak."

"You mean my words don't sweep you away?"

He grinned. "Not now. Remove your glasses and speak to me; it might be different."

"But then you'll be able to read my mind."

"Does that frighten you?"

She hesitated, then reached up and removed her glasses. Her light brown irises sparkled like crystals around a perfect black sphere. Billy felt himself pulled in the abyss beyond, where her thoughts echoed for him to hear.

I'm afraid, Billy. Please don't look at me like that. I'm afraid of what you will find.

I don't care what anyone thinks of me, but I care what you think about me, Billy.

"Can you . . . hear me?" she asked.

"Yes."

"They say the human mind can only store a handful of events or thoughts in the immediate, short-term memory. Are you going deeper?"

"I don't know. No, I'm just getting what you're thinking on the surface. Say something to me."

They were staring into each other's eyes like partners circling in an intimate dance.

"I am saying something."

"No. Tell me to do something. Persuade me. Don't you want to know how this gift of yours works? It might have some perks."

"Okay," she said. "Hop on one foot."

Billy felt nothing that compelled him to do so.

"I don't feel anything. Try something else."

"Stand on your head. Jump out the window."

"Isn't that a bit dangerous?"

"Clearly I don't have the authority to make you do anything of the sort."

"No, but if you did . . ."

"Then I would have seen you attempting to jump and stopped you with as much authority. So you can read minds and I can do nothing, is that it?"

"No, I felt your pull on my mind this morning. Try something else. Maybe something I'm predisposed to do. Or may want to do without realizing it."

She stared at him, thinking. A fire lit her eyes. "Could be a bit dangerous, don't you think?"

"Why is that? We're just trying—"

"Kiss me, Billy. Please shut up and kiss me."

The urge to step up to Darcy and gently kiss her lips pulled at him like an undertow. His fingers began to tremble. He couldn't kiss her, of course. That would be absurd, having just reconnected after so many years estranged from one another, never mind that they'd kissed before, in the dungeon.

"Kiss me, Billy," Darcy whispered.

Billy stepped in and kissed her lightly on the lips, pulled by her words. The moment his lips touched hers, his desire swelled until he could hardly resist her lure. And then he couldn't resist it at all.

He put his arms around her waist, pulled her against him, and kissed her deeply.

She returned the affection. His heart was pounding in his ears, flooding him with such a strong desire to love her, to protect her, to hold her that he thought he might do something rash.

Time seemed to stall.

He pulled back, disoriented.

"Well," she said, wearing a coy smile. "Was that me? Or was that you?"

"I . . . You. Both, maybe both. I'm sorry, I didn't mean to do that."

"I think you did."

"Maybe you should put your glasses back on," he said, turning away. "I don't know how much of that I can handle."

He felt himself blushing. He'd tipped his hand, hadn't he? Was that really how her voice worked? Persuading others to do what was really inside of them to do rather than something against their will?

It was all a bit dizzying.

"I like you too, Billy," Darcy said. "Just so you know."

He didn't know what to say. So he kept his mouth shut and walked back to the couch.

Darcy slid onto the seat opposite him. "Now what?"

They spent the afternoon catching up, respecting each other's boundaries, yet breaking down the past with a freedom Billy hadn't felt for a long time. That one kiss had melted thirteen years of ice that had barred him from realizing just how close he and Darcy really were.

They had been taken into a monastery as infants, two of thirty-six orphans who'd been rescued from various parts of the world and brought to Colorado, where a group of priests led by David Abraham had brought them up in the ways of virtue, protecting them from any form of evil. Noble savages, sequestered away as unknowing participants in an experiment between primitivism and morality. The overseers had known all along that a terrible kind of evil waited in the tunnels below the monastery.

Billy had been the first child lured into those tunnels where he'd discovered the ancient books responsible for these unique gifts. And Darcy had been right by his side. The consequences of writing in the pages had been disturbing enough for Billy to spend a lifetime hiding from, but the worst of it could still lie ahead.

"Marsuvees Black isn't dead," Billy said.

"You can't know that."

"You said you feel a snake in your gut, waiting to come out?"

"Something like that."

"So do I. And I think it's him. I think he's alive and after us."

"The Catholic Church is after us," she said.

"Could be. Or it could be Black, masquerading as the church."

She hesitated, not ready to abandon her conviction that the church was living up to its reputation by trying to squash them.

Billy glanced at the clock. "Six o'clock. Kinnard should be here."

The doorbell chimed.

CHAPTER TWELVE

KATRINA KIVI looked at the slip of paper the man named Johnny had written the address on: 1549 Inspiration Canyon Drive. The bus had dropped her off at the end of the street, a good ten-minute walk. Johnny whoever-he-was lived on the edge of the old district in one of the wood-frame houses that still stood.

Kat had finished her first day at the shelter and hit the road at five, but not before finding out more about the man who'd mysteriously appeared, broken up the fight with Asad, and then vanished.

Tobias, an Indian janitor at the shelter who liked to talk, had filled in a few blanks. Johnny wasn't a priest, not technically, no. But he often wore a collar and nobody seemed to mind. They called him Father Johnny or *Padre Juan*.

According to Tobias, Johnny was a quiet man who volunteered every other week, usually in the kitchen or cleaning up in the rec hall. Never to be seen without them glasses, said Tobias. Never.

Johnny had become somewhat of a legend around the halls of the shelter after subduing two armed men during a robbery a few months earlier. Bravest nut Tobias had ever seen. Spread his arms like he was some kind of savior, walked right up to them speaking in that low voice of his and then, *bang!*, he had both of them flipped over on their bellies, squealing like pigs. He shoved the guns into his belt like a man born with holsters in his skin and hog-tied them in ten seconds flat using an extension cord from one of the lamps.

Father Johnny.

Kat had spent the last five hours rehearsing every possible angle of her ostensibly simple predicament, and best as she could figure it, she was toast. The judge could reverse her previous order, but there was no reason for her to do so. Nevada's violence laws were some of the strictest in the nation. Three strikes and you're out. End of discussion.

This was Kat's third strike. She was out. There was a jail cell in Clark County with her name on it. Four to a cell. The idea had grown uglier as the hours ticked by. She'd never actually considered the possibility that it could come down to this. One lousy fight, a justified one at that, and here she was.

The idea made her palms sweaty.

Kat stopped on the porch and looked around. Streets were empty, large lawns, brown lawns. Not exactly your typical suburban neighborhood settled by rich Indians or Arabs like so much of the city. But not poor, either.

She lifted her hand and was about to knock on the door when a faint moan drifted to her on the wind. A sob. From behind the neighbor's house?

It came again, a cry and then a strange grunt that sounded angry. No one on the street that she could see.

Kat stepped off the porch and crept to the corner of the house. Then around and down the wall. A tall fence bordered the backyard, but the wooden gate was wide open. She stopped in the opening and studied a grassy lawn, at the end of which stood a white shed with a red roof.

The sob came again, from the direction of the shed, she thought. This time it was joined by a soft thump.

Three soft thumps, something hitting wood. Still no sign of anyone except for this one lonely voice crying softly on a slight breeze.

She almost returned to the front door, but the next cry was so sharp and laced with pain that she felt compelled to rush to the aid of whoever was in such trouble.

Kat hurried across the lawn toward the shed, one of those ready-made ones you could buy at Home Depot if she had to guess. She eased her head around the corner and blinked.

A blonde woman dressed in jeans and a sleeveless red blouse kneeled on the dirt, facing the shed's back wall, forehead pressed against the siding. A soft moan escaped her gaping mouth, though there were no tears that Kat could see.

This was the crying she'd heard. The woman was softly thumping her forehead on the shed in anguish.

The sight pulled at Kat's chords of empathy and terrified her at once. The woman looked clean and well groomed, not abused or hurt.

Kat pulled back, undecided about how to proceed. She could ask the woman if she needed any help, but anyone hiding like this obviously wanted privacy more than help.

The wail continued, and Kat thought she might start to cry herself. What kind of man was this Johnny? Maybe she'd gotten the wrong house.

She ran back to the gate and turned back to the shed. The afternoon seemed unnaturally quiet except for the sound of the woman's moaning.

"Hello, is there anyone back there?" she called out.

The crying stopped immediately.

"Hello? Is this Johnny's house?"

For a moment only the breeze blew, and then barely. The woman stepped from behind the shed. A genuine smile spread across her mouth.

"Hello, you must be Katrina Kivi. I was just getting some work done." The woman walked toward Kat, exhibiting no sign that she'd been crying and beating her head against the wall.

"My name's Kelly." The woman stuck out her hand and Kat took it.

She had blue eyes, the haunting kind that women who'd been around the block typically had, though she couldn't be older than thirty.

"Johnny told me all about you. Come on, he's been expecting you."

Kelly stepped past Kat and led her back around to the porch, through the front door, and into a living room filled with antique furniture.

The whole thing was downright freaky, Kat thought. But the woman had the right to her own privacy, she supposed. Kat had her own struggles that she wanted to keep to herself, and she wasn't interested in nosing about Kelly's business.

"Have a seat," Kelly said.

"No thanks, I'll stand."

Kelly's brow arched. "Really? You're not staying?"

"I don't even know why I'm here."

"Probably because you're in a jam, if I know Johnny. And I do."

Kelly smiled. The woman was pretty enough. Even confident, despite the shed incident. For all Kat knew, Johnny had taught *her* how to hog-tie gunmen.

"You're his wife?"

"Not yet."

"I see you've met my fiancée," a voice said from behind. Johnny walked in, as blond as Kat remembered. He'd changed into khaki cargo pants and a loose black T-shirt. Still wore the same glasses, framed in black, like the glass itself. The expensive, stylish kind.

"Hello, Katrina." He took her hand like a gentleman and shook it once. "You hungry?"

"Not really."

"Eat anyway. You need some meat on those bones. You got tapeworm or something?"

"I'm not a pig," Kat said. "That a crime?"

"Not the last time I checked."

"You always so frank?" Kat asked.

"I speak my mind," he said. "That a crime?"

She was beginning to like him. "Not the last time I checked."

"Next time you check, it just might be. Kelly, could you get the pizza out of the warmer?"

"She didn't want to sit," Kelly said with a slight smile. Then she retreated into the kitchen.

"Sit," Johnny said, sitting on the sofa. He rested his feet on a large leather ottoman that doubled as the coffee table. "Mind the furniture, it's not mine. Came with the house."

Kat sat on the edge of a chair, elbows on her knees. "Would you mind telling me why I'm here?"

"I was under the impression you were in trouble. Something about a judge who plans to throw you in jail."

"Assuming that incident is—"

"Too late," Johnny said. "It's already on her desk."

Kat stood. "What? You said you could help me! You know very well that the moment she sees that footage, I go down."

"Yes, I do. Sit."

"Then why am I here?"

"I assume it's because you're toast. Please . . . sit."

Kat eased to her seat, confused as to his intentions. "Okay, stop being so cryptic here. Why did you give me your address?"

Kelly came in with a large Pied Piper Pizza box and three bottles of water.

"So that you could break some bread with my fiancée and me," Johnny said. "We'd like to know how serious you are about getting our help."

"I defended myself from a guy who was trying to beat me to a pulp," she snapped. "I wasn't knocking off a casino. You really think I deserve to go to jail for that?"

He took a slice of pepperoni pizza from the box, took a bite, wiped the corner of his mouth with the back of his hand, and then gestured toward her. "Have a piece."

But she was too frustrated to consider her hunger.

"I'm not the one who decides if you deserve to be locked up. We have judges for that. They look at all the evidence, your priors, and your attitude, put it all on their scales and make a judgment. In your case, I do believe the scales of justice will weigh in the favor of jail time." He took another bite.

"Why?"

"Because of your attitude," Johnny said. "Which is why you're here. To see if you really do want our help. Tell me, do you have something in particular against Indians?"

What kind of question was that? "No."

"Muslims?"

"No."

"How about Arabs?"

She hesitated. "No."

"So then that incident was race related?"

"I said no."

"But you do hate Arabs, don't you? You would never admit it in school, maybe not even to your friends. Everyone knows that anything less than tolerance isn't tolerated these days. I can see why you would lie about it."

He wasn't easily fooled. "You don't think the towel-heads have ruined our country? Talk to them about tolerance."

"As a matter of fact, no, I don't think Arabs have ruined our country. And I think most of them are as tolerant as their neighbors. Perhaps more so. But you're being honest. You hate Arabs."

He left it at that, and Kat didn't see any need to confuse the issue.

"So let's say, just for the sake of argument, that I do really want your help," she said. "You said the judge already has the report. How would you propose to help me?"

"I'll tell you what: you have a piece of pizza, pretend you're grateful to be here sharing food with us, and then maybe I'll explain why I invited you."

Kelly sat down next to him, a slice of pizza in hand. She put her feet up on the ottoman, bit into her slice, and watched Kat while Johnny rubbed her back with his free hand.

Kat felt like a goldfish in a bowl, but she wasn't exactly in a position to turn her back on him yet. Her mother had often cursed her stubbornness, but she wasn't a complete fool.

Kat withdrew a piece of pizza, leaned back into the cushions, and crossed her legs, pretending to be interested in the oil paintings of lakes and mountains that hung on the walls.

They ate in what Kat found to be a very awkward silence for a few minutes. Johnny seemed content to stare out the window through those glasses of his, either lost in thought or busily manipulating her, tempting her to ask the one question that burned on her mind until she could no longer resist.

"Why the glasses?"

It was Kelly who answered. "I'm afraid that's just a bit too personal, Katrina."

"Kat," she snapped.

"Well, Kat, you're going to have to wake up to the fact that you're in a world of trouble here. Johnny can help you, trust me. But I have to agree with him, you don't seem to have a clue about how abrasive your attitude is. I'm not sure I'd blame the judge."

"You want me to pretend I'm someone I'm not?"

"No," Johnny said.

"And you? Are you allowed to pretend you're someone you're not?"

He stared at her, slowly smiling. "Now we're getting somewhere."

"Why the glasses?" she asked again.

"They're for your sake. I was involved in a bit of trouble and came out blind. But let's not talk about that."

"You're blind?" The revelation surprised her. "I'm . . . I mean, you don't seem blind."

"Tell me, Kat, do you believe in God?"

"God? What does God have to do with any of this?"

"Humor me."

"Seriously?"

He refused to answer.

"I'm a witch. Not the hocus-pocus kind or the Satan-worshipping kind, just the plain old love-the-earth-and-smoke-some-grass-when-you-get-the-chance variety. As for Allah"—she shrugged—"God, whatever . . . it all sickens me. Just being honest."

"Fair enough. Then where do you get your sense of right and wrong?"

"What's wrong today is right tomorrow," she said. "The world is full of hypocrites crying about what's right and wrong. I'll tell you what's wrong." She felt her temperature edge up. "God is wrong. Telling people to hate their neighbors because they don't have Jesus or Allah or Buddha."

"I see. And evil?"

"Like I said, I don't go for all the hocus-pocus."

"I see."

Johnny stood and walked to the kitchen, leaving Kelly with her legs curled under her on the sofa, smiling. That infuriating plastic smile.

"Okay? So now what?"

"Now you can go home, Katrina," Johnny said, washing his hands.

"You'll help me, then?"

"I'm afraid not."

She stood again. "What do you mean?"

"I mean I don't think you're very interested in being helped. I'm sorry you had to come all the way out here. Would you like a ride to the bus stop? Kelly?"

Kat's anger boiled to the surface. "What kind of nut are you? How the heck do you know what kind of help I'm interested in?"

"He knows," Kelly said quietly. "Trust me, he knows."

It was all Kat could do to keep from picking up a cushion and throwing it at the woman. *Easy, Kat. Don't do anything stupid.*

Johnny came back into the room, drying his hands on a towel. "I'm sorry, really, I am. Kelly?"

"I'll give you a ride," Kelly said, unfolding herself.

"No. Forget it. Where's your bathroom?"

"Down the hall," Kelly said, gesturing to it.

Kat walked across the brown carpet, dizzy with anger. She might have been tempted to think that the bait and switch had to do with her skin color, but she knew this false priest would never have invited her if he had any issue with blacks or Indians or whatever she was.

She walked down the hall, pushed her way into what she thought was the bathroom, and found herself in a bedroom instead. Queen-sized bed, overstuffed chair, drawn curtains. Looked unlived in. On the far side was a door that she thought might open to a bathroom.

Without a second thought she crossed to the door and pulled it open. But it wasn't a bathroom either. Rather, a very large walk-in closet. A dozen articles of clothing hanging neatly, several boxes piled on the right, each labeled with a month: January, February, March . . .

She saw all of this by the light filtering in from the door she'd opened. But the closet was deeper on her left, cloaked in darkness. She hit the switch on the wall and blinked.

A rack had been fixed to the wall. Seven or eight weapons sat in the rack, and next to each, several boxes of ammunition. Two rifles, an automatic weapon of some kind, three pistols, several knives . . . There was enough here to start a small war.

Whatever Father Johnny was, she doubted very much that he was blind. Unless this belonged to Kelly. But from what Kat could tell, Kelly didn't live in this house.

Kat took two steps toward the rack and stopped. Her right hand began to shake. She might not believe in God, but God may have just believed in her.

It was a crazy thought. The kind only a desperate person would even consider. But she was a desperate person, wasn't she? There was something about the mystery surrounding Johnny that could get her out of this fix. She hadn't come here to eat pizza before being sent to jail.

Kat moved up to the rack, ran trembling fingers over the pistols, and pulled one of them off the wall. Its black steel gleamed in her hand, cool to the touch. She'd fired several guns in the desert before, with boys showing off their toys. A tug on the slide revealed a round chambered. He was the kind who would leave his weapons loaded, she thought.

She stared up at the automatic weapon on the wall. Set the pistol down and reached for the larger gun. Held it gingerly.

Then she slid the pistol into her belt at her back, cradled the automatic weapon in both hands, and returned to the living room.

CHAPTER THIRTEEN

THE COUNCIL.

Kinnard led Darcy and Billy to the basement of Constitution Hall across Eighteenth Street from the U.S. Department of the Interior. They entered through a supply dock and made their way down a service elevator—all new over the last several years, Kinnard said—and into a large conference room.

Seated around one end of an oval cherry table, nursing drinks in crystal glasses, sat four men and two women, leaning back and talking in familiar tones. A couple of dozen high-backed chairs surrounded the table. Variable indirect lighting was set on low. The Hyundai plant in Lewistown had half a dozen similar conference rooms, all built to impress visitors and presumably to improve efficiency. Though with a full bar near at hand and such comfortable leather chairs, Darcy wondered how much of a priority efficiency really was here.

The conversation stalled, then stopped entirely. All eyes turned to them. All heads, to be more precise. Darcy couldn't see their eyes because they all wore dark glasses.

Yes, of course. She still had a hard time believing this ability she supposedly had was real. What had she really done to prove it? Talked Billy into kissing her. She was a girl, he was a guy, they'd shared a crush the last time they'd been together. Did it really take some kind of super-human power to talk him into kissing her?

"Ladies and gentlemen, I'd like for you to meet our guests," Kinnard announced with a knowing grin. "Billy Rediger and Darcy Lange." Then to Billy and Darcy, "Meet the Council of Seven."

"Council of Seven," Billy said. "I thought this was more of an infor-mal group."

"Well, yes. But if I'm right, that will all change tonight." He pulled out two chairs. "Have a seat."

Darcy sat at the head next to Billy and crossed her legs under the table.

"Forgive the glasses. I took the liberty of insisting they all wear pro-tection. We don't want all the Capitol Hill secrets bared to the world." A chuckle. "Not yet, at any rate."

There were six plus Kinnard. The four men all sported white shirts and ties; two wore navy blue jackets. The two women wore blouses, one pink silk and one white cotton, pants or skirts beneath the table, Darcy couldn't tell. At first glance she would place all but Kinnard and one of the women over fifty. All meticulously groomed and comfortable.

None of them had yet spoken. They simply stared from behind their protective lenses. David Abraham may have confided in Kinnard or another one of these power brokers, but that didn't necessarily make them all cozy bedfellows.

The room seemed robbed of air.

"Maybe introductions would be appropriate," Kinnard said. He went around the room clockwise using two fingers to point out each member.

Lyndsay Nadeau, attorney general, the older woman in white. Looked nearly anorexic.

Ben Manning, Democratic senator from Nevada. The only black man in the group.

Fred Hopkins, Democratic representative from New York. Overweight and short.

Annie Ruling, White House chief of staff, the younger woman in pink. The prettiest of the bunch by far.

Sanchez Dominquez, Republican senator from Illinois. Looked like a brother to the Hispanic president, Cesar Chavez.

Newton Lawhead, associate director of the FBI. Gray hair, pale face.

Brian Kinnard, with the CIA. And that's all he would share. Probably the only one here who could handle a gun with ease.

He smiled. "You're probably wondering how such a powerful and diverse group of leaders ever managed to agree on a meeting place. Let me assure you, it wasn't easy."

"Well, you got us here," the senator from Nevada, Ben Manning, said. "The question is, can you keep us?"

"I only have a few minutes," the chief of staff said. Annie. She kept her eyes on Billy. "Why don't we cut to the chase?"

They were a skeptical lot, and Darcy didn't blame them. She wondered what kind of favors Kinnard had called in to get them all here.

"Of course," Kinnard said. To Darcy and Billy: "Like I told you, this may take some convincing."

The attorney in Billy rose to the surface. "So, in essence, we rushed down here to meet with six highbrows who are a breath away from throwing us out on the street?"

"Close," Annie Ruling said.

"Then I'd have to advise my client to reserve her thoughts," Billy said.

"Client? Is that what you are, Miss Lange? I was led to believe you haven't seen each other for thirteen years." So Annie wasn't used to being handled by people who wore jeans.

"You think I would walk into this den of snakes without proper representation?" Darcy said.

The attorney general, Lyndsay Nadeau, smiled from the far side. "Feisty. That's a start. But can you bite, darling?"

Billy stood. "I think it would be best for us to leave."

"And go where?" Kinnard snapped. "Into the arms of Ricardo Muness?"

"He's got a point," Lyndsay said.

Darcy stood to show her solidarity with Billy.

"No," Billy said. "But once Muness understands what we can offer him, I think he'll be friendly enough. We appreciate your efforts in rescuing us this morning. The flat was a nice place to rest up. The food was excellent. But I'm afraid we're in the wrong room now. We really have to be going."

He started to turn. Posturing, Darcy thought. All posturing, and she loved Billy for how smoothly he did it.

"Sit down, son," the attorney general said. "None of us can say how Brian managed to pull this off, but you have the ear of seven of the most powerful people in the United States. Let's at least examine the reason for this rather unusual gathering, shall we?"

He looked at her. "To what end?"

"Well . . . If you can do what Brian says you can . . . Trust me, we'll be interested."

Billy looked at Darcy, who was feeling quite good about the way the meeting was going down. She'd never understood herself to enjoy conflict of this sort, but she certainly couldn't deny that at the moment she felt positively exhilarated.

She sat and Billy followed her lead. "So you want a show-and-tell, is that it?" she asked.

"Something like that."

Now Kinnard was smiling.

"Fine, then let's start with Annie," Darcy said. "Chief of staff, right? Do you mind taking your glasses off, Annie?"

She hesitated, then lifted her hand.

"I warn you, this could get embarrassing," Billy said.

Her hand stopped on her glasses. "Is that so?"

"Please try not to think about any . . . say, inappropriate relationship you might have engaged in during the last few years. Any derogatory thoughts about your neighbor's appearance, or any parts of your own body that you might find embarrassing. As long as you don't think about it, you should be fine."

The chief of staff sat speechless.

"You wanted a show-and-tell," Billy said. "You show, I tell. Unless, of course, I'm bluffing."

"Can he really do that?" Annie asked Kinnard.

He shrugged, but he was grinning.

"Think of a number, Annie. Do you mind if I call you Annie? Think of a number between one hundred and one million. Write it on the notepad in front—"

"Please, we didn't come here for parlor tricks. This is ridiculous."

Billy studied her for a moment. "You're right, it's been done, hasn't it? Then just remove your glasses, all of you, remove your glasses and let's see where this takes us."

No one did.

"How does it work?" FBI man Lawhead asked.

"You already know how it works. I see your eyes, I see the thoughts in your consciousness. Not the ones stored in memory banks, but those you are actually aware of at any given moment. Usually no more than five or six thoughts."

He'd explained his theories to Darcy earlier, and after a quick search on the Net and some testing she'd agreed to under the strictest conditions, they confirmed that those theories were at least likely.

Annie pulled her notepad forward, scribbled something under a cupped hand, and turned it over. "Okay, what number did I just write?"

"Think about it, remove your glasses for a second, and look at me."

Annie reached up and lifted her glasses. The moment they'd cleared her forehead, Billy spoke. "127,333," he said.

She froze, glasses hovering over her forehead.

"And now you're trying to figure out how I could have done that. You're efficiently running through a list of possibilities. Mirrors, no. Cameras, no. Other surveillance gadgets, but you know the room was swept before this meeting. No chance. And you're reminding yourself that you don't know me, never met me, besides, the number was completely random, not your birthday or something those who know you might be able to guess at. Should I go on?"

Annie lowered her glasses. Turned the notepad over for them to see.

127,333

Lawhead stared at the number. "So you're saying you can actually read thoughts as if they were in a book."

"The thoughts in your immediate consciousness," Billy said. "Care to try?"

Lawhead removed his glasses, stared at Billy for a few seconds, then replaced them.

"Your grandmother is in Saint Gabriel's Hospital, Columbia, Ohio. You're hoping the Vitamin B therapy they administer this afternoon will mitigate the adverse affects of the selective radiation administered last month."

"Anything else?"

"Fragments."

"What kind of fragments?"

"A hangman's noose. Doubts. Fear."

"You can read emotions?"

Billy shrugged. "I don't know. Thoughts about emotions maybe. I'm not exactly practiced yet."

"Does it come and go?"

"Not so far, no. I see your eyes, I pretty much know what you're thinking."

"This is absolutely incredible."

"Ladies and gentlemen," Kinnard said, "think of the implications."

Ben Manning, the black senator from Nevada, was frowning. "I am, and I'm not sure I like them. What about her?" Nodding at Darcy.

She glanced at Billy. Compared to him, her ability was virtually untested. Apart from the kiss, of course. She wasn't about to seduce anyone in this room.

Again, Billy came to the rescue. "Darcy can . . . what shall we say . . . help people do what they want to do. Or know they should do. Or what is logical to do. Or something like that."

"So you don't actually know what you can do?" Annie said.

"Well, evidently I can be persuasive. You'll have to ask Billy. He kissed me this morning." She dropped the admission in his lap and sat back to see how he would deal with it.

"Not exactly what I'd call a miracle," Lawhead said.

Billy's face had reddened a shade. "Trust me, sir, her ability to persuade isn't tied to any adolescent fantasies. Her words can be quite influential."

"You can persuade people to do what they're predisposed to do," Annie said. "As Newton said, that's not exactly a miracle."

"What do you want me to do, fly around the room for you? I'm not some freak on the Net. Please, take your glasses off. Just for one second."

The president's chief of staff plucked her dark lenses off and stared Darcy down with baby blues.

"Surely there's at least one person in this room you'd love to slap for the way they've conducted themselves lately. This is, after all, Washington. Slap them now."

At first there was no change in Annie's demeanor. "Don't be ridiculous."

"Just one slap, honey. He deserves it, you know he does."

Sweat beaded on Annie's forehead. She tapped a French manicured nail on a glass half filled with amber liquor. "This is ludicrous. What a juvenile suggestion." Her lips were trembling, just barely, but enough to betray her struggle. "The fact that you would even *think* of this shows just how immature you are. Yes, this *is* Washington—not some sorority house!"

Darcy leaned forward, speaking low, enunciating each word clearly.

"He deserves it, you know he does. And you know he would slap you if I asked him to. Under the plastic smiles in Washington, everyone wants to slap his neighbor. Do it now, Annie."

The war being waged in Annie's mind was now not only unmistakable but a bit frightening. No one rose to her position in this town without having extraordinary control of her faculties.

"This is ridiculous . . ."

But that control was slipping.

"Okay, I think you've made your point," Ben Manning said.

"Slap him, Annie. Do it now."

"I can't! Don't . . ." She stopped, closed her eyes, trying to maintain the last threads of control. When her eyes snapped open, Darcy knew something had changed.

Annie reached over and struck Ben Manning on his shoulder with an open hand. "No!" She struck him again, unleashing a fit of anger directed at the Nevada senator. "No, no, no! How dare you threaten to expose the president's university binges over his stand on the health-care bill? He was just a kid!"

Annie stopped, stared at Darcy with wide eyes, slipped her glasses back on, and then lowered her head into her hands.

Okay. Awkward.

"Please tell me I didn't just do that," Annie mumbled, face red.

Ben Manning had paled. The rest didn't know how to react except to look between Darcy and Annie.

"Forgive me, Ben," Annie said, turning to the man. "I . . . I don't know what came over me. I didn't mean any of it . . ." She swallowed. "Well, yes, I did mean it, actually. Every word. But I had no right to act so unprofessionally. I'm sorry."

Lyndsay Nadeau smiled. "Well, well, well . . ." The attorney general looked like she was enjoying herself. "My deepest apologies, Brian. I'm impressed." She addressed Darcy. "Can you make people do things they don't want to?"

She was about to say no when Billy spoke. "It's too early to know."

"You may find all of this amusing, Miss Nadeau," Ben Manning said, "but I find it troubling. Setting these two loose in our nation's capital would be incredibly irresponsible!"

"Which is why we are here," Kinnard said.

"Ben's right," Annie said, arms crossed now. "This could be dangerous."

"Unless they work for us," the overweight senator from New York, Fred Hopkins, said.

"We're not guns for hire," Darcy snapped.

None of them seemed too interested in her comment.

"Imagine these two on the Senate floor," someone said.

"Heaven help us all."

"Whatever the advantage, two minds with these abilities would destroy Washington," Manning said. "We can't allow it."

The attorney general faced him. "What are you suggesting?"

For the first time, the full extent of their predicament settled over Darcy. She and Billy presented a real danger to the men and women in this room. One that might push them to extreme measures.

She turned to Billy and saw that a trail of sweat marked his temple.

"Yes, Ben, what are you suggesting?" he demanded. "That we should be suppressed somehow, knocked off?"

The senator just stared at them.

"Why don't you bolster my trust in you by removing your glasses so that I can see what you're really thinking?"

But Manning made no move to remove his glasses.

"Don't be foolish," Lawhead snapped. "We're looking at what might be this country's most valuable asset. I suggest we put our minds to protecting that asset!"

"Agreed," the attorney general said. Lyndsay Nadeau watched Darcy with a smile. "Don't you worry, dear. Argument is just part of the whole process."

"You're right," Annie said. "This could be good."

Manning shook his head. "If you're thinking we should use them to manipulate discussions made on the hill . . ."

"Come on, Ben, no one's suggesting we waltz Darcy into the White House to seduce the president," Lawhead said. "There are other ways to test the waters, so to speak."

"Assuming our two guests are in favor of working with us," Lyndsay said. "This is more about them than us."

They looked at Darcy and Billy.

"Yes, assuming," Lawhead said. "Brian?"

Kinnard had worn a perpetual grin. He might not hold the most power in this room, but he was clearly the mastermind.

"Our proposal is simple," Kinnard said to Darcy and Billy. "Commit to this council. Change Washington with us. Change the world. In exchange, we will provide for you without limitation. More importantly, we will guarantee your security. You are already in the crosshairs."

"That simple, huh?" Billy said.

"If you choose to go it alone, you're free to leave after this meeting."

"And if we stay? What would we do? Besides sit tight up in our glass box?"

Both Lyndsay and Lawhead spoke at once, then stopped. No shortage of ideas, naturally. The other members still sat in shock, trying to figure out if what they'd just witnessed was somehow rigged. But they were also reeling over the implications of the power, assuming it was real.

Lawhead looked around the table. "If I may?"

Lyndsay Nadeau nodded. She was the top authority here, Darcy thought. They would argue, but she would cast the final vote.

"I admit, this could . . . There's no telling what the repercussions of . . ." Lawhead shook his head. "It's hard to believe." He stood and walked to the bar. "We have to be cautious. See what we really have here. You've probably heard of these lynchings in Missouri. Homicide motivated by both race and religion with an intent to elicit revenge."

Darcy had heard it on the news just last night. Disturbing.

Lawhead poured himself a drink. "Two persons of color have been hanged in the last week, in and around Kansas City, one on Kansas soil, one on Missouri soil, making the case a federal one. Both victims were abducted immediately following the religious services they'd attended and found hung behind the church. Someone clearly has a beef with black Christians."

He faced Billy and Darcy, drink in hand. "What would you think about helping the FBI stop the killer?"

"No," Ben Manning snapped. "Not before we know more about these abilities."

Lyndsay Nadeau came to their defense. "Please, Mr. Manning, the suggestion seems reasonable to me."

"They should be locked up, not escorted around the country by the FBI."

They all turned to the senator from Nevada.

"Some respect for our guests," Kinnard demanded. "I don't think you appreciate—"

"I appreciate the fact that I was just slapped by Miss Ruling because of this woman. I appreciate that she has no business out in public. Even less business mixing with anyone who has any power in this country."

Darcy felt the blood drain from her face. She didn't know quite what to say.

Lawhead set his glass down. "You're overreacting, Mr. Manning."

But Manning wasn't easing up. "I insist you put them both under armed guard."

"They are," Kinnard said.

"And kept there."

"So now you want to incarcerate us?" Billy demanded. He faced Kinnard. "This is what you bring us to?"

"Actually . . ." Fred Hopkins, short and plump, wiped his beaded brow with a hankie. "Ben has a point. I realize this is awkward for all of us, but if the wrong party got their hands on Darcy in particular . . ." He didn't bother finishing the thought. "And she could do some major damage on her own."

The room fell silent. Darcy suspected that Billy was as taken aback as she over this assault.

Lyndsay Nadeau was the one who settled the issue.

"I appreciate your concern, and I'm sure that the FBI will take it under advisement. For the time being, let's keep you two under tabs, shall we? If you're not with Kinnard it would be best to stay in secure quarters."

"You're actually imprisoning us?"

"We are protecting you, just until we can figure this out."

"Nonsense!" Darcy cried.

Billy's hand on her arm immediately settled her.

"She's right, Darcy. It's for our protection."

But Senator Ben Manning's stern scowl spoke nothing of protection, she thought. He looked like a man who wanted their heads on a platter.

CHAPTER FOURTEEN

THE AUTOMATIC weapon trembled in Katrina Kivi's hands as she walked down the hall toward the living room where Johnny and Kelly waited for her.

Jumbled thoughts pounded through her mind. Wrong, *wrong*, she was a fool to even think she could . . .

. . . do *what*? What did she think she would do?

. . . force them, force him, force anyone to just listen!

. . . she'd never aimed a gun at anyone. This wasn't her, not her, not Katrina Kivi, so why?

Because she had to do something, anything. She was only doing what he would do—pretend—because whoever Father Johnny was, he wasn't a priest.

Her hands felt slimy on the steel of the automatic. She nearly turned and ran back to the closet. She could still get back there and dump the weapons before they had any clue she'd gone this far.

But she kept on walking, ignoring her mother's voice in the back of her head mumbling that mantra about how her stubbornness would get her into real trouble one day. That one day was here. It was now.

Her eyes stung, blurring her vision, and she knew, she just knew this was a bad, bad idea.

But she'd done it. It was too late.

A strange concoction of fear and rage screamed through Kat's head, and then she was around the corner, facing the back of Kelly's head on the couch. She stood behind Kelly, momentarily affixed to the carpet, gun extended.

". . . never know how it could turn out," Johnny was saying from the kitchen.

Again Kat nearly fled.

Again she forced her feet forward.

And then the gun was only three feet from the back of Kelly's head and Johnny was exiting the kitchen. "I think we . . ."

He saw her and stopped, bottle of water half raised to his mouth.

Kat stared at his black glasses. "Don't move, or she dies." Her words weren't hers, they couldn't be, because she wouldn't really say that, not really. She was a sixteen-year-old girl who had run into some bad luck with the Muslims; she was not a killer!

But she had said that. And now that she'd said it, her fear gave way to all the rage holed up for years.

Kelly turned her head.

"Don't move!" Kat screamed, gripping the gun more firmly. "Neither of you, don't—"

Kelly moved fast, whipping around, knocking the weapon aside with a brutal chop. The weapon flew from Kat's hands.

Kat may have been stalled by her lack of experience when it came to guns, but she'd been in her share of fights, and now on the defensive, her instincts returned.

She had the second gun out of her waistband before the automatic weapon hit the carpet. Fired one shot into the wall, surprised by the noise. The tremendous recoil forced her to take a step backward.

"I said don't move!"

Kelly now faced her, standing just beyond the couch with her hands half raised. Johnny still hadn't moved.

"Don't think I won't shoot," Kat cried. Her hands were still shaking, but now due to the adrenaline coursing through her veins.

Johnny slowly lowered the bottle in his right hand. She swiveled the gun to cover him, but then thought better of it and trained the barrel back on Kelly. Oddly enough, neither of them seemed too put off by her show of force, and this angered her more.

"I swear, I'll shoot."

"What do you want, Katrina?" Johnny asked in a soft voice.

Yes, what do you want, Katrina?

"Sit down. I want you to sit down."

"Why?"

"Be careful, Johnny," Kelly said. "This isn't why we are here."

"You think?"

She glanced at him, hands spread, but otherwise seemingly unconcerned. "She's nothing but a high-school student with a grudge."

"Is she? I don't know."

"You see something I don't?"

"Don't I always?" Johnny said.

"Yes or no?"

"I see a scared girl who was put into our path. I like her. She has a strong backbone. She needs some discipline, but I think she has a good heart."

Kelly faced Kat and studied her. They were obviously trying to distract her with all this nonsense. Kat took another step back, keeping the gun trained on the woman. "I just need your help," she said. "I . . . You have to listen to me!"

"I think we can trust her," Johnny said.

"Don't be foolish, Johnny!"

"They aren't after us—"

"You can't know that!" Kelly snapped.

"Stop it!" Kat shouted. "You think you can just talk nonsense and get me to drop my guard?"

"Please, Kat." Johnny set the bottle on the kitchen table and stepped into the living room, hands elevated by his sides. "You're far too intelligent to think shooting one of us might encourage the judge to extend you any leniency. It's the kind of thing dopers and pimps might try because they have a few burned circuits between the ears. You, on the other hand, know very well that harming either one of us will only ensure that your sentence is upgraded from months to years. And not jail, either. State prison."

He stopped by the couch in full view. "Am I wrong?"

"Then help me," she said.

"I offered you help, but you didn't want it."

"What are you talking about?" she cried. "You keep talking like that, but what did I do to make you hate me so much?"

"So you do want help in changing who you are?"

"What are you talking about? I am who I am! You can't tolerate who I am?"

"I can't tolerate your intolerance for Arabs, no. Or your hatred and fear of other people in general."

Here she stood, pointing a gun at a blind priest who wasn't really a priest and who couldn't possibly be blind, discussing *tolerance* of all things! The absurdity of it was as maddening as the fact that she no longer felt compelled to pull off this stunt.

But there was no way out now.

"You want me to stop hating Arabs? Fine, I swear to stop hating the towel-heads that've taken over Las Vegas and forced my mother to work long nights just to put macaroni and cheese on our table. Good enough? I'm a changed woman."

"You see? That's what I'm talking about. You want out of your predicament, but you don't want to change the person who got you into the predicament in the first place."

"Listen to me, honey," Kelly said. "If he's talking to you like this, you really should listen. Don't ask me why, but you've managed to get his attention. And trust me, it has nothing to do with the gun. He's faced far more than that toy in his days."

"Don't try to confuse me," Kat snapped. "I'm warning you . . ." But she stopped because even to her, her words sounded ridiculous.

"Kelly's talking about a time when I could make things do what they weren't supposed to do," Johnny said. "But it was temporary, a kind of surge, as best we can figure out."

"Don't let him fool you," Kelly said. To Johnny, "You sure you want to do this?"

If their intent was to distract her, they were succeeding with ease, Kat thought. They showed no fear, no real concern even. She might as well be holding a noodle. Their only dilemma was this business about whether Johnny should take her into his confidence.

"I don't know, Kat . . . What do you think? Are you willing to trust me on this?"

"Why should I?"

"Because you know it's the right thing to do. And because you have no other reasonable option."

"Okay. Fine. I'll trust you."

"Then lower the gun."

"Exactly!" she said. "You think I'm stupid?"

"No. Which is why you will lower the gun."

Her stubbornness had hit a wall. And Kat's curiosity had grown larger than her anger. So she lowered her gun, knowing that she could always lift it again.

"Give it to Kelly."

"That's not what you said."

"I'm saying it now."

Kelly held out her hand. Kat hesitated only a moment, then handed the weapon to her, relieved to be free from it. Kelly gathered up the automatic weapon and set both on the counter beside Johnny.

Kat felt weak in her knees, but she stood strong. Because that was what she'd always done. Stood strong.

"So who are you really, Father Johnny?"

"The real question, Kat, is who are you? If you can understand yourself, then you'll know where my journey started. Do you believe in God?"

"We already—"

"So then, I was once who you are today," he said. "If you want to understand me, you have to understand yourself. Why don't you believe?"

"For starters? Because everyone runs around killing in God's name."

"But that's a child's answer and you're already sixteen. You don't know much about religion, do you?"

"Should I?"

"Do you know the difference between Christianity and Islam?"

"Why are we talking about this? You're trying to get me to convert? There's a good reason why religion is not allowed in the schools. Because it brings out the kooks!"

"Please, humor me. The difference between Christianity and Islam?"

"How should I know? One prays in a mosque, one prays in a cathedral."

"So you know nothing. To you God is simply an extension of foolish religion. And if religion had much to do with God, I might agree with you. If you want to accept my help, the first thing you'll need to do is set any notion you have of religion aside. Put everything you think you know about Islam, Judaism, Christianity, Buddhism, all of it behind you. If you can do that, I may be able to help you."

"What are you trying to do? Convert me?"

"You've demonstrated that you have no true moral compass. No fundamental beliefs that guide what is right or wrong in this world. How can you hope to recognize good and evil for what they truly are if you have no belief in a moral authority greater than yourself?"

"Spoken like a true blood—"

"No!" Johnny snapped, cutting her off. "Please don't use that word in this house."

"Sorry. But you're saying that I'm going to jail because I don't believe in God."

Kelly stepped up beside him. He absently took her hand and kissed it.

"That's a bit simplistic, but yes. Because you haven't opened your eyes to see him. To love and be loved by him. 'For him who has eyes to see, let him see.' Jesus said that. Would you like to have your eyes opened?"

She had never heard such a preposterous line of argument. She knew the gist of God, naturally. Big guy in the sky who made it all and forgot to tell his subjects not to rape, kill, and destroy. But Johnny was right: she hadn't searched out the meaning behind any of the world's major religions.

The only religion she was truly familiar with was one called tolerance. Now the false priest was asking her if she wanted her eyes opened.

"How do you propose to do that?"

"I have a shortcut."

"Fine."

Johnny walked casually to the fireplace, something you wouldn't find in most homes in Nevada these days. But it was an old house. Kelly picked up a pair of sunglasses that sat on the kitchen counter and slid them onto the bridge of her nose.

"You're absolutely sure about this, Johnny?" Kelly asked.

"No."

He looked down at the floor, removed his own dark glasses, and stared straight down at the lenses.

Johnny lifted his head and stared at Kat with white eyes.

Not a speck of color, no retina, no pupil, just pure white eyes. The sight stopped her cold.

"You like?"

Like? She wasn't sure how she felt. He was blind after all.

"Can you see?"

"The question is, can you see? Really see?"

"Your . . ." Did she dare just blare it out? "Your eyes are white."

"That's their natural color, yes. And I can't see the world the way you see the world. It's more like heat signatures and geometrical shapes. But the power in these eyes of mine has more to do with you than me. They can help you see things differently."

On cue, his white eyes were gone, replaced by bright blue ones, as clear as sapphires.

Kat blinked, expecting them to change back, but they didn't. Johnny lifted his hand and snapped his fingers. An apple appeared in his palm.

"You like apples? If you try to eat this one, it will taste like air because it doesn't exist."

Impossible. Kat stepped up and put her hands on the back of the couch. "I . . ." She didn't know what to say.

"An illusion," Johnny said. "I can make you see what I want. I can either deceive you or let you see the truth."

He tossed the apple into the air and caught it, but now it was a snake, writhing in his fist. He struck the snake against his other palm and it became a wooden cross. He snapped his fingers and the cross vanished.

"That's incredible."

"No, it's commonplace. Half of what you think you know has been subjected to deception. You think you know so much about what matters: we all do. But we're blind to the real issue facing us. We've been sold a magic trick."

She was watching him, not six feet from him, when he vanished. She caught her breath. Kelly stood by the kitchen table, watching her, smiling.

"What happened?"

Kelly shrugged.

Kat studied the space that Johnny had occupied just a moment ago. "Is he . . . I mean, is he there?"

Johnny reappeared. "Exactly! Just because you didn't see me didn't mean I *wasn't* here, any more than seeing the apple meant it *was*."

The simplicity of Johnny's point struck Kat broadside, like a locomotive on full steam.

"For him who has eyes to see . . ." she said.

Johnny finished the quote. "Let him see. Are you ready to see the truth, Kat?"

"Ummm . . ."

"It could change everything, I warn you."

"How do I know what it . . . What am I supposed to say to that? How could anyone say they don't want to see the truth?"

"You'd be surprised." He smiled. "Just say yes, Kat. Please say yes."

"Yes."

"Hold on to the couch."

She gripped the back of the couch, wondering what about the truth could possibly require her to hold on.

Johnny closed his blue eyes. When he opened them again they were white. But then they were black and then they weren't eyes at all.

They were a pool of darkness, drawing her deep, deep into hot black water, suffocating her. Pain ripped through her spine, and she heard herself—the self gripping the couch—gasp.

And then scream.

She was in a black lake, unable to breathe, smothered by the shock of it all. And yet she was screaming.

Kat doubled over and sucked at the blackness. Vile bitterness seared and flooded her lungs. Entered her capillaries. Seeped into her bloodstream.

And she knew then that she'd breathed evil. Raw, unfiltered evil.

From her own soul.

She felt herself falling, here by the couch. She was shaking from head to foot, unable to close her eyes, staring into Johnny's black eyeballs.

Screaming. Screaming.

From the corner of her eye she saw Kelly's mouth yelling at Johnny to stop, stop, stop, but Kat couldn't hear Kelly over her own screams.

And Johnny did not stop.

Kat wasn't sure how she knew, but she knew that she was seeing herself as she really was. Nothing more, nothing less. Just the truth of Katrina Kivi.

This evil within herself washed her mind with unrelenting waves of horror.

The water turned blood red. She was still screaming by the couch, but it occurred to her that she didn't need to scream any longer. The horror still clawed at her mind, but the pain and bitterness was soothed by the water.

A baby before birth.

Her voice caught in her throat. She stared around at the red water, stunned by the absence of pain. The change was so great, so overwhelming that she wanted to cry. To sob like a baby, safe, just safe in the belly of the . . .

A distant cry came to her ears.

The cry swelled to a scream that was not hers. The water around her was screaming. Oh the anguish, the pain, the remorse, the horror in the wail flogged her mind.

She rolled tight into a ball and began to scream with it, crying her remorse, her terror. She wanted to be out of this red lake, breathing new life, reborn.

And then Johnny closed his eyes and Kat was back in the room, behind the couch, screaming at the top of her lungs, shaking violently, standing only because her fingers had latched on to the cushion and refused to let her collapse.

But now she was here, just here, and she relaxed her grip. She fell to the carpet like a bag of rocks.

CHAPTER FIFTEEN

MARSUVEES BLACK stopped on the street curb, cracked his knuckles, and looked first to his right, then to his left. Twenty-ninth Street was quiet, too quiet, terrifyingly quiet for his own considerable tastes. He'd long ago discovered that he liked hanging out with people, particularly when their necks were doing the hanging. The small church across the street, however, was not quiet. Seventy or more parishioners were inside the converted watering hole being faithful, most of them were colored folk.

These seventy-or-more colored folk were about to help him change the course of history.

He had nothing against colored folk, no he did not. No sir. He himself was a colored folk, really. White skin, but his trench coat was black, his boots were black, his hat was black. If he'd had a choice, he himself would have been black because from his experience, most black folk were smarter than the white trash he'd run across. Take Arabs, take Indians, take Mexicans, take Africans, take whites, throw them all in a bowl and the dumbest of the bunch always came out as white as a pancake.

Another reason he wished he could have dark skin was because being white as a bowl of flour lumped him in with a group of people who were known to be more devious. He would be less likely to draw suspicion if he were black.

At one point in history, some had erroneously associated dark skin with certain negative, even criminal tendencies. The trend was now precisely the opposite. Being white was a distinct disadvantage. His timing was off by fifty years.

Hitler, now there was one fine white fellow who'd attempted to show the world the truth about whites. And despite being dead wrong in the end, he'd effectively demonstrated how to sweep away the sentiments of a whole country.

Marsuvees had no issue with skin color. Christianity, on the other hand, was a different matter altogether. He spat to one side. But the fact that these particular Christians were also colored was of the utmost importance. It was a two-for-one sale, and he intended on selling the whole lot to the world.

Satisfied that the quiet night was ready to accept him, Marsuvees Black stepped across the street.

Practice makes perfect, it was said. It was time to practice.

He stepped up to the entrance, cracked his neck, put his hand on the door, and entered the Holy Baptist Church of the Resurrection.

The crowd inside did not stop humming and swaying as a bass player and an organist filled the small, dimly lit, bar-turned-church with a disturbing tune he'd heard a time or two in his life. None of the faithful turned to stare at the white guy who'd just entered. Indeed, no one seemed to have even noticed that Marsuvees Black was among them.

He suppressed a tinge of irritation—the briefest temptation to do some immediate and exquisitely painful damage to the lot of them. Although it was true that he found most colored folk more intelligent than pasty whites, his general hatred of all people by far superseded any respect he had for the people in the Holy Baptist Church of the Resurrection. And the fact that they had as of yet returned none of his respect only reinforced that hatred. He'd undoubtedly selected the right church for his deed.

One rather thin man with graying hair who might be considered an usher was smiling at Black from behind the bank of chairs set up on the right.

Black strode up to the man, black alligator-skin boots clunking upon the wood floor with each step. He stopped, keeping his eyes on the platform. "Christians," he said.

"Yes, that's right," the man returned.

Black again restrained himself, mission clearly in mind. He strode up the aisle, keeping his gaze on the bass player.

He spoke plainly but just loudly enough for those on either side to hear as he passed. "Shut up, shut up, you pathetic black bloodsuckers. Shut your black holes, every one of you stinking hatemongers. Die in hell, you filthy black bloody suckers."

The reaction was what he'd expected, stares and angry glares. They were obviously stunned by his choice of words, thinking perhaps that a lunatic had escaped from an institution and found himself in the wrong building. In this age of tolerance, walking around uttering such language was unthinkable to all but complete fools. He particularly liked the word *bloodsucker*, a useful slur popularized as of late that called into question the absurd habit Christians had of taking communion, of drinking Christ's blood to celebrate Christ's death.

Black held his tongue, having sown just enough bitterness to suit him, and stepped up on the stage. Four brothers were playing a bass, an electric guitar, a piano, and a set of drums. He mounted the stage and strode up to a microphone not in use.

The music went on as if he hardly mattered. But that would change.

He'd selected the church because it was located only blocks from Union Cemetery and was frequented by blacks, many of whom represented the city's key circles of influence. Judging by their dress, the place looked to be full of professionals tonight, though in a church it was always hard to tell.

He leaned into the mike, tapped it, and was rewarded with a loud *thunk*. The organ and bass were still in full swing, but he spoke over them.

"Thank you, Bill. Fantastic, fantastic. Let's give our well-groomed players a hand, shall we?" He applauded loudly and smiled at the organist, a proud-looking woman with high cheekbones whose fingers now stalled on the keys.

A smattering of applause spread among those who didn't yet realize that they were about to get more than they bargained for.

"Thank you. Not often do you get such superb playing from monkeys. Bravo!"

The place fell quiet. Nice. Issue any similar statement directed to whites in a gathering of rednecks, and they would be hollering threats of retaliation. Here, Black would have to dig deeper.

"Thank you all for coming out tonight. In addition to the freak show on my left we have a very special treat for you tonight. Me. Here to set the record straight for all of you brothers and, uh . . . sisters."

A large, well-muscled man who might well be the preacher was approaching the stage. "Please, this isn't the place."

Black could have toyed with him, but he chose not to. He drew an old Smith & Wesson six-shooter he favored and shot into the air.

Boom!

"Actually, I do mind. Just hold your horses there, you fat pig," he drawled.

The man pulled up sharply. Somewhere a Bible or a hymnal thumped softly closed.

"Now, I realize that my words aren't the kind our society takes in stride, but you know as well as I do that plenty of people out there are thinking what I'm just saying. Not even ordinary types of people, but politicians and lawmen. Am I not right? The whole world hates you Christians."

Anther man, whom Black now guessed was the pastor, stepped out, both hands stretched high in a plea for caution. "Sir, put the gun—"

"Shut up, gimpy. I'm here to help you, not hurt you. And don't bother calling the police. I'm leaving soon enough."

Now he had their fullest attention. The door banged as several scurried out the back. He let them go.

"Now, I'm not one of those who would put you back on the ship and send you back to Africa were it in my power to do so. I'm a man who realizes that blacks should probably run this country. All things being equal, they're smarter, they have more patience, they aren't as lazy, they are better lovers, they know how to entertain on the field, on the stage, you name it. Blacks rule, baby. But this Christianity bit . . . It's a bit much, don't you think?"

"Sir, I'm—"

"Please, sir, don't be so white. I'm trying to make a point. The time has come to deal with the race and religion issue once and for all. You've all heard about the lyncher."

Unless they were living under a mattress, they had, all of them. As had Black, who was, in fact, the very lyncher who had been making national headlines.

Marsuvees grinned. "You think this is the work of some lone psychopath? Not a chance. It's a calculated effort to enrage the black community, if not the community of believers. And if it doesn't work, you're not as intelligent as all the latest studies say you are. The first shots of a new cultural war have been fired. Pony up. Fire back. Or at the very least have your less restrained brothers fire back. For heaven's sake, don't be such wimps. The time has come for a cultural revolution. Black power!"

Black shoved his gun back into the holster under his arm.

"If my words haven't successfully enraged you, then I hope the lynchings will. They won't stop, not until riots turn the streets red."

He let them chew on that for several seconds.

"I have it on good authority that not one but two people in this room at this very moment will find themselves hung from a tree in Union Cemetery by morning."

He tipped his hat. "Thank you kindly for your attention."

Marsuvees Black stepped off the stage, exited through the side fire door, and receded into the dark. It was going to be a busy, busy night.

CHAPTER SIXTEEN

Day Three

DARCY WOKE to the annoying ring of the telephone. It was 7:00 a.m. by the clock on her wall. She assumed Billy had picked up from his suite after three rings, and rolled over for more sleep. They'd agreed on a nine o'clock pickup.

She was just beginning to slip away again when a rap on the door jerked her from sleep. "What is it?"

Billy poked his head in, eyes covered by dark glasses. "Kinnard's on his way."

He looked sophisticated in his white bathrobe. "What happened to nine?"

"Change of schedule. Lawhead has a plane fueled and waiting to take us to Kansas City. Kinnard wouldn't say, but something went down last night. He'll be here in half an hour."

"Nice of them to let us out of our cage early," she said bitterly.

He frowned, pulled his head out, and closed the door.

She rolled from the bed and dragged herself into the bathroom—an expansive living space with double doors, a large round Jacuzzi dead center, sinks on either side, a five-foot shower encased in clear glass, and a separate room, which housed the bidet. Fluffy white towels, slippers, bathrobe, all the bubble bath and body soaps she could possibly use.

The maid would clean the entire apartment once every day.

Billy's room had identical accommodations. This was how royalty lived, Darcy thought, the kind of lifestyle she'd railed against on more than one occasion. But standing in the middle of the bathroom this morning, she wasn't sure she entirely disapproved.

Billy sat at the breakfast bar scanning a Net feed on the wall monitor when she came out twenty minutes later. A silver tray rested on the table, neatly arranged with raspberry and vanilla Danishes, sliced apples, oranges, and a pot of something hot.

"That was quick. Coffee?"

She shook her messy mane. "Do I strike you as the kind who needs an hour to curl my locks? Coffee would be nice, thank you."

She watched him pour the steaming liquid from the white pot into a black porcelain mug. He gestured to the wall. "Another lynching in Kansas City last night. Front page."

She glanced at a headline: Two Dead from Kansas City Church.

"Someone's trying to make a point." She took a sip of coffee. "Pretty sick."

Billy stood, picked a black blazer off the back of the bar stool, and laid it on the sofa. Dressed in a pressed white shirt tucked smartly into black slacks, he undid his tie, pulled it free, and faced her. Her Billy, all grown up and dressed for success. She thought he looked handsome.

"You think I'm underdressed?" she asked. She'd chosen a stylish throwback to gothic dresses. Her standard fare. Charcoal.

"You're you. I think it may take them a day or two to get used to the idea, but anything different would be a mistake."

"Was that a yes or a no?"

"A no. Not at all. Not for my tastes anyway."

THEY FLEW to Kansas City in a government-leased supersonic Citation 25, one of the newer models that covered the thousand-mile flight in less than one hour.

Darcy sat next to Billy, arms and legs crossed, listening as he engaged Lawhead and Kinnard on all the pertinent facts regarding the Kansas City lyncher, as if this sort of thing came as naturally to him as tying his shoes.

How race could still be an issue with some people was beyond Darcy. There were some areas in which society had actually made progress over the years. Race was one. Surely those who thought race had any more to do with their value than the color of their underwear deserved to be locked up in a loony bin.

"... which, as bad as it may seem, isn't our primary concern," Lawhead was saying.

"No?" Billy asked. "Then what is?"

"The potential spillover."

"Others jumping on the bandwagon," Billy said. "Copycat crimes, vigilante justice, revenge."

"Correct."

"Over race?" Darcy asked. "Last time I checked, we do live in the twenty-first century, *please*. I would think the religious tension would be greater than any racial divide."

Lawhead's brow arched. "Maybe. Hard to separate them at times. But race has *always* played a major role in any nation's evolution, including our own. Rwanda, Somalia, Sudan, Indonesia, Uganda, Croatia, Palestine, Germany—if history teaches anything about race it's that humans are hardwired to feel superior to their fellow men and women, and nowhere is that sentiment as easily expressed as in matters of race. It only takes a spark to provoke the minds of one race against another."

She'd never thought of it in those terms.

"We've had four sparks in the space of eight days," Lawhead continued. "The drums are beating already. Every Net feed in the country is featuring the story, top of the hour."

"Surely people have the sense to realize someone is purposefully stirring this up."

"That's not the point. A thousand editorials on the Net are ranting about the injustice—"

"As they should be," she said.

"As they should be. But the editorials take the rhetoric further, railing against any white supremacist who would dare stoop to this. In an issue as deep-rooted and tragic as race in America, passions are easily inflamed. More people have lost their lives over the race issue than any other issue in human history. Just counting our own Civil War and Hitler's extermination of Jews . . . well, I'm sure you get the point."

"I do. And religion?"

"Clearly someone hates Christians. But Christians aren't striking back, so the situation is stable. If there is any retaliation, however . . ."

"Then Christians will be as culpable as any race," she said. "Even if they aren't to blame, you'll have a true mess on your hands."

"God forbid," Lawhead said. "No pun intended."

"So, what exactly is the point of this?" she asked in a moment of silence. "Me and Billy, I mean. What exactly do you expect your two little lab rats to do? You really think we can solve this case for you?"

Perhaps she was just a bit harsh.

Lawhead glanced at Kinnard, then back to her, pushing the bridge on his sunglasses to snug them against his forehead.

"This trip is not about this case," Kinnard said. "It's about you. We would like to better understand exactly what you're capable of. In the field."

"You saw what we could do last night."

"If you can do in a group, under pressure, what you did last night . . ." He stopped there.

"We can take over the world," she finished.

Kinnard smiled. "Maybe not, but you get the picture."

They landed at nine and drove in an armored FBI Cadillac to the vicinity of Union Cemetery, just off Warwick Trafficway, two miles south of city central. The street was blockaded by several police cruisers, but onlookers were crossing into the large cemetery from the perimeter. Streams of people walked or ran toward a grove at the center of the burial grounds.

Lawhead swore and made a quick call on his cell. He snapped the phone closed. An officer who was trying his best to keep the road clear for authorized traffic waved them through the barricade.

"How long have they had the scene secured?" Billy asked.

"The bodies were discovered by a jogger at six thirty this morning. We were on-site with the local authorities shortly after. The crime scene is secured, but the cemetery is open access. They can't secure the whole thing."

The hanging had occurred among a group of large trees at the heart of the cemetery. Darcy saw the ropes hanging from two adjacent trees before they crossed the yellow tape that cordoned off the crime scene. Federal Bureau of Investigation—Crime Scene—Do Not Cross.

Two dangling ropes with nooses at the ends of each. The thick fiber ropes were twisted around themselves atop eighteen-inch loops, which were stained dark brown with blood. Her stomach turned. Whoever was behind this had chosen one of the most offensive symbols in American history to elicit precisely this kind of reaction. It was all far too sick for her tastes.

And as for those gathered . . . Gazing around, she wondered why they weren't rioting already.

"You really think it's wise to keep those up?" she asked. "Everyone can see the ropes. Even from the perimeter."

"Follow me," Lawhead said. He climbed from the car and walked to a white tent. Darcy and Billy followed with Kinnard, wearing glasses.

The two bodies had been laid out on white evidence mats in the center of the tent. A porous mesh cloth was tented over the bodies of each. A black woman in a purple dress who looked to be in her early twenties, and an older man who could have been her father. Their faces were bloated, eyes open, mouths gaping. Rope-burned wrists, bloodshot stares.

Darcy turned away, nauseated. She took one look around the tent, saw that the crime scene investigators had the situation covered, and stepped back outside.

A thousand stares met hers. People lined the perimeter, twenty, maybe thirty deep, set back fifty yards from the tent. If they weren't staring at her, they were looking up at the ropes. An eerie quiet gripped them all.

"You okay?" Billy took her elbow.

"Not really, no. I don't belong here."

"I know how you feel."

A fire truck was extending its ladder to remove the ropes.

"What kind of monster would do this?"

"The same kind of monster who was in your house two nights ago," Billy said.

Her head spun with the memory of the long night. So much had happened in such a short space of time. It was hard for her to wrap her mind around it all.

"Trust me, the world is full of people who would just as soon hang their neighbors as put up with them. I should know. I made my living defending some of those people."

Kinnard emerged from the tent with Lawhead. "You two okay?"

"Darcy was just making a good point," Billy said. "Remind us again exactly what it is you want us to do here."

Lawhead scanned the onlookers at the perimeter. "More than likely he's out there now, watching." His eyes settled on Billy. "You're looking for a white male, middle-aged."

Kinnard and Lawhead looked at him like scientists studying a new specimen. They both had worn glasses for the duration of the flight, unwilling to subject themselves to whatever forces probed Annie Ruling at the council meeting.

"You sure you're up to this?" Kinnard asked. "It's entirely up to you, as agreed. You say the word and we're gone."

"What about Darcy?" Billy asked.

"You're welcome to join us," Kinnard said to her.

Billy nodded. Plucked off his glasses, baring his green eyes. "Wait here for Darcy and me."

"No," Kinnard said. "I go with you. And I don't want you any closer to the perimeter than ten feet."

Yes, of course, their protector.

"Isn't this a bit dangerous? Seeing as there are people who might want us dead?"

"No one could possibly know you're here. Washington would be a different matter. Ready?"

"Go ahead," Lawhead said. "I have a call. I'll catch up with you."

Darcy followed Billy and Kinnard toward the perimeter, feeling even more out of sorts than she had earlier. Not because she was useless here, although she certainly felt like a third leg, but because they were now part of the spectacle. Three white goons walking around inside the perimeter, returning the stares of those gathered with hate in their hearts.

And she was the straggler, dressed like some kind of hippie behind the clean-cut attorney with his armed guard.

"Anything?" Kinnard asked.

Billy grunted and walked on, scanning the crowd, slowing at each white face. Darcy nearly turned and cut back for the tent several times but reminded herself there was nothing in the tent that was her business either.

"Anything?" Kinnard was impatient.

"Plenty. Frankly I'm not sure how much of this I can take."

"Meaning?"

"Meaning you have a problem here, my friend. Somebody better start talking to these people about why . . ." He stopped and stared at a man who held a noose in his right hand, twirling it in small circles, eyes fixed on them.

"You okay?" Kinnard asked.

Billy walked on. "Fine."

Darcy turned and headed back toward the tent. "I'll see you when you finish."

She stood by one of the ambulances and watched as Billy and Kinnard slowly made their full circuit before regrouping at the tent with Lawhead.

"Well?" the FBI man asked.

Billy slid his glasses over glazed eyes, hands trembling. He looked back at the crowd, as if testing the waters to see if the glasses were protecting him from their thoughts.

"Billy? You okay, son?"

"I'm fine."

But he wasn't, she thought.

"What did you get?" Lawhead pushed.

"More than I bargained for. How long are we going to be here?"

"They'll keep the scene secured for a few days. The heavy lifting will be done in a few hours. No reason to believe he's out there?"

"No. If he's out there, he's either not thinking about the crime or our eyes didn't meet."

"So it's working, then," Kinnard said.

"Working, yes."

Lawhead took Billy's elbow. "That's good. But before you go again, I want you to make a sweep inside the tent."

"Again?"

"You know as well as I do there's a good chance he's close by. You know how explosive the situation could get. Please, if there's even a small chance you can expose him . . ."

Billy hesitated. "Once more. That's all I think I can handle."

CHAPTER SEVENTEEN

DARCY DIDN'T think she was up to hanging out with two dead bodies or she would have followed them in. But she wasn't up to being the object of so many stares either.

She found her predicament positively absurd! Enraging even.

Without allowing herself another moment's hesitation, Darcy headed for the gap in the perimeter where two police cars controlled access to the crime scene.

She strode up to the barricade where an officer stepped in her path. "May I help you?"

"Yes, you can let me through. I need to get some air."

"I understand. Maybe I could get you an escort."

"No, I don't want an escort. I'm fine, these people have nothing against me."

"I really think you should wait for an escort, ma'am."

Darcy pulled off her glasses and stared him in the eyes. "You have no authority to keep me here. Let me pass."

He blinked. Twice. Then he stepped aside. "Of course, ma'am."

"If they ask, tell them I'm waiting in the trees over there."

"Yes, ma'am."

She stepped past him, wondering if she'd really done that. Of course she had! The power she held in this new voice of hers was a bit stunning. She put her glasses back on and headed for the public restrooms, eyes fixed ahead, refusing to be intimidated by a dozen angry stares.

There was no way she could know for certain that this ability of hers worked every time. In fact, of the three events thus far, only Annie's reaction to her suggestion she slap Manning was irrefutably linked to a power beyond her comprehension. Billy's kiss and this passing could be explained by other means.

Why are you so resistant to the idea, Darcy?

Because it was too much. Who'd ever heard of such a preposterous thing? The world turned on its axis, round and round without even the slightest pause, regardless of what anyone did. Some things did not change. Movies of superheroes who'd evolved, or vampires who fed on the living were one thing. This . . . this was another.

Then again, so was writing in the books below the monastery with Billy as a child.

The bulk of the crowd was gathered around the scene a hundred yards to her back now. Dozens, maybe hundreds, were still hopping the fences and pouring into the cemetery from all sides, coming to see what all the fuss was about. But the main entrance was guarded and lay directly behind the trees she walked to. Large gravestones rose from the ground like guards for the dead.

Darcy walked around a few of the monuments.

David Wilber

1999–2023

Who Loved Truth More Than Life

Rest in Peace

Another to Zephaniah Smith. Where did these names come from? America was a mishmash of a hundred cultures all thrown into one giant pot and stirred slowly over the fires of time. A delicious stew of harmonious humanity celebrating diversity and tolerance. Naming their children Zephaniah Smith.

"You lost?"

Darcy turned around, startled by the low voice. Five men stared at her from a distance of ten feet, two with their feet planted on headstones. She recognized the one who appeared to be their leader by the noose stuffed half into his jeans pocket. He'd stared at her from the crowd earlier.

"No, not really. You?" she asked.

"You look lost to me," the man said. They were blacks, gangbangers with red and blue bandanas wrapped around their upper arms. Silver chains with crosses hung heavy from their necks.

"Last I checked we were in Union Cemetery, close to downtown, Kansas City," she said. "You need directions somewhere?"

One of the others chuckled. "Man, she got it going, James."

"Shut up, fool." He jerked his chin at Darcy. "You think a smart mouth makes you any better?"

Darcy glanced at the rope. "What's the noose for?"

"They're used for hangings. Or did you think your kind were the only ones who knew how to have fun?"

It occurred to her that she might be in a bit of trouble here. She looked at them all, eyes fired for violence. Maybe she'd spoken too soon. There were times to fight back and times to walk away, and although she wasn't very good at the latter, this was shaping up to be a time for it.

"I'm sorry for your loss," she said with as much sincerity as she could. And she meant it.

James walked slowly up to her, grinning. He reached out for her chin, and although every bone in her body begged her to snap, she made no attempt to stop him. His finger traced a line down her cheek, down her neck, over her shoulder.

Darcy began to tremble.

"What's a lily-white party girl like you doing in our town? Hmmm?"

She swallowed. "I'm trying to help you out."

The one who'd chuckled earlier looked back at the crowd, then stepped up with the others. She took a step backward, then another, and ran into Zephaniah Smith's large tombstone. She thought about screaming Billy's name but knew he'd never hear her.

"All dressed up like a rock star," James said, plucking at the straps on her dress. "You came down here to rock out with the monkeys, celebrate the lynching. Huh?"

"Sing for us, rock star," one dressed in a red shirt said.

They pressed closer, forming a tight circle that prevented her from seeing past them. Her fear spiked and she began to sweat.

"You're mistaking me for someone else," she said. "I don't have a racist bone in my body."

"That so? How many times have I heard that? I saw the way you walked around all high and mighty."

"Come on, sing for us, lily-white," the one in the red shirt repeated.

"Disappointed by the turnout, party girl?" James said. His gleaming white teeth and wet lips were close, covered in the smell of tobacco. "I knew that girl you have in the tent back there. She was the valedictorian at my high school four years ago. You people never get it, do you?"

Darcy felt smothered. She could smell their deodorant, their breath, feel the heat from their bodies. Trapped. Boarded up, sealed tight, no way out.

"Please . . ." She felt her reserves of courage waning and closed her eyes. "Please, please . . ." Her own shift from defiance to dread sickened her, but she felt powerless to stop her sinking emotions.

"You heard him," James said. "Sing and we might let you walk away." She felt something touch her head, then slide down over her face. The noose, she saw with a glance. He'd slipped the noose over her head.

"How does it feel?"

She cowered against Zephaniah Smith's tombstone, hands flat against the surface on either side. She should sing, she thought. Just sing. How she'd found herself in such a predicament was no longer a relevant question. She had to get out, that was all that mattered now.

"Go on," James said, mouth hovering an inch from her face. "Sing like a bird."

"Please . . ."

"Sing!" he screamed.

She flinched and began to sing through a flood of tears. Random words unconnected to any tune she knew. "Please, don't hurt me, please save me, please, I beg you, I beg you, I beg you."

"What else, huh, baby? What else you beg us to do?"

She could barely think straight. Fury pushed her fear back—but then it returned, even more tangible than before.

"Sing for us that lily-white lullaby, baby," James said, lifting the glasses from her face.

Darcy clenched her eyes and tried to sing again, but the words refused to form any tune. "Please leave me alone. Please . . ."

She couldn't do this. Any moment and she would crack; she could feel the outrage coiled inside her mind, straining against good sense. When she snapped she would launch herself at them fingernails first, take some skin with her, and then be beaten to a pulp, she knew that. And she didn't want that. But she just couldn't cower here and sing for them.

"Please . . ." she whispered. "Billy, please. Please don't do this."

"Please don't do this," he mimicked. The noose tightened. "Don't do what? Make you sing or hang you by the neck? Isn't that what you people want us blacks to do for you? Perform like a bunch of monkeys?"

"No, no, that's not me."

Their leader leaned forward and licked her cheek. Her control broke then, while his tongue was still on her face.

"Don't!" She lowered her head, shoved both arms out, and pounded into his gut like a battering ram. "Don't. Don't you dare touch me! Don't, you sick beast!"

"Mother of . . ." Hands grabbed her and pinned her back against the tombstone, but she kicked out with both feet.

However noble and courageous her attack, it yielded nothing but rage from them. They smothered her, punched her in her gut. A hand slapped her face.

One of them got his arm around her throat and began to choke her so she couldn't breathe, much less beg for . . .

Then Darcy remembered her voice. A distant abstract detail floating on the edge of her mind. *Save yourself, Darcy! Look in their eyes and speak to them and save yourself!*

She snapped her eyes wide. James grabbed her face in one hand and squeezed her cheeks tight. "You're going to pay for that, lily-white."

Darcy tried to scream at him; nothing but rasping air came out.

"Back off, James. You can't kill her," one of them said.

"No?" His fist slammed into her gut and she jerked forward against the arm coiled around her throat. She tried to suck in some air, found none. Her oxygen-deprived head pounded; the world began to fade.

She was going to pass out! She wanted to look them in the eyes and use her voice, but now she was going to pass . . .

James grabbed her hair and jerked her head back so that she was forced to stare into his face. "It's nothing personal, lily-white, but we're going to send a message. And you're our messenger."

His eyes were only a few inches from hers when the arm around her throat relaxed.

She forced a single word from her lungs with her last reserve of air. "No," she breathed.

Then she sucked at the air. Her lungs filled with oxygen. James continued to drill her with his malignant stare. *It isn't going to work.* Tears blurred her vision. And then Darcy did the only thing left in her heart to do, knowing that they were going to kill her.

She screamed her rage. "No, no, no!" she screamed, each word growing in volume. "Let me go, you sick dog, you have no right to touch me,
no, no . . ."

The arm tightened, cutting off her voice.

James froze, breathing hard. His eyes were wide.

"Let her go," one of the others said.

The guy with his arm squeezing her neck wasn't getting the message.

James pulled back, confused, still fixed on her. "Let her go."

"What? What do—"

"Let her go!" he snapped.

The arm released its grip.

Darcy doubled over, gasping. Oxygen flooded her lungs, seeped into
her blood, swarmed her with life. She breathed deep and hard, and they
watched her.

"What's wrong with you fools?" the one who'd choked her said. "You
think this will bring Samantha back from the dead? We have this whore
dead to rights here and I'm be—"

"Shut up!" Darcy screamed, jerking her head around to face him.

He returned her stare, speechless.

She stood up, rubbing her throat. The anger she'd felt before dread had
set in returned with a vengeance. "You want me to sing? Is that what you
want? You want your pretty little rock star to sing for you? Huh?"

Darcy glanced over their shoulders. A few from the edge of the crowd
were looking their way, but no sign of the cavalry.

"Go ahead," she said, glaring at them again. "Beg me. Beg me! Beg me,
James. Beg the rocker girl you tried to kill for forgiveness."

His faced had lightened a shade. "Please . . ."

"You should be ashamed of yourselves, all of you!"

"I—"

"Shut up. Get on your knees."

They hesitated, so she put it another way. "You know you should grovel at my feet for what you've done. It's unforgivable! Get on your knees! Now!"

They sank to their knees, all five of them, and Darcy learned then that she didn't need to look at each one as long as they were looking at her eyes. They seemed to be more responsive than Annie Ruling. Why? Because of her own passion, perhaps.

She paced in front of them, breathing deeply. "You're petrified, aren't you? Well, you should be. You should feel terrified by yourselves."

Tears sprang to the eyes of the one in the red shirt. "Please, oh please, we're so sorry."

They were like putty in her hands, she thought. Not robots who would do whatever she wanted them to do, but minds inclined to do what she could convince them was the right thing.

"I'm leaving," she said. "And I don't want you to tell anyone what happened here. You don't tell them you tried to lynch me, and you don't tell them you broke down like a bunch of babies. You hear?"

They all nodded except for James, who still looked like he'd been hit by a comet.

"James? You hear me?"

"Yeah."

"Good. Get up."

They stood.

"Now shake my hand, so anyone watching believes we were just messing around."

She shook their hands one by one, then left them standing by Zephaniah Smith's tombstone.

So . . . now she knew. She most certainly did have a gifted voice and it wasn't giving out. The power of it made her dizzy.

CHAPTER EIGHTEEN

BOULDER CITY High School had been flattened to the ground and rebuilt three years earlier to accommodate the swelling student body, a move that had sparked outrage from those who thought adding trailers to the old school would suffice in the face of rising taxes.

From the air, the academic halls looked like a plus sign, a Swiss cross, with a large circular atrium at the center. Directly to the west stood the gymnasium and lunchroom. All new, all beautifully furnished thanks to the taxpayers.

But the real beauty of the campus lay outside the buildings. Here the desert had been transformed into a lush greenway that could be mistaken for a golf course at first look. Twenty acres of manicured lawn, broken by small pockets of desert landscape and gazebos where students could escape the sun to study or loiter.

The greenway ended at a small concrete pond with a twenty-foot-high fountain that sprayed water behind a placard: From the Desert Rises a Fertile Mind, Never to Be Wasted.

As was so often the case, when the dust settled and the buildings stood proud, the tax-hike controversy had been long forgotten.

Other controversies among the 2,429 students that roamed the beautiful new campus, however, were new every morning.

Like every school in the United States, the race-religion controversy was more felt than spoken, because the public school system had long ago learned that some things were best left out of the classroom. Issues like freedom of religious expression, which had taken a brutal beating early in the century. Like politics, which was best discussed at home. Issues like racial prejudice, which had come full circle in its failure to be resolved. After all, whites, the historical perpetrators of most racial discrimination in the United States, were now a minority.

But the lynchings in Kansas City over the past week had sparked a flame among the students in most schools across the country, and Boulder City High was no exception. Principal Joseph Durst had used the public address system for a reasoned speech about the absurdity of racially motivated hate crimes. "Tolerance, students, is the pathway to harmony. Diversity should be celebrated, not snuffed out. Just remember we live in the twenty-first century, not the Dark Ages."

Although his intentions were undoubtedly sincere, the announcement only highlighted the news of the two latest lynchings in a Kansas City graveyard this morning.

Katrina Kivi walked down the covered walkway that led to the first set of gazebos in the yard, as they called it. The fountain rose majestically a hundred yards directly ahead. Carla walked beside her, noisily popping gum, rambling on about how Mexicans were worse than the whites and if there was anyone the cops should suspect, it should be a Chicano.

Katrina Kivi couldn't say that she didn't care, but compared to events that had forever altered her own world these past twenty-four hours, two hangings in a Kansas City graveyard, however tragic, seemed distant.

In fact, most of the day had felt disconnected from Kat. Like everything around her was actually part of a world to which she didn't belong. She'd awoken to discover that she was really an alien and had been sent here at birth by the mother ship as part of an experiment.

She dressed the same: blue jeans, black blouse. Still had the snake tattoo on her shoulder blade that could just be seen slithering around her neck when she wore a T-shirt. Same dark hair, same hazel eyes, same skull ring on her left forefinger.

But she didn't feel like the same person who walked down this very same outdoor walkway with Carla and Jay yesterday. Kat's friends had long ago agreed they were three of the school's twenty-seven "true" witches, who didn't dabble in the craft but lived by a respectable code.

It was the kind of hogwash Kat normally would have shot down in flames, but she went along with this to be included. A person had to belong somewhere. Today, though, she knew that she was a foreigner even among her own clique.

"So you gonna tell me?" Carla asked.

"Hmmm?"

"C'mon, Kat. Don't you try to tell me nothing's wrong. Why you being so quiet today? You sick?"

"No, I'm fine." She wasn't fine, of course. She was far better than fine.

"Okay . . . so what happened?"

The events of last night spun through her mind for the hundredth time since leaving Johnny's house late last night. Her eyes had been opened to another world. She'd seen herself as she truly was, but that wasn't the main thing.

The main thing was that for the first time in her life she became completely and utterly aware of a greater reality, of which she was a part. Simple statements she'd once heard as distant, annoying barking dogs in the night, yapping, yapping at the world, had thundered through her mind. A huge monster had grabbed her by the hair, spun her around, and roared in her face with enough power to rip her skin off.

Okay, that wasn't the way Johnny had put it, but it was what had happened. Only the huge monster had turned out to be God. Not in a million years would she have figured. How ludicrous.

God.

Walking next to Carla now, the word sounded so . . . strange.

"God," she whispered.

"What?"

"What?" She remembered that Carla was waiting for an explanation. "Never mind." But then Kat couldn't keep it back any longer.

She smiled, gripped her books tight against her chest. "Carla, what if I told you that everything you thought about life was wrong?"

Carla was looking at Charles Wright, who loitered with a group of football jocks. All blacks. "He thinks he's so hot." But the devilish grin on her face betrayed her infatuation with the running back, who was watching them.

He smiled and nodded. Carla lifted her fingers in a tempered acknowledgement, then turned back to Kat.

Carla feigned nonchalance, but her crush on Charles was well known to the group. "You see that look?" she said.

"I saw it." But Kat wasn't interested in it.

"Sorry. You were saying?"

Kat had thought through countless ways to spill the beans to her fellow witches, and none of them seemed particularly compelling.

"What if I told you that God was real?"

"Yeah? So what?" Carla glanced back at the group of jocks.

"I mean, really real? Like in Moses-in-the-ark real?" Or had she gotten that mixed up?

"Moses? I'd say you were starting to sound like a Muslim." Her friend grabbed her arm playfully. "Don't tell me you've decided to put aside your witchery and follow hard after Moses and Jesus! Oh, that's just wonderful news, Kat."

"Muslims? Do they follow Jesus?"

"'Course they do." Carla's voice was tinged with bitterness.

"Where'd you learn that?"

"Before my father converted to Islam, my family used to go to church. Trust me, I've had an earful. Muslims think Jesus was the only sinless person, prophet, whatever, to live. They worship the ground he walks on."

"They do?"

She shrugged and grinned. "What would I know? I'm just a witch."

After picking herself up off the floor last night, Kat had sat on the couch and wept in Kelly's arms for two hours as Johnny served them tea and talked about the truth of the matter, as he put it. But he hadn't spoken much about religion.

But what did that make her? She couldn't be a witch, surely. Was she a Christian? She supposed so. She was most definitely a follower of Jesus, because in the world that her eyes had been opened to last night, there was no difference between Jesus and God. Together they'd ruthlessly and yet so lovingly ruined her to this old world, with its cars and boyfriends and designer jeans.

How could she express all of that without sounding like a complete fool?

Carla punched her arm. "You're not serious, right?" They reached the gazebo and ducked out of the sun's hot rays.

"I . . ." *As a heart attack, honey.* But could she just say that? "As a heart attack, honey."

"Serious about what?" Carla asked. "Being a Muslim, or this bit about thinking God is real?"

"About God."

"Two black crows alone in their nest, eh?" Carla and Kat faced the familiar voice, surprised to see that Asad had appeared out of nowhere with twenty or more of his friends.

"Who you calling a crow, towel-head?" Carla snapped.

A square white bandage covered Asad's cheek where Kat had cut him with her fingernails yesterday. He hopped over the wall, joined by the others, mostly Arabs.

"I am calling you a crow, you black witch. In my father's court you would be nothing more than a slave for mopping the floor." His eyes moved to Kat. "And you, with your milky brown skin, might make for a good whore."

Some of them had straddled the wall, others hung behind. All watched expectantly. And Kat didn't have a clue what should be done.

"This coming from the desert donkeys who have nothing better to do than to hack each other to pieces over women and oil."

Had Carla lost her mind?

Asad's face darkened. "We are Muslims who follow the Koran and do only the will of Allah. If he commands us to kill the infidels, do you suggest we turn our backs on him? If he gives us the gift of a slave like you, do you suggest we throw his gift back in his face? You filthy crow."

"My father's a Muslim, you fool!" Carla shouted. "He'd come down here and twist your creamy little neck if he heard your militant, fundamentalist garbage."

The fact that Carla's father was a Muslim seemed to stall Asad.

"Not all Muslims follow the will of Allah," one of the others said.

"No, only those who blow themselves up for the virgins, I suppose," Carla shot back. "Your brand of extremism is dead!"

"What's going on here?" The black jocks had come up behind them. Seven of them, Kat saw. "You girls okay?" Charles asked, glancing at Carla. It didn't take Kat much to imagine that he could do as much damage off the football field as on.

"I don't know, are we?" Carla demanded, staring at Asad.

Asad was surrounded by his people, and he didn't back down easily. "From the beginning and in the end all your type will be good for is entertaining and serving the true followers of Allah."

"You got a death wish, boy?" Charles snapped.

Kat finally found herself. "Stop it! Both of you!"

She inched away from Carla, putting herself between the boys. "This isn't right, it can't be. And I'm to blame. So I'm going to fix it."

Carla stared at her as if she'd lost her marbles.

"That's where you're wrong," Asad said. "We're going to fix it for you."

"No, Asad, you can't, not like this. I'm sorry for cutting you. I'm sorry for hitting Leila." No sign of the girl in this group. "It was wrong of me."

No one seemed to know what to do with that, so Kat continued.

"This isn't what God would want."

"What could a witch know about Allah?" the boy to Asad's right said.

So here it was, the moment of truth.

"I'm not a witch," she said, looking at Carla. "Not anymore. I met God yesterday and learned of his world."

"So now you expect us to believe that you're an expert on Allah's world?" Asad said. "What do you know about Allah? Christians and Hindus don't follow Allah!"

"*Allah* means *God*, right? I may not be familiar with who prays to which God yet, but I know that this isn't his way. If you were to see his world, you'd fall on your faces, crying out in fear and love!"

The words sounded idiotic here in the gazebo. Carla was still staring at her, dumbstruck. The jocks looked like they'd rather be slamming into a defensive line than facing off with a girl spouting Allah talk.

Johnny had introduced her to Jesus, so she dispensed with the God-Allah talk and spoke to the heart of the matter.

"You worship Jesus, right?"

"I worship no one but Allah."

"Okay, whatever, you worship the ground Jesus walks on if I remember correctly. You think he'd go for this?"

"Since when are you into Jesus?" Carla asked.

"I'm just saying, Carla, we got witches facing off Muslims and Arabs facing off blacks. Where does this end? Where's the room for love in that way of thinking? We should be loving each other, not trying to figure out how to cut each other's throats."

"Not if those throats refuse to pray to Allah," Asad said.

Kat whipped her head back to the boy. "Come on, you really think that's what Jesus taught? Don't Muslims believe he's the sinless prophet? Shouldn't we all follow his teachings?"

She was hardly the expert on Islam or Jesus, and undoubtedly she was full of mistakes that Johnny would help correct, but her reasoning sounded decent to her. And she knew that the love she'd felt last night after her initial meltdown was available to Asad and Carla as well.

"As Allah wills it," Asad said.

"And he does!"

They all just stared at her.

"Trust me, I saw him. Or myself as he sees me. My eyes were opened to the world the way God sees it, and it's changed me. I can't be the same ever again. I can't, because I believe in God."

"Even the demons believe in God and tremble," one of the Arabs said.

Now it was Kat's turn to be silenced.

"As to the infidels . . ." Asad said, regaining some confidence.

"Okay." Kat nodded. "Fair enough. I have a challenge for you. Rather than cut each other up, let's call a truce. On Monday we'll reconvene for a debate on the true will of Allah. If I lose, you may beat me to a pulp off school grounds without any retaliation from any of my friends."

When the idea had first presented itself to her it had sounded brilliant. But already she wondered just how brilliant. And all of this assumed that Johnny Drake could talk the judge out of a jail sentence for her.

Maybe the jail sentence was a better idea.

"A debate," Asad said.

"Yes. On Monday, after school."

Asad glanced at his line, seemed to receive no help either way. He evidently took this as a positive sign.

"Fine. On Monday." And then he added for good measure. "Infidel."

CHAPTER NINETEEN

Day Four

"I'M TELLING you, Billy . . ." Darcy turned from their apartment window with the Capitol's dome framed in the backdrop, folded her arms, and drilled him with a hard stare. "I've never felt anything like it."

"So you've told me," he said. She had woken him early, unable to sleep, all wound up. He tilted his shades down, stared past her to the graying Washington sky, then replaced them. He was losing interest in the prospect of living in the perpetual shade of sunglasses.

"This was different. Are you even listening to me?"

"Of course I am. I'm out of bed at six in the morning listening to you."

"Then *listen* to me. This was different. I had them in my hands." She made a fist. "I mean . . . I felt it this time."

"Okay, Darcy, I'm not being insensitive or anything, but both of us have had our worlds turned upside down this week. It's catching up to you, I get that. But it's not news." He paused. "Coffee?"

She uncrossed her arms, then crossed them again. "Well, it's news to me. And yes, coffee would be nice."

Billy left her standing by the window and retreated into the kitchen. She hadn't told him about her episode at Union Cemetery until they returned last night, and then she told him as if it should be a secret. It hardly sounded any different from her persuading Annie Ruling to slap the senator. But her perceptions of the cemetery event seemed to have shifted her understanding of her power. Maybe he should be more understanding.

"Look, I'm sorry if I sound impatient," he said, pouring the coffee. "But I'm starting to feel like a rat trapped in a glass cage. They whisked us off to Kansas City yesterday and what? Nothing. What are we, their sniffing dogs?"

"That's my point!"

But she'd made no such point. "It is?"

He placed her cup in her hands, but she set it down on the coffee table so she could use her hands to speak.

"Okay, so maybe I'm trying to make sense of this . . . these powers of ours, but I'm telling you, we have more power than either of us realizes, Billy. This ad hoc council of theirs may be scrambling around trying to figure out how to use us for their personal gain, but I don't think even they understand what kind of power we have."

"I think Kinnard knows exactly what we are capable of," Billy said. "He's been dreaming of this ever since he met Johnny. I think the council is over there plotting right now while we sit here like two rats trapped in this cage."

"Think of what we could do!"

"I have been. I've been thinking about it ever since I stood in the courtroom and—"

"I think I could have killed them, Billy," she said.

"Really?"

"I don't know. But I'm sure the power increases with my own emotion and forcefulness. No, I don't think I could have killed them, but I'll tell you what, this power is absolutely incredible."

So that's what this was about. The implications of her ability were finally sinking in. The only thing that had really changed was Darcy's perception of her gift.

"So, tell me again, why are we doing this?" she asked.

"Last I checked, there are people out there who want us both dead."

"And Kinnard and company can protect us?"

Billy arched an eyebrow. "They seem to be doing a decent job so far."

"So you're okay with being their sniffing dogs then?"

Billy sat on the couch and put his cup beside hers. "No, but that's not going to last."

"Oh?"

"They're just getting the feel of things themselves."

"And just who put them in charge?" she demanded.

For a moment she looked exactly like the thirteen-year-old Darcy he remembered from the monastery. She was showing her true feelings. And honestly, Billy preferred her this way.

"You find this funny?" she asked. "I'm trying to make a point here!"

"I was just remembering how beautiful you are when you get aggressive."

That stopped her.

"So tell me, Darcy, what exactly is your point?"

She thought about it, then turned to face the window and stared out at the rising sun.

"My point is that we should think about us, not them. We should use what we have for us. The gifts were given to us, not to them."

A bell went off in Billy's head. They'd been here before, only then it had been him trying to convince her. *Reach out, take the forbidden fruit.* And they had done it together.

He stood and walked up behind her. Put his hands on her shoulders and looked at the majestic buildings that housed Washington's power.

"Does that make sense?" she asked without turning.

Billy rubbed her shoulders gently. "Maybe more than you know."

"It's just that we should look out for ourselves, Billy. Not for the criminals in this town."

"We could do a few things, couldn't we?"

"We could become filthy rich."

He slid his hands around her belly and whispered into her ear, "Do you want to rule the world with me?"

She threw her head back and chuckled, exposing her neck to his lips. "Why not take over the universe while we're at it?"

Billy kissed the soft of her neck. "Become God."

She turned into him and traced his cheek with her finger. "Now there's an idea." Their lips met like two silk pillows, and Billy knew that he would follow Darcy to the grave for kisses like this.

The phone buzzed. Darcy bent for the receiver and spoke quietly into it, keeping her eyes on him.

"Hello?"

She listened for a moment, then hung up.

"What?"

"There's a car downstairs waiting for us."

"What is it?"

"Two more bodies were found lynched in the Union Cemetery last night. They were white."

"So they want their sniffing dogs in Kansas City again?"

"Kansas City is rioting."

"LISTEN AND observe," Kinnard said, marching Darcy and Billy through a sea of cubicles at FBI headquarters. They had taken a ride down the street, past the White House to the J. Edgar Hoover Building and been assigned visitors' passes upon arrival. "This is all seat of the pants, but Lawhead's eager to bring you inside."

So you can poke and prod your sniffing dogs some more, Darcy thought.

They passed a bank of computer stations manned by agents, most of them glued to their phones.

"Mind you, the others don't have a clue about you, and we'd like to keep it that way. Play along, be discrete. This way." Kinnard led them up a flight of stairs where glass walls overlooked a large conference room lined with large screens. She could see Newt Lawhead inside, bent over a conference table with a dozen other suits, intent in discussion. It looked like a war room from a movie set.

Kinnard stopped with his hand on the door and faced Billy and Darcy. "Keep your glasses on. I'm sure you understand. Lot of sensitive information floating around this building. Observe only. Speak only when you are addressed."

They entered the conference room and stood with him at the back, doing as instructed. Observing.

Now the sniffing dogs were muzzled, she thought wryly.

But she quickly lost herself in the scene on the large screens. All the news services were carrying live feeds of the riot in Union Cemetery. CNN, FOX, BBC, IRN . . . they all showed different views of the scene, some from the ground, others from the air.

She locked on to the footage taken from a helicopter high above it all. Smoke boiled skyward from at least five separate fires set to buildings around the cemetery. Dozens of fire trucks and police cars had formed a perimeter around what looked to be about a ten-block radius, but none were going into the battle zone.

Darcy stared at the scene, stunned by the destruction. All of America was seeing this? And over what? Race?

Several thousand rioters ran through the streets in gangs, smashing windows and overturning cars. The crime scene they visited yesterday had been overrun by several hundred rioters who looked to have set up a defensive position under assault from at least two fronts.

"Unbelievable," Billy muttered. "It looks like a war zone in Lebanon."

Lawhead heard and looked up. He nodded.

"Gentlemen, if I may . . ." He motioned them forward as the others seated around the table turned. "Meet Billy Rediger and Darcy Lange. We've brought them in as consultants on the case. I wanted them here to observe in the event they might be of assistance. Thank you for coming."

"Observe in what capacity?" A stout man with bushy eyebrows watched her with pale blue eyes. One look and Darcy decided she didn't like him.

"None that concerns you," Darcy said. She had half a mind to tell the man where he could put his area of specialty.

Lawhead glanced between them. "Actually—"

"Then you can observe from the observation room in B wing. Let's get back to work, gentlemen. They're waiting for our—"

"I'd like a rundown," Darcy snapped, striding around the table. "Just the essentials. Starting with who's rioting, specifically."

"Blacks, presumably Christian—"

"I doubt it. Christians might not be completely right in the head, but they wouldn't attack law enforcement. The fact that the media is spinning this as a religious matter doesn't help. Maybe you should shut them down." A breath. "Why aren't the police evacuating the area?"

The room stilled to the sound of a buzz from the monitors. The FBI's upper echelon looked at Lawhead.

He nodded at a thin man with a bald head. "Pete?"

"Do you really think this is the time, Newt?" the man with bushy eyebrows demanded.

"Humor her."

Pete cleared his throat. He picked up a laser pen and directed the beam at a three-dimensional rendering of the riot zone. "First responders have set up a perimeter along Holmes Street to the east, Main Street to the east between Twenty-sixth and Thirty-first Streets. We have substantial gunfire from at least a dozen buildings along those lines. Fifteen dead that we know of so far, and that's just along the perimeter. No estimate from inside. They seem to be organized, well armed, and intentional. If there is a command center inside the perimeter, it's likely coming from this building and the original crime scene. The assault will have to come from the west—"

"Assault?" They'd brought her to observe, right? "You're considering waging war on the ground?"

The walrus wasn't liking her. "I really don't think you're in a position to question—"

"We're here to observe, sir," Billy interrupted. "Please let the sniffing dogs do their tricks."

Darcy took comfort in his support. "Well?"

Pete looked at Lawhead, who gave him a barely perceptible nod.

"The National Guard is on its way from Jefferson City," Pete continued. "Plans for an assault have been drawn up with consideration for collateral damage."

"So basically you're in a pickle either way," Billy said. "You let them fight it out and you have maybe a hundred dead. You roll in with tanks to stop the fighting and you end up with the same."

"Something like that, yes."

"We can't, as a matter of policy, allow rioters to take our streets hostage," one of the others said.

Billy was right, Darcy thought. She was staring at a scene on one of the small screens. A shaky camera operator had caught a man running for the perimeter with a child in his arms when a bullet blew off his hand. He dropped the child, who jumped up screaming. The man stared at his bloodied hand for a moment, then grabbed his child with his good hand and resumed his run.

"What about gas?" Billy asked.

"So you're a military expert as well?" the stout man asked. "That's not our call. Please, Newt. We really don't have time for this."

"I'm going in," Darcy said.

The statement was absurd; Darcy could hardly blame their silence.

Lawhead was the first to speak, asserting his authority. "I'm sorry, Ms. Lange, but I can't allow that."

She faced him. "Daylight's wasting. I need to know how to get to whoever in there has a say."

"Darcy . . ." This from Billy. "I'm not sure this is the wisest course of action here."

She could persuade him easily enough later. "I don't need this right now, Billy."

Lawhead wasn't buying it. "There's absolutely no way. This is not a good choice."

"You don't *have* a choice! Would you like me to prove my point?"

By the look in his eyes she knew that the truth of her statement had sunk in. She could remove her glasses and speak to them all, persuading them more pointedly. Maybe Lawhead had underestimated her. And maybe he'd begin to see her as a threat, the last thing she wanted.

So she quickly covered. "No disrespect. I really need to do this. If you'll allow me. Please."

"It's a war zone."

"I can see that. I insist."

CHAPTER TWENTY

THERE WAS good news and there was not-so-good news, Kat thought.

The good was that Johnny had talked to the judge and received a court order placing Kat under his supervision. As long as she bided by the terms of her six-month probation, which among other things strictly forbade any kind of violent behavior, she would remain a free woman.

She was required to stand before the judge first thing Monday to receive the instructions directly from the court.

The not-so-good news was that Johnny wasn't exactly thrilled about her challenge to debate Asad bin Salman.

Per their agreement, Kat hurried to Johnny's home at ten o'clock sharp Saturday morning, eager to share the details of her first day walking in the light, as he put it. She paced the carpet, a bundle of exuberance, overflowing with questions and opinions.

Kelly served them all iced tea and seated herself next to Johnny on the couch, where they watched Kat moving about the room like a kid who'd just discovered she won the lottery.

"Yes, of course it's all about the truth," Johnny said. "But the question is wrong. What exactly are you debating?"

"The true will of Allah, like they always say. God versus Allah. All of that."

"The question is Jesus."

"Perfect. Then the truth about Jesus."

"The truth isn't best shown with words. Particularly not when you're trying to determine God's will. Truth is an issue of the heart, not merely the mind."

"Of course it is. But you start with the mind, don't you?"

"You can."

"And on that note, why don't you just come with me, we'll get into it, and when the right time comes, you can just take off your glasses and get them all to see the truth. For that matter, why not just show the whole world, end all of this fighting over who knows what's right?"

Johnny frowned. "It doesn't work like that. Just because someone sees the truth doesn't mean they will accept it or allow that truth to change them. Fact is, most have seen the truth about themselves a thousand times, the truth about God even more often, and remain unchanged. Seeing that same truth in a more spectacular way didn't change the hearts of the crowds who saw Jesus feeding the five thousand. They still killed him."

"Sure, but you're showing them the truth all in one overwhelming shot. It nearly killed me! They'd fall to their faces, how could they not?"

"Maybe. It's not my habit to cast pearls before swine."

"Swine?"

"It's what Jesus said about not putting the truth in front of people who refuse to hear it."

"You showed me."

"I figured you would hear it and I was right. But the kingdom of light is foolishness to most, just remember that. Your friends . . . what did they think of this sudden change in you?"

"Carla?"

"Sure, Carla."

Kat shrugged. "She thinks I'm nuts."

"Exactly."

Kat walked to one of two chairs facing the couch, thought about sitting, then walked behind it and paced. "Exactly. I just can't get over how, two days ago"—she lifted her fingers at them in a peace sign—"just two days ago, I was as stupid as them."

"Stupid?"

"Whatever. I couldn't see it. There's this light all around us . . ." She smiled at the ceiling, unable to see it now but remembering what Johnny had shown her for a moment after she'd spent herself crying.

"It's here and I can feel it. I know it's here. This kingdom of heaven thing. The light." She glanced at him. "Can you show me again?"

"Maybe. Sometime. And how do you know it's not just another apple in my hand? An illusion?"

"Because I *felt* it! You showed me the apple and I thought, *Wow, that's incredible.* But when you showed me the light . . ." Tears sprang to her eyes.

Now she slipped into the chair, crossed her legs, and let the emotion come. A painful knot clogged her throat.

She looked at Kelly, the more mysterious one here, really. What did she know about Kelly, other than she smiled all the time?

Johnny, on the other hand, was crying. Tears ran from under his glasses, leaving thin trails down his cheeks.

Kelly followed Kat's eyes, and she rested her hand on his thigh when she saw his tears. She'd clearly been here before, supporting him. The image of Kelly crying behind the shed now seemed as unreal as a childhood nightmare.

"We'll have to work on your theology." Johnny smiled. "But I think your heart is doing just fine." He looked out the window and spoke in a soft voice. "The Book says that eternity is set in the hearts of men. But so is evil. That was Billy's problem; he let the evil get the best of his world. And it never seems to go away, not for good."

"Billy?"

"Billy," Kelly said. She'd remained quiet, but at the mention of Billy she'd come alive, eyes round. She blinked, catching herself, then offered an explanation. "Billy, a figure of speech as much as a real person. The common man who spawns evil and leaves it to roam through his life until it one day comes back to wreak havoc again. Billy."

Johnny looked at her, then nodded. "Yes, Billy. Question is, does the evil he created still walk among us? I think so."

Kat didn't know what he was talking about, and she said so.

Johnny sighed. "It doesn't matter right now. You know, when I was first given this gift it confused me. Of course, it was different then. The whole thing came on very strong, but then it all settled into this ability to help others see things. The truth about themselves. An apple. The light. But I myself can't look at a person and know the truth about him. I can't see God or see the evil. The light, yes, glimpses of the light, but that's all."

He faced her. "What I would give to be able to see what you saw again, Katrina Kivi. To feel what you felt."

"You don't feel it?"

"I do, yes, but not like a blind-born man seeing the world for the first time. The moment of freedom is mind blowing, isn't it?"

"It is."

"I'm a prophet to this world, though only God knows what my purpose is. I suppose one day it'll be clear. But now I live in the dark, knowing truth, frustrated by the inability of others to see what you and I have seen. Does that make sense?"

Kat was so taken aback by his admission that she couldn't answer. He was the most wonderful person in the world, living in this small house on the edge of Boulder City, Nevada, hidden from the world. He could change the world with his blind white eyes!

Instead, the man who'd saved her sat on his couch wearing glasses. Humbled.

Kat stood and crossed to him. She eased herself to one knee, leaned forward, and wrapped her arms around him, resting her head on his chest.

"You're a hero to me, Johnny. I love you. I love you with all of my heart."

Johnny put his hand on her head and they cried together for a few minutes. Kat eventually stood, wiped her eyes, and returned to her chair.

"It's infectious, isn't it?" Johnny said.

"I'm still trying to figure out what *it* is."

"Yes, well, we'll work on that. But it's your heart you have to guard, Kat. Most Christians have their facts cinched down pretty good. It's their hearts that are up for grabs. Really, most of the news about the kingdom of heaven can be summarized in a few words."

"Which are?"

"The kingdom of light is among us, and his name is Jesus. Follow him."

She felt a wry smile pull at her lips. "That's it?"

"It also helps to know what he taught."

"To love," she said.

"Yes, to love. Which is what we'll focus on today."

"So you'll help me prepare for the debate, then?"

Johnny smiled. "On the condition you promise that none of the knowledge we stuff into that brain of yours will make you cry any less."

She stood and raised her right hand. "I swear. On one condition."

"Which is?"

"That you cry with me."

He hesitated.

"Swear it," she said.

"I swear it."

CHAPTER TWENTY-ONE

THEY USED a QP-505 news helicopter borrowed from an ABC News affiliate for the flight in, so as to avoid any appearance of military aggression. Whoever controlled the whites, who were hunkered down in the center of Union Cemetery, would likely fire upon army green but be friendly toward news coverage that might spread their cause. No military personnel, no police, no one but her, she'd insisted. She had to go in flying friendly flags and she had to do it quickly.

At least that was the plan, and it sounded reasonable to Darcy. Maybe the only reasonable part of what she was about to attempt.

The blades chopped through the midday air above Kansas City as the helicopter moved closer to the green blotch of land spotted with a thousand graves. Billy sat beside her trying to hide his concern. One airman had accompanied them to operate the ladder.

"It's not too late," Billy said. "Please, Darcy, this can't go well."

She'd avoided speaking to him plainly without her glasses on, because she didn't want him to love her because of some spell she'd cast on him. At the moment his words seemed more convincing than her own.

"It is too late," she said. "Lawhead sold them on this attempt at negotiation. The governor and the commanding officer of the National Guard have acquiesced. They've held off the assault in hope that I can do something to prevent further bloodshed. I probably already have blood on my hands."

"No, that's not true! For all you know, delaying the assault has saved lives." He peered at the approaching cemetery from his side window. They tried to talk him out of accompanying her, but he'd been adamant to the point of belligerence.

"This is nuts."

"Please, Billy! You're not being helpful here!"

Billy saw the tremble in her hands and took them in his own. "Okay. I'm a nervous wreck. But you're right, this is precisely the kind of situation we can do some good in."

She nodded. "So much for looking out for just us."

"Beats being a sniffing dog." He brushed her hair back from her cheek. "You're not doing this for Washington. You're doing it for us, for them." He looked out the window. "Forget what I said—that's just me being me. The truth is, I couldn't be more proud of you."

They each wore one earpiece, which now crackled. "One minute." The pilot was from the Air National Guard, dressed in civilian clothes. "I'm going to drop like a rock right over the friendlies. Nick, you ready?"

The airman slid the door open, locked it into place, and readied a rolled aluminum ladder. The sound of the engine roared. The whole scenario felt horribly wrong out here in the air. She'd forgotten how much she hated heights until they climbed aboard the helicopter.

"Ready when you are." Nick faced her. "Just like we practiced. Let the ladder do the work. Just step off on the grass, easy." He tapped his palms. "Gloves on."

She could have hooked in but after some discussion decided that the risks of getting hung up outweighed any risk of falling. Looking through the open door, she wasn't so sure.

Darcy took the gloves from Billy and slid them over her hands.

He leaned over and spoke into her ear. "You can do this, Darcy. Just don't stop talking. Make them look into your eyes and talk. Just . . ."

"Here we go."

The helicopter dropped like a stone. Nick took her hand, ready to pull her into place as soon as they hovered over the clearing.

"Hold on . . ."

They fell for what seemed an eternity before the blades flared, slowing their descent like an elevator braking to a stop at the bottom floor. Nick threw the first few feet of the ladder out.

"Go, go, go!"

She adjusted the flak jacket she'd donned, flung her glasses off, and slid off the seat with Nick's and Billy's help.

They're white, I'm white, they won't shoot. They won't shoot.

She grabbed the ladder, shoved first one, then her second foot into the third rung. "Okay."

The ladder began to uncoil and she swung into open air.

Darcy looked down, saw the grass twenty feet below. Bodies were scrambling to get out of her way. She kept telling herself that no one would shoot, that all she had to do was get her feet on the ground and everything would be okay. They were rioters armed with a few popguns and pipes, not an army with machine guns.

She kicked her feet out and dropped when she was still ten feet from the turf. Hit the ground hard and rolled as they'd shown her.

The helicopter's thumping deepened then faded as it climbed. Leaving Darcy on her belly in the grass, staring at a large tombstone ten feet from where she'd landed.

She shoved herself to her knees, looking for someone, anyone, who could do what she needed done. The clearing was roughly thirty yards across, encircled by the tombstones of those who had paid the most for the largest monuments to their loved ones. Perfect cover for a hundred or so rioters who'd taken up position on this side of them.

The tent that had housed the crime scene investigation just yesterday had been reduced to charred balls of plastic. A group of seven or eight men, at least two of whom were armed with rifles trained on her, hunkered down behind a row of gravestones.

A glance to her left showed another group with several handguns and three rifles, pointed in her direction.

She lifted her hands high above her head. "Don't shoot! I have critical information!" Her voice rang out above the sporadic popping of distant gunfire.

"Keep your hands high or we'll blow your head off."

"Just don't shoot! I'm unarmed. Just the messenger."

Based on her limited experience, her persuasive power seemed to work only in conjunction with a person's own intentions. She didn't think she could force a person to do something they knew to be wrong unless they harbored a deep-seated desire to do it.

She made eye contact with one of men who had a rifle trained on her. "I'm here to help—you don't want to shoot me! You hear me?"

She couldn't see his immediate response from this far away, but she felt exposed here, so she stood and went for the large group, hands lifted high.

"Look at me, all of you," she screamed. "Just look into my eyes, see if I'm not telling you the truth. You do *not* want to shoot me. You *will not* shoot me." She kept walking but turned her head to face the men behind the gravestones.

"You hear me? You don't want to harm me."

An unnatural stillness had gripped the clearing, and she knew that she was connecting with them. So she turned around, walking backward now. They looked to be a loose gang who'd taken advantage of the lynchings to express their own hatred or mistrust of blacks. Most if not all of the hundred or so gangsters were watching her.

"All of you listen to me," she cried out. "No one wants to harm me. No one will shoot. You all want to listen to every word I have to say. You hear me?"

Darcy stopped and looked around at the circle of men staring at her, dumbfounded. She couldn't tell who their leader was, or even if there *was* a leader, but learning this wouldn't be difficult.

"I have information that is going to change your day, my friends. You will want to do what I've come to suggest." Turning, she said it again. "I have information that is going to change your day, my friends. You will want to do what I've come to suggest. Show me who's in charge."

No one jumped to her wishes.

She turned, more angry than fearful now. "Show me, for heaven's sake! I need to speak to your leader now!"

A man armed with an automatic weapon stood and stepped out toward her. His pitted face frowned and his dark eyes seemed to sear her with hatred, but he came willingly.

"What's your name?"

"What do you want?"

"I want you to get everyone over by your position so I can address them."

"Are you nuts?"

"Don't be a fool." She threw the words at him in a flash of anger. "I'm here to save your rotten white skin and there's nothing more precious to you than your own skin. Now get everyone over here immediately."

He hesitated a moment, nodded once, and waved at the men across the clearing. "Get over here, all of you." When they hesitated, he cursed and raised his volume.

They hurried to his side, ducking behind the tombstones as they ran. An occasional bullet slapped into the tombstones surrounding them, but most of the firing came from the streets surrounding Union Cemetery. They had placed their command in the safest part of the field.

Darcy approached and stared at them all, tapping her cheek. "Look at me. Don't remove your eyes from mine. I know all hell is breaking loose out there, but you want to listen to what I have to say."

They watched her, attentive as dogs begging for a steak. She had them in her hands and the power was intoxicating.

"You're all going to lay down your weapons and leave this place. You're going to do that because you know in your gut that this is a dead-end fight. You don't want to die today. And you're not going to die today, because you're going to help me stop this standoff. Every one of you knows that's the right thing."

"Robby?" A skinny kid with one of the rifles was shaking, looking at the pitted-faced man for guidance. "Robby?"

"Shut up!"

"Listen to Robby," Darcy snapped. "Tell them how they can save themselves, Robby."

Their leader looked confounded and disturbed.

"Robby?"

"She's right," he said.

"Of course I'm right. You're going to leave this place now and run as fast as your legs can move."

How her words worked their effect she didn't know, but whatever power they carried had now fully engaged them. First a dozen and then twice as many dropped their weapons and began to run west, toward the warehouses and Main Street just beyond, the closest and safest line of exit.

"No, not that way," she cried.

They pulled up, disoriented. Others were dropping their guns and pipes. Standing, eager to be gone. But she needed more from them.

Darcy pointed east and north. "You're going to run that way, into the houses, spreading the word to everyone who will listen. You'll say, 'The riot's over, lay down your weapons, and run while the running is good.'"

"What?"

She didn't know who called the question and she didn't care. "If you go west, the National Guard will be waiting to clean you out. Go east, undo what you've done here, tell them all that it's over. Lay down your weapons and run, run, run! Go north and tell them to spread the word; get out now before it's too late."

The skinny kid who'd called out for Robby was the first to move. He threw his gun on the ground in a fit of panic, whimpering and swearing at once. And he ran pell-mell into the graveyard, headed due east.

Then they all ran. All except for Robby, who'd dropped his weapon and stood staring at her. It was as if his mind knew what to do, but his muscles were in shock and refused to move.

"Run, Robby," Darcy said, walking toward him. "You will yell the loudest."

He turned and jogged after the others.

BILLY PACED the street at the intersection of Main and Twenty-ninth, where Darcy would emerge. *If* she emerged.

He'd bitten his nails to stubs, pacing behind the line of police cars, waiting. If she'd succeeded, she would have been out by now. Unless she'd decided in all of this newfound confidence of hers to head farther into the war zone.

Her first plan had been to meet with both black and white leaders, but they'd talked her out of it. A white heading into a black zone couldn't turn out good. But what if she'd gone anyway?

A news van stood at the ready, filming the empty street. If Darcy managed to calm the storm, they would make sure the entire country knew. Already there were reports of vandalism in St. Louis, Miami, Detroit, and Los Angeles. Nooses with hangman's knots were found in half the universities across the country. Putting an end to the Kansas City riot was really about nipping a much larger problem in the bud.

Billy looked up to see Kinnard walking toward him with quick strides, phone plastered to his ear. Billy had removed his glasses, intent upon knowing the truth, however ugly it might be. Kinnard, however, still wore shades.

He covered the mouthpiece while he was still twenty feet off and called to Billy. "She did it," he said. "I think she actually did it!"

"What? Where is she?"

"Spotters are reporting a flood of rioters running east and north." Into the phone: "Say again . . . Let me know the moment you hear anything." He snapped the phone shut.

"Any word on Darcy . . ."

"Look alive, people!" someone shouted. "We have incoming."

Billy ran up to the line of cars. A solitary figure was jogging toward them from around a warehouse a hundred yards out. There was no mistaking her long, dark brown hair, flowing in the breeze as she ran.

Darcy.

"You getting this?" someone said. The news crew.

Billy hopped over the barricade and sprinted toward her. An officer started to protest, but Kinnard shut him down. The rioters were headed east. Only Darcy was headed west.

He saw her beaming smile fifty yards off. And her wide brown eyes, glistening, uncovered in the sun.

"You made it," he said, slowing to a walk.

"And you were worried?"

"It's over?"

"I think so, Billy. I think they will do whatever I tell them to."

"You're alive," he said, stopping in front of her.

"Then kiss me."

She wasn't wearing any glasses, and looking into her intoxicating eyes, Billy realized that he desperately wanted to kiss her, more than he'd ever wanted to kiss anyone in his entire life.

"Do you love me?" he asked.

He heard her thoughts before she answered. *Of course I do, you silly boy. I never stopped loving you.*

"Yes," she said.

He took her into his arms, lifted her from her feet, and spun her around. Their mouths met and he kissed her deeply.

CHAPTER TWENTY-TWO

Day Five

THE COUNCIL sat around the same conference table, in the same order, wearing the same glasses the next morning. Oh yes, they would definitely wear the glasses now, wouldn't they? *Maybe they should consider getting the lenses surgically implanted,* Darcy thought.

Most of the rioters had vacated Union Cemetery and the surrounding area within an hour of Darcy's pep talk. Without an enemy to engage, the lingering hostiles slipped out during cover of darkness that night. Thirteen arrests were made, a fraction of the guilty, but by all accounts, the FBI's last-minute intervention was a smashing success.

Footage of Darcy jogging in from the war zone of Kansas City like some kind of Special Forces hero made the news, and that news spread fast and far, a byproduct of her feat that concerned Kinnard deeply, he said. Putting her to the test in the field where any potential enemy wouldn't likely see her was one thing, but exposing her to the nation was troublesome.

They covered her as best they could. She wasn't with the FBI or the SWAT team. She was a negotiator, a highly trained mediator who specialized in talking common sense to combative personalities in the most difficult situations.

Cued by "sources," talking heads throughout the Net extended Darcy's credit beyond this one situation. There was no telling how often the State Department dispatched negotiators to conduct secret meetings deep behind enemy lines. Or barter for trade policy, for human rights advocacy . . . the list was endless. And Darcy set an example for them all.

With just a little common sense and tolerance, any conflict could be avoided.

But the message fell on deaf ears. And the dawn brought unnerving news after a night of peace.

Sunday morning, three blacks hung from a tree behind a Pentecostal church in St. Louis.

Two whites hung in a graveyard next to a Catholic church twenty miles east of the first.

No rioting. Not yet. But the media was both stunned and expectant. The nation was a keg of gunpowder, silent and dormant.

"They're wrong," Lyndsay Nadeau said. The attorney general wore her perpetual smile. "It's not one spark, like the one in St. Louis, that will set off this keg. It's a thousand sparks. We all know that."

Darcy scanned the others for reaction: Ben Manning, the black Democratic senator from Nevada who had demanded they be kept locked up, stone faced.

Fred Hopkins. No better.

Annie Ruling, White House chief of staff. A slight amusement nudged the right side of her mouth northward.

Sanchez Dominquez. Might as well be a rock.

Associate director of the FBI, Newton Lawhead. Frowning, watching Darcy like a hawk.

Kinnard had excused himself after delivering them, explaining that he had someone else to pick up. Some mystery guest. For all she knew the president was coming.

She and Billy sat at one end, hands on the table, drumming their fingers lightly on the wood. She hadn't felt so alive in years and she decided to point this out.

"It's good to be alive," she said.

"Excuse me?"

"Nothing, just thinking aloud. We enjoy freedom in this country. That's a good thing. Hopefully we can all keep it that way."

"Random," Billy said.

"Ain't it great?" They were both smiling. Their moment of shared humor was lost on a few of them.

"I'm not sure you appreciate the gravity of the situation we're facing in this free country," Annie Ruling said. "So tell us—I'm curious—what was it like?"

"What was what like?"

"Doing your . . . thing in Kansas City yesterday."

"I spoke, they listened. They were persuaded."

"So you can just persuade anybody to do anything?" Ben Manning asked.

"Shall we test it with you?"

His flat lips curved downward. "It's that kind of ego that concerns me."

It had taken Darcy the better part of the week to wrap her own mind around her power. Manning and the members of the council were finally catching up. Perhaps she did owe them an explanation. The last thing she wanted was the council itself gunning for them.

The moment the thought occurred to her she knew that she'd hit on something. Kinnard feared that people like Ben Manning were as great a threat to them as the Catholic Church.

"To answer your question, no. I can't randomly persuade anyone to do anything. I'm not God."

"From what we can gather she can only persuade others to do what they know is right, or what they have a desire to do," Lawhead said.

She nodded once. "That's right. The rioters either realized that my suggestion to disband was the right thing to do, or deep in their minds where it counts, they wanted to disband."

"So what was it like?" Annie asked again. "I mean, having this kind of power must be quite exhilarating. Are you sure you can handle it?"

"Do we have a choice?" Billy asked. "We are what we are. The only question for this council is whether we will use our power to help you."

"This isn't an arbitration, Mr. Rediger," the attorney general said. "We're not a court of law. We're simply trying to determine if you can serve your country in a capacity never before appreciated."

"Are you?"

She removed her glasses and looked at him with sincere eyes. "I don't know, Billy. You tell me. Am I?"

"Yes. You at least believe you are."

"Thank you." She replaced her glasses. "This country is facing a crisis it hasn't faced since the Los Angeles riots or even the Civil War. We could use your help."

So at least the attorney general was being straight, Darcy thought. Maybe she'd been too quick to distrust this group.

She continued. "Annie, why don't you help our friends understand the scope of the crisis."

A knock sounded on the door behind Billy and Darcy. She turned as Brian Kinnard stepped through and a well-built man with blond hair, dressed in black slacks and a white button-down shirt filled the doorway. He wore glasses, no surprise.

Darcy didn't recognize him. Was she supposed to?

"My friends, please meet Johnny Drake."

Darcy's heart skipped a beat. A tremble overtook her fingers and spread to her hands. *Johnny?* This was Johnny from Paradise?

"Hello, Darcy. Billy." Johnny stretched out his hand. "Good to see you."

Billy stood and took the hand. "Johnny Drake . . . no kidding, is it really you?"

"In the flesh."

Darcy stood and he embraced her gently, then stepped back. They stood in an awkward moment of silence.

"Johnny heard the news, made contact with me yesterday, and agreed to come out. We consider Johnny to be a survivor of Project Showdown, though he was not a student there. As some of you know, Johnny is also quite . . ." He paused. "Special."

Darcy stood next to Billy, speechless.

Lyndsay Nadeau was the first to stand and take Johnny's hand. "Lyndsay Nadeau, attorney general. Good to meet you, Johnny. I've heard a few things here and there."

"Not too frightening, I hope." He smiled.

She grinned and turned to the others. "Our government has some classified history with Mr. Drake. Suffice it to say we can all be grateful for the sacrifice this man has paid on our behalf." She began pointing the others out, making personal introductions as they shook his hand.

"Okay, sit." Kinnard pulled out a chair next to Darcy's. "Like I said, you'll have time later."

Johnny looked at Darcy. "You okay? You look like you've seen a ghost."

"I'm sorry, I just never . . . Frankly, I'm a little speechless."

"Well, there's some hope for us all then," Annie laughed.

Johnny folded his hands on the table. Strong hands, but not rough like a bricklayer's. Certainly not the frail hands he'd had the last time she'd seen him as a boy. Darcy couldn't figure out how she felt about his dramatic reappearance.

"And what is your special gift, young man?" Ben Manning asked.

Kinnard spoke for him. "He can open the eyes, Mr. Manning. To see what the natural eye can't. Does that about cover it, Johnny?"

"Close enough."

They faced each other in an awkward stalemate. So Johnny had a backbone, Darcy thought. She liked that.

"Well then, can we continue?"

"Please," Kinnard said.

"Continue with what?" Billy asked. "Forgive my confusion here, but I still don't quite understand what you want from us."

Darcy pried her mind away from Johnny and glanced at Billy. True enough.

"You've seen what we can do," she said. "I think Billy's asking what your intentions are now. At the risk of imposing, of course."

Again Annie grinned, and Darcy grinned back. She liked the woman.

"Fair enough." The chief of staff slid her chair back and crossed one leg over the other. "Although I have to point out that forty-eight hours ago we didn't even know you existed. You can hardly blame our caution."

"Fine, Annie. But now we all know, so how are we going to help you change the world?"

Judging by the amusement on the faces of Annie Ruling and Lyndsay Nadeau, neither of them seemed to mind her boldness.

"President Chavez's primary concern extends beyond the recent hate crimes, however tragic they might be," Annie said. "Our real concern is in the news coming out of Los Angeles and Miami and a dozen other metropolitan cities. Racial and religious prejudice has been emboldened by the lynchings. We face a war of murderous words. Newton, what were those stats you had for us?"

Lawhead pulled a sheet out of the briefcase by his chair. "As you're well aware, both the CIA and the FBI track certain kinds of content on the Net. Over the past forty-eight hours, the incidents of racially and religiously motivated denigration have increased 437 percent."

He slid the paper onto the table. "A big number, and it's already out-dated. That stat is from two hours ago. What's most disconcerting is the rate at which it continues to grow. The charts are all there; we can track it by the minute if we want. If our analysts are correct—and they are—as things stand, the rate of incidents will double again in the next twenty-four hours."

Johnny sat in silence. He struck Darcy as someone who'd seen far more than most men his age. And hadn't they all? But with Johnny, there was more. It was his statuesque stillness, his very slow breathing, the way his fingers were interlaced without so much as a slight twitch, the lean muscle on his bared forearms.

She was listening to the others, but behind her glasses she was watching him.

The attorney general continued. "Nothing less than racially and religiously motivated hate speech."

"Let's not forget the First Amendment," Manning interjected. "Free speech—"

"The president is the first to defend every citizen's right to free speech, Ben," Annie interrupted. "We're here to calm a storm, not generate one." She took a deep breath. "Wouldn't you agree, Mr. Drake?"

Johnny considered thoughtfully and answered in a soft voice. "Hatred is your enemy, Ms. Ruling, not racial insults."

"But hatred must find expression before it can affect daily life, isn't that right?"

"In a social arena, yes. But it can just as easily eat a man's heart out and leave him dead long before his pulse stops."

It was the simple truth, Darcy thought. Spoken by the man with hands that looked like they could strangle anyone in this room, perhaps with the exception of Kinnard, who'd proven he knew a thing or two about killing.

Annie smiled. "Well spoken. But we all know that this kind of hate mongering has to be stopped. Maybe these lynchings will allow us to finally change the law to curb certain kinds of speech. Someone has to muzzle the bloodsuckers."

All eyes turned to Annie. Darcy wasn't sure she'd heard correctly. *Bloodsuckers?* Meaning Christians, of course. It was strange to hear such an offensive word spoken in a place of such power. Clearly there was no love lost on Christians among this so-called council.

She could hear each breath.

Annie forced a smile to offer her apologies. "Pardon the French. The president is going on the air at six eastern tonight to address the nation, urging restraint. He will promise that any violation of our nation's laws will be prosecuted swiftly and with force."

"Messing with free speech will cause an uproar," Billy said.

"And what do you call the riots?"

"Do you know how long it's been illegal to display a Swastika in Germany?" Lyndsay Nadeau said. "Since Germany's constitution was changed at the end of the Second World War. A sensible restriction on free speech, I'm sure we would all agree."*

"Just a tad different, don't you think?"

She pressed on. "The United Kingdom's restriction of free speech has proven to be an effective deterrent to runaway bigotry in that country. Even here, speech is already restricted in some ways: perjury, contempt, treason, and sedition are all forms of spoken communication and are illegal in the United States, for good reason."

No one argued.

"We all know our history well enough to remember the highly debated so-called Noose Bill of 2008, which very nearly made the public display of any symbol offensive to race, religion, sexual orientation, and gender a hate crime.* The day is coming, ladies and gentlemen, when offensive remarks, gestures, and/or symbols will be—must be—considered hate crimes. Some freedoms must be sacrificed on the cross of social progress. Frankly I can't believe that this country still allows pundits to get licenses from the federal government to broadcast offensive hate speech."

Manning drummed his fingers on the table. "Offensive to whom? Hate crimes are nothing more than a nice tag for anything that offends anyone."

"Surely you can see the harm caused when a radio show host is allowed to get on public airwaves and berate a whole class of citizens for their religion. Or when they are allowed to rail against a class of people for their particular sexual orientation, going so far as to claim God hates their particular way of life and will send that whole class of citizens to hell. Our country should have put an end to this kind of overt discrimination a long time ago."

"That's the cost of freedom," Manning said. "That and the blood of those who've fought to protect those freedoms, or have you forgotten *your* history? Thank God for our Constitution."

"What does God have to do with it?" Annie said. "Common sense is what makes this a free country. Religion, on the other hand, has always fueled hatred. Isn't that right, Johnny?"

He looked at Billy and Darcy. "Did you know I was a chaplain in the army once?"

The revelation surprised her. "You're a religious man?"

"Not particularly. But I understand a few things about good and evil."

"And God?"

"Is good."

So there it was. Johnny didn't share her hatred of all things religious. But she wouldn't hold that against him. She was sure his reasoning was compelling enough, given his own experience.

"The crisis we're facing today is fueled in large part by hate speech," Annie said, pushing forward. "The keg that could explode isn't filled with gunpowder; it's filled with vocalized bigotry. The president's going to urge calm. The question is, Darcy, can you do the same?"

"That's it?" she asked. "You want me to calm the world one riot at a time?"

"I think what Annie's asking," Lawhead said, "is how good you are in front of a camera?"

Darcy had never considered the possibility that she could affect her listeners over the Net. But why not? Assuming they were watching her eyes.

The notion swept through her like a warm blast of wind. And all she could think to say was, "Wow."

"No," Billy said, standing. He stepped out and faced Kinnard. "It's too dangerous, you've made that clear."

"I agree, it's not what I had in mind," Kinnard said.

"We agreed to leave it up to Darcy," Annie was quick to say.

"Absolutely not," Manning snapped. "I can't stress the danger of this, not to her—although I take your point—but to the country. If it works, are we to turn over the minds of this land to this girl? It's irresponsible!"

"People are dying, Ben!" Annie cried. "Open your mind for once."

"How would this be dangerous to me?" Darcy asked.

Billy slid back into his seat. "Because being subjected to your voice is an unmistakable proposition. Your power is felt, not just heard."

"And just how exactly is that dangerous?"

"It would essentially 'out' you on a grand scale! Granted, most people would never realize *why* your words had such an impact on them, but some would begin asking questions. Once the questions start, your life is over, not only as a private citizen, but maybe quite literally."

"He does make a point," Lyndsay said. "Speaking to Congress might be one thing. But addressing the nation could change your life."

Darcy was concerned to realize she liked the idea.

"Johnny?" Annie asked. "You've lived with your gift for some time, I gather. Besides the obvious, any downsides?"

"There's always a price. But you'll both figure that out soon enough. I wouldn't do it if I were you. It could ruin you."

Ruin her? And who was he to judge?

"Assuming it works," Lawhead said. "It would be easy enough to find out. Let's put you in front of a closed-circuit camera."

And what if it didn't work?

"No," she said. "I think Billy and Johnny are right. I can't do it. Not now."

They just stared at her.

"No," she repeated. "I'm not some kind of mind-numbing ray gun you pull on whomever you want."

"I think you have a responsibility to your country," Annie said. "What did you expect to do here in Washington? You need to use your powers as much as we need you to use them."

"Don't patronize me."

"You want it, Darcy," Annie said softly. "You know you do."

How dare this woman speak to her like this?

"You love the power, I can see it in your eyes."

Johnny stood, looked at them for a moment, then dipped his head. "Excuse me, I'll have to be leaving." He faced Billy and Darcy. "Brian knows how to get in contact with me; please come out and visit."

"I take it you don't approve," Annie said.

"That's not for me to judge. I've just been reminded why I fled to the desert." To Billy and Darcy again: "Anytime you like, my house is open. Be careful, very careful."

"Just like that?" Darcy demanded. "You fly all the way out, stay for half an hour, and leave?"

"It was a mistake to come. Remember, the enemy is within. Don't think you're isolated from danger in these ivory towers of theirs."

He walked to the doors. "I'll take a cab." And then Johnny Drake was gone.

The room felt suffocating.

"So will I," Darcy said, standing.

Billy followed quickly. "And me."

Kinnard was already on his feet. "Not a chance. We'll take your no for now. I'll take you home."

ANNIE WATCHED the door close behind Brian Kinnard, unable to hide the amusement on her face. Simple fact: she liked them. Even without their gifts, she found Darcy in particular superbly suited for life in the capital. Not a career politician who thrived off the foggy landscape of compromises, but a real voice for change. The kind of person best suited for Washington was often the kind who hated it enough to suffer all that was required to effect change.

People like Darcy and Billy. So hard to attract, but oh so valuable if you could.

She kept her eyes on that sealed door. "Well, that went well. What do you think?"

"I think you're way out of line, even speaking about muzzling . . . Christians." Ben Manning spread his fingers out on the table and tapped a large gold ring on the wood. "Or any religion for that matter. And Darcy presents a significant problem. We have to end this."

The ice clinked in Deputy Director Newton Lawhead's glass. He took a sip, set the tumbler down, and slid his sunglasses into his pocket. But he offered no comment.

"I would say this is the beginning, not the ending," Lyndsay said.

Manning continued as if he hadn't heard. "I'm the last one to suggest extreme measures, but I hope all of you can appreciate the delicate nature of our problem here. We have to silence her."

Annie faced the senator, surprised by his bitter tone. "Silence her? What exactly are you suggesting?"

He pulled off his glasses and met her stare head-on. "I'm suggesting that all of this is horribly irresponsible. I can't be a party to it. That child could walk into any bank and leave the wealthiest woman in the world. Imagine what she could do in a war, or a presidential race, or . . . or . . ." Manning was too flustered to elaborate. "She could single-handedly bring this country to its knees in the worst of ways. She has to be stopped."

"No, Ben, she has to be guided. If she fell under the wrong influence, yes, then we'd have a problem. But she's not a child, and I don't see her as the kind who will easily fall under anyone's influence but her own. We work with her, not against her."

"Agreed," the attorney general said. "And for goodness' sake, we protect her."

Ben Manning stood abruptly, scowling. "You can't protect her. No prison can hold someone who has the power to seduce the first person who looks into her eyes. You're flirting with disaster. A vial of the deadliest virus. Drop it and we all die."

Lawhead cleared his throat. "You're suggesting we kill her, Ben?"

He didn't answer. He didn't have to. If they couldn't find a way to win Darcy and Billy's complete confidence, they could indeed have a very awkward problem on their hands.

But kill them? The very idea seemed ludicrous to Annie.

"We protect this country at all costs," Manning said. He walked around the table and strode for the door. "It's your job to figure out how to do that."

He turned back with his hand on the knob. "And if you don't, I will."

CHAPTER TWENTY-THREE

Day Six

KELLY DROVE the car down the street that wrapped around the school yard. Kat sat quietly beside her. Johnny was unexpectedly called out of town Saturday night, so Kelly had agreed to take her to the courthouse and return her to Boulder City High during the lunch hour.

It had been four days since Kat's change, and those days had passed like a dream. She really did feel as though she'd been birthed into a new world. Everything was new to her.

The debate, however, had become a familiar fear. She'd imagined her face-off with Asad a hundred times, and each time it brought a tingle to her fingers. Who was she, to engage in such a debate? But she would do it anyway, in just a few hours when the bell rang at day's end.

During her time with Johnny Saturday, he'd shown her an account written by a prisoner named John the Apostle, who had actually been with Jesus while he was on earth, thousands of years ago. The basic truths of Jesus's teachings hurried through her mind like soft echoes in a deep canyon. Big words that sounded strange but right. Perfect.

Love the Lord your God with all your heart. Love your neighbor as yourself. Simple enough. Jesus was all about love.

The kingdom of God is among you. I am the Light of the World. The Truth, the Way. No one can go to the Father but through me. Again, simple enough. Truth was all about Jesus.

Others were less obvious. *The gate to heaven is narrow; only a few will pass through it. Unless you leave your mother and your father for my sake, you cannot enter the kingdom of heaven. Unless you eat my body and drink my blood, you cannot follow me.*

The world will hate you if you follow me.

Clearly, following Jesus wasn't a casual affair. She'd never imagined such startling, narrow-minded teaching could follow so easily in the path of love, love, love, all you need is love.

But it made perfect sense to her heart if not her mind. Jesus wasn't merely a good and wise prophet; he was God, and he was pointing the way *to* God. To himself. As it turned out, following that way came at a price few were willing to pay.

It cost their own pride, as Johnny put it. Their self-interest.

You won't make it through the narrow gate because your eyes are on yourself and your own endless arguments and you'll run into the wall, O blind one. That's how she had put it, and Johnny smiled.

So then, the debate. Johnny had been right in saying that truth was best shown, not simply argued. She had no idea what kind of words she could use to show Carla and Asad and the rest of them that Jesus was the Way.

It would be foolishness to them. Which, appropriately enough, was another one of Jesus's teachings.

The car rolled to a stop in the parking lot and Kat opened her door.

"So I can come over after school then?"

"Johnny will be back this afternoon. Why don't you come for dinner?"

"Really? I'll check with my mom, but that should work."

"What does your mother think of all this?"

"We haven't really talked about it. I mean, she knows something's up, but I wanted to wait until we actually have some time to talk it through. Not sure she would believe me, you know what I mean?"

"Cried wolf a few too many times?" Kelly said. "Don't worry, she'll see the change."

Kelly said it all with a smile, that perpetual smile, so constant that at times Kat wondered if it had been surgically affixed to her face.

She'd told Johnny about finding Kelly behind the shed, crying, but he only turned away. Kelly had been through hell in Hungary, he said. She had been caught up in an underground training camp for assassins hired out to the world's largest governments. Her mind had been stripped and forced into a mold that she'd since rejected.

She'd been his handler, he said. Forced to manipulate him before they'd fallen in love and gone on the run together. Without her, he'd be dead or worse, a vegetable. He owed his life to her. Johnny said it all with a knot in his throat and then dismissed the subject.

Kat wondered if whatever had happened hadn't blinded him just a bit. Not that she was jealous, but . . . just who *was* Kelly anyway? She never talked about Jesus. She never joined in the discussion. She never did anything but sit there with that flat smile, rubbing Johnny's back.

"That's what I was hoping," Kat said. "Okay, see you."

"Six?"

"Cool."

Kelly left Kat standing in the parking lot. The school grounds were quiet this time of day. A man on a riding mower was cutting the grass around the fountain pond, and two groundskeepers had weed cutters out, trimming the edges of the walkway around the concrete slab that surrounded the water.

Blue sky above, sun blazing hot. She headed for the lunch wing.

Tires squealed past her and she saw a news van brake to a hard stop. A camera crew spilled out and began to run toward her followed by a blonde woman dressed in a blue business suit.

They ran past.

"What's going on?"

"Stay outside," the blonde woman said.

Kat ran after them.

"Where is it?"

"In the lunchroom," the reporter said. "From what I've heard it's a mess in there. You need to stay back!"

Odd, here Kat was, basking in the light of this new kingdom, and all around her the world was coming apart at the seams.

The back entrance to the lunchroom was around the other side by the gym. She cut across the lawn, rounded the building, surprised to see no students on the greenway. The reason became immediately apparent: someone had rolled a large garbage bin in front of the cafeteria's fire door, blocking any exit.

Whatever was occurring inside had been planned.

She threw her weight against the bin, but it refused to budge. Fists were pounding on the other side of the door. She could hear screams.

"Does this door lead to the lunchroom?" the cameraman demanded, running up behind.

"Yes, push! We have to clear it."

With three of them pushing, the Dumpster rolled free. The door burst wide open with a bleat from the fire alarm, spilling a stream of students. The screams from the lunch hall weren't all cries of fear. There was as much anger in the voices as panic.

The cameras were already rolling behind her. "We're here at what appears to be an emergency exit at the Boulder City High School lunchroom, where students have been trapped for the last five minutes." The reporter spoke rapidly. "It appears that the exit was blocked before the riot began. No sources have come forward yet to reveal the nature of this conflict, purportedly a racially instigated conflict between Arab Americans and African Americans within the student body . . ."

Kat saw an opening in the flood of students and ducked inside. The sight that greeted her made her catch her breath.

The new lunchroom was set up food-court style, with hundreds of small round tables situated around a dozen stations that offered everything from pizzas to salads to sandwiches, some for a price, some as part of the school's free-lunch program.

Most of the tables were on their sides, a few broken. The food stations had been destroyed by thrown chairs, which appeared to be the weapon of choice.

A group of roughly fifty blacks were scattered along one end, facing off Hispanics who clutched chairs, shielding themselves from a fusillade of ketchup bottles, mustard tubes, glasses, and silverware. The floor was covered in condiments and bottles.

A line of Arabs headed by Asad and his gang stood along the wall to Kat's left, turned toward both the Hispanics and blacks on either end. It was a three-way face-off.

Of the seven hundred students in this lunch shift, only a hundred seemed to be directly involved. The rest had taken shelter behind stations or had taken up chairs to ward off flying objects.

She'd expected to see the Arabs and blacks going at it after last week's run-in. But Hispanics? Granted, there had always been some rivalry between black and Hispanic gangs, but that rivalry had been limited to a war of words.

She couldn't imagine what had pushed things to this level.

The principal's voice was screeching over the PA, demanding calm. It wasn't working. The camera crew piled in through the exit. The reporter was at her shoulder.

"Can you tell what's going on? You see anyone you know?"

Then Kat saw the fourth group on the far side, opposite the Muslims, mostly Indians huddled behind a makeshift fort made of overturned tables.

A four-way battle, and she could hardly tell who was against whom. Hispanics against blacks, Muslims against Hindus? Watching the projectiles, it looked more like all against all. Chaos.

An older Indian student she recognized as a Hindu was screaming at the Arabs. He cocked his arm back and hurled a bottle at the group.

"Death to Muslims!"

Two of his compatriots stood from behind their tables and hurled the same words, chasing them with a glass saltshaker and some cutlery.

The first projectile slammed into the wall behind Asad and shattered with a loud pop. A large blotch of ketchup splattered on the baby-blue wall, erasing *Is* from the large motto painted on the wall: Tolerance Is Beautiful.

Asad didn't bother ducking. No fewer than ten of the Arabs heaved a volley of condiments and silverware on the ducking Hindus.

"Death to the infidels! The Hindus are warmongers! *Allah akhbar!*"

Kat felt panic welling up in her chest. It didn't take much of an imagination to see how blacks against Hispanics versus Arabs could mutate into Christians against Muslims against Hindus, not when religion and race were so closely connected. Not when they all knew that they all secretly despised each other in spite of the tolerance preached in every classroom.

A small Indian girl suddenly stood from behind the tables, eyes fixed on the Arabs across the room. Kat had seen the dark-haired girl around a few times, a freshman who looked as green as a foreigner who'd just flown in from Calcutta. The wide-eyed girl looked at the open door behind Kat, stepped out from the makeshift fort, and scooted out into the open, angling across the open floor for the exit.

"Stop!" Kat cried, waving the girl back. "Get back, get back!"

The girl did not stop. Instead, she began to cry. She shuffled in fast, short steps with her arms by her sides. Crossfire whizzed past her and she began to run, white dress flapping around her thin tan legs.

Kat broke from her safe corner, holding her arm out to the Arabs. "Don't throw! Stop!"

A single glass ketchup bottle shot from the line to her left, covered the gap to the Indian girl in the space of one breath, and struck her on the side of her head.

The girl dropped to the ground.

Kat sprinted, screaming at the top of her lungs, "Stop! Stop!"

They weren't stopping—she could see that in her peripheral vision—but her eyes were on the young girl who hadn't moved.

She waved her arms over her head and raced into the cross fire. "Stop it, she's hurt, you're gonna kill someone! Stop this!"

A bottle flew past her head as she dropped to her knees beside the girl. The freshman was moaning now, rolling to one side. No sign of blood.

"You okay?"

A spoon struck her on the shoulder and clattered to the floor.

Kat stood up and faced the gang of blacks, knowing that they thought of her as one of their own.

"Stop this!" she screamed. She met their eyes and spun to the Arabs. "Just stop it!"

They seemed momentarily stalled by her boldness. The decibel level of the cacophony dropped. She seized the opportunity and cried out, facing the Hispanics. The Arabs had fired the ketchup bottle, but she knew that confronting them directly would only inflame Asad, who believed, as others once had, that a bloody crusade was the only way to convince people of anything.

"You've hurt a girl who only wants to be safe with her father!" she cried. "Is that what your mothers taught you?"

No bottles flew. All four sides stared at her. An older Indian girl raced out, weeping. "Hadas, Hadas!" She slid to the fallen girl's side and brushed her hair from her face. Touched the swelling bump on her head. "Speak to me, Hadas. What have they done, what have they done?"

The young girl tried to sit, and her friend helped her. "Are you okay? Are you sure you are okay?" She cradled her, and the young girl began to cry, soft moans.

By the door, the news camera rolled. Otherwise the room was still. She had to keep the focus on race rather than religion, Kat thought.

"Blacks and whites are lynching each other out there, is that what we're here on this earth to do? Hang each other because we're different? You're a black man in a Hispanic neighborhood, they rope you up, is that what you want? You're Hispanic in a black neighborhood, they lynch you, is that what you want?"

A single mustard bottle sailed out. She stepped aside and watched it bounce off the floor, unbroken. It slid to a stop at the feet of a Hispanic student, who picked it up.

"Go ahead, throw it back," she cried, pointing at the boy. "But throw it at me, not them. I'm black. Or am I Indian? For all you know I'm Hispanic! Go ahead, throw it."

The student looked at his people and received no encouragement.

Only now did Kat face Asad and his band. "We were made to love each other, not to fight. You think you're throwing ketchup bottles at the enemy, but you're not. You're just giving them more ammunition to throw back at you. Races have been doing that for centuries. The school teaches us to tolerate each other. But I say we should *love* each other! Tolerance is not enough! Blacks, Hispanics, Arabs, whites, Hindus, Muslims, Christians—love each other."

The Arab boy dropped his stare, and she decided to take her words a step further, right here in front of them all.

"This is my debate, Asad. *Love!* Love your neighbor as yourself; *that* is the teaching of Jesus. It's a narrow way, but it's a simple way and the whole world ought to listen."

For nearly twenty seconds, no one moved or threw a bottle.

"To hell with your debate," Asad finally said. "*Inṣhe'allah.* The will of Allah will be done."

Then he turned and walked toward the door, followed reluctantly by the others. The last few scrambled after.

A teacher came out from behind a salad kiosk. "Someone, call an ambulance."

Just like that, the riot at Boulder City High School was over.

And the news coverage of the girl named Katrina Kivi, who'd risked her neck to speak sense into a crowd of angry students, had just begun.

CHAPTER TWENTY-FOUR

Day Seven

DARCY FELT a bit lost. Powerless even. Which to her way of thinking was a bit terrifying. She'd gone from the highest peak of confidence and power to this miserable state of denial in the space of two days.

One day, God's gift to the world, the next day, scum of the earth.

She knew none of her feelings were justified. She hadn't lost any power, and even if she had, since when did she need this gift, this drug, to help her through the day? She'd made a perfectly good life for herself before all of this, thank you very much. And it didn't include performing for others at their whim.

And yet . . .

She'd fully expected the council to demand another meeting on Monday, but they left Billy and Darcy in their glass prison to stew and watch the Net.

Billy had spent Tuesday morning scanning the Net while she finished reading *Birthright*, the Frakes vampire novel. She eventually joined Billy on the couch, scanning the reports and blogs. Johnny's visit seemed to have stirred up fresh concerns about Marsuvees Black in him.

Interesting, yes, but something else had taken charge of Darcy's mind.

She simply could not dislodge the idea of speaking to a million people at once over the Net. A hundred thoughts, some of which might disturb Billy, buzzed through her mind, simple *what ifs* that she immediately rejected as preposterous.

But . . . what if?

It was one o'clock in the afternoon before the badgering thoughts became too much for her. She stood from the couch, intending to do something about it.

"I want to test it," she announced.

Billy tapped the remote and muted the Net. "Test what?"

"The Net. Me speaking over the Net."

They'd maintained a rule that at least one of them would wear glasses at all times unless both agreed to bare themselves to each other; at the moment she wore hers.

Billy retrieved his sunglasses from the table, slid them on, and sat back. "You mean your power, over the airwaves."

"We have to know, right? I'm not saying I would ever expose myself on the Net—it's dangerous, you've already established that." She walked toward the phone. "But it's stupid not to know."

"You sure you really *want* to know? I mean, even knowing that you have that kind of power could mess with your mind."

There, he'd said it. Darcy suppressed an urge to snap at him and picked up the phone.

"I have you to keep me in line, dear Billy." Maybe a little too much bite in her voice. She sighed. "I need to do this. It's driving me crazy."

He frowned and nodded. "It would be a trip, wouldn't it?"

There's my Billy. She smiled and dialed Kinnard.

IT WAS three o'clock before Kinnard broke free, set up a room at CIA headquarters for the test, and arranged secure transportation to Langley.

They stood in a communications room, essentially a small television studio without the sets. A single camera faced a stool from a tripod ten feet away, blinking red. The technicians had been told that Kinnard wanted to do a simple camera test, which he would personally conduct. Billy would be in the adjacent room separated by a glass wall, watching a secured, closed-circuit image of her during the test. Both rooms and the adjacent corridor and technical offices were cleared of all other personnel.

"Okay, Darcy, you ready to do this?"

She'd reconsidered a dozen times since calling Kinnard, but not for the reason Billy had cited. She wasn't afraid of the possibility she had a power that could reach into every home in America. She was afraid the test would fail. Which is why she still wore her glasses and would wear them until Billy was safely out of the room.

They already knew that he couldn't read the thoughts of those on the Net. Which made sense: thoughts didn't travel thousands of miles or through wires, right? But her gift was different. Her voice could travel thousands of miles and be heard by millions. There was no reason she could see that it wouldn't work.

Still, her palms were moist and her heart was racing.

"Billy?"

"Okay." He headed for the door, then spoke over his shoulder, grinning. "Just don't make me do anything crazy. Like undress."

Darcy sat on the stool and chuckled nervously. "Scout's honor, dear Billy." She waited for him to enter the adjacent room, sit with his back to them, and face a black screen on the wall.

Kinnard stood behind the camera, sunglasses safely in place. "Okay, light goes green, you're live."

"Okay."

"Here we go."

The light changed from a red blink to a green blink. She looked to her right, saw the image of herself with her sunglasses fill the monitor. Billy had freed his eyes.

Now she did the same.

Darcy looked into the camera lens, silent for a few seconds. She hadn't considered what she would say. It had to be something definite. Unmistakable. Something that would get a physical reaction from him so that she wouldn't have to depend on his word.

"Billy . . . you're afraid of Black, aren't you? He terrifies you, because you know as well as I do that he's your brainchild. You created him. All of this is your fault. You're to blame. If Black is evil, then you are the father of that evil, isn't that right? You should be on your knees, weeping, begging the world for forgiveness."

Her own breathing had thickened as she slashed him with her words. She dared a glance but couldn't see if he was reacting, because his back was toward her.

She had to take him to his knees!

"Billy, you useless scum, get your lousy, worthless self off the chair and beg; beg like you deserve to!" She was shouting, letting herself go. "You did this to me! It was your idea—you went down first, you deceitful little runt!"

Darcy surprised even herself at the emotions that she'd put into those words. Is that how she really felt? She sat on the stool, breathing hard. Kinnard had turned and was watching Billy. She followed his gaze.

Billy sat upright, hands on his lap. Then he replaced his glasses, stood, and calmly exited the room.

He hadn't been affected? How could he not have been wounded by her words? They'd hurt even her, just saying them!

He stepped inside her room and stopped. Perhaps he had been too distraught to weep.

"Anything?"

"No."

"That's impossible."

"Did you mean what you said?"

But she wasn't listening to him. "Maybe the words mean nothing to you! Maybe I was wrong!" Only one solution presented itself to her. "Take off your glasses."

"Darcy, it didn't work."

"I have to know! Take off your glasses. Now!"

He slowly lifted his hand. Slid his glasses off.

"Now you listen to me, you beast, you are *terrified* of Black because you brought him to life, here in this world. This is all your fault; you did this to me! I've spent the last decade paying for your selfish ambitions, weeping like a child, running scared from my dreams, waking up drowned in sweat. Now, you get on your knees and weep like you have made me weep!"

Billy's shoulders had started to shake after the first sentence, and by the last he was falling. Not to his knees as she'd demanded, but to his side, where he curled up in a ball and began to sob.

"I'm sorry . . . Oh Darcy, I'm sorry. I'm so sorry . . ."

Tears flooded her eyes and she blinked them away. The test had failed, then. Her power was localized and therefore drastically inferior to what she'd hoped.

She'd accomplished nothing but to wound the one man she loved.

"Leave us," she snapped at Kinnard.

He stared at her for a long moment, then walked for the door. "Take your time. I'll be outside."

Darcy waited for him to leave, watching Billy writhing on the floor. What had she done? If there was a guilty soul in this room, it was her!

She rushed to him, fell to her knees, and threw herself over him. "No, Billy, no! I'm sorry, I didn't mean it. Please don't cry!"

But he didn't let up. So she held him tight and cried with him. What had she been thinking, leveling this kind of brutality at him? It had only been the truth, that much was now clear. Or at least, Billy believed it to be the truth.

She held him for a long time and begged him to be still. The test had failed. She'd destroyed Billy and the test had failed. Anger flushed her face.

It occurred to her that neither of them wore glasses. If she'd wounded him with her voice, she could heal him with it, couldn't she?

She knelt beside him, hushing him gently. Took his head in her hands so that he faced her.

"No, Billy, listen to me, you don't have to do this. Look at me, look at me, baby. Please look at me."

But his eyes were clenched and he was still sobbing.

"Look at me!" she snapped.

His eyelids opened slowly and she stared into his tearful green eyes. "Don't cry, Billy. Please don't cry. I am as guilty as you are. This isn't your fault. You don't have to fear Black. It's true, you wrote him, but what you did, you can undo. And I love you, Billy, I love you. Hear my mind, hear my heart, do whatever you do, climb inside my head. You know that I love you! Stop crying, please stop crying."

She said it all so quickly, flooding him with her power. He stilled immediately.

"You see? I'm sorry, I didn't mean to hurt you." She quickly added, knowing he could read the truth in her mind, "And if I did, I was wrong. Please forgive me, tell me you forgive me."

He swallowed. "I forgive you. Tell me, Darcy. Tell me that you love me."

She did, washing him with her gift. "I love you, Billy. And you love me. You love me more than you've ever loved any woman."

Darcy brought her lips to his and they kissed deeply, smothered each other with comfort. She'd never been so direct with him, never presumed to tell him how he should feel. Only what he should do for her. Meddling with his mind was stepping on hallowed ground.

But the moment called for it.

Billy pushed himself to his knees and looked around, disoriented. "We're alone."

"I sent him out." Darcy stroked his hair.

"So the test failed."

And with those words Darcy felt her mood shift, subtly, but enough for her recognize it.

"Evidently." She looked away from him. "I really am sorry for this, Billy."

"Don't be. We both know there's plenty of truth in what you said."

He stood and walked out to the middle of the room, hands on hips.

"Have you ever wondered if this is all part of a much larger plan?"

"I think that maybe you've been talking to Johnny," she said pushing herself to her feet.

"No, really. What if we were actually drawn to Washington by forces we don't understand yet?"

"Maybe. So what?"

He turned around and faced her. They were still both bared to each other. "Maybe we should leave. Just pack up and run. We could—"

"No!"

"No?"

"Just because Johnny does his thing in anonymity without obligation doesn't mean we need to go chasing after him."

"That's not what I meant."

"We can't leave."

Billy looked into her eyes and read her mind, she could see it in him. So she countered quickly.

"Don't tell me you haven't thought about what our power could accomplish here, Billy." She stepped toward him. "Deep down inside, you feel it as much as I do. Who wouldn't? The desire to see just how far we can take this."

His eyes were wide, drinking in her words. She took his hand.

"I want us to do this, Billy. We're here for a purpose, we have these powers for a purpose. We have no reason to be their sniffing dogs any more."

"We could go a long way . . ."

"Think of the good we could do!" Darcy knew that she was exploiting him, but she did it because she knew he wanted it. She walked around him, turning him slowly, her hand over his.

"We've already skated on thin ice. Let's dance on it—with this power; what do you say?"

"We do have a lot of power," he said, grinning.

"So my powers don't work through the Net. There's more than enough good to be done locally."

"We couldn't be too obvious, you know," he said. "We don't need more enemies."

"That's right. But we could make more friends. We'd have to start with something very calculated. Something the council approves of. But something quiet."

"Work our way through this town like ghosts in the night."

"Exactly."

Billy grinned. "I can see you've given this a lot of thought." And he meant it literally. He'd taken the thought right out of her mind.

"I have." And then she said something she hoped he would forgive her for if the need ever arose.

"I need for you to go with me on this, Billy. I know you want to, but I want you to promise me that you'll trust me and do whatever it takes. Promise me. Whatever it takes."

He hesitated only a moment, and then answered with a coy grin.

"Whatever it takes. I swear it."

CHAPTER TWENTY-FIVE

Day Eight

ANY ILLUSION some may have fostered that the nation was not facing a crisis of monumental proportions was shattered Wednesday morning when the nation's capital woke to find six victims, all black, hanging from six consecutive streetlights on First Street, directly in front of the Capitol.

The victims: three males between the ages of thirty-five and sixty, two females in the same age bracket, and one older female in her sixties. They were discovered when security officer Joseph Custer arrived at his station at six. Three guards, whose names had been withheld from the press, were found dead in a Dumpster behind the National Gallery of Art, little more than a block away.

Five of the six bodies found hanging from the streetlights had not yet been identified to the press. But the identity of the sixth could not be hidden for the simple reason that most of those who lived in Washington and half of those who lived in Nevada knew him.

He was the well-heeled and occasionally outspoken Democratic senator from Nevada, Ben Manning.

By six thirty, footage of the lynched bodies taken just before dawn, presumably by those responsible, had been widely circulated on the Net. The victims looked unreal, like scarecrows floating against a gray Halloween sky, until the camera zoomed in on each face, each crooked neck, snapped by the heavy ropes from which they hung.

Darcy had woken, showered, dressed, and walked out into the living room to find Billy on the phone with the images frozen on the screen behind him.

He hung up. "Gotta go, come on."

"What's going on?" The images on the Net screen behind him answered her question in a matter of moments. Six had been lynched in front of the Capitol. She felt nauseated and turned from the pictures.

"Take a look."

He stared out the glass wall overlooking the corridor that extended from the Lincoln Memorial to the Capitol. A sea of people pushed in on a perimeter that had been established around the entire corridor, including the White House.

"What happened?"

"Over a hundred thousand. It hasn't turned violent yet, but nobody's holding their breath." Billy paused. "One of the victims was Senator Ben Manning."

"What?" She was stunned. "*The* Ben . . . ?"

"From the council. Yes."

She blinked, unable to come to grips with the idea that the man was actually dead. Had she had any part in that? Her thoughts refused to connect.

Fire trucks and police cars lined the streets along the Mall below, lights flashing. Several dozen military response vehicles, likely from the National Guard, D.C. Police, and monitored by the Secret Service, crept along Pennsylvania and Constitution Avenues. Several armored vehicles had been stationed around the White House.

"The keg of gunpowder is blowing up," Billy said. "I'll explain more along the way."

"Kinnard's here?"

"Downstairs. Annie Ruling is waiting for us at the White House."

Darcy's pulse spiked. "We're meeting the president?"

"I don't think so."

He hurried to the door, yanked it open, nodded at the armed guard stationed at the door, and quickly crossed to the elevator, followed closely by Darcy. She started again the moment the door slid shut.

"The council?"

"I don't know."

"Then who, just Annie?"

"I don't know, but she called us directly and insisted no one know that we were meeting."

"Other than Kinnard?"

"Other than Kinnard."

Darcy stared up at the floor lights as the elevator car dropped. "She's making an end run."

"Maybe."

The bell chimed, and they stepped out into the basement loading zone, where Kinnard waited, phone fixed to his ear. As dark as it was, she wondered how he could see anything with those glasses on. Then she remembered that her sight was darkened as well.

He rounded the truck's hood and climbed in behind the wheel as guards opened their doors for them.

Billy told her what he knew as Kinnard piloted the car up Arlington Boulevard, headed for Theodore Roosevelt Memorial Bridge. They were stopped at a checkpoint and quickly waved through when Kinnard flashed his ID.

He shut his phone and activated the bulletproof glass partition between the cab and the back. "Morning, kids. I'm sorry, it's just a tad busy out there."

"Why are we going to the White House?"

"Because that's where Annie Ruling and Lyndsay Nadeau want to meet you. But I'll let them speak for themselves, if you don't mind. Don't worry, our route is safe. The crowds are contained north of the White House. Just sit tight."

The glass partition rose, sealing them off.

They pulled onto Constitution in silence. No tour groups or crowds gazed upon the Lincoln Memorial or the reflecting pool on their right. Ahead, the Washington Monument pointed to the sky, tall and stately, like a lighthouse for the nation.

They took a left on Seventeenth before the monument. Darcy had shrugged into a charcoal cotton dress with spaghetti straps and a lace hem—not exactly White House material. Her dark hair hung past her shoulders, slightly disordered by design, but if she was to become a regular in this town, she might want to consider a new style. She thought about sliding off the silver snake bracelet that coiled around three inches of her right wrist. And the silver choker chains around her neck.

But then, who did she think she was? Miss Polyester Pantsuit?

Billy looked just as causal, dressed in jeans and a black polo shirt. His dark reddish hair was as ever, neatly ordered over his ears, the perfect gentleman. But too young to be anything more than an intern in this town.

Listen to you, Darcy, the Capitol is practically under siege and you're thinking about what you're wearing. This thing is getting to you.

As it turned out, Kinnard didn't take them to the White House proper, but into the Eisenhower Executive Office Building, just across the street from the White House's West Wing, and then into a back door that led into a basement.

Other than the guards, there was no indication that they had entered the halls of power in the world's most powerful nation. The protest was too far away to disturb the quiet, and she imagined that the staff had mostly stayed away this morning because of it.

"Watch your step."

They walked down a flight of steps into a dim white hall that needed a fresh coat of paint to cover the chips along the borders. Large framed photographs lined the walls, mostly old black-and-white images of people and buildings.

"This way." Kinnard led them down a second hall toward a white door with an old brass handle. "Don't let the lack of elegance fool you; more work gets done behind doors like this than you might realize." He smiled and twisted the knob.

They entered a large office, plainly decorated with several large paintings, a colonial-era wood desk, and a round conference table to one side. The attorney general, Lyndsay Nadeau, and Annie Ruling, the White House chief of staff, were both on their cell phones in different corners. They each glanced up and moved toward the conference table.

"Just keep a lid on their names," Annie was saying. "Promise me at least that much. Thank you, Charles."

She pocketed her phone and crossed to Billy and Darcy. Shook their hands. "Thank you for accommodating us on such short notice. As you can see, the world is falling down around our ears out there."

The attorney general offered her wizened smile. "Darcy. Billy."

Kinnard joined them at the table.

"Here we are," Darcy said.

"Here we are."

"Ben Manning . . ." She didn't know what do say.

"Tragic," Annie said. Her face was pale with concern. "It's gotten way out of hand."

"Why Manning?" Billy asked.

"Maybe you can tell us that, Billy. When we get to the bottom of this."

They looked at each other in silence. Both were out on a limb, Darcy thought. They all were.

"You're doing an end run?" Darcy said.

First Annie, then Lyndsay took off their glasses. "Let's just say we want to bring you in. No hidden agendas on our part. We need your complete confidence. No glasses."

Billy looked from one to the other. "All of us?"

"If you don't mind." Kinnard tapped his temple. "I have just a few sensitive details I can't expose."

"As do we all, Brian. Okay, all of us but the company man. Read our minds, speak carefully, do what you have to do. We aren't interested in playing any games. No more cloak-and-dagger among the four of us."

Billy pulled off his glasses and stared into their eyes for a moment. He set the shades on the table. "Fair enough. Go ahead, Darcy."

His was the more ominous power in some ways. Particularly in the town of a thousand secrets. Darcy bared her eyes.

The attorney general's light blue eyes smiled. "I hope you realize the significance of this gesture, Billy. You could walk out of this room with more classified information than even the president is privy to. And you will. But that only puts you in the crosshairs of more scopes than you can count. We will depend on each other. I for your confidence, you for my protection."

"I get it, ma'am. Really, I do."

"And we respectfully ask that you hear us out without any attempt to persuade, Darcy," Annie said. "None of us, not even you, knows just how long the effects of your persuasion last, but we have no interest in being at your whim, even for a few hours."

There was a veiled threat in there somewhere, Darcy thought. "You wouldn't do what's not in you to do. But I won't betray your trust, you have my word."

"Good. Lyndsay?"

The attorney general stood and walked around the table, arms crossed. Eyes on the walls. "You're probably wondering why the rest of our so-called council isn't here. Washington is all about arguing. Posturing. Frankly, knowing what we do about some of the others, we don't have the time to argue. Need I say more?"

"No," Darcy said.

"Good." Lyndsay faced Billy. "The only way to deal with hatred is to contain it through discipline. What do you tell a naughty child who has screamed at his sister over a toy? Used to be they would get a smack. Now we say, 'If you can't play nice, you can't play at all.' Put them in a time out. In this country we call that prison."

"What she's saying," Billy said, "is that the time has come to expose the hypocrisy of certain so-called freedoms and force adults to follow the same rules they impose on their own children."

Lyndsay smiled. "And what else am I thinking?"

"That you can't stop people from hating. But you can limit the freedom they have to express that hatred, just like we do with our children."

"And?"

"We're facing this crisis today because the children have been allowed to scream at each other for far too long. Everyone knows that screaming children eventually turn to sticks and stones. The only way to keep the sticks and stones on the ground is to end the screaming."

Her breathing thickened. "Bravo. My, that's a stunning gift you have."

"Thank you."

Won't you just listen to them, Darcy thought. *So taken with Billy.*

"And the solution is a constitutional amendment that would limit certain kinds of free speech," Darcy said. "Doesn't take a mind reader to guess that."

"That's right," Annie said. "Our current hate-crime laws only affect sentencing in racially motivated events. These laws used to be adequate for localized bigotry, but they don't and can't expand the definition of *what* those crimes are. Especially at the federal level. Our only option is to make certain kinds of *spoken* hate crimes illegal, punishable by law. And for that, we need to amend the Constitution."

The attorney general's eyes were on Billy again. "You know why we have to do this now?"

"That's a little more convoluted. One, the country needs a serious change to throw it off balance. A thundering shot across the bow to snap it out of all this racial idiocy. Martial law would likely inflame the country. Most protesters don't have the stomach for prison. Shut them down by making inflammatory racial remarks a prosecutable crime, and most of them would go home, unlikely to return."

"And the other reason?"

"The country's already reeling. Radical action like this is more easily digested in times of crisis."

"That's right."

It all made sense to Darcy. "When you say 'certain kinds of speech,' you mean racial slurs," Darcy said.

"And inflammatory expressions of faith."

So there it was. They were out to muzzle the religious as much as racial bigots. Considering how many citizens hated the faithful, it was only a matter of time. And that time was now. All things considered, it was a reasonable course of action, Darcy thought.

"Okay. When do we start?"

Kinnard spoke from his seat. "You do understand, Darcy, that what Annie and Lyndsay are suggesting constitutes a change of staggering proportions to the very fabric of this country."

"Of course she does," Billy said. "But the fact is, we've already discussed this, and we happen to be in agreement. Certain kinds of religious and racial speech should be subject to boundaries."

She and Billy hadn't so much discussed the particulars as they'd agreed to capitalize on something precisely like this.

"You realize that the opposition will be staggering," Kinnard said.

"Which is why Billy and I are here," Darcy said.

They fell silent.

"So. How do we go about this amending the Constitution thing?"

"Okay." Annie seemed skeptical that they'd been so easily convinced, but her small smile didn't say she was disappointed. "For starters, we do it quickly. I mean very quickly. And that, my friends, is where you come in."

"Quickly for two reasons," the attorney general interjected. "This crisis may be the only means we have to accomplish our objective; we also believe swiftness is the best way to end this crisis. Half a week, while the U.S. economy is still on level ground."

"Three days?" Billy said. "Both the House and the Senate have to repeal the applicable portions of the First Amendment with a two-thirds majority. And it has to then be ratified by three quarters of the states. That's a lot of representatives, a lot of senators, a lot of governors, and the president. Not to mention the inevitable judicial block at the Supreme Court. Laws typically take months, even years, and that's not even taking the enactment and enforcement into account. It's impossible."

Lyndsay confirmed the process. "And that's just repealing the amendment itself. We need a federal law that gives us the teeth to enforce the amendment."

"So you're thinking five days."

Annie held up her hand. "Please, this reading of the minds is cute, but for the rest of us, maybe we could revert to straight dialogue? Billy?"

"Okay. Why don't you just lay it all out in layman's terms so we can all understand, Lyndsay."

Was that a dig at Annie? Darcy glanced at him and winked.

The attorney general took her seat and pulled out a red folder. "Okay, from the start, then."

ERECTING THE framework for their carefully calculated plan took more than an hour with several interruptions for updates on the crisis surrounding the Capitol. The protesters, as they were now being called, had been mostly dispersed, but four smaller riots had broken out in California, Alabama, and Missouri again. The president had activated a nationwide order for National Guard units to respond at the first signs of any violence in any city, but the order did nothing to silence the war drums.

Darcy was surprised to see Annie Ruling pull out a pack of cigarettes and ask if they minded her smoking. The stress, she said. Legislators had all but banned smoking in the United States ten years earlier. But the fact that Annie smoked to relieve stress only endeared her to Darcy more.

And she was a smart one. The plan she and the attorney general laid out (assuming it was them and not Kinnard who'd engineered it) might be completely unthinkable without Billy and her to grease the wheels, but with them, the plan just might succeed.

They *needed* Billy and Darcy. The whole notion didn't merely energize Darcy, it thrilled her. Isn't this why she had this gift, to change history? Not to calm gangsters and seduce Billy, although that wasn't a bad thing. She hadn't asked for the power, unless you held a thirteen-year-old responsible for an impulsive decision to scratch a note in a book.

Fate had given her the power to be used for the good of all. And by *all* she meant herself as well.

Darcy looked at the notepaper strewn over the table, listing names and flowcharting the multipronged approach. She noticed that her fingers were trembling and she pulled them off the table.

Lying before them on a white sheet of paper were two versions of the First Amendment as adopted as part of the United States Bill of Rights, inspired by Thomas Jefferson and drafted by James Madison in 1791. At the top of the page, the original.

Amendment I
Congress shall make no law respecting an establishment of religion, or prohibiting the free exercise thereof; or abridging the freedom of speech, or of the press; or the right of the people peaceably to assemble, and to petition the government for a redress of grievances.

And below it, the amendment as proposed.

Amendment I (Amended)
Congress shall make no law respecting an establishment of religion, or prohibiting the free exercise thereof; or abridging the freedom of the

press; or abridging the freedom of any speech that does not publicly defame, slander, or libel another person's race, national origin, or religion; or the right of the people peaceably to assemble, and to petition the government for a redress of grievances.

The only material change was the addition of the clause that removed defamation, slander, or libel in the context of race and religion as a form of protected speech.

The media's rights were still protected; so long as they didn't slander anyone's race or religion.

Religions were still protected, so long as they didn't preach inflammatory accusations against other ideologies or the faiths of their neighbors.

The right to assemble was still protected.

Honestly, the huge amount of effort required to make such a small, long overdue change struck Darcy as a bit ridiculous. The ACLU would have a cow, naturally, as would most religious institutions, fearing the erosion of their rights to rail against whomever they wished to rail. But in the end, they would bow to the winds of change, just as so many other Western nations already had.

"So that's it, then?" Billy said. "What do you say, Darcy? You've been quiet for the last ten minutes."

She cleared her throat. "Me? You know what I'm thinking, Billy."

"But do they?"

She looked at them. "I'm thinking we're going to change history."

Annie smiled. Then spoke carefully. "Tell us how, Darcy."

"You need convincing?"

"No. But I could use a little pick-me-up, and I can tell you have it."

Annie had felt her voice before and was now asking for it again. What, she was Annie's personal drug now? But the idea appealed to her.

"All right. You're going to open all the doors we need, Annie, beginning with the president and the Senate Judiciary, who will sponsor the bill. An emergency session of Congress will be called and the bill will be presented tomorrow for debate. I will address the House of Representatives, because you will see to it that I am allowed to. And I will also address the Senate. Once the bill is passed and signed by the president, the states will have forty-eight hours to ratify the amendment in compliance with a deadline passed in the House by common vote. Do you need more, Annie?"

"I do."

Her words were like a soothing balm, reinforcing what Annie already knew and desired. Like a preacher reassuring a choir shouting, "Amen, brother, preach it!"

"A new law based upon the amendment will be voted on and signed into law within forty-eight hours of the ratification. Yada, yada, yada . . ." Darcy leaned forward, drilling Annie with her stare, knowing that Lyndsay was watching her with as much interest. "I could go on and give you all the little twists and turns as you've outlined them, thrilling you with details that would bore an average person to tears."

She returned Lyndsay's stare. "But I won't. Instead I'll tell you what's really interesting here. It's the part you play. You've always dreamed of making a difference. Of being remembered as a figure that changed history. Which is what you're going to do, because you're going to make sure Billy stands in front of every single undecided politician so that he can find out exactly—and I do mean exactly—*all* those nasty secrets, which is what I need to persuade them to vote the right way. He's going to do that because of you. Do you need more, Lyndsay?"

"Yes."

"Do you need more, Annie?"

Sweat beaded her forehead. "I do, Darcy." She said it softly, without apparent emotions, but Darcy knew that she was only covering up a deep-seated pleasure that probably surprised even her.

"You're going to make sure I get to speak into the hearts and minds of each and every man or woman whose vote we need for a two-thirds majority. We're going to succeed, Annie, because Billy and I will know which buttons to push and how to push them. We'll try not to make enemies, but if we do, we'll protect ourselves by holding information about them that would be released in the event we were ever harmed. The kind of information that Billy will have in reams and reams. The kind he already has on both of you, or will have in the next few seconds now that I've brought it to the surface for you to think about."

She paused for that dose to work its bit, and then continued.

"In the end we will convince the House, the Senate, the president, all nine Supreme Court justices, and, maybe most importantly, the governors of those states who sit on the fence if we need their vote. And we will succeed, because of you. Because of us. Because of our commitment to each other."

She stopped, then pushed further. "This is your day, both of you. You will stop at nothing to accomplish the objectives you've laid out for us. Do you hear me? Nothing. And you will owe Billy and me a great debt for helping you achieve this plan. Wouldn't you both agree?"

"Yes," Annie said, struggling now to maintain an air of calm. "I would say that puts it accurately."

"Wouldn't you say, Lyndsay?"

"It think that's fair, yes." She looked like she'd been slapped.

"And if we help you achieve your objective—changing the first amendment in the Bill of Rights so that it limits protected speech—if we do this for you, you *will* agree to give us something in exchange, and you will be bound to that agreement in good faith."

Kinnard put his hands on the table. "Darcy—"

"No," Annie interrupted. "No, it's okay. She's right. What did you have in mind, Darcy?"

"Billy?"

He winked at her. "Anything permitted by law."

She nodded once. "There you go, then. Anything permitted by law. Is that fair?"

"I would say so."

"You don't have any resentment toward me for asking this while you look in my eyes, do you? I don't want you to feel compelled unless it follows your true feelings. You do want to do this for us, right?"

Of course, the phrasing put Annie in a bit of a bind, unless she really did think the request completely unreasonable, which Darcy knew she would not.

"No." Annie looked at the attorney general, who was grinning. It was the first time she'd felt Darcy's power personally. "Lyndsay?"

"No, not at all. Oh my, I think we might actually have a shot at this."

"Then you both swear to give us what we want, permitted by law?"

"Yes."

"Yes."

"Okay." Darcy looked at Billy and spread her hands. "Anything else?"

"No, not from me. I think I get the picture." He slid his glasses back on, and Darcy followed his example.

"Where and when do we start?" she asked.

Annie took a deep breath, replaced her own glasses. "With the president. In fifteen minutes." She pushed her chair back and stood.

"I think history's going to like you, Billy and Darcy. I think I'm going to like you very, very much."

The Books of History, Darcy thought. *She's thinking of the Books of History.* And her heart skipped a beat.

II

WORDS OF POWER

The Apostle who saw the Light with his own two eyes said this:

I came to you in weakness
and fear and with much trembling.

My message was not with wisdom
or persuasive words,
but with power . . .

First-century letter written by
Paul to those in Corinth

CHAPTER TWENTY-SIX

Day Fourteen

THEY WERE calling the last week "the five days that changed America," but to Katrina Kivi, nothing had changed. Certainly not the kingdom of light that greeted her every morning, so to speak. In fact, nothing had changed except the newscasts on the Net, and for some reason the news never really felt very personal. Secondhand data from secondhand sources. Long before this so-called crisis, Kat had seen a thousand images of flag burnings, street violence, and Molotov cocktails exploding against cars, even if it was in other countries. And now it was coming to America, for real.

But it still didn't *feel* real, not next to her new real.

It had been all constitutional and civil liberties dialogue, all day, all night, all on the Net. Worse than a sci-fi marathon, only real.

Kat stood on the cliff's edge next to Johnny and Kelly, overlooking the valley before them. Except for the chirping of birds and the occasional rattle of lizards dislodging pebbles on the rocky surface beneath them, the day was quiet up here in the mountains.

Johnny stood still, breathing in the scent of pines and clean air, staring at the small Colorado town they'd come to see.

Paradise.

A large crow settled on a bare branch to Kat's right, eyed them with a beady eye, and cawed. Its head jerked a few times as it hopped down the branch, holding firm with long clawed feet. *Caw, caw.* Jet black. It leaped into the air and flapped away, calling out over the valley, as if announcing their presence to all who might be interested.

Kelly stood to one side, staring south, not looking terribly comfortable. But Kat hardly blamed her; it had been clear from the beginning that Johnny's hometown held a nearly mystical, very personal place in his mind.

"So, this is it, huh?" Kat said.

He didn't bother answering, because they all knew the question was rhetorical. Of course this was it. The real question was what *it* was.

Upon learning two days earlier about Johnny's occasional pilgrimage to this spot, Kat had talked her way into accompanying them. By helicopter.

"This is it," he said. "The place where I lost my sight. And saw for the first time."

Kat looked at the town. A single black strip of asphalt ran down the center, bordered by the kinds of buildings she would expect in any small town like this. A church complete with a steeple, surrounded by a huge lawn. A large community center. Gas station, odd shops, maybe a bar and a grocery store, though she couldn't actually see clearly enough from this distance.

Beyond the center of town, fruit farms filled the valley before it rose again to the mountains across the valley. Several green fields spotted the otherwise wooded landscape. A couple hundred homes dotted the valley, in rows around the town and like scattered seed beyond.

"And why are we here again?"

Johnny swiveled his head and faced her. "Because a very good friend of mine, Samuel, suggested that I have a date with destiny here."

"Now?"

"He seems to think so, yes."

"Samuel?" She waited for him to explain.

Johnny frowned. "A friend from Paradise a long time ago. I talked to him yesterday. He would have been here, but he seems to think I should face this alone."

"Face what?"

Johnny didn't seem eager to elaborate.

"Why can't you just tell me what happened here? You don't trust me?"

Johnny looked at her for several long seconds, then looked down the valley and told her about the birth and death of Project Showdown.

When he finished, Kat stared at him, stunned by his casual account of such improbable events. Who would believe that such books existed?

But then, who would believe that the kingdom of light existed unless they had seen it with their own eyes?

She cleared her throat. "What happened after that? The town doesn't look like it's on its knees any longer."

"No. No, the town pulled out, but at a high price. And Black escaped unscathed."

A crow cawed again, but Kat didn't know from where. She was fixed on the town below, mind lost on what must have happened here not so long ago.

"We're linked, Johnny. You know that, don't you?"

"Is that so?"

"You brought me into this kingdom."

"No, I don't think so . . ."

"And I'm not about to let you just drop me off at the nearest bus station now that we're here."

A slow grin twisted his lips. "I like the way you speak, Kat. I really do."

"That's a promise then?"

"It's a promise."

"What about you, Kelly? Did Johnny bring you into this kingdom?"

She chuckled. "Not exactly, no."

"But you do believe."

"Of course."

"You're with Johnny. I mean in heart and soul."

"Yes."

Kat scolded herself for asking such an obvious question that could only be interpreted by both of them as a kind of childish jealousy.

"Not to worry, you two," Kat said, gazing out. "I'm not suffering from a bout of youthful infatuation. Just to set your minds at ease."

"Infatuation? With whom?" Johnny asked.

The blind man was indeed quite blind when it came to matters of women, Kat thought.

Kelly was still smiling. "With you, dear," she said.

"Yes, with you," Kat said. "I'm sixteen, you know."

"My, you are a straight shooter," Johnny said.

It occurred to her that none of this was remotely necessary. She just felt so comfortable around him. Maybe she *was* developing a crush on him.

"Awkward," she said.

"Not at all," Johnny said, deadpan. "Thank you for setting my mind at ease." Then he offered her a smile. "Think of me as your spiritual father."

That was it, of course. The realization set her completely at ease. And if he was her spiritual father, then she had every right to look out for him as any daughter might. No question was out of bounds. Starting with why he was going to marry Kelly. Just to be sure.

"That's good, because I don't have a father, not one that I know anyway."

Kelly stepped up, arms crossed, and stared at the valley. "So then, it's begun."

"So it seems," Johnny said. "The supernatural reality that so many pretend to believe in has crossed over in physical form. The books did that for us. And now the stage is set for a new kind of conflict."

Kat's only experience with the kingdom of light revealed in Jesus had been quite physical, but she knew that very few had been exposed to such a dramatic unveiling as she had.

"You don't mean a physical conflict?" she said. "Or do you?"

Johnny nodded at the valley. "What do you see, Katrina?"

"The town that you grew up in. Paradise."

"But that's the same answer you would have given me two weeks ago. You know better now."

Realization dawned. "I see a valley filled with the struggle between good and evil. To be more precise, I *wish* I did, because I know it's there even though I can't see it. If you would just open my eyes again . . ."

"So much of what really happens in this world can't be seen with those round balls in our eye sockets. You could pluck them out and still see as bright as day. Or you could walk around with the prettiest blue eyes carved from the sky and be as blind as Black himself."

"Exactly."

"The valley is teeming with every sort of wraith from hell you can imagine, you just don't see it. Light defeated the darkness in this valley once, but I do believe that darkness is coming again."

Johnny frowned. "Samuel thinks the monastery existed for the sake of what will happen here. This final showdown."

"When?" Kelly asked.

Johnny's jaw muscles flexed. It was always hard to guess what he was thinking because of his dark shades, but that he was emotional about the prospect of returning to Paradise was obvious.

"Now," Johnny said.

Now? Alarm spread through Kat's chest. "You can't! There's the court order, you have to watch over me!"

"We'll have to speak to the judge."

"No. Just what's this all about anyway? Kelly, you can't just up and leave your home because he says it's time! What's so important about Paradise anyway?"

"It's not Paradise," Johnny said. "You may not realize it yet, but our lives changed when the Constitution changed."

"What are you talking about?" she demanded. "So you can't trash another person's race or religion. You yourself said the light is best shown, not just talked about. I don't see how our lives have changed, other than you think you have to come to Paradise to face this wraith of yours."

It was crucial he realize just how important he was in her life at this time. The thought of him abandoning her was terrifying.

"I'm not sure you understand, Kat," Johnny said. "This change in the Constitution allows Congress to create new laws that make it a crime to express your faith in public. What may seem like a good thing on the surface opens the doors to laws that could make following the teachings of Christ a hate crime."

What?

"Seriously? How could talking about the love of God be a hate crime?"

"Because saying that he is the only way to enter the kingdom implies that another's path is wrong. You're saying your faith is better than another's faith. They will say it's no different than a claim that black skin is better than white skin. Both will be interpreted as hate crimes."

She understood in a single flash that sent a buzz through her skull.

"So saying, 'Jesus is the only way, follow him,' is like calling those who don't follow him fools. An insult."

"Yes."

"But Jesus claimed he is the only way. The whole kingdom is based on teachings like that. Even by following him you could be judged as saying that others are fools for not following him the way he insisted the world follow him!"

"That would be an extreme interpretation, but yes, you get the point. What few Christians realize is that you can't follow Jesus without actually following his teachings—none of which include denying him with silence."

"Meaning what?"

"Meaning that we are in a bind, dear Kat. There will be challenges, but any public support for the narrow teachings of Jesus will likely be deemed by the courts as a personal attack on other religions. Take my word for it." And then he added under his breath, "This reeks of Marsuvees Black."

Kat's whole mind-set changed. Johnny's need to make a stand in Paradise, however that looked, had nothing to do with her. Her eyes had been opened to an incredible new world two weeks ago, a reality brimming with light and truth. The realization that Jesus was who he'd claimed to be. The Light of the World. The Truth. The only Way.

She would never abandon that light!

She'd only just learned that her whole life was oppressed by a great dark lie, and now some law was going to attempt to force her back into that darkness? How could she even consider not walking in the light?

She'd read about a dog named Rutt who was so severely beaten every time he left his cage that when he was finally set free he found his way back to the cage, entered it, and died of starvation.

Unlike Rutt, she would not return to the cage, not under any circumstances.

"We can't let that happen!" Kat paced along the cliff, mindless of where her feet landed. She spun back to Johnny.

"Someone has to tell them. This is what following Jesus means, they can't make following him a hate crime."

"Someone *is* going to tell them," Kelly said.

Kat hardly heard her. "And what about the Muslims or the Hindus? Are they going to take this, just . . . lying down? Doesn't this affect them?"

"The clerics will scream foul, but like nominal Christians, nominal Muslims don't actually follow their faith to the letter. In the face of this tide sweeping the West, most will argue for tolerance. As will most Christians."

"It's obscene!" Kat's voice rang out over the cliff so that a careful ear in Paradise might have wondered if they'd heard a hawk's cry. "Tolerance, yes, but tolerance for the darkness? Are we bats?"

They let the echo fade. Johnny faced Paradise. Kat recalled Kelly's last statement: *Someone is going to tell them.*

"Who's going to tell them?" she asked.

"Johnny is," Kelly said.

"Then so am I," Kat said, marching back to him. "I'm going to Paradise with you."

"I really don't—"

"I don't want to hear it. You promised me, you promised the judge."

"You're in the middle of a school term."

"There's no school in Paradise?"

"Your mother—"

"Will agree. And don't tell me about how dangerous standing up for my faith will be. I've done it."

They stood in silence once again, and Kat knew that the matter was settled. She suddenly felt quite emotional about going with him to stand up for all the world to see, because surely, knowing him, that's what would happen.

Johnny was this day's John the Baptist, a voice crying in the wilderness. Only this time John had himself an apprentice.

"Thank you, Johnny," she said.

"It could get very bad, Kat. You know that."

"No, thank you for showing me the light." Tears welled up in her eyes. "It's the kindest thing anyone has done for me."

He put his hand on her right shoulder and pulled her close. Kissed the top of her head. "You're welcome."

"When do we go?" Kelly asked.

CHAPTER TWENTY-SEVEN

DARCY STOOD at the podium in the United States Senate chamber staring out at ninety-seven senators, prepared to convince these men and women to pass the National Tolerance Act, the first federal law to be based on the amended Constitution. Ninety-seven—a full house, less three, compelled by Billy to abstain or have their abuses of power exposed: Brian Clawson (D-Utah), whom Billy had persuaded to either vote for the law, miss the vote entirely, or pay the fallout when the real purpose of his frequent trips to Thailand were made public; Nancy Truman (R-Texas), who was missing under similar pressure; and Rodney Walton, senior senator from Arkansas, who was in the hospital with a prostate flare-up. All other members were present, including two who had been escorted in by Capitol Hill police for a mandatory quorum call, the first time the Senate had enforced a quorum using compulsion since 1995.

Her mind flashed over the last five days. While she and Billy toiled around the clock, working their magic, the riots had spread, picking up steam over the weekend with nine separate national incidents that resulted in the death of at least one party.

Racial protests were joined by freedom-of-speech protests. It was all a bit jumbled. One image of a mob marching down Pennsylvania Avenue showed protesters carrying signs that read Stop the Hatred, No Tolerance for Bigots right next to signs that read Americans for Free Speech.

The outcry from all sides of the social and political spectrum was inevitable. Liberal social-progressives found themselves agreeing with archrivals, even though neither group shared any other common idea.

The Human Rights Watch, along with the Religious Action Center, attacked the constitutional amendment from both sides, one arguing that the legislation didn't do enough, the other that it was a step in the direction of national socialism.

The National Association for the Advancement of Colored People condemned the lynchings on one network and decried the constitutional amendment on another. A group calling itself the Nontheists of North America emerged from the political woodwork, hailing the amendment as a "bold new shift in social strategy."

Elliot Marshall, president of the National Association of Broadcasters, stated at a televised national conference that the government had just committed "the most flagrant act of legislative irresponsibility in U.S. history" by amending the Bill of Rights, which began with the specific phrasing "Congress shall make no law . . ." but that the American people deserved such severe repercussions. "Let us hope," he said, staring past bushy eyebrows into the camera, "that history forgives us."

The bottom line was that everybody wanted to be heard and nobody wanted to listen. But Darcy had changed all of that here in Washington. And now she would make them listen in the most sacred of all halls.

Located in the north wing of the Capitol building, the Senate chamber was a massive expanse that dwarfed the White House in both spaciousness and prestige. Royal blue carpet mapped the floor, surrounded by eggshell-white walls and populated with rich brown desks. A broad center aisle separated each political party, and three rows of chairs overlooked the room from the balustrade above.

She'd dressed in a blue business suit, one of seventeen of varying designs and fabrics that Annie had tailored for her five days ago, immediately following their successful meeting with the president. Darcy knew within ten minutes of sitting down across from President Chavez that as long as they could gain access to the right people over the next five days, they would succeed. He'd breathed in her words, converted wholeheartedly, and offered unlimited support in the initiative's passage.

Today, Billy sat behind and to her right, legs folded beneath a Queen Anne chair that had been given to the Senate as a gift by the Duchess of Wales before Darcy was born. His weapon was his mind, and he wielded it with a small PDA that transferred the notes he thumbed into the keypad to the prompter in front of her.

Hardin, D, 2 + 2. Religious Right concerns.

Which meant that Senator Hardin, a senior Democrat who sat two rows back and two seats over, was struggling under the excessive strain that had come from both his office and the House of Representatives.

The tension was a welcome advocate for Billy and Darcy. Together, they would motivate the Senate toward a resolution, like Mozart conducting an orchestra—every note and strain had to be perfect, he with his ears, she with her voice. There would be no second chances.

Darcy looked at the white-haired senator, who sat back frowning, tapping his pencil's eraser on the desk. "I realize that the Religious Right has come out of the woodwork regarding this resolution," she said. "The Christians and the Muslims are screaming bloody murder as we have expected. Try to muzzle a Doberman and he will try to bite your fingers off. Try to silence a bigot and he will turn his hatred on you. God himself understood this when he gave the Ten Commandments, restricting free speech. False witness in court was treated with stoning. This law we have before us today doesn't call for the stoning demanded in the biblical times, but it is critical we level appropriate punishment at those who spurn the Constitution of these United States as amended yesterday."

She watched his lips flatten, his throat bob as the conviction in her words resonated with some deep place of agreement in his psyche.

Darcy had spoken for less than ten minutes, and she already knew that they had the majority votes needed to pass the National Tolerance Act. It would provide federal provisions to enforce and prosecute the new terms of the Bill of Rights as a public bill, with the necessary appropriations included, to be voted on by the House of Representatives that very afternoon.

But she pressed them with her gift in this final push to change history, speaking in this language she now affectionately called *Washington lingo*.

"I have no doubt that each member of this Senate has been exposed to more hate mail and public contempt than ever before. With the power vested in each of you comes the responsibility to act, to engage in direct interdiction with these events. Yes, we've seen the vitriol on the news networks. Even out front of this building. There are rabid fanatics who have plagued your office lines with threats simply because you responded to the president's—no, the nation's—call to this session. I would ask you then, senators, delegates of our union—if the call to action has been heralded by civil unrest, social upheaval, and rampant crime, then when is the time more appropriate to call for a vote to stem the tide of recent violence and social distrust? When?"

The sensation of power had become her drug. Sweat veneered her face and cooled into ice from the air-conditioning and the wide-eyed stares of the Senate before her. Yes, it was her drug. She made no attempt to deny Billy's caution.

"Both houses have passed the resolution to amend the Bill of Rights. The president has signed it. Seven out of nine Supreme Court Justices have defined its interpretation as necessary and true to the durability of the Constitution. What we are asking of you, what *I* am asking of you today, is that this resolution, the National Tolerance Act, be acknowledged according to the urgency of the nation's need."

She paused and allowed a few breaths. Enough time to convey the exhaustion brought on by her passion, enough time to scan her prompter for an update from Billy.

She scanned the room slowly, seeking the strong to weaken, but she'd weakened so many over the past five days that only a few remained fixed to their convictions. Sixty-six men and thirty-one women, all dressed for business, watching her with glassy-eyed stares.

With great conviction comes great emotion. Perhaps more than anything it was this emotion that attracted Darcy to her undeniable power. Never had anger and contempt flared so hotheadedly than before she'd taken the stage when they'd gathered to vote four days earlier.

And then never so many tears.

"The power of the vote brings all of us into this chamber. The responsibility of legislation. As an American citizen today, I ask . . . even *demand* that you act to de-escalate the conflict. Make examples of yourselves as legislators by voting to support, enforce, and prosecute the National Tolerance Act. Sign it into law. History will remember you, but only if you act with definitive unity and decisive speed. A nation of hurt and disaffected people look to you to put your feet down and say 'This is enough.' It stops here. If you do not, thousands of municipal, state, and federal law-enforcement officers will be abandoned, without the support of the nation and the provisions and appropriations that this act supplies."

She loved the flow of words over her tongue.

"I realize that I'm only one voice, brought here to address you as a favor to the Senate Judiciary Committee; but when you look into my eyes you will *know* that I am the voice of the people," Darcy said. "This great country called the United States of America was founded because a few sought true freedom. They sailed for this land and endured terrible hardship for that freedom. They were the outcasts, the few who cried out for the right not to be trampled by oppressive beliefs. Now to preserve that freedom, not for a few who are black or white, Muslim or Christian, but for all, regardless of race or religion, you must pass this act"—she held up the sheaf of paper and shook it—"this law, which will deny any man the right to insult, defame, or degrade anyone's right to be black or white, Christian or Muslim!"

Her voice rose, and the truths mixed within her words washed over them with a conviction that they could not possibly understand.

"We are Americans, and that is enough for us to cling to. We *can* unite, as one body. As one voice. With one thing in common. We are states, united in freedom, and I say that our freedom comes from our unity, and *not* from our differences!"

Tears snaked down the cheeks of some. A few still retained set jaws, but not without a struggle.

"I say let no man be called unequal for the color of his skin! Let no woman be called a *witch* for her faith! Let no child be denied the sanctuary that this land offers their sacred beliefs."

She was almost yelling now.

"Stop the bigotry. End the violence. Break the impasse. Pass this law. Make history. Today!"

The chamber erupted in thundering applause. A senior senator from Connecticut was the first to stand to her feet and call out her support. "Hear, hear!"

She was joined by five, then fifty, then all but a dozen.

Brian Kinnard watched from the balustrade, emotionless, arms crossed, dark glasses affixed to his face.

Darcy lowered the transcript of the resolution and raised a hand to silence them. She read the summary at full volume, aware that the power behind her words was seeping into their minds like an addictive intoxicant.

"'This resolution, the National Tolerance Act, is a public bill, enveloping the national body of the United States and territories governed by the federacy. As by law, any occurrence of public expression that implicitly defames, denigrates, insults, or otherwise casts aspersion upon the race of persons of similar or dissimilar race shall be considered a personal attack of heinous nature upon that person's intrinsic value as a citizen as well as upon the moral character of that person, and as such, is to be considered a hate crime in that it brings into question the equality of all persons. The unalienable rights of all people are as protected as they are endowed, and each person is entitled to embody those things that are in their ethnic nature without harassment, molestation, denigration, or defamation.'"

A slight pause for effect, though she hardly needed it.

"'As by law, any public expression of religious faith that implicitly defames, denigrates, insults, or otherwise casts aspersion upon the beliefs of persons of any other religion shall be considered a personal attack of heinous nature upon that person's intrinsic value as a citizen as well as upon the moral character of that person, and as such, is to be considered a hate crime in that it brings into issue the equality of all persons. Similar expressions of religious faith made in the privacy of individual places of worship or within the freedom of private domiciles are protected by the right to assemble and the right to free speech as provided by the First Amendment in the Bill of Rights of the U.S. Constitution. A place of worship shall be defined as a publicly recognized structure that has been licensed by each state in accordance with federal laws. A private domicile shall be defined as the private dwelling of any persons in accordance to each state's residential zoning requirements.'"

Darcy dropped the document on the podium.

"Give an example for the House of Representatives to follow. Give your country this law today, and history will smile on you all."

Then she left the stage, sweat standing out on her pores like dew. It had completely soaked her blouse.

Billy squeezed her elbow as they left. The drowning roar of the Senate followed them. "Congratulations," he whispered in her ear. "I think you just sealed the deal."

And she did, one hour and thirteen minutes later, with a vote of 83 to 17.

CHAPTER TWENTY-EIGHT

Day Seventeen

THE EPISCOPAL church on Main Street, Paradise, Colorado, was packed to the collar on Friday night, although there was only one liturgical collar in the building that Kat could see. That being worn by Father Stanley Yordon, who stood at the podium, trying to hush the excited crowd of three hundred who'd filed in over the past twenty minutes.

The auditorium's ceiling rose thirty feet to a single center beam, from which hung three huge bronze chandeliers. Pews padded in a maroon upholstery ran down both sides of a center aisle. A large wooden cross hung at the focal point in the center of the stained glass wall behind the platform. It was the first time Kat had actually been inside a church, and she found the environment rather moving. The church was at least symbolic of her new faith.

"Okay, ladies and gentlemen, please take your seats." The priest's voice boomed over the black speakers on either side of the platform. "No need to turn this into a barn. Please take your seats."

Kat sat between Kelly, who sat quietly with her hands folded, and Paula Smither, who'd taken it upon herself to introduce her around since their arrival earlier this morning. Her husband, Steve Smither, owned Smither's

Barbeque, the local gathering place for a closely knit community of Paradise's movers and shakers.

Before her trip to Paradise, Kat had never set foot outside of greater Las Vegas and Boulder City, but she'd seen enough movies and been exposed to enough U.S. history to imagine that Paradise was trapped in a thirty-year-old time capsule and had made no attempt at escape.

For example, although their lives were tied to the Net like the rest of the modern world, in the Smithers' home, where Kat was staying, the computer Paula used to do her shopping was wired to an old flat-panel monitor rather than the all-in-one wafer screens that had replaced the bulky boxes ages ago. She'd even seen a juke box in Smither's Barbeque.

More than the old technology that seemed prevalent in Paradise was the age of the people themselves. There were plenty of gray heads and plenty of children, but very few people between the ages of twenty and forty, which apparently was the popular age for locals to leave the time capsule for a taste of the new-fandangled world, as Paula put it, before they returned to settle down.

Mostly white. A few of mixed race like her, but even then, Kat stood out. Paula had spent the better part of the afternoon traipsing her around the town, meeting the neighbors, visiting the tiny grocery store, the salon, the recreation center, the few mom-and-pop shops. She'd advertised Kat as if she were a prize from the local fair. Kat had never felt so important in her life. She'd asked Paula why all the fuss.

"No fuss, they're just friendly." Paula paused. "And you have to understand that Johnny's a bit of a legend in this valley. You have to be something pretty special to come home with him."

There had been no helicopter, not this time. Johnny, Kelly, and Kat flew into Grand Junction and took an hour-long cab ride to Paradise. The street was deserted when they'd placed their bags on the boardwalk and walked into Smither's Barbeque unannounced. Steve Smither was there with half a dozen others, eating lunch. Johnny's mother, Sally, was there.

You'd have thought that Moses had just come home. The image of Sally flying across the room, chased by her own shriek, and throwing her arms around Johnny's neck was one Kat wouldn't forget.

Steve had his cell phone out and started a chain of calls that brought twenty people running to the bar and grill. In the space of five minutes, Paradise had come fully awake.

They made a tremendous fuss over Kelly, Johnny's fiancée, demanding to know all the arrangements and heaping him with suggestions when he said that there were no arrangements yet. They demanded it be a fall wedding on the church lawn. Kelly would be a beautiful, stunning bride. Johnny had really caught a fine woman.

Kelly took it all in, blushing, saying all the right things, but to Kat she looked out of place. Like a high-society type in Mayberry. Then again, that could be the instinctive protectiveness coming out in Kat. She was, after all, Johnny's spiritual daughter. He'd said so himself.

Guest accommodations were settled after a lot of back and forth over who got to host whom. Johnny would stay with his mother, naturally. Sleep in his old room.

Everyone else wanted *both* Kat and Kelly, but they divided themselves between Katie Bowers and Paula Smither. Katie would put Kelly up in her son's old room. He lived in Amarillo with his wife now, she was proud to point out.

Paula Smither staked a claim for Kat by hooking her hand around Kat's elbow and letting it remain there for a good ten minutes. She would put Katrina up in Roland's old room, she said.

Then Johnny left with his mother and Kat hadn't seen him since. That's what the meeting was for, to see Johnny. Hear his plan. The news had spread.

Father Yordon's call for quiet hadn't stilled the conversation between the pews.

"Never changes," Paula said to her, leaning so that Kat could hear. She swept her dark brown hair behind one ear. "You give people a little money and they lose all their manners, even the ones who had manners to begin with."

Most of the residents were farmers who grew exotic Paradise apples that were exported to Japan, where they sold for ten times the price of domestic Fuji apples. The valley's soil composition had changed thirty years earlier, resulting in an unusually sweet fruit unique to this single valley. Only so much land could support these trees farmed by these people. Their apples were rare; supply and demand dictated the rest.

When Kat had asked Steve why they sent the apples all the way to Japan, he'd winked and told her that no one in Paradise was beyond taking a healthy profit. The farmers might look dated, but they were by no means poor. Paradise was a small Eden, as rich as an oil field and much more beautiful.

Kat had no idea what they did with all their money. They all drove late-model cars, the only real sign of progress in the town, but not the flashy kind she would find on Las Vegas Boulevard any night of the week.

Johnny had managed to talk the judge and the school into granting her variances for a two-week sabbatical, which he claimed was critical to her progress and emotional stability—all true, because she wasn't sure she could have stayed in Boulder City, not knowing what she knew.

Which was what?

That the kingdom of light was buzzing all around them.

That the darkness she'd once walked in wasn't taking it without complaint.

That Johnny wasn't going to take it lying down, so neither would she.

"People!" Father Yordon kicked it up a notch. He probably faced the same unresponsive crowd every time he took the platform. There was no frustration on the gray-haired man's narrow face. This was only part of the ritual, and both he and the congregation had their roles to play.

"Now he yells at them, they'll listen," Paula said. But even her expression of disapproval included a wink and a nod.

Kat looked at the woman's twinkling eyes set in a comfortably round face. Steve sat by her side with arms and legs crossed, dressed in jeans and a black shirt. That was another thing—none of the farmers dressed much like what she imagined farmers would. Jeans, sure. But they likely shopped at Dillard's rather than Wal-Mart. Dresses, but not cheap ones. No flannel shirts. Lots of expensive leather jackets. No cowboy hats or even boots. But then, what did she know about rich farmers who sold exotic Paradise apples to the Japanese for a killing?

He caught her stare and winked. "She's right."

"People! I know this is a Friday night, but we have business here!"

Now they quieted.

A tall man built like a tree trunk remained standing. "Where is he, Father?"

"Well now, Claude, if you'd just have a seat I'll bring him on, won't I?"

Claude Bowers sat and put his arm behind his wife, Katie Bowers, who smiled back at Kat. She ran the beauty salon across the street, a pretty strawberry blonde who looked much younger than her sixty years, but Paula had been guessing on her age.

"Thank you, Claude."

The man dipped his head once, without showing a hint he'd understood the gentle rebuke.

Father Yordon sighed. "Thank you all for coming on such short notice. But I can promise you, you won't be disappointed. We've seen our days in here, haven't we?"

The place stilled to the sound of breathing.

"Well . . ." Father Yordon smiled at them, formed a teepee with his fingers. He didn't seem to know quite what to say. "So then . . ."

The back swinging door creaked, and as one, the congregation twisted in their seats. Sally Drake, Johnny's middle-aged mother, walked in with her son on her arm. She was a full foot smaller than he, but her smile was larger than both of them put together.

Johnny was dressed in the black slacks and knitted T-shirt he often wore, and with the dark glasses over his eyes he looked like some kind of misplaced superstar. But then he was, wasn't he? The white eyes behind those sunglasses said so.

He kissed his mother at the front pew, then hopped onto the stage. Took Father Yordon's hand. They shook too long, and Kat suspected it was the priest's doing.

"Folks." Yordon stepped up to the microphone. "Folks, I couldn't be more pleased to welcome Johnny home."

The congregation broke out in thundering applause, taking their feet, to the last man and woman.

Paradise did indeed love Johnny.

He stepped up to the microphone and stared at them through the shades. "Thank you." But the applause drowned him out.

"Thank you . . ."

"Okay, let the man speak!" Claude Bowers thundered.

They settled and began to sit.

"Thank you, it's good to be . . . home."

He put his hands on the podium and looked down at them. For a long time he just stood there. He swallowed hard and a tear leaked past his black glasses. Silence smothered the room.

But he still didn't move, didn't apologize, didn't lift his hand to signal he needed a moment. He just stood there, hammered by emotion.

Somewhere a woman started to cry softly. Then another.

Kat glanced over at Paula and saw tears streaming from her eyes. There was a bond among the people in this room that Kat couldn't begin to understand.

But she could, she realized. She could! She'd stepped into the kingdom of light and been washed away with tears.

She wished he would take off his glasses and show all of them his eyes. Not the pain but the light. Show them the light!

Instead he just stood there, frozen by emotion.

There couldn't possibly be a dry eye in the room, and Kat was crying with them. Johnny had said he was blind, like Samson. She could only wonder at all the times this blind man had encountered the truth with those eyes of his. What memories were rushing through his mind.

Gradually he seemed to relax, and finally he lifted his head.

No apology. "The light came into the darkness, but the darkness did not understand it," he said. "It tried to crush the light. We've all seen the face of that darkness. We've all felt the horror."

Paula began to cry silently, shaking beside Kat. Kelly sat still, hands folded.

"But the light prevailed. It revealed to us the true reality that we now live in, a world crackling with power and light and more love than any one of us could dare ask for. Do you know this?"

"Yes! Yes, yes." The room filled with hushed yeses.

"Then you know why we can't now turn our backs on that love or deny that the light is our sole hope. Do you know this?"

"God, yes!" Father Yordon stood from his seat behind the podium that had blocked Kat's view of him. His face was wet and his eyes blurry. He stood there shaking. "Yes."

He seemed to come to himself, then eased back down out of her view.

"I've come back to Paradise to stand in the face of the darkness. They are telling us that we must hide our faces and our voices, that if we speak of the love that has rescued us from darkness we are guilty of hate and will be put in dark cells."

"Black!" someone in the back cried. A murmur rushed through the crowd. So they knew too.

Johnny let the statement stand.

"But I can't turn my back on the one who has saved me, nor on the kingdom of light, which he's led me into. For me, it is the source of life. I would have to die before I denied the truth, even with silence."

Johnny took a deep breath.

"I've come back to Paradise to ask you to stand with me, to stand in the face of the new law that our government has passed prohibiting us from following the teachings of Jesus. Will—"

Paula stood. "We will!"

"They're trying to do that?" Claude demanded.

"He's saying they've done it," Paula said. "And yes, we will stand with you, Johnny. We're not letting darkness back in this valley, never again!"

Father Yordon was out of his seat again, stepping forward. "What are you suggesting? Each denominational leader has posted Net bulletins, urging calm. They say the new act will be tested in the Supreme Court and overturned. And until then we should just worship in private."

"Well, you know where they can put that bulletin, and their new law," someone said.

"No!" Johnny stepped out from behind the podium. "No, Ben, this isn't about resistance or harsh words. This is *only* about staying faithful to the Way. The Truth. The Light that crushes darkness. I'm sure that millions of people of faith are screaming foul at this very moment, arming themselves to the teeth with legal briefs and signatures to force a repeal of the new law. Muslim clerics all over the world will condemn it, Mormons will march, Christians churches all over the country will denounce the law and work against their elected officials. And all of that will only satisfy the bitter while they *wait* for change."

He scanned the people. "But we will do none of that. We will simply hold up the light for all to see. And they will see it. The whole world will see the light shining out of this one small valley in the Colorado mountains. Paradise will be a beacon of truth, and they will see it above all others because they will see us, living in the light. And I will show it to them."

They weren't shouting their support, but at a glance Kat could see that to a man, woman, and child they were pinned to his every word, and the look in their eyes was resolute.

"We will use the Net and boldly announce our love of Jesus, our only hope. And they will know that Johnny Drake and the people of Paradise will not be muted."

His breathing had thickened.

"Our stand will grow beyond the Net. Others will come."

Dead silence filled the room.

"And then . . . then the darkness will come, like a torrent, to crush this light shining so brightly in the land."

Okay. That was the challenge, wasn't it? Kat wanted to jump up and tell them why they had to do what Johnny was suggesting. If they'd seen what she'd seen, felt what she'd seen.

"How?" Johnny's mother, Sally, asked in the small voice of one who'd faced too much suffering.

He faced her. "I don't know, Mother. But it could get bad."

What if they wouldn't support him? Kat couldn't sit a moment longer. She jumped to the stage next to Johnny and spun around.

"You can't let them shut us up! Two weeks ago I didn't know that this kingdom even existed, but then my eyes were opened and I saw it!"

The moment of her conversion swept through her again and she began to tremble. She hadn't been prepared for the emotion, and she couldn't stop the tears.

"It's like magic!" No, that wasn't quite right, but she couldn't think of a better way to put it. "The whole world has to see! How can we not scream out the truth from the tops of these mountains? We've found life! They have to know!"

Her voice rang out in the auditorium, greeted by silence.

Slowly, Sally stood, smiling. "But we will, Katrina. We wouldn't even consider turning our backs on the truth. We're in already."

Kat blinked. She'd misjudged them?

They began to stand, one by one, then in groups, then all.

Johnny reached out and placed his hand on her shoulder. By her, with her. To the congregation: "Remember the darkness and remember that it is dispelled by the light," he said to them. "Hold your children close. Love your wives. And pray, Paradise. Pray that the light will illuminate the world."

CHAPTER TWENTY-NINE

Day Eighteen

FOUR DAYS had spun by in a frantic buzz since their monumental victory in the Senate, and Darcy was feeling exceptionally pleased with herself. Pleased with Billy. With the power she'd used to bring justice to millions of people. Like a surgeon, she'd wielded a scalpel to cut out a life-threatening cancer. Not just any surgeon, but a specialist who alone could operate and alone could change history.

She couldn't have done it without Billy; he was the CAT scan, revealing layers of truth hidden beneath the skin so that she could apply her skill to rid the tissue of disease. To bring wholeness. However crucial he was, she had received most of the praise, as it had been her speech that convinced minds and secured votes.

Prior to the Senate vote, half of the lawmakers in Washington knew she could be very persuasive, flexing logic and leveling coercion in a kind of manipulation that they understood—they all practiced the same form of control, minus the uncanny gift. After the Senate vote, Washington knew without a doubt that Darcy Lange was also a supremely gifted orator. Maybe the best ever.

The notion that there was a supernatural component to the compulsion they felt to follow her suggestions was beyond the reach of most, but many surely sensed that there was more to her words than persuasive articulation. She'd given them all something to keep them awake at night.

She, on the other hand, was sleeping like a baby. The potential danger to their well-being had been drastically elevated in the last week—as Kinnard put it, "You don't coerce half the U.S. Capitol and then not expect these power-mongers to plot ways to eliminate you; you're a threat."

But Billy had done a good job identifying those whose minds were filled with nasty thoughts, and Kinnard was already working behind the scenes to discourage them from taking their thoughts too far.

The president signed the National Tolerance Act into law the day of the Senate resolution, before Congress had made its landslide vote to appropriate funds official.

The president addressed the country that night, promising instantaneous judicial response to any person, party, association, or denomination caught actively infringing upon the federal statute. Net-broadcasted sedition, even disguised as dissent or protest, would be subject to federal investigation by the U.S. Department of Justice and the FBI. Prison time would be administered; due process would be expedited from Maine to Maui. It wasn't just an amendment now, it was the law of the land, from the top down.

Knowledge that even ethnic slang could mean incarceration for a minimum of ninety days spread through the country like the ripples of a shockwave.

After sixteen days of social mayhem, the United States woke to an eerie calm on Wednesday morning.

In Darcy's mind the results were tantamount to liberating Poland at the end of World War II. The entire operation was a smashing success.

Even the Net was quiet as the talking heads took extra precautions not to violate the new laws with their blogs and editorials. There had been the rash of outcries and denouncements from the expected sources, naturally. Saber rattling that would eventually find its way into the courts.

But at least it was all off the streets. More importantly, Caucasians were no longer calling Arabs towel-heads, and if anyone was calling Christians bloodsuckers, they were doing it behind closed doors.

Peace had come to America.

Saturday Darcy rode the elevator to their penthouse suite, holding in both hands a box containing the $40,000 titanium Rolex she'd purchased for Billy. Her first major purchase. Kinnard had said no limit, and Darcy intended to test his words.

They'd celebrated late last night over a lobster dinner catered by Rosario's, an exclusive Italian restaurant that Annie insisted they try. Too dangerous to go into such a public place, Kinnard insisted, so they ate by candlelight, overlooking the city. It had been a perfect evening.

Better still, Billy didn't know she'd made arrangements with Kinnard to pick out the watch for him. With any luck, he was still asleep. She'd pounce on his bed, smother him with kisses, and pull him from under the covers before presenting him with her token of appreciation.

Just because Billy was Billy. And because she loved him, loved him desperately.

She nodded at the guard, slipped though the front door, and tiptoed through the vestibule.

"I will." Billy's voice sounded from the kitchen and she stopped. He was up. Change of plans. She'd slink in with the watch behind her back and kiss him hard before presenting it.

"This isn't good." A pause. "Right."

Darcy only half heard. She walked around the corner and saw that he had his back to her. He must have sensed her, because he turned and stared, eyes wide, and not because of the Rolex behind her back. Something was wrong.

"What?"

"Johnny called Kinnard an hour ago," he said.

"Johnny?"

"He's in Paradise."

"So? Good for him." She took another step, but there was more, wasn't there? Johnny going to Paradise wasn't the bad news.

"He's making a stand against the National Tolerance Act."

Her heart slogged through one heavy beat.

"Is that right?"

"He says the town has decided that they can't or won't deny their truth with silence."

Darcy's past came back to her at once, as if the monastery itself had been dropped from the sky to crush her. Johnny was defying them again. In Paradise.

"Making a stand, how?"

"By publicly claiming that Jesus is the only way to God."

She lowered the watch to her side and swallowed. "He can't do that. That defies the law. Right?"

"The attorney general thinks so. Hard not to interpret it that way." Billy's eyes dropped to the Rolex. "He posted a blog on the Net this morning—he's made his position very clear."

"His position?" She wagged her head. "Listen to him. *His position.* What position? And who cares? Just what does he think he's doing?"

But she knew that Johnny could make plenty of people care.

"Read it yourself."

Darcy saw that the large Net screen was open to a document. Not that it mattered; she already knew what he'd written. Light into darkness, blah, blah, blah. She could *kill* him for pulling a stunt like this!

She set the watch on the counter and crossed to the couch in spite of herself. Grabbed the remote and scrolled down the one-page statement, noting by the counter that the site had already been hit eight thousand times. After only a couple of hours, at most.

The blog was exactly what she'd expected, a run-on about the Way, the Truth, the Life, the Light of the World, Jesus, Jesus, Jesus.

"Jesus!" she snapped, slapping the remote down.

"Slow down, Darcy." Billy crossed the room. "He did go out of his way to make sure he didn't specifically deride any particular religion. He's only talking about his faith in Je—"

"Which is now legally the same as denigrating Muslims, Hindus, Buddhists, the lot of them! He knows very well that Christianity is exclusive. *Jesus* was an exclusivist!"

"Maybe, but he has some pretty direct words for all religions."

"Which is in itself a flagrant violation of our law."

"*Our* law?"

"You know what I mean," she said, standing and dismissing him with a wave of her hand. "The Tolerance Act."

"This kind of thing's going to happen all over the place for a while. We haven't exactly declared martial law. Let's give it some time to settle in."

"This isn't just any old place, Billy. This is Paradise. This is Johnny! And he's already got eight thousand hits; if this gets picked up—and knowing Johnny he'll make sure it does—it'll top the Net posts by the end of the day. How many people live in that town now?"

"About three hundred."

"You can bet they'll lap up whatever Johnny serves them."

"You're overreacting."

"And the fact that he called Kinnard makes it clear he's challenging us directly."

"We don't know that."

"He's breaking the law already! He's defying us. And he knows what he's doing. Johnny probably doesn't floss his teeth without a backup plan; do you think that this was just a *mistake*?" She was half tempted to take off her glasses and set Billy straight.

"You're right, he's defying the law. The attorney general agrees. I don't see how any court could interpret it differently. We crafted a pretty nasty little law. But we need to be thoughtful about how we proceed."

"Okay, that's more like it," she said. "So you agree we can't just leave this up to whatever local police they have up there? Does Paradise even have a sheriff? Do we have to wait for the state patrol to round him up?"

"What do you suggest?"

"Let's shut down the blog. Censure his statements and send in the FBI or whoever Kinnard has access to. We squash this before it has time to breathe!"

"Not that simple. We have jurisdictional considerations. The law would be enforced first by local authorities. The National Tolerance Act is still brand-new. It'll take time to work out the kinks."

Billy looked at the Rolex.

"I'm sorry." She walked up to him and they stared at the watch together. "I bought it for you. It's a Rolex. A kind of, you know, gift of appreciation. It was rude of me to get sidetracked."

"Thank you," he said. "I've always wanted a Rolex. That was kind of you."

"You're welcome."

But neither of them picked up the watch. Johnny had taken the air out of their celebratory mood.

"Kinnard had a suggestion."

"Let me guess," she said. "He wants us to go to Paradise."

"That's right."

Of course he would. Fly to Paradise, talk Johnny down, nip this whole thing in the bud before it grew out of local proportion. Wasn't that the skill she and Billy had perfected?

"I'm not sure I can go back to Paradise," Billy said.

She knew what he meant. The very idea of meeting Johnny in Paradise sent shivers down her spine. But the sound of fear in his voice betrayed something deeper than simple anxiety. Billy perhaps had more reason to fear Paradise than she; after all, he'd been the first to fall. The first to push the line between reality and terror. Black was his own evil progeny, and Black had been born in Paradise.

"He would agree to meet us outside of Paradise, don't you think?"

His eyes darted over to her. "Not the canyons."

"Of course not, no, not where the monastery was."

"I don't know why it makes me so nervous," he said. "It's just a place."

"A place that gave me nightmares for years," she said. "I understand perfectly well why you'd be terrified of it."

Darcy realized her mistake immediately. "I didn't mean to suggest that you're to blame any more than I am," she said, crossing quickly to him. She took his hand and lifted it to her lips. "We all made choices. Just because you were the first to defy the monks . . ."

Darcy stopped there, realizing that she'd already dug a hole of blame. She thought about using her eyes to comfort him, but they'd agreed not to manipulate each other without being invited. And she wasn't eager to have her mind read, though she had no apparent reason to fear it.

She brushed his hair from his forehead and spoke in a soothing tone. "Do you know what the best part of what we've done is, Billy?"

"We've stopped a string of lynchings."

"We've stopped priests from wandering around this country condemning people to hell."

Billy didn't share her resentment of the church, but neither did he lose any love on religion.

"Instead we have *Johnny* condemning people to hell," he said.

"Then let's go to Paradise and change that, once and for all."

"Talk him out."

"And if he doesn't talk out?"

Billy answered with fire in his eyes. "Then we burn him out."

JOSEPH HOUDE, a rail-thin, blond-cropped freelancer whose sudden rise in blog rankings a year earlier had led to significant demand for his stories on several larger Net feeds, was the first reporter to arrive in Paradise. His small yellow Volkswagen hybrid had quietly rolled into town at two on Friday afternoon after a four-hour drive from Denver.

He'd made the decision to cross the mountains after receiving an e-mail from one of his Washington sources, who had it on good faith that one of the many potential infractions of the new hate-crime law might bear a closer look. The e-mail had included a link to Johnny's blog, which in turn led Joseph to twenty-three similar blogs that had originated from the same geographical location.

Without coming right out and denouncing the National Tolerance Act, the blogs had unashamedly broken the law by doing precisely what many feared would test the law. Without naming any religion or group of people, the blogs asserted in a very public forum that when Jesus had repeatedly claimed to be the Way, the Truth, and the Life, who alone provided access to the Father, he meant precisely that.

It was a narrow-minded perception of the prophet's teaching, Joseph thought, but then the same prophet had also claimed that the path to God was indeed narrow, missed by most.

The legal conservatives were sure to wage full-scale war on the new law. The American public had choked it down in a time of crisis, but more than a few would vomit it back into the courts. The notion that people could not stand up and say whatever they pleased about their faith might make sense on paper, but two hundred fifty years of complete religious freedom would not be so easily squashed.

Indeed, similar positions were even now starting to pop up on the Net.

Then again, suppression of free speech in similar categories had been accepted with surprising calm in other countries already. Most European countries had put the brakes on freedom of expression years ago in an attempt to keep the peace between Christians and Muslims.

The Europeans had learned that it was one thing to say, "Starbucks makes the best coffee in the world." Such opinions, freely stated, had never been contested.

It was quite another thing to say, "White is by far the best color of skin in the world." Or, "Christianity is a better religion than Buddhism." Or even, "Islam." Or even, "Jesus is the only way."

Fighting words, all of them.

Regardless, as of today, running through Harlem screaming, "Whites rule!" was a crime. And so was holding up a sign in public claiming that Jesus was God. Which was what Johnny had done, albeit a virtual sign.

Hits on blogs were updated hourly, and on Johnny's blog they numbered eight thousand at 9:00 a.m. When the counter rolled over to seventy-six thousand at 10:00, Joseph threw his recorder, his computer, and a few clothes into a bag and scrambled down the stairs for the parking lot.

He'd been in the business long enough to recognize a story when he saw it, and this one had history in the making written all over it. Oddly enough, in dire need of a distraction the night before, he'd downloaded an old classic titled *300* off the Net and filled his mind with an hour and a half of raw heroism or foolishness, depending on how one viewed the movie. Either way it was a enjoyable flick, if a bit violent.

Although he knew it was purely coincidental, it amused Joseph that the current population of Paradise, the epicenter of this blog, was also three hundred.

The three hundred Spartans had taken their stand against impossible odds and been memorialized on film. Now the three hundred Paradisians were gathered in the valley, and if Joseph's nose told him anything, it was that the number would grow to three thousand. He wondered if a memorial would be built to honor them.

The town looked like a typical mountain community abandoned by progress and youth. One church, one grocery store, one bar and grill, one salon, four fruit stands. Nothing about his first drive down Main Street suggested that he was at the epicenter of any ideological struggle destined to be memorialized.

His research told him that the average income of Paradisians was nearly fifty times the average income of other American farmers, but only the expensive cars parked about town provided evidence of this.

There were no mobs standing around with pickets, no signs on the walls of the buildings denouncing the U.S. government, no prophets walking up and down the street with bullhorns, crying for the world to repent. In fact, there were no signs that anyone from this town had done anything to draw attention to themselves at all.

He spent the first hour speaking with residents, pretty much down-to-earth Americans eager to shake his hand, extraordinary only in their apparent simplicity and unapologetic appreciation for the light that had come to destroy darkness. It all sounded a bit kooky to him, although no one met his expectations of a kook.

Then Joseph met Katrina Kivi, the girl who'd hit the wires after her breakup of the Boulder City High School riot a week or so earlier, if he wasn't mistaken.

"You're a journalist?" she asked, eyes bright as the moon.

"I am."

"Really?" The news seemed to delight her. "What brings you here?"

"I was going to ask you the same question. Aren't you the girl from Boulder City—"

"In the flesh," she said. "Kat."

"And what brings you here, Kat?"

"I'm glad you asked. Do you want to meet him?"

"Who?"

"Johnny Drake. You're here because you read his blog, right? Is the word getting out?"

"Umm . . ." Her lack of guile was disarming, to say the least. "I would say yes. Are you sure you want that?"

"Of course. Why write a blog if you don't expect anyone to read it? Do you want to meet him?"

"Yes. I would."

"Come on."

She led him to a white house across from the church and informed him along the way that Johnny was staying with his mother for now.

Katrina bounded up the steps, rapped on the front door, and stepped back when a tall, well-built man wearing dark glasses answered the door.

"Hello, Kat."

She looked at Joseph, smiling coyly so that he couldn't help but to think he'd been set up for something.

"The press is here," she said.

"They are, huh?"

"His name is Joseph."

Johnny Drake studied him, then stepped to one side. "Come on in, Joseph."

Joseph Houde spent thirty minutes with Johnny, but he knew within the first three that he was sitting on top of a time bomb. The man had in mind an epic showdown between good and evil, and he held an utterly compelling conviction that he'd been born to make his stand here, in Paradise, Colorado, today, for all the world to see. There wasn't a breath of backdown in him.

Even worse, Joseph found himself strangely drawn to the man, wanting to believe his soft-spoken rhetoric.

He left the house thinking that if there was such a thing as a devil, Johnny could probably stand toe-to-toe with him and not bat an eye. He returned to his car, fired up his sat link, composed his first story for immediate release, and sent it to his clearing board.

Two minutes later he received a confirmation that Sapphire, the largest of the Net news services, had accepted the story at his regular rate.

When Joseph checked Johnny's blog, he discovered that the hits now numbered 989,498. Even more interesting, a few hundred bloggers outside of Paradise had picked up the cause and posted their own bold declarations of faith.

He looked out at the sleepy town before him. The Paradisians would indeed be immortalized.

CHAPTER THIRTY

Day Nineteen

IT HAD been a mistake to wait for all the arrangements before leaving Washington, Darcy thought, as they hovered far above the valley of Paradise. It had taken Kinnard four hours to reach Johnny by phone only to be told that he was unavailable before Sunday morning. Johnny was posturing. She had paced the carpet in the suite, telling herself that the bitterness she felt toward him was unreasonable, that this was just a simple misunderstanding, that even he had sat with the council and all but offered his support!

It was almost as if he wanted this showdown of his. But it would all work out. They'd all been through too much to let one little protest from one little man deny them now.

Billy sat beside her, staring out the window, brow beaded with sweat. At first glance, from three thousand feet above the town, Paradise looked deserted and untouched by time, still the same as she remembered.

But on closer inspection she could see one small difference. A dozen cars lined Main Street, more cars than she thought should be there. And now one of those cars was uploading information to the Sapphire News Network.

Darcy tapped the pilot on the shoulder. "How far?"

He fanned his fingers out: five minutes. Johnny had suggested a lunch at Smither's Barbeque, of all places. Billy refused, and they settled on the plateau above the canyons to the south, at noon. Johnny had the gall to offer to bring sandwiches.

Billy was still staring. His return to Paradise was beating him up more than he let on, she thought. She had expected to be the one slicked in cold sweat, but he seemed more deeply affected.

Darcy lowered her eyes to the red folder on her lap, flipped the file open, and stared at the first few lines from the Net report that Joseph Houde had filed from Paradise last night.

From the desert has come a voice crying in the wilderness, and his name is John. Johnny Drake to be more precise. But ask his disciples and they will tell you his mission is no less defined than the mission of John the Baptist, who first introduced the Light from heaven to the world over two thousand years ago. The multitudes listened to John, who told them that Jesus of Nazareth was the Way to God. Then Herod took John's head.

Now the question begs us: Will the world listen to Johnny Drake? And who will take his head?

It went on to characterize the town's stand as some kind of beachhead—yada, yada, yada.

How those sneaky reporter rats got around so quickly, she didn't know, but the story had spawned a flood of activity on the Net. It hadn't exactly become the media's focus, but it was enough to warrant a call from the attorney general first thing this morning seeking and receiving assurance that Darcy and Billy could handle Johnny.

Darcy was tempted to drop down there and tell this Joseph Houde exactly what he should do with his stories. And he would listen, wouldn't he?

Darcy put her hand on Billy's thigh. "You okay?"

He didn't answer, which was answer enough.

The helicopter gave the canyon ridges a wide berth, as Darcy had instructed, and homed in on the green plateaus to the south. Large groves of aspens interspersed with grassy fields covered the land. She picked out Johnny's helicopter sitting idly between two stands of trees that bordered one of the many small lakes on the high mesa. And not far from the helicopter, a white blotch.

A tent, she saw on closer inspection. Johnny had set up a tent. What did he think this was, a summit with Abraham, Isaac, and Jacob?

With some reluctance, Billy had agreed last night to the strategy she'd suggested. They had to handle Johnny on his terms, not theirs. They'd both learned a thing or two about negotiation over the past two weeks, and this was a time for seduction, not blackmail.

The helicopter settled on the ground forty yards from the tent, which turned out to be a canopy. Billy slid out, walked around, and helped her to the ground.

She took his hand. "You sure you're okay?"

"I'm fine." The chopper quickly wound down. "Perfectly fine."

"Then let's go."

Johnny had set up a table under the canopy, complete with a white tablecloth, a bowl of fruit, and a pitcher of water. Four chairs faced each other in pairs next to the table, and in one of these chairs sat a blonde woman.

So Johnny had brought his lover too. The woman could be anyone, for all Darcy knew, but she rather liked the idea that she had some competition. So to speak.

Johnny stood and waited for them at the edge of the canopy, dressed in what appeared to be the same black slacks and white shirt he'd worn on his visit to Washington. He wore his glasses, as did they all, even his lover or whoever she was.

Darcy dropped Billy's hand and walked up to him. "Hello, Johnny."

"Darcy. Billy." His hand was large and warm around her palm. "I'd like you to meet Kelly."

Darcy walked over to the pretty woman, who stood. "And who might Kelly be?"

"I'm a friend," she said. "Johnny and I go back a ways. It's good to finally meet you." Kelly turned to Billy and took his hand with both of hers. "And you, Billy. I've heard so much about you." She held his hand a bit too long, Darcy thought. "It really is such an honor to meet you, Billy."

No, this couldn't be Johnny's lover. If Darcy didn't know better, she would think the woman was attempting to seduce Billy right here in front of them all. But then again, Darcy's wary nature had always turned sparrows into hawks.

"And why exactly are you here?" Darcy asked.

"Because she's the only other person who knows everything," Johnny said. "I thought you'd want to meet her."

She thought about a clever retort, but then dismissed it. They were here to win Johnny, not threaten him.

"A drink?" Johnny asked, walking behind the table. "Fruit? The best apples in the world, they say."

Darcy took an apple and turned it in her hand. "Well, it's nice that something good has come out of Paradise," she said, eyeing him, then bit deeply. The apple's juice was surprisingly tasty. "Sweet."

"As sweet as the first time?" he asked.

What was he saying? They'd eaten apples together before?

"I'm sorry, I've put most of my memories of our childhood in a room and sealed the door." She smiled and took another bite. "Therapist's order, you know."

"Sometimes remembering isn't such a bad thing."

She glanced at Billy and saw that his jaw was fixed. Only then did the significance of the apples come to her. Billy had been the first to taste the proverbial forbidden fruit when he'd used the Books of History to write Marsuvees Black into flesh and blood. Johnny had brought the apples as some kind of cute object lesson, and the fact hadn't been lost on Billy who was now seething.

Darcy had to calm herself.

"So, what can I do for you?" Johnny asked.

"That's a low blow," Billy said softly.

"No, it's simply the truth. We've turned Paradise into the valley of truth and light, or hadn't you heard?"

"And we'll bury this valley!" Billy yelled.

"The truth isn't easily buried," Johnny said.

Billy's anger surprised even Darcy. This wasn't the right approach.

"Please, can we put the testosterone back in the bottle? Why don't we take a seat and discuss this reasonably. We're not children any longer."

Kelly eased into a chair, but neither Johnny nor Billy moved.

"Okay, then we can stand," Darcy said.

"I don't mean to be antagonistic," Johnny said. "But I've decided that I can't deny the truth we all know." He crossed to his chair, sat, and folded one leg over the other. "Until I saw Darcy on the Net, I was alone with this . . . gift. Finding you was like finding a long-lost brother and sister."

"And it was to us as well, Johnny," Darcy said, setting her apple down and sitting opposite him.

"I couldn't put my finger on what bothered me then—Kelly tells me that my ability to help others see makes me blind in more ways than I realize. But when I learned that you've been behind—"

"It doesn't have to be this way," Darcy interrupted. "You could join us. Imagine the good we three could do for this world. We'd be using our gifts to help millions!"

She looked back at Billy. "Come, Billy."

"This isn't going to work," Billy said, sitting. "Can't you see that, Darcy? He's here to reject any proposal before we even put it on the table."

"You're reading minds through glasses now? There are only three people in the world who have the gifts we have; surely we can see our way past fighting each other with them!"

"But you're wrong, Darcy," Johnny said. "We aren't the only three."

"No? Some of the other children also—"

"Black," Billy said. "You'll never let me live it down, will you?"

"It's not my intention to blame you for anything, Billy," Johnny said. "Only to help you remember the consequences of following the other path."

Darcy was having difficulty controlling her frustration.

"And just where has your path led you?" she asked as calmly as she could.

"To the same place yours has led you," he said. "Back to Paradise."

"But you see, that's where you're wrong! This is no paradise! The whole *idea* of a heaven was never based on reality, and it never will be."

"Not in this life, no."

She could feel the heat rise in her face. "If you think the message or manipulations of a man in a white collar can in any way lead to a paradise in this life or the next, then maybe your lover is right. Maybe you are as blind as a worm."

Then she thought twice about her haste to show her frustration.

"Speaking loosely, that is. So that you understand how *I've* been able to cope since being set free from the monastery."

"Your problem is that you've always blamed the monastery, Darcy. The monks weren't to blame. They gave you everything you needed and more. The *only* thing they forbade were the dungeons. They knew of the danger there. They tried to protect you from harm."

"They could have sealed it!" she snapped.

"But you couldn't stay away, could you? *You* went down into the dungeons, opened the ancient books, and brought the evil upon yourself. The priests weren't the sinners, *you* were the sinners. The books gave us three these gifts to be sure it never happens again, and all you want to do is crucify monks."

Billy stood, trembling. "Would you have done any different? Would you have stayed away?"

"I don't know. Maybe I'd have done the same as you. But I hope I would accept blame for what I'd done and learn from it."

It was too much for Darcy. "How dare you?" she screamed.

Birds took flight from the nearby scrub oaks.

"How dare you turn the pain we've suffered because of those monks against us, as if it's all *our* fault, as if we *chose* to be experiments, as if they aren't culpable, as if the dungeons had no blame! No child deserves to be put through that."

Johnny sat quietly for a moment.

"What have you come to say to me?" he finally said.

Billy was right, Darcy realized. Johnny had no intention of even considering any proposal from them. But they *had* to turn him away from his plan.

"We've come to say that what you're doing will end badly," she said. "Sit down, Billy."

Instead he turned to his left and headed toward the trees.

Darcy let him go.

She turned back to Johnny. "You really don't see the damage you're doing here, do you?"

He just looked at her from behind those glasses. She wondered what would happen if they both removed their lenses and spoke frankly.

Kelly stood. "Excuse me." So Johnny's trophy hadn't forgotten how to speak. She walked after Billy, but if she thought she could calm him down, she was even more foolish than Johnny.

"Maybe we could start over," Johnny said. "I think we know where we stand, but maybe there's a way we can understand each other better. I doubt you came all this way just to threaten me."

Now it was just the two of them.

Darcy took a deep breath. "No. No, that's not why we came. Tell me how we can work this out."

"The light came into the world, but the world did not understand it. Perhaps I could help you understand."

"You forget, I grew up having my head stuffed with all of that *understanding*."

"Then maybe I can help you remember."

"I've spent a lifetime trying to forget. Please, Johnny, you know as well as I do that this has nothing to do with understanding. I realize that you believe differently about the nature of things than I do. That doesn't give us the right to even attempt to change each other. Why can't we leave the world to believe what it wants to believe in peace without degradation or accusation? That's all this law does. It stops the finger-pointing. You have a problem with that?"

"Did you read my blog?"

"Half the world has probably read your blog by now."

"Did it call the Muslims *fools*?"

"Yes! Not in so many words, but by publicly claiming that your way is the *only* way, you're calling their way wrong. And in matters of race and religion, calling someone wrong is as inflammatory as calling them *fools*, or even worse. Can you imagine me walking around spouting off that all blacks are immoral or unequal because they are black? We'd have riots again!"

"You're making one mistake in equating the two."

Darcy held up a hand. "Stop. I know. Blacks aren't wrong because they're black any more than Hitler was wrong because he was white. Where you split hairs is that you believe that Muslims *are* wrong about some things, right? But that's *your* belief, Johnny! You have no right to force your morals down their throats."

"When did speaking your beliefs become synonymous with forcing them upon others?"

"When they involve explosive issues, like deciding who's going to hell!"

"Perhaps you're still misunderstanding. I'm condemning no one. I'm only saying that I will follow Jesus."

"But Jesus condemned all who refused to follow him!" Darcy cried. "His was a narrow, bigoted, exclusive faith that has no place in the world today."

"I'll let his words stand on their own," Johnny said. "He died for what he said two thousand years ago, and nothing in this world has changed

since then." He paused, then took a new approach. "Are you also denying the supernatural?"

"Of course not. I'm a living example of the extraordinary. Call it mystical, paranormal, whatever; that doesn't mean the church understands
it any better than the rest of us."

"I'm not speaking for any particular church. Only for the kingdom of
light that has reversed my understanding of reality."

"And you have to throw the *Jesus* element in there? He's the problem,
Johnny, not the light."

Johnny unfolded his legs and stood. He walked to the edge of the
canopy and stared out at the trees into which Billy had disappeared.

Darcy approached him from behind, struck by the broadness of his
shoulders. No telling what kind of hell he'd been through to make him
the man he was today. An intelligent man who understood the wisdom
of her words, with or without glasses.

She drew next to him and followed his gaze. No sign of Billy or Kelly.
"We can change the world, Johnny. I know we can. We could probably ban
war, stop global conflict, even eradicate poverty or disease—if we put our
minds to it."

"The scope of our power is an amazing thing," he said softly. "I would
love to see the Senate stare into my eyes."

She chuckled. "A sight to behold."

"We really do have the power to overcome evil, wherever it shows its
ugly head."

"To rid the world of poverty."

"And disease." He looked down at her, and she could smell his spicy
cologne. "You would use your gift to save the world at any cost,
wouldn't you?"

"I must!"

He turned and walked back into the tent. "And so must I. Which is why
I have to lift up the Light of the World by which *all* men can be saved.
Doing anything less would be like walking away from a dying leper."

He'd set her up.

Darcy decided then, as rage washed through her, that she would not let this man manipulate her again. Not ever.

He bit deeply into an apple and sat back down.

"You're assuming that the world has a disease, Johnny," she said, fuming. "You're also assuming you have the cure. And that, my friend, is the deadliest sickness to face humanity. Arrogance."

"You're forgetting again, Darcy," he said without a hint of reconsideration, "I have seen that disease with my own eyes, before I went blind. I've battled that disease. I've watched how this disease ravages life. And I've seen the cure to this disease. I would be a coward not to warn the world of the disease or to withhold the cure from the afflicted."

"So then that's that. You're flat refusing to listen to sense."

"I'm doing the only thing that makes any real sense."

"By defying this nation's laws? And make no mistake, the law will be held up and what you're doing will be judged by the courts as strictly illegal. Is that what your precious faith has taught you?"

"I'm simply refusing to dim the light that showed us both the way."

"Whatever happened to tolerance?"

"Tolerance of evil *is* evil. That's Black's new game." He faced her. "And I do believe that you, Darcy, have your tongue down his throat."

Her fingers shook.

He took another bite.

"This is going to end very, *very* badly, Johnny Drake."

UNTIL JOHNNY spoke, Billy wasn't sure why the idea of returning to Paradise had struck such a deep chord of horror in his mind or why the chorus rising out of that chord had refused to be silenced.

He long ago assumed he'd pretty much put his childhood to rest. Darcy was the one who still struggled. Sure, he had his bouts with nightmares, his flashbacks, his days of regret, his flogging sessions, but who didn't? Had he ever met a man or woman who did not have mistakes they wished they could take back?

How did it go? To err is to be human, be it a bite out of an apple, or a spilled cup of coffee. Error was a quintessentially human quality. Right?

He'd told himself that his fears were only of the unknown, and that once he returned to Paradise, he would put them to rest. The whole experience could be healing to them both. Put a lid on the past once and for all.

Seeing Paradise from the air had only made the fears perfectly real.

But not until Johnny recounted exactly what had happened in the monastery did Billy realize what that fear actually was.

Himself. He feared himself, because Johnny was right; he had been the one to first take a bite out of that apple. He'd been the one to drag Darcy down into the dungeons to join him.

He was the first sinner.

And he still was, wasn't he? He was afraid he would return to the vomit, like a hungry dog. That he, having once tasted, would want to taste again.

He wouldn't, of course, he'd learned his lesson. But the fear that he might, just maybe might, crushed him with more weight than he'd borne in many years.

The meeting with Johnny was a bust, he knew that already. All their efforts were coming down around them. They would have to enforce the law here in Paradise. Johnny had come here to make his stand, because he knew that more than poetic justice awaited them all here. A confrontation in Paradise would end it all for good.

But Johnny didn't realize that it was he who was going down this time.

Billy walked into a small clearing among the aspens, trying to clear his head. He'd walked away because he didn't trust himself to contain the rage that had welled up in him as Johnny reminded them all who had written Marsuvees Black into existence.

Which only confirmed how much Billy despised Black. He'd never doubted that.

Wanna trip, baby?

Billy shuddered.

"Billy?"

He spun, surprised to see that Kelly had followed him into the trees.

"Sorry, I didn't mean to startle you." She glanced back the way she'd come. "I just wanted to make sure you were okay."

"I'm fine." But it was just one of those meaningless rote statements. They both knew he wasn't within a radar's distance of fine.

"Billy . . ." She turned back to him and studied his eyes. "You sure you're okay?"

It was an awkward moment, he thought. Standing in a clearing with a friend of Johnny's while Johnny spoke to Darcy in dead-end negotiations.

"I think you should go back," he said.

"Yes. Yes, of course."

But she didn't leave. She stood there staring into his eyes with her blue ones. They misted and he realized that she was fighting back tears.

He hadn't considered what those surrounding Johnny must feel like, caught up in his predicament. Kelly realized that things couldn't turn out well here in Paradise, and she'd come to plead on Johnny's behalf. He hardly blamed her.

"Johnny's the one you should talk to," Billy said. "You realize that our hands are tied. We're here out of respect for an old friendship. But if we can't talk Johnny down, the authorities will step in. Laws that aren't enforced are worse than no laws at all."

A tear slipped from her right eye and broke down her cheek. At first glance he'd assumed Kelly was a confident woman, the way her blonde hair framed strong cheekbones. There was a firmness to her eyes suggesting anything but weakness.

But seeing her cry, he wondered if he'd misjudged her. Maybe she was fragile, vulnerable.

She looked away and wiped her cheek dry.

Billy didn't know what to say. "I'm sorry, really. This just isn't—"

"I love him so dearly, you know," she said.

"I'm sure you do. Unfortunately, there really is nothing I can do."

Kelly looked at him again. A slight grin crossed her face. She stepped closer. "You know that's not true, Billy." The grin flattened. "If there's anyone who can do something here, it's you."

"I'm not sure you understand."

"I understand better than you." Kelly lifted her hand and touched his face with a gentle finger, tracing his chin. "I understand him. We've been through hell together, Johnny and I. Do you know how many tears I've wept on his account?"

She walked slowly around him, brushing Billy's shoulder with her fingers.

"I know Johnny better than he knows himself, because in so many ways, I helped him become the man he is today. And I know how far he will go."

"Ma'am, I'm sure—"

"Call me Kelly." She looked into his face again. Tears rose to the rims of her eyes. "Johnny won't stop. I've seen him suffer through torture that would have even you screaming like a baby—he suffers without so much as flinching a muscle. He's a very, very powerful man, Billy. Did you know he was once known as the world's most dangerous assassin? They called him Saint."

He hadn't known, but then he knew very little about Johnny. An assassin named Saint. Go figure.

"What would that make me, Sinner?"

"My Johnny was put on this planet for a very special purpose."

Tears spilled from both eyes now. For a brief moment her resolve to keep from breaking down waned and her lips quivered. But then she drew air through her nostrils and regained what composure she could control.

"You can't stand in his way, Billy."

He wasn't sure what she was asking of him, but the conviction in her voice cut to his heart.

"And I mean that literally," she said. "You can't, because you, too, were put on this planet for a very special purpose."

"Forgive me for not—"

"Shh, shh." She placed a finger on his lips. Traced his mouth. "Don't pretend you don't know what I'm talking about. Don't try to say you don't believe in the power that swims all around us. Do you think your gift came from monkeys?"

What was he supposed to say to that?

"You're very special, Billy. Very, *very* special. Even more special than Johnny."

He was now at a complete loss. She knew something he did not, and it appealed to him like water to a fish.

Kelly leaned forward and kissed him lightly on his lips. "Promise me you'll remember that, Billy. For his sake, remember that."

Then Kelly turned and left him alone in the clearing.

CHAPTER THIRTY-ONE

THE TOWN'S inner circle gathered inside of Smither's Barbeque for their first ad hoc meeting as dusk grayed the western sky, twenty-two men and women by Kat's count, including Joseph Houde, who wasn't really an insider. But then neither was she.

Then again, Steve and Claude and Paula, all of them had a way of making even total strangers feel like insiders within minutes of arriving. Her understanding of friendship had been formed through cliques and alliances forged by kids of similar race and beliefs, and then only after a formal invitation to join the group.

Someone had forgotten to tell Paradise that the customs of society had become more complicated than theirs, which was simply: *Hello there, friend, how you doing this afternoon? Have a seat. Have a bite of my pie?*

The informal meeting had come about for two reasons: One, Johnny had headed out of town with Kelly for a meeting at ten o'clock this morning, and no one had heard a word from him since.

Two, people were coming.

Ben Ringwald, who had to be ninety if he was a day, chuckled. "Well, if we'd a'known this day was coming, we might have built us a few hotels with all that loot everyone's holdin' on to."

"I don't see it being a problem," Claude said. "We have over two hundred homes in this valley. And another hundred barns."

They hung around the bar and two round tables, half of them nursing drinks or popping the peanuts Steve had put out. The restaurant was once a proper bar before they'd converted it, and the old lights behind the counter still advertised Bud Light.

"We aren't putting visitors in barns," Paula said. "Not if I have anything to say about it. We can use the church if we have to, but we have plenty of room to house a hundred guests."

"A hundred? And what if no one turns this tap off? I'd say we already have fifty. Give it a couple of more days and we could have five hundred. You ready for that?"

"Well, it's not the housing I'd worry about. We can put ten to a house if we have to. It's food."

"Got ya covered there," Ben rattled with a twinkle in his eye. "Me and Charlie got us a few extras."

They looked at the old geezer. Richest in the valley on account he owned seven fields, Paula had told Kat. He glanced at their questioning gazes.

He shrugged. "You know Charlie. He's a bit of a survivalist. Trust me, food won't be a problem. Could prob'ly feed five thousand for a week out of that basement."

Kat spoke up. "Umm, excuse me?" They glanced at her. "I'm not sure you guys are getting the whole picture here." She thought Joseph Houde did, judging by his smile. "Any of you been on the Net in the last couple of hours?"

"Sure," Claude said.

"This thing's blowing up out there. I mean really, *actually* blowing up."

"That's just the Net, honey," Paula said.

"Just the Net? The Net is America. People live on the Net. And it's not just Johnny's blog, it's thousands of blogs. It's news stories. It's dialogue centers, chat rooms . . . Half the country is talking about Paradise."

They just looked at her, still not comprehending. To them, life was about getting a kick out of what junior did last night during supper. To the rest of the country, life was quick exchange over the Net about what Johnny did last night.

"Tell them, Joseph."

The reporter chuckled. "She's right. As of a half hour ago, Johnny's blog had over two hundred million hits worldwide and has been referenced over fifty thousand times on the news feeds. Today alone, his name has been viewed over a billion times if you include public chat rooms, unrestricted e-mail, and the rest of it."

"A billion?" Katie Bowers asked, as if she hadn't heard right. "How is that possible?"

"Think about it. One post on a bulletin board might use his name a half dozen times. Turn that into a hundred-page thread. Multiply it by a thousand threads. And that's just bulletin boards."

"Okay, so Johnny's gone and gotten famous on us."

"But it's not *just Johnny*," Joseph said. "There are threads cropping up suggesting that believers who support Johnny should join him in Paradise."

Kat watched realization settle over them.

"I'd say fifty people have rolled into town this afternoon, some of them press. It could be five hundred tomorrow. And it could be three thousand in three days."

"No, that's too much," Paula protested. "What in the world are we supposed to do with three thousand people?"

"Like I said," Claude replied, "We have plenty of barns."

"What do you expect them to sleep on, dirt?"

"The church won't hold that many either," someone said.

"We could set Johnny up on the old theater's roof and let him speak from there," Claude said.

The suggestion came from left field and had little to do with the point.

"I hate to point out the obvious," Joseph said, eyeing Kat as if only he and she were really in the know. She liked the man. "But accommodations are the least of your problems."

"Well, you can't just throw people into a barn and then expect them to live like human beings," Paula said. "What are we going to feed three thousand hungry mouths? Grain?"

"I think he means to say that these people will never arrive," Kat said.

"I thought you said three thousand people would arrive in a couple of days."

"Could," Steve said from behind the bar. "If they aren't stopped."

"Who would stop them?"

No one seemed to want to speak out the obvious, Kat thought. Were they really that naive?

"The law," she said. "The law's gonna come to Paradise."

"Claude's the law," Paula said. Paradise had no real law—they'd elected him as their "sheriff" two months earlier when the spot became vacant. But really, he was just the grocery store owner.

"She means the real law," Steve said.

Joseph stood and walked around the table, cracking his knuckles. "I still don't think you're getting the whole picture here. You do realize that you've broken the law. Not just a little law. Not like running a red light or being drunk in public. The law Congress just passed makes everything you're doing here illegal. A federal offense. They're not just going to sit by and let you keep doing it."

"Well, that's fine, Joseph," Paula said. "We know that. They'll try to keep us from saying what we know to be the truth, and we'll keep saying it, and then who knows what happens? Johnny will help us figure all that out. But in the meantime we have to figure what to do with all these people."

"And if they come in here tomorrow to arrest all of you? What will you do?" Joseph asked.

"Are you asking on the record?" Kat asked. "To publish, I mean?"

He shrugged. "Unless you don't want me to publish it."

Steve set his glass on the bar. "Publish what you want. Johnny will make the call, but I think if they come to arrest us, we'll lock ourselves in the church."

"You'd resist arrest?"

"Not with force, no. Call the church our prison."

"And if they demand that you surrender yourselves?"

"Then we'd have to go," Katie said.

Her husband shook his head. "Well, I ain't walking. If they want to throw me in prison, they's going to have to pick me off the floor."

"What good would that do? You're going. You're going one way or the other."

"Do you really think they would come in here and arrest the whole town?" Paula asked. "Three thousand people?"

"That's the whole point: they won't let it get to three thousand people because they know they can't deal with that many," Kat said. "Which is why they'll probably come in tomorrow and deal with five hundred."

"Even five hundred. They're going to arrest five hundred people?"

"They won't have to arrest five hundred." They all turned and stared at Sally, who sat quietly at the back with her cell phone on the table before her, waiting for a call from her son.

"They'll come for Johnny," she said.

"If they take Johnny, they take us all!" Claude said.

The screen door slammed behind Kat and she twisted around. Johnny faced them from the entry. Kelly followed to his right and slightly behind him.

Sally rushed past Kat and embraced her son. "You're back," she whispered.

"I'm fine, Mother," Johnny said, kissing on her cheek. And then he walked in, like a prophet, come to set his people straight.

"Hello, Johnny," Kat said.

"Hello, Kat. Claude." He scanned the rest. "Looks like the town's growing."

"The newsman thinks we'll have five hundred by tomorrow," Paula said. "We were just talking—"

"Five hundred isn't enough," Johnny said. "We need a gathering of three thousand by morning. Can you do that, Joseph? Tell them that Johnny Drake is calling for three thousand followers to drive through the night and join him in Paradise valley by sunrise."

"You might get more than three thousand."

He acknowledged Joseph with a single nod and faced the old geezer, Ben. "That food you told me about will feed them for a week?"

"Should."

Johnny looked at Steve. "There are still only two roads into this valley?"

"Only two."

"I want you and Claude to get a few men together and go house to house. Collect every weapon in this valley. Every gun, every hunting knife, all of it. Take them all up the road three miles and leave them in a pile, right in the middle of the road. You think you can do that?"

A thin smile crossed Steve's face. "Sure."

"We're going to have us a showdown," Johnny said.

"CRUSH IT!"

Darcy leaned forward in an overstuffed chair and faced Attorney General Lyndsay Nadeau across her dark wood desk. Darcy glanced at Billy, who sat beside her. He hadn't smiled once today that she could remember.

"She's right," Kinnard said, speaking from the couch next to FBI Deputy Director Lawhead. "Crush it. Question is, how? You're not suggesting we roll the National Guard in there."

"That's exactly what I'm suggesting. How else do you enforce the law, with threats? He's blatantly defying the laws of this country. If we don't respond now, send a clear message, we could face much worse than the Kansas City riots. Surely you see that."

Lyndsay watched them, perpetual smile fixed in place. The defiance on the Net was growing exponentially by the hour, but so far it had been contained to the Net. Except for Paradise.

"The president wants this shut down," the White House chief of staff said, turning from the window.

"Of course he does, Annie," Lyndsay said. "We expected something like this, maybe not in quite the same form, but we always knew the first challenges would come over the Net."

"And Johnny Drake's activities clearly break the new law, correct?"

"I've had a team of ten of the country's best attorneys on the case since this broke. There's a lot of noise out there, but the law the president signed isn't the most difficult to interpret. Trust me, what is happening in Colorado right now clearly defies the law in a most egregious manner. It's blatant and purposeful, done to make a very specific point."

"Johnny threatens to test our system in a way it's never been tested," Billy snapped. "This is spreading like fire out there. What are the stats?" He stood and waved off Kinnard. "Forget the stats, we know the problem. And it's going be almost impossible to shut down. You mess with people's faith and they tend to get just a bit lopsided on you. I've been there."

"Precisely why we wrote the laws," Annie said.

"If we don't shut Johnny down in the next twenty-four hours, it's going to be too late."

"I'm afraid I don't see the urgency," Lyndsay said.

"Think!" he snapped. Billy had indeed changed since his visit to Paradise, and Darcy liked him this way. "Today he was joined by roughly fifty people, so as of this moment the three hundred heroes standing in the gap number three hundred and fifty. I guarantee you that will swell to ten, even twenty times that number. Johnny isn't going to be talked down—he'd die first. That's what Darcy and I learned in Paradise today. We have two choices: either accommodate Johnny or silence him with force."

He took a breath.

"I know you won't accommodate him, so the question is whether you want to go in there with force tomorrow, when you only have to deal with a few hundred, or go in later and deal with thousands."

She nodded. "Point made."

Yes, point made, Darcy thought. But that wasn't Billy's true motivation. He'd always supported the new law, but not with the passion he wore on his sleeve now.

She'd tried to engage him on the flight home, but he stared out of the window most of the way, lost in thought. He said that Kelly had made a plea for Johnny, and at first she wondered if he was considering it. But Billy said that Johnny would get exactly what he had coming to him.

"The law will prevail," Darcy said. "We all know that getting the act passed was bound to happen anyway, just like similar laws have been passed in Canada and Europe. Billy and I just greased the wheels. The world can't afford certain freedoms any longer, and it just might take as much blood to purge them as it did to win them."

"And now Johnny is trying to put the brakes on it all," Annie said.

Billy waved his hand. "Keep this isolated to Paradise and Johnny won't be able to do a thing. Let Darcy and me handle this our way."

"Which is?"

"To roll in tomorrow and seal off the valley before we issue our ultimatum. Ignore the hundreds of thousands of voices joining Johnny on the Net and go after him now, before they actually join him on the ground."

"And then?"

"And then enforce the law using whatever force is necessary."

"And just how far do you suggest we take that force, Billy?"

Darcy answered for him, making her support clear.

"As far as it takes to silence Paradise. We want carte blanche from the governor of Colorado, the president, the Justice Department, and whoever orders the National Guard around in situations like this."

"Stop," Lawhead said. "Giving you that kind of authority could undo everything we've accomplished. First of all, activating the National Guard to do anything but assist the Justice Department will demonstrate to the American people that we are enforcing domestic laws with military force. We simply can't afford that for two reasons: One, engaging an American populace with military force is like trying to squash a bee with a sledge-hammer, which will take weeks of preparation and will effectively drive Americans toward insurrection at the national level. Enforcing change with troops will only convince people that they are no longer free *at all.* Secondly, because the National Tolerance Act is a federal statute, it needs to be handled by federal law enforcement."

"Which puts a quick response out of the picture?" Darcy snapped. "We can't afford to let this situation grow. We don't even have time to deliberate. We have to move *now.* Time is on Johnny's side, not ours."

"That's why we sent you two in first," Annie said. "And Johnny sent you both home."

"I'm not saying there isn't a solution," Lawhead said, glancing between them. He stood, clicked a remote, and began to highlight points on a digital map. "Paradise is in a valley, which is to our tactical advantage. Containment by the Colorado National Guard should be simple enough and shouldn't cause a PR disaster. Assuming that the governor will pro-vide us with support from the state patrol as well, we can cordon off the town within hours."

"He will," Darcy said.

Lawhead nodded, understanding her. "Fine." He clicked his remote and brought up another aerial image of Paradise Valley. "With medical and support troops in play, the FBI can begin a systematic sweep from both ends of the valley in coordinated tactical groups. We can fly them out from Quantico if necessary. A component of the Air National Guard can provide overwatch and strategic direction. The state patrol will put out descriptions, the guard will hold the line, and the FBI will prosecute the arrests while air support provides intel. It could work."

"It has to," Billy said. "What are the challenges?"

"Warrants and timing." Lawhead dropped his pencil on the table. "Justice won't arrest on suspicion alone. We need federal papers authorizing these arrests. And getting interagency cooperation will take twenty-four to seventy-two hours. In the meantime, the Net will be counting their score while we're still putting our pieces on the board."

Pause. "I didn't say it would be quick. But this is legal, and it could work: the FBI serves the warrants, the guard provides medical support and overwatch, and the DOJ and state get to preserve credibility."

Darcy removed her sunglasses, set them on the table for all to see. "Seventy-two hours is two days too long."

Lawhead planted his palms on the table and eyed her through his own spectacles. "I can't make miracles any more than you can talk Johnny Drake into a truce. You asked me for a legal solution that involved timing, force, and terrain. This is what I've got."

"Enough." Kinnard stared at them. "You have several points that I think could be refined for our purposes. One, the attorney general can supply—or demand—the warrants to make this legal. Two, the sedition currently growing in Paradise is still small enough to contain without diverting traffic. Three, because Paradise is in a valley, we can divert or block over 80 percent of the satellite-based communications, and simultaneously shield outgoing calls and uplinks."

Darcy bit into the idea. "No coverage means no media. No media means we can act without hesitation."

That settled them all.

"How far do we take this?" Billy asked.

Darcy frowned. "As far as we have to."

"Legally . . ." Lawhead dipped his head and thought a moment. "With the warrants and the timing . . . It could work. But we need the governor, the Justice Department, and a good window of timing. The public spin we can handle later."

"We can get all that," Kinnard said softly.

"Billy and I can," Darcy said, "make this happen."

"You're actually suggesting we place part of our national armed forces in your hands?" Lyndsay asked with a hint of incredulity.

None of this had been planned, but Darcy saw no reason to mince words. "Why not? We all know that using force on Paradise is the right thing to do given the laws of the nation. Would you prefer that I speak to you more directly, Lyndsay?"

The attorney general was quiet for a moment. "Be careful, Darcy. You're on very thin ice here."

"Get over yourself," Billy said. "Everything Darcy's suggesting is going to happen anyway. Tell me where we're wrong."

"You're not," Annie said, "unless you're actually hoping to spill blood in that valley."

Billy tipped his head back with exasperation. "I'm not suggesting you drop a bomb on Paradise. But Johnny has to believe that I could. *I* could. Not some commander who has no personal stake in the operation. Only then do we stand a frog's chance in the boiling pot of getting him to roll over."

"You're suggesting a bluff," Lawhead said. "Knowing that these people won't actually die for their position. And I tend to agree, Lyndsay. For all their talk, I can't imagine too many Americans willing to give their lives for the right to follow a guy who's been dead for two thousand years."

"They don't believe he's dead," Annie said.

"Yes, well, follow a ghost, then. Point is, they will capitulate if led to believe that the alternative is a prison sentence or a bomb."

"It only works if the bluff has teeth," Billy said.

"You'd do nothing without my personal approval," the attorney general said.

"Naturally."

We don't need you, you old prune, Darcy thought. *You don't think we could rip off those eyeglasses and make you do this anyway? I could probably make you commit suicide. Who doesn't believe, deep down inside, that they deserve to be dead?*

She'd never considered the possibility before. Maybe she should try it out on Johnny. Looking at Billy's set jaw, the dark circles under his eyes, the pale green eyes, she thought Billy just might approve. She was being influenced by his hatred. And honestly, it was all a bit exciting.

CHAPTER THIRTY-TWO

Day Twenty

"NOW, YOU get your pretty little head down when I say," old Ben said, eying Kat with a twinkle in his eyes.

"Got it."

He winked at her in the dawn light. "Time to go boom."

She winked back. "Boom, boom."

Steve placed his hand on her arm and pulled. "Down."

Kat gazed up the road one last time. It hadn't taken much to twist Steve into letting her tag along. She was from the city, she'd argued— used to much worse than any of this.

They'd laid out the plan with Johnny last night. There were only two roads leading into Paradise, this one heading west toward Delta, and the same one heading north out of Paradise. They would welcome visitors through the night, explain their plan, turn all weapons over as a symbolic gesture caught on film by Joseph and three other news crews, then blow both roads at daybreak. If anybody wanted out or in, a helicopter would be available.

Johnny was locking Paradise down and locking its artillery out.

As instructed, Steve and company had gone house to house, collecting two pickup loads of weapons, which now sat a hundred yards outside the blast zone with a large sign in the window that read: *Please don't lose. We'd like these back.*

Claude Bowers and Chris Ingles were blowing the northern road. Steve and Ben had selected this particular spot on the western road because of the cliffs on either side. Bring down all that rock and it would take heavy equipment at least a few days to clear the rubble, then another couple to rebuild the road.

It had taken them a couple of hours to rig the dynamite along the cliff walls and rig the detonator lines.

"You ready, Ben?"

He glanced at Jeremiah and Brodie, who'd been scurrying around like mountain goats for the last hour, setting charges.

"We're good. Let her rip."

"Cover your ears," Steve instructed.

Kat ducked low on her knees and pushed her palms against her ears. Beside her, Ben, who'd said plenty about how he preferred the old ways over all the fancy electronic wireless gizmos, gripped an ancient plunger with his wrinkled hand. "Fire in the hole."

He shoved the handle down.

Ka-boom!

The earth shook and the booms kept coming as huge slabs of rock tumbled from the cliff and slammed onto the road. Small pieces of gravel rained on them.

"Stay down!" Steve covered her back with his big arm. "Just stay down!"

But there was no need. The debris stopped falling and the show was over. Kat was the first on her feet, staring at the road.

Where the road *had been*, to be more precise. Now a mountain of rock at least fifty feet high filled the gap between the cliffs.

"Well now, that oughta discourage any pranksters," Ben cackled.

"You think the trucks got it?" Jeremiah asked.

"I guess we'll find out in a week."

They piled into Ben's new Lexus SUV and sped back into Paradise, a mile down the road.

As it turned out, 2,713 supporters had responded to the call to join Johnny in Paradise, mostly driving in from the Four Corners states but also as far as Los Angeles, California, to the west and Springfield, Missouri, to the east. (Jamie Peterson, the college kid who'd driven from Springfield, admitted to breaking every possible speed limit law on the way, just managing to fly past the checkpoint in his cobalt blue Corvette at dawn.)

Four people had elected to leave the valley, one of them pregnant, two more who'd just wandered in the day before to see what all the fuss was about, and one hitchhiker who was trying to get to Denver.

The gathering in Paradise stood at just over 3000, up from a population of just under three hundred twenty-four hours earlier. And despite all of her worrying, once Paula Smither settled for making do, she'd gotten them all situated just fine. The regulars opened their homes to as many as could sleep comfortably, seven or eight, which took care of two-thirds of the visitors. The rest preferred the church, the rec center, or the barns anyway. They were here because they'd been born into the kingdom of light, not because they wanted a five-star vacation getaway.

Ben and Charlie's food stash consisted mostly of dried soup packages. Pea soup, corn soup, tortilla soup without the tortillas, chicken noodle soup, turkey soup. And those were just the ones Kat could remember.

Looked like they would be eating soup and fruit for breakfast, lunch, and dinner. Which, again, was fine, Paula had decided. Wasn't no five-star resort, wasn't no five-star food.

Kat rode into Paradise at six thirty with Steve and Ben. The street was still quiet this early, but she immediately noticed two changes.

First change, the sheer number of cars. They were parked everywhere except for the town center, which they were keeping clear. Had to be a thousand cars strewn throughout all the alleys and surrounding fields.

Second change was the plywood platform Father Yordon and a team of a dozen men had built along the side of the old theater, looking out over the center of town and the church lawn. They'd built it tall, at least five feet, so that the whole town could see whoever was talking up there. They'd even set up a sound system with two black speakers balanced on top of crates.

Word had gone out: they would gather at eight.

Short on sleep, Kat slipped into the Smithers' house on Main Street, rolled onto her bed in the back bedroom, and was asleep before the first sounds of waking could mess with her mind.

She woke to a "Check, check, check," over an amplifier at 7:59 by the wall clock, and sat up with a start.

They'd started?

"Could I have your attention?" Yordon's voice rang out over the town. "Ladies and gentlemen, your attention up here please."

Kat splashed water on her face, dabbed it dry, ran out the front door, and pulled up sharply.

She gasped. The crowd started at the bottom of the Smithers' porch and stretched across the whole center of town to the field on the other side of the church lawn. No street that she could see, no lawn, nothing but people standing and looking up at Father Yordon on the platform.

Ordinary people dressed in everything from jeans to skirts, even a few business suits. A black boy of about ten stood beside the planter at the bottom of the porch steps, staring up at Kat. His closely shaven head was almost perfectly round.

Kat smiled and nodded. The boy grinned back, all gum except for one buck tooth.

Father Yordon was welcoming the people, giving them some basic instructions about keeping order. Sanitation. Food.

A helicopter chopped overhead, and Kat saw with a glance that there were two, actually, in army olive-drab green.

She returned her gaze to the crowd. It struck her that so many people had traveled so far at the drop of a hat to stand up for what was to them the essence of life. She remembered stumbling across a quote by George Washington saying that it was ". . . impossible to rightly govern a nation without God and the Bible," and she'd wondered what that meant about governing a school. And what about a town?

Johnny had made it clear in his blog that he wasn't as interested in politics as he was interested in matters of the heart. Faith in God. Following Jesus.

So all of these people had read that blog and come to follow Jesus with Johnny. To Kat, who'd only just stepped into the kingdom two weeks ago, the sight was an incredible thing.

The kingdom of truth wasn't just her alone in the high school.

It wasn't just her and Johnny.

It wasn't just a church full of old people in the Colorado mountains.

It was these 3,000 pilgrims who'd traveled hours to stand and be heard for Jesus. He'd been slain two thousand years ago, but he'd left the world with this.

Kat felt such a surge of gratitude that she didn't think she could contain it. Why the whole world didn't rush here and stand as one was beyond her.

Father Yordon was still going on about organization, which she knew was important. But she just couldn't bring herself to care. The helicopters were flying overhead, pilots' jaws probably dropped at the scene below. The Net was flooded, yes indeed, truly flooded with blogs and news from this very small town. The whole world had its eye on Paradise, and she was here because one blind man had shown her the light.

"Go, Johnny!" she screamed.

Her cry rang out over the crowd, which turned as one and stared at the dark-skinned girl standing on the porch next to Smither's Barbeque.

She'd actually screamed that?

"Go, Johnny!" The toothless black boy had seen fit to match her cry.

And then they all did, a dozen at first and swelling to three thousand voices calling for their leader.

"Johnny! Johnny! Johnny!"

But Johnny was nowhere to be seen.

Not yet.

CHAPTER THIRTY-THREE

"HOW LONG?" Billy demanded.

"Three days, four tops." Kinnard stood on a plateau high above Paradise, eyeing the wrecked roads through his glasses. "Assuming the Army Corps of Engineers can get their gear here before nightfall. You gotta hand it to Johnny—he knows what he's doing."

Darcy stood to one side watching Billy pace, white-faced.

"I don't care when they arrive, they can work by lights if they have to. We need those roads clear."

"And they will be. Three days," Kinnard said. "We'll have plans for an extraction long before that. We can't wait three days to deal with Johnny."

Darcy lifted her binoculars and stared at the valley again. They'd gotten the thumbs-up to bring in the National Guard late last night—no martyrs, not even one, Lyndsay warned—and immediately issued the orders to close the valley. But Johnny had beaten them to it. The first unit of the National Guard of the 947th Engineer Company arrived from Grand Junction to find both ends of the highway into the valley completely blown.

Apart from the single gathering earlier in the day, there had been no organized activity. Darcy wondered what they were eating. No sign of

Johnny, not even at the meeting. He was wisely staying out of the line of the snipers brought in by the FBI's Hostage Rescue Team and the Colorado National Guard, 5/19th Airborne Special Forces. They had the area mapped and scouted, but . . .

"Somehow I doubt extracting Johnny will be that easy," she said, lowering her binoculars.

Kinnard nodded. "Saint."

"You know about his days as an assassin?" Billy demanded.

"He was known as Saint. From what I can gather, Johnny was one formidable opponent, especially with a rifle."

"Johnny was an assassin?" Darcy asked. "So then what makes you think we can waltz in there and take him out?"

"No martyrs, remember?"

"Not take him out as in kill him," Billy snapped. "She means extract him. And that's not the point, Darcy. The point is to show him what he's up against, make him second-guess himself."

A large double-bladed helicopter thumped in from the north, settled to the ground behind them, and emptied its cargo onto the high mesa. Several large tents had already been erected in the guard's staging base, and this load brought another dozen with three times that many soldiers armed to the teeth.

A perimeter had already been established around the valley with seventeen carefully placed teams dug in and armed. Only two of these teams were responsible for the roads. The rest had taken up positions that protected any traffic in or out, on foot or by horse. They had enough rifles trained on Paradise to make the president pucker right up, no doubt about that.

"Yes, of course, give time for negotiations, we've all heard that," she said. "But we all also know that Johnny's not going to negotiate. Not without some juice."

"We'll force him to negotiate!"

The National Guard were being led on the ground by a Ranger battalion flown in from Fort Carson and commanded by a Colonel Eric Abernathy.

Kinnard took a call from the colonel, something about rules of engagement, civil response, and logistical support. Darcy eased over to Billy and
took his arm, guiding him away from Kinnard.

"Is it really necessary to go through all these motions?" she whispered
quickly. "I can change them all!"

"You don't know that. We can't change Johnny!"

"No? Maybe not, but his bringing all these people will work with him,
I'm convinced of it."

"If you think you can change their minds—"

"I can! Drop me in the middle of that crowd down there and I'll
show you."

"And if you can't? You expect them to revolt against their beloved
Johnny?"

She was appalled by his lack of confidence in her.

"Did I or did I not convince the whole of Congress to revolt against
their beloved Constitution?"

"Half of them already wanted to change it. I'm just saying"—he faced
the town far below, scowling with bitterness—"Johnny wants a fight, and I
swear, I'm going to give him his fight. And this time it won't just be with
words."

"So you're just going to give up on me?" she demanded.

"I'm going to save you!" he cried. And she knew then that he was
starting to lose it. His whole past had caught up to him in the last week,
and he was starting to set reason aside to protect himself from it.

As are you, Darcy.

She ripped off her glasses. "Take off your glasses."

"Now?"

"Yes, now!" she screamed.

Kinnard spun around, ear still plastered to the phone, but he meant
nothing to her now. She stepped forward and plucked Billy's glasses
from his face.

Bore into his eyes with her own.

"You love me, Billy, but if you think you can save me you're not think-ing straight. I'm here to save *you*. What have you ever done to save me? It's not in your blood—accept it. You've always been an impetuous gam-bler, willing to throw yourself to the wolves for the chance to be crowned the wolf slayer. This time we will do things my way, you hear me? You're not taking me down with you again!"

Billy's face wrinkled with pain. She knew she'd been far too harsh, pushing him to the point where he might resent her words and obey her out of pure obligation.

But she was honestly afraid for him. He was beginning to lose himself in this whole affair.

"I want you to make them take me down there now, set me in the middle of the town down there"—she shoved a finger down toward the valley—"and let me deliver this ultimatum of yours in person."

Kinnard took a step toward them. "Are you two—"

"Shut up, Kinnard!" she snapped.

Billy's eyes leaked trails of tears. He looked both terrified and bitter at once, and Darcy felt a tinge of regret.

"Sorry to put it like that, Billy." She shoved her glasses back on. "I'm just a bit out of whack myself."

Billy spun to Kinnard. "Tell them we're going down."

"I'm not sure that's really a good idea."

Darcy drilled him with a glare. "Do you want an earful as well?"

"Just thinking of your safety."

"Johnny isn't going to guillotine us, you idiot. We're going to guillo-tine him!" she said. "It's time he learned what the stakes are."

THERE WERE only a couple hundred people milling about the center of town when the old Apache settled onto the church lawn and barely waited for Darcy and Billy to tumble out before screwing back into the sky.

She stood next to him beneath the pulsating air, long hair flying every which direction, calf-length black dress buffeted about, arms limp by her sides. She scanned the eyes that watched her from the perimeter.

"Take your glasses off and tell me what they're thinking," she instructed.

He did so, but must have gotten nothing, because he stepped closer to a group loitering by Smither's Barbeque. Used to be Smither's Saloon, if she remembered right.

Darcy followed by his side. "Anything?"

"They're wondering who we are. Some fear. Mostly curiosity."

"Who has the fear?"

"The one in the white shirt."

Darcy strode toward a woman in her forties, dressed in jeans and a white, sleeveless blouse and tennis shoes. No sunglasses, that was good. Hardly any of them wore sunglasses.

She plucked her own from her face. "You there in the white blouse, what's your name?"

The woman blinked, already aware of some subtle change in her own disposition. Darcy bore into her with her eyes and clearly annunciated each word.

"What is your name?"

"Holly."

"You're afraid, aren't you, Holly?"

Tears sprang to the woman's eyes, but she didn't respond.

"Fact is, you're all afraid," Darcy said, running her eyes over the group. "You're so afraid, that I think you'll demand to be taken out of here, to safety."

The woman in the white blouse had frozen, though confusion batted at her eyes.

Darcy had done this enough to know that her power was at its greatest when she exerted the full force of her own passion into each word. And at the moment, her passion was fueled by the frustration of Johnny having compelled her halfway across the United States not once, but twice now because he wanted men in clerical collars to be able to point their fingers at the world.

She ground her molars and looked into each of their eyes. "The National Guard is preparing to invade this valley. People will die. Innocent lives will be lost. But you've forced their hand, and so now you may die."

"No."

"Oh yes, Holly. Yes, *yes*." She'd exaggerated for effect, and Holly responded.

The woman was trembling head to foot, as were five others, hands to their mouths, shaking without being able to fully comprehend where the extreme emotion was coming from. Without realizing it, they were facing more than the simple fear of the National Guard.

"They're coming for you," Darcy said. "You're all terrified for good reason, and you're going to demand that Johnny take you out of here." She offered them a gentle smile and stopped ten feet from them. "Aren't you?"

"Leave?" one of them asked. A thin brunette.

"Yes, leave this valley."

"No," said Holly. She was crying earnestly now. "No, you don't understand, we can't leave."

Darcy blinked. "Oh? But you *will* leave!"

"No."

"Yes, yes, you *will* leave."

A moment of silent stalemate.

"No!" the woman screamed. "No, you can't make me leave. I will *not* be silenced! I will *not* deny the love of my Christ! Take my head, take my home, take my husband, but you will not take my heart!"

Darcy was too stunned to reply. The woman was resisting her? Her mind scrambled for better reasoning. Surely she could find and act on the morsel of doubt in this woman's mind. That sliver of fear. That spot that resented God, even.

"You've betrayed Christ before," she said.

"Yes!" The woman's hands flew to her face and she wept into them bitterly. "Yes! And I can't betray him again. Never!"

She was being defied? For the first time since Darcy had understood her gift, she feared that it might fail her. But she couldn't let that happen.

"You'll all leave!" she screamed at the women. "You're all whores who have no understanding of how dangerous your own betrayal really is, and you're terrified to stand here one more moment."

Holly began to wail through her hands, and the moment her volume rose, the rest of them began to weep with her.

"Run. Out! Get out of this valley. Don't be stupid, you hear me? Don't you dare be fools for the sake of a Christ you can't even see!"

She might have pulled the plug from their resolve. But instead of running from the town, screaming about their own foolishness, they fell to the ground, writhing in sobs, praying—*praying!*—begging to be forgiven.

"Have mercy on us sinners, Son of David! Have mercy on us sinners, Jesus Christ!"

She realized too late that she'd pushed them toward their beliefs, not away. Watching these women, she wasn't sure she *could* push them from their faith.

Darcy became aware of a murmur mixed with soft cries behind her. She spun, half expecting to see Johnny standing there. But it wasn't Johnny. Another five hundred at least had gathered and were watching the women on the ground, crying with them, some kneeling, some with their faces in their hands, some just staring with wet eyes.

The sight sliced through her chest like a white-hot blade. She didn't dare speak. Billy was beside her, eyes wide, truly afraid.

"Call the chopper," she managed. "Get us out of here."

"Darcy!"

There was no mistaking the sound of Johnny's voice. She turned back to Smither's Barbeque, where Holly and the others were now sobbing softly, and saw Johnny standing to the right of the building.

"I have something to show you."

"No," Billy shouted, but his voice sounded like a hoarse whisper.

"Take one look, Billy," Johnny challenged. "If you don't like what you see, then leave."

Billy thrust out his right arm and pointed at Johnny. "You have twenty-four hours from sunset today to surrender yourself before we use force." His fiery eyes scanned the crowd. "All of you, twenty-four hours, and then this game of yours comes to an end. You've been warned!"

"Then we have some time, Billy," Johnny said calmly. "Or would you prefer the camera told the world"—he indicated a newsman who was filming them—"that Billy and Darcy have forgotten how to negotiate?"

Darcy felt heat sting her face.

"We have to go with him," she said softly to Billy. "We're on. *Live.*"

"He's . . . he's . . ." Billy voice was laced with panic. "He's manipulating—"

"We have to give negotiation its due course." She turned and looked into his eyes. "I love you, Billy. I will be with you all the way. We're stronger than Johnny. You can do this. You can set aside your fear of Black and the memories that haunt you, because I am with you."

His face melted like snow under the heat of each word.

Darcy took his hand, at the risk of appearing juvenile in the camera's eye, and strode toward Johnny.

CHAPTER THIRTY-FOUR

THE SUN had sunk below the surrounding cliffs by the time Johnny's chopper settled into the old canyon above Paradise. Billy and Darcy had dutifully climbed aboard the helicopter behind the old theater. The flight to the upper canyon that had once housed the hidden monastery took seven wordless minutes.

It occurred to her that they had Johnny in their grasp. They could force the pilot to fly them to the staging plateau, where several hundred armed National Guardsmen awaited a command from the Special Forces within their indirect command.

But a single glance told her that Johnny was ahead of her. The pilot wore a helmet with a dark visor that shielded his eyes from the sun and, more importantly, from her. The helmet had been fixed to a strap that ran under his arms. There was no way they could get it off without brute force.

The chopper settled on the sand long enough for them to step out before being snatched back into the sky by blades that bit hard into the air.

"Follow me," Johnny said, heading up the canyon.

Darcy let her eyes follow the sheer rock walls on either side as silence replaced the chopper's whine. The white sand was littered with chunks of granite that had tumbled from the cliffs. The center of the canyon reminded her of a huge bowling lane strewn with broken balls. Larger boulders, taller than she, stood along the canyon walls.

"I don't like this," Billy said. "We shouldn't have gone down to the town in the first place, and we shouldn't have come up here."

"Yeah, well, sometimes you have to take the bull by the horns," she said.

He walked forward, face set. They followed Johnny up the canyon ten paces behind.

Around the bend.

The cliff on their left had been brought down in a landside and now covered the whole section of canyon that had once housed the monastery. A small cabin sat at the base of the slide.

Darcy was staring at her childhood, and the memories she'd worked so hard to bury now exploded to the surface.

Monks hurrying up and down the halls, gathering the children for dinner.

Classes with the others in an expansive library, learning of virtue, always virtue.

The dungeons that Billy had led her into. The worms. The Books of History from which all three had gotten their powers. All there, beneath the pile of boulders that had obliterated it.

"Doesn't look so bad," Billy said, stepping closer.

Johnny turned around and faced them, dark glasses in place. "Not so bad, Billy." He spread his arms wide. "The birthplace of unique evil never looked so innocuous."

"What evil? I see rocks and sand and a cabin. Your finger pointing won't change the fact that you have three thousand people trapped in a valley, facing their deaths." He flipped open his phone.

"I wouldn't do that," Johnny said, easing toward a boulder half his height.

"You don't think they know exactly where we are?"

Johnny suddenly had a pistol in his hand. "Problem is, so do I." He spun the weapon and caught it neatly in his palm. "I suggest you tell them to give us some space. We need to talk."

Billy hesitated. Judging by the way Johnny handled the gun, the rumors about him were true. Darcy had no doubt that he could kill them both before they had the time to notice.

"I could shoot the phone out of your hand, but you might lose a finger—it's been awhile. Please, Billy, tell Kinnard you're fine. We're just trying to understand some things."

Billy frowned and spoke into the phone. "Yes, we're fine. No, leave us here in the canyon."

"Pull back any observation posts," Johnny said.

"Pull back the spotter on the north face. I'll call for a chopper when we're ready." He snapped the phone closed.

Johnny tossed the gun into the sand and held up his hands in a sign of good faith. "Thank you."

Darcy clasped her hands behind her back and walked to her right, gazing at the piles of rock, trying to imagine the old entry to the monastery. "You really think dragging us back here will help you? I hate to disappoint you, Johnny, but we're here about our future. Clearly, our past is buried."

"On the contrary, this is all about the past," he said. "It's about what happened two thousand years ago. What happened twelve years ago. What happened last week. The truth doesn't change over time."

"Is that what lies under that pile of rocks? The truth? I think we were fed lies."

"Then why don't we put it to a test?"

She knew immediately what he had in mind.

"You want us to remove our glasses and see what happens, is that it?"

"I want you to use your gifts. They were given to you for good, not evil. Billy, search my mind, show me where my doubts hide. Darcy, persuade me of the errors in my way of thinking. I'll remove my glasses and let you speak to me clearly."

The notion put Darcy on guard. Why would he subject himself to such a baring of his soul?

Then she remembered Holly down in Paradise.

"If you don't see the sense of our way," she said, "you only prove that your deception runs all the way into your bones."

"Who cares about that?" Billy said. "He intends to make us look into *his* eyes." To Johnny: "Do we look like morons to you?"

"You do. But looks can be deceiving. My eyes are harmless. They will expose only truth, unless I decide to show you more."

"More?"

He hesitated. "Nothing that will hurt you. But I want you to see your souls, the way they really are, and that sometimes can be painful. You're not afraid of yourselves, are you?"

Darcy found the idea of staring into her own soul a bit esoteric but nonetheless unnerving.

"No," Billy said. "No, Darcy, I'm telling you this is a bad idea."

She looked at Johnny. "You heard him. It's a bad idea."

"Why?"

She faced Billy again. "Why, Billy?"

"Because he's not telling us something. He knows that his eyes can do something . . ." The tightness in his voice betrayed his fear.

"My eyes can show the truth. And only then if you are open to it."

Johnny lifted his hands and removed his glasses. His eyes were as blue as the sky. Nothing that looked threatening.

"You're not seeing my real eyes," he said. "I have the power to do a few tricks, like turn my eyes blue. Basic illusions. But that's not what we're interested in here, are we?"

"It doesn't matter what we see, then," Billy said. "How would you expect us to think that anything you show us isn't just an illusion? A hundred false faith healers have turned the world into cynics. So what are you, the ultimate miracle worker for the entire world to see? You're a fake!"

"Then you'll be fine, Billy. You'll know if what you see is just an illusion. Skeptics aren't easily won over."

Darcy stared at his blue eyes. Here it was then, three grown children with special powers facing off in the very canyon where they had been granted those powers. The world gathered on the Net for one of the largest global ideological battles it had yet faced, but this was the epicenter.

In the end there was Billy, Johnny, and Darcy.

Johnny took a step toward her, eyeing her with deep pools of impossible blue. "You've rejected the faith, but surely you remember your lessons. The account of the leader who swore to kill every follower of the Way, these so-called Christians, after they'd crucified Jesus. He rounded them up wherever they could be found, do you remember?"

"A story," she said.

"Verified by numerous historical documents. An accurate account."

"So what?"

"He took a journey to Damascus to bring followers of the Way to justice, just like you and Billy are doing here. But that journey changed his life dramatically. Instead of stomping out the Way, he vowed to spend his life speaking the truth about Jesus. What happened to bring about such a radical transformation from hatred to devotion, Darcy? Do you remember?"

"Of course she remembers," Billy snapped. "What are you now, an angel of light?"

Johnny kept his eyes on Darcy. "That's right, Billy, the apostle Paul saw a light on the road. A blinding shaft of truth that bared his soul and threw him to his knees."

Darcy reached up and snatched her glasses from her eyes. "Fine, Johnny. Show me your light. Do your tricks. The world's waiting."

He stared at her for a moment, then looked at Billy.

"And you?"

Billy's voice was laced with bitterness. "You think dragging us through the mud, shoving our pitiful failures in our faces, spitting on us when we're down will do anything more than prove what Darcy convinced me of a week ago?"

He meant that freedom from hate speech was grounded in hate, not love. But at the moment, Billy seemed to have cornered hate speech. He'd lost a bit of perspective, Darcy thought.

"Just because the truth disturbs someone doesn't make speaking that truth hate speech," Johnny said.

"It's nothing more than *your* version of the truth."

"Then take off your glasses, Billy, and see if it should be your version as well . . . or not."

Billy ripped his glasses off, and Johnny's thoughts flowed into his mind like a torrent. They locked eyes for a few long seconds that stretched into ten.

Darcy guessed by the deepening scowl on Billy's face that he was learning what they already knew: Johnny was indeed deceived by his own rhetoric. To the marrow of his bones he believed that he was speaking not only the truth but the only truth.

"Look at me, Johnny," Darcy said.

He blinked and turned his eyes to her.

She started to slowly walk toward him, light on the sand. "You will not use your eyes on me, Johnny. You respect me too much to force me against my will, and really, I don't want to hear any more of what you have to offer."

He took a step back, undoubtedly unprepared for the power in her voice. She pressed.

"Even if your version of truth has merit, you have to respect those who dislike it. Speaking of it in any arena where it is uninvited, such as in this country, is wrong."

Johnny's blue eyes did not blink. She wondered what it was like to see the way he saw, in lights and shapes rather than in color or texture.

"I do not want you to be rude to me, Johnny."

"Was Jesus rude to the money changers he drove from the temple?" Johnny asked.

"Yes. As a matter of fact, he was. And I don't want you to treat me that way. This is America, not ancient Palestine. We've grown up since then, don't you think?"

"The world has fallen into a dark pit. Is it rude or hateful to point the way to the light?"

She reached him and lifted her hand to his face. Rubbed her thumb on his cheek. His flesh was hot to her touch, closely shaven, smooth.

"I think the world likes this dark pit. So please shut up and let us all grope around in the dark if that's what we want to do."

He was feeling the full brunt of her words; she could see it in the sweat on his forehead. But she hadn't tested him yet, not really.

"I must follow that light," he said softly.

"You should join us, Johnny."

Why did she keep coming back to that? Because she liked Johnny, deep down where she had no business liking him. He was so wrong, so misguided, and so deceived, but she found his conviction nearly irresistible.

"Would you like to kiss me, Johnny?"

He didn't respond, so she turned back to Billy, smiling. "Does he want to kiss me, Billy?"

She realized in a flash that this tack was entirely inappropriate. Billy frowned bitterly and his eyes were dark with anger. But before she could backpedal, his frown morphed into a wide scream of raw terror.

It was as if a bucket of black fear had been thrown in his face, so sudden was the change. He stumbled back a step, threw his hands to his face, and shredded the air with a scream that made her hair stand on end.

She spun back to Johnny. His eyes were fixed over her shoulders on Billy. Black eyes, as black as polished coal.

She'd asked him not to use his eyes on her, but she'd said nothing about Billy, and now Billy was seeing whatever Johnny showed him.

"Stop it!" she cried. But he stared on, unaffected.

She slapped his face. "Stop it, I said!"

He blinked and looked at her, now with white eyes.

"It's just the truth, Darcy," he said, swallowing hard. "Please let me show you the truth. For their sakes, for the sake of those in Paradise. For all of our sakes!"

"Oh, God!" Billy wailed behind her. "Oh, my God, my God . . ." He sounded like a father who was helplessly watching his children being brutalized. Weeping uncontrollably.

"God, God, God!"

She whirled back and watched Billy fall to his knees, gripping his hair with both hands, eyes clenched.

"What did you do to him?"

"The truth . . ."

Darcy spun back. "If that's the truth, the world doesn't need it! Let him go!"

"I don't—"

She slapped him again. "Let him go, now!"

"I don't have him!" Johnny yelled. His eyes flashed blue.

"Oh, my God, my God," Billy sobbed. "What . . . what was . . ."

"Me, Billy." The voice came low, guttural like a rolling boulder from the direction of the cabin behind Johnny, flattening all other sound in the canyon.

Darcy's heart crashed into her throat at the sound of his voice. A voice she couldn't possibly forget. The one that had haunted her nightmares for thirteen years and made her weep on the therapist's couch so many times.

Black.

Johnny jerked around, and she saw Marsuvees Black over his shoulder even as he turned.

Black stood in the cabin's opened doorway, dressed in a black trench coat, black polyester pants, black Stetson hat. Silver-tipped black boots.

He stood there, leaning on the doorjamb with one ankle crossed over the other, chewing on a small twig. The left corner of his mouth suggested a grin, and his sparkling eyes confirmed it.

"You do remember me, don't you? Billy?"

He looked at Johnny and the grin faded.

"Keep your tricks, John-John. I've been staring at myself for thirteen years and I'm getting to like what I see. Granted, some of the older mes didn't cut the mustard, so to speak, but I do think I've hit upon the right ingredients this time. Don't you?"

"Tell him to tell you who he really is, Darcy," Johnny said. "At least give me that much."

"I know who he is."

"Pray, do tell," Black said, and stepped from the cabin, strutting toward them. "Who am I, Darcy?"

"You're something written from the books, words that have taken flesh."

"More, baby, more. Don't shortchange me now after all we've been through."

She said what was on the top of her mind. "You're an incarnation of evil." Then louder: "The demon in the dark, the ghost who whispers in the night. The bogeyman, if you want. One iteration of the figment of all our imaginations."

He stopped at that, as if disappointed, then walked on. "You reduce me to something that goes bump in the night? I expected more from you, Darcy. I'm not that plastic, not by a long shot."

"I want you to stop where you are," she said. But he continued as if he hadn't heard her, impervious to her voice. She began to fear him in earnest.

"Raw evil," he said. "Like a raw steak, just meat and blood. The devil incarnate. But there's more, baby, so much more. You've gone and saved the juiciest detail for last, you naughty little girl."

Darcy was struck by the undeniable fact that Black's very presence validated at least part of what Johnny had claimed.

"Tell me who I am!" Black snarled, lips twisted and wet. Darcy wanted to run. Her hands went cold and her breathing stopped.

Only then did she realize that he was staring past her at Billy. He was demanding that Billy confess the full truth.

"Tell me, you worthless brat. Tell me!"

"You're me!" Billy cried. He was on his knees and his arms were spread and his face was twisted in anguish. "I made you!"

Black strode past her and Johnny as if they didn't exist. His focus bore into Billy, who cowered on the ground, shaking.

"Almost. Let's be precise here. *You* are *me*, Billy. Say it."

"I am you!" Billy cried. "I am you!"

"You need me, Billy. Tell them."

He shook, robbed of breath.

"Leave him!" Johnny yelled. "You have no right to him."

Black halted midstride, slowly turned around, black eyes like holes in his face, head tilted to one side. "*Au contraire.* I *own* him."

He turned, grabbed Billy by the collar, and jerked him to his feet. But instead of verbally abusing him as Darcy expected, he wiped the tears from Billy's face, then pulled him close and hugged him.

"It's okay, Billy. You're okay now. I'm here."

Billy hung on Black's shoulder, limp like a rag doll and sobbing.

Darcy felt numb. She couldn't fathom the desperation that had brought Billy to this point, and seeing him reduced to such a pitiful state made her want to cry. She had to help him. But they'd come here to talk sense into Johnny, not face Billy's demons.

What if this was all just a trick played by Johnny's eyes to make a point?

As if he'd taken on Billy's gift and heard her thoughts, Johnny leapt to his right, snapped up the fallen gun, and spun to Black.

"Let him go."

Black whispered something into Billy's ear, and he immediately began to calm. The man appeared not to have heard Johnny's threat.

"Back away from him!"

But Black pulled back, gripped Billy's head in both of his hands, and then kissed him full on the lips.

Johnny cried in outrage and pulled the trigger. The gun bucked in his palm with a thunderclap. Black jerked once. Released Billy and turned slowly.

For a moment Darcy thought that Johnny just might have hit him.

Black's face twitched like a horse's hide, twitching at a fly. Billy stood with his head hung low, completely quieted.

Marsuvees Black strode back toward the cabin, black eyes fixed on Johnny. And as he passed them he spit something out of his mouth.

A copper-jacketed bullet plopped on the sand.

"Welcome to the real world," he said.

CHAPTER THIRTY-FIVE

Day Twenty-One

"NO, MA'AM, there's not a bit of bend in him," Billy said. "Do I need to explain to you how I know that?"

In the National Guard command center, Darcy watched Billy talk on the phone with the attorney general while eyeing a string of monitor panels he'd ordered set up for his personal surveillance. His eyes flickered from aerial surveillance to thermal images from one of the observation posts and back again. His transformation from wounded soul to enraged tyrant had become complete over the twenty-four hours since their encounter with Marsuvees Black, Darcy thought. And it frightened her.

But this is what they'd signed up for, and she wasn't about to backpedal now.

Brian Kinnard leaned over a backlit table on which the incursion plans had been drawn up, speaking quietly with the captain, who was dressed in camouflaged BDUs. The Ranger battalion's CO listened in but let them run with the conversation unless directly addressed.

Billy walked to the corner, and Darcy hung close. He'd taken the lead and she wasn't sure how she felt about that. Slightly resentful, but she couldn't very well reprimand him for doing exactly what she'd begged him to do when they were back in Washington. He was forcing Johnny's hand, and he was doing it with surprising command.

His face reddened momentarily, and then he spoke into the phone with black-ice calm. "Then Congress will just have to get used to the fact that laws are worthless unless they are enforced," he said. "Are you saying that you disagree with the use of force?"

He nodded at whatever she said.

"Exactly. My point. And as I've said, I've been inside his mind and I can tell you that this is going to get bloody. He has no intention of walking out of there with his hands up. The whole valley is drunk on his Kool-Aid. They'll die for their cause and they'll take down the first responders with much more than the pop guns they dumped outside the town for everyone to see."

Another pause.

"Don't worry about the Net. I know the movement is significant, but the backlash has already started. Over half the country thinks of Johnny and his cult as a band of lunatics. Darcy assures me that the sentiment will grow. If anything, this new hatred toward Johnny demands we take action before people start acting on their hate."

Billy faced Darcy and studied her with his green eyes. Glasses were a thing of the past for him: he wanted to know the thoughts of everyone in the command center at any given time. Only Kinnard and Darcy guarded themselves from his probing eyes, Kinnard because he insisted, Darcy because she didn't want to unfairly influence Billy, though she wasn't sure he cared any more. Maybe he thought he could resist her charm as Black had.

"That's fine, Lyndsay. But I'm asking you to expand our authority to the use of reasonable force. We gave them twenty-four hours from sunset, but we might as well have been speaking to the dirt. The Net feeds have the whole world glued to that valley, and they saw me issue the ultimatum. If we don't execute justice—"

Billy listened for a moment. "Hold on." He handed the phone to Darcy. "Talk sense to her, please."

She took the black cell and lifted it to her ear. "Hello, Miss Nadeau."

"Darcy," the attorney general acknowledged her politely.

"Why the hesitation?"

"No, dear, no hesitation. But I can't just turn over our police and military forces to two civilians, I'm sure you understand. I'm just establishing some ground rules."

"I think you're missing the point. It's time to make the president good on his word to deal swiftly with extreme prejudice. To do that, we must have certain authorities, surely you understand."

"Of course. Yes, but I want any decision you or Billy consider to pass through me. I, in turn, will need to get the president's—"

Darcy snapped at that. "How dare you throw the president in my face? He's indebted to *me*. We know his dirty little secrets, and don't think that we haven't put them in a very safe place. Are you already forgetting your promise to let Billy and me do what is necessary to effect this change?"

Her own anger surprised her, but the thought of smug Lyndsay Nadeau sitting in Washington, second-guessing them now, made Darcy want to fly back and forcibly remind the woman of her power.

"You're not suggesting that this is the favor I promised," the attorney general said. "You're asking for the head of Johnny Drake?"

Darcy had all but forgotten their agreement to be granted whatever they asked in exchange for their help. That had been a last-minute negotiation, thrown into the pot for good measure.

"No," she said. "Don't be stupid. I'm demanding that you give Billy the authority he's asking for. Tell Kinnard to pass the order. Neither of us has any intention of abusing that power; *please*, you know it's only a fraction of the power we already have. Or would you rather I rip Kinnard's glasses from his face and tell him myself?"

That brought silence.

"I'm not threatening you," Darcy said. "I'm just telling you that Billy and I are two people you have no choice but to trust."

Or kill, she didn't say. An unnerving thought. A very real thought.

Black's statement to Johnny spun through her mind. *Welcome to the real world*, he'd said. Meaning what? No amount of thinking brought clarity.

"Put Kinnard on," the attorney general said.

Darcy crossed the room. "Thank you, Lyndsay. We'll keep you up-to-date. I can promise you no force will be used except in the most extreme case."

"If you do use force, remember, Mr. Drake first," she said. "He's already used force to resist arrest by blowing up the road and refusing to turn himself in. There would be some fallout, but frankly I wouldn't mind. Someone has to take the fall for this."

"So you do agree, then."

"I never said I disagreed. The world has to accept the full enforcement of the law at some point. It might as well be now, before half the country gets swept up in this movement."

Hearing it like that, Darcy realized that the exchange wasn't just about Billy jockeying for position. Paradise was much closer to an escalation involving violence than any of them realized.

"Let's hope it doesn't get to that," she said, and handed the phone to Kinnard. "The attorney general."

Is that what she wanted? Johnny killed? Or worse?

Darcy returned to where Billy stood by the window, looking out over the tarmac, where six or seven helicopters waited in the dusk. The deadline was less than an hour away—they would go in under the cover of darkness.

"You okay?"

Billy's jaw muscles bunched. "Sure."

He'd refused to talk about his encounter with Black. The attack was nothing short of a rape, and Darcy had decided to give him space to deal with it on his own before interfering in any way. But she couldn't ignore the incident any longer, regardless of what wounds it would open.

"Walk with me."

She led him from the command center out onto the tarmac. A few army personnel carriers that had been used to transport guard forces to the perimeter around Paradise, roughly fifty miles south, now sat behind a barbed-wire fence, silent. Dozens more like them were parked along the two roads leading into the valley. Between the small operations base here and the staging area above the valley, the National Guard had the capacity to put a thousand soldiers on the streets of Paradise within thirty minutes of the order.

The plan was to arrest Johnny and the town council peaceably unless they resisted. The three thousand who'd entered Paradise would be released with a stern warning, only if they went peacefully.

But no one expected either Johnny or the three thousand to leave peacefully.

Darcy walked along the fence. "She's instructing them to give us the authority to use force. But we won't, Billy. Not yet."

"No, not yet."

"You're sure Johnny will resist? It doesn't seem like him."

"And if I'm not mistaken, you seem a little distracted by him."

His accusation surprised her. "Don't be ridiculous. I'm just saying that he's had his chances to fight and hasn't, even though we know he has the skill."

"But he is resisting. He's defied us both!"

She couldn't deny that. And why did she even want to?

"Yes, he has. And Lyndsay Nadeau says we have full rights to use force if he doesn't comply in the next hour." She took a deep breath and let it seep out through her nostrils. "But you and I both know there's more to this story than what the rest of the world sees."

He didn't agree or disagree.

"So what really happened yesterday, Billy?"

"You tell me."

"I mean with Black."

"Ask Johnny."

"Why?"

Billy shrugged. "It was all his doing."

"You mean his eyes."

"That's right."

"So we didn't really see Black walk out of that cabin? It was just a figment of our imaginations?"

"That's what I'm saying."

She'd pondered the possibility all through the night.

"I'm not sure it adds up."

He stopped and turned, eyes fiery. "And your voice does add up? My hearing? What about any of this adds up, Darcy? The way we got these powers? The monastery? The fact that over half of this planet's population believes in some supernatural God or force that can bend spoons and open a blind man's eyes and make another man blind with light? Does any of that add up?"

"No. But the man we saw yesterday came from our own pens, Billy! We saw him ruin Paradise once. He's haunted us ever since that day, and now he's returned to destroy us!"

"You mean Johnny," Billy said. "Black's come to destroy Johnny."

She blinked. "So you acknowledge that he's real and he's really here."

He shrugged again. "You checked the cabin with Johnny after he walked back in. You tell me where he disappeared to."

"Judging by the way you're acting, I might guess he crawled up inside of you."

Billy's face paled. She might as well have gut-punched him.

"I didn't mean that. That was unfair. But you have to tell me what happened, Billy. He . . . he kissed you, for heaven's sake!"

"Stop it!" he yelled. Tears sprang to his eyes.

His silence on the matter had been out of shame, and her speaking of it was like salt to the wound. But she had to know what Black's role was here.

"I'm sorry. But if Black's real and really here, in the flesh, then shouldn't we take that into account?"

Billy turned away. Walked a few feet and then back. He grabbed Darcy's hand and spoke quickly, eyes frantic.

"He's after us, Darcy. He's come back for the sinner. It's either Johnny or it's us."

"He said that?"

Billy didn't respond. "This is all Johnny's fault. I know I was the one who wrote Black into flesh, but now Johnny's using him to tear us down."

He wasn't speaking with any sense. "Listen to yourself, Billy. First you deny Black is real. Then you insist he's out to kill us. Which is it?"

Billy shook his fist. "Both!"

"How can it be both? You're not stable."

"Is the devil here, floating around us? Is he really here?"

She wasn't quite sure what to say.

"Is the devil out to kill us?"

"What's your point?"

"He's here, he's not here, he's out to kill us, it's all true, and it's all not true. That's Black for you, and I should know. I wrote him!"

Billy turned and strode for the door, both fists by his sides.

"Billy?"

He walked on.

"Be careful, Billy."

"Don't worry your sweet little backside, Darcy," he said without turning back. "I haven't lost my mind."

Watching the door close under the words Authorized Personnel Only stenciled in yellow, Darcy knew what she had to do. What she wanted to do.

She had just under an hour to get through to Johnny using every means at her disposal.

She spun and strode for a helicopter, where a pilot who'd just returned from a run was still filling out paperwork in the cockpit.

"Do you have enough fuel to take me to Paradise?"

The pilot glanced at her and grinned. "I'm sorry, do I look like a taxi to you?"

She snatched her glasses off and drilled him with a ruthless gaze. "You will fly me to Paradise or you will choke on your own vomit tonight in your sleep."

His eyes went round.

"And you'll do it without filing a report."

Three minutes later they were in the air.

CHAPTER THIRTY-SIX

BILLY LEANED over the light table, staring at the map of Paradise valley, which highlighted the location of the forces as currently deployed.

Small blue circles indicated the location of each of the thirteen snipers and scouts hiding in position around the hills and cliffs. Four larger green squares represented the units that waited inside the perimeter near the roads that had been blown.

The bulk of the forces waited on the plateau above Paradise and would be airlifted in if needed.

"I would strongly suggest we cut off their links now," said Ranger Captain Adams, speaking of the impulse generator they'd installed on the mesa. It would interfere with all conventional wireless communications within a ten-mile radius, cutting Paradise off from the world. The guard would rely exclusively on laser communications, a military-grade system that bounced beams off of satellites and back to receivers at specific GPS coordinates. Scrambler/transceivers gathered the signals and channeled them to tactical units within line of sight.

"For tactical reasons, but you might want to also consider the public relations side of things."

"Do it," Billy said.

Kinnard nodded, effectively under Billy's thumb.

"There's a call for you, sir." A staffer of some lower rank handed Billy a phone. He took it and walked from the table, grateful for the distraction. He couldn't just stand around and let his mind itch the way it had ever since Black had forced himself on him.

The clock was ticking. Forty-one minutes and counting.

"Hello?"

"Hello, Billy." A woman's voice. "How are you holding up?"

The voice was only vaguely familiar.

"Who is this?"

"I'm waiting for you in your room, Billy. We don't have much time."

He glanced over at the light table and saw that Kinnard was watching him through those annoying obsidian sunglasses.

"I'm sorry, who did you say this was?"

"I didn't." She paused. When she spoke again, her voice sent a chill through him. "You know me, Billy. You know me better than you know yourself."

The air left his lungs and the room seemed to tilt. Billy jerked the phone from his ear and disengaged the call.

"You okay, Billy?" Kinnard had walked over to him.

"I just need a minute."

"Who was that?"

"I . . . Nothing. Just Darcy. I'll be right back."

He took a breath, frozen by indecision. The compound comprised half a dozen buildings including the armory and officers' quarters, where they'd been put up for the last two nights—Darcy must have retreated to one of them. She wouldn't be standing outside where he'd left her twenty minutes earlier.

But the voice wasn't Darcy's, was it? This itching in his mind was clouding his thoughts.

"You're sure you're okay?"

He headed for the door and crashed through it without giving Kinnard an answer. An old barracks on the north side of the compound had been renovated to accommodate VIPs and visitors. Billy glanced around, saw that he was alone, and took off for his room.

It's you, Billy. You're the sinner.

Black's voice had washed into his body yesterday like a cool drink after a long hike through the desert.

I'm you and you're me, baby. And you know what we want, what we need.

Blackness had filled him from his mouth, chilling his body from the inside out. Billy didn't know if the man who'd shoved his mouth against his own was real or not—how could a person know that? But he did know that something had changed in that moment.

You know you wanna trip, baby. It's just you and me and we're going to slam this town.

A slight buzz had settled into the base of his mind with that voice, the cause of what he'd come to call the itch. The cold had reached down into his bones. But more than either of these had been the hatred of Johnny, the self-appointed prophet who'd forced Billy to face his past once again.

He thinks he's Johnny the Baptist, Billy Boy. He thinks he's come to introduce the world to salvation.

Billy shuddered and ducked into the dark hall that led to his room, number 105, on the left. He swiped his key card through the lock, pushed the handle down, and swung the door open.

"Hello?"

No answer.

He flipped the light on. Nothing. She'd lied to him. Billy felt a sting of bitter disappointment. There was no way anyone could have gotten in. He was hearing voices now. That buzz at the base of his brain wasn't only itching, it was whispering lies.

The clock on the nightstand glowed red. Thirty-three minutes till six.

Billy was about to turn when she stepped out of the corner shadows next to the curtains. He jumped back, startled, half expecting her to morph into Black and kiss him. Dump more of that cold blackness in his belly.

"I knew you would come," Kelly said.

Kelly. Yes, it was Kelly. She'd come with terms of surrender from Johnny.

The woman wore a sleeveless white dress that hung to her calves and swung evenly with each step. Her bare feet were white and her neck was pale even in the dim light.

"What are you doing here?" he asked.

"I think you know, Billy." She smiled. "I'm here to make sure you don't fall apart at the last minute."

"Johnny's surrendering?"

"No," she said. "But we both know that he isn't going to use force."

It occurred to him that he couldn't read her thoughts. She was staring at him with bright eyes, and he didn't have a clue what she was thinking. How was that possible?

"No we don't." But the likelihood that Johnny would not use any force had gnawed at him all day. Johnny himself had never suggested he would use force, which Billy suggested was an intentional omission for the attorney general's sake.

"He said it would get bloody. He didn't say that Johnny would draw that blood."

Billy felt the blackness creeping in. "Who said that?"

"*He* did."

"Black did? How do you know what Black said?"

"Because he and I go way back, honey. Not as far back as you do, but far enough."

"You're . . ."

Then Billy knew that he was looking at another person like Black who'd stepped into human form with the stroke of a pen. Kelly, Johnny's Kelly, was from the pages of Black's book.

She walked up to him and reached for his face, smiling. Her fingers were hot. Flesh. She leaned forward and kissed him with soft warm lips.

Fleshy lips. She was more flesh than he'd ever known flesh.

"Johnny isn't going to cooperate, Billy. But he's destined to die. He needs to die. And you're going to kill him."

She kissed him again, longer this time, with more passion. Her lips smothered his. Once again he felt the chill pour into his belly and begin to fill him up. But this time he didn't resist. He welcomed it.

"You know why, Billy," she whispered into his mouth. Her arms reached around his back and she pulled him closer as she kissed his lips passionately, feeding on him. "You know why. Tell me why. Come on, baby, tell me why."

"Because I'm the sinner."

Sorrow engulfed him and he felt himself go.

"Because I was born to sin."

"That's right, baby. Say it again, tell me like you mean it. Tell me who you really are. Say his name." Her hands were in his hair, pulling him so hard against her lips that he could hardly speak.

He started to cry.

"Tell me! Tell me!" She pulled back just long enough to slap his face with an open palm. Then she gripped his cheeks in her fingers and kissed him again, biting his lip.

"Black," he whimpered.

"Say it like you mean it!"

"Black!" The full truth slammed into his mind, crushing him under its weight. Any self-pity weakening his resolve was rolled under by rage.

"I am Black! Black came from me. *We* are the sinner!"

"Yes! Say it again."

"It's me, I made him!"

"And you love him."

"I love him . . . I love him."

"You love me because I'm like Black. He made me. You made me. Tell me, tell me."

Billy felt it more than he could remember feeling anything. The authenticity of his confession brought such relief, such . . .

"I love you. I love you because I am Sinner."

Kelly immediately relaxed. Kissed him gently now, just barely touching his lips. "And so am I, Billy. I didn't even know he'd made me until just a few days ago. I didn't understand why I felt the conflict, the temptations, the inevitable pulling at my soul. Then he came to me, and I knew that he'd made me just like you made him."

He stepped back, panting. Trembling.

"Johnny—"

"I hate Johnny." Kelly ground out the words as if they were dirt. "Now that I know the truth, he makes me want to throw up. Black put me there to love him so that he would end up here—and that's all I knew until Marsuvees came to me. So I loved Johnny, and now I hate him for it. The Johnnys of this world have to die, Billy. They stand in the path of humanity. But we all know who will win."

Her words cut deep into his mind, cold steel penetrating flesh.

"You wrote Black because he was already in you." She flung her arm behind her, pointing at some imaginary enemy. "Now this kingdom of light, or whatever they insist on calling it, wants you to think that this is all your fault!"

Kelly was pulling at the air through her nostrils. He'd never seen a woman quite so enraged.

"That's why you have to kill him, Billy," she said. "You have to kill this Jesus freak or die with all those he condemns. I can't stand his bigoted, hateful nonsense about the narrow gates of heaven."

Kelly's hands trembled and her pale face had turned red.

"You made Black. Johnny's defying your creation. Now you kill him, you hear me?"

"Yes."

"Kill him!"

He felt his face screw up in hopeless acceptance. "I will."

"Kill him!" she yelled.

"I will, I'll kill him!"

"Kill them all, Billy. Do whatever it takes. Swear it to me!"

"I swear it." And he meant it with all of his heart. She was like a lover to him, and he would follow her to hell if he must. He didn't understand why he felt this way, but he embraced the sentiment and let the confusion fall away.

"I swear it on my life."

"Order a preemptive strike on the town. Kill them all."

"I will."

Kelly stared at him hard for a full ten seconds. Slowly the hard lines in her face softened. A smile tugged gently on one corner of her mouth.

She stepped forward, placed her mouth against his, and bit his lip hard enough to draw blood.

"I'm with you, lover. I'm with you all the way."

CHAPTER THIRTY-SEVEN

KATRINA KIVI stood on Main Street in the same spot she'd stood for the last half hour, facing the makeshift stage they'd built against the old theater, listening as first Father Yordon and then Paula Smithers spoke to the gathering about love.

The kind of love she'd seen with her own eyes when Johnny had opened them. She could feel it now, not like she had the first night three weeks—seemed more like a year to her—ago, but here, very much here, like static on the charged air.

She looked around, unable to wipe the slight grin from her face. Home, she thought. I've found my home. How else could she describe the feeling of knowing without the slightest shadow of a doubt that she had found what she'd been made for?

They'd called the meeting that morning because they all knew that the government had given them until sunset to throw up their hands and go home. Four people had already flown out by helicopter. But a strong resolve to stay here, where Holly and the others had fallen on their faces and cried out for mercy, had swept through the valley yesterday afternoon. News spread about what had gone down when Billy Rediger and

Darcy Lange delivered their ultimatum, and the town quietly prepared for whatever might come.

Now three thousand gathered in the town center, crowding the space between the stage on which Johnny stood and the trees that bordered the church lawn a hundred yards away. Kat sat on the Smithers' porch and watched those who hadn't taken a spot on the lawn earlier in the day trickle in. By four thirty the town center was a sea of people.

News came an hour ago that all wireless reception in the valley was gone. Joseph and the other crews were filming from both sides of the stage, but their footage was not going out live.

Her small friend with the toothless smile had taken up his spot next to the porch, grinning up at her. Paula kept busy, hemming and hawing about supper, but no one seemed interested in when or how dinner would be served. Claude paced the front of the stage, assuming the local-law role, which, as far as Kat could tell, was simply to assure those who asked that, yes, he supposed that they were breaking the law.

Steve had been tapped to handle sanitation, control the crowd, and make sure traffic didn't become a problem. Which meant he pretty much sat on the porch outside Smither's Barbeque, because apart from Mary Mae's clogged toilet, neither sanitation, crowd, nor traffic had presented anything remotely similar to a problem.

The town had remained hushed all afternoon as they gathered. Everyone knew something was going to go down. Something big.

This was the gathering. This was the 3000, as the reporters called it.

Now the crowd stood in complete silence, fixed on the stage, staring at Johnny, who stared back through his sunglasses, feeling with them.

Feeling what Kat felt. The electrical charge of expectancy. But she felt more than that. She knew because she'd *seen* this feeling before.

They were feeling the kingdom of light, which raged bright around them, just past their eyesight.

Beside Kat, a thin, gray-haired woman was crying silently from eyes that said she'd been here before. It was about time.

Kat swallowed and looked back at the platform. The two towers of speakers stood to either side, silent now. Two spotlights had been rigged to shine on center stage, and someone had set a potted fruit tree with some apples on it to the back.

Otherwise it was just Johnny. And those sunglasses, which everyone attributed to some kind of affliction that made his eyes sensitive to light. But Kat knew the truth.

Johnny could see best in the dark.

"Take them off," she whispered to herself. "Show them the light, Johnny."

The gray-haired woman glanced down, then faced forward again.

Johnny had already spoken for ten minutes, calmly explaining that if the authorities came, no one should lift a finger against them. If police wanted to take them to prison, they should go. Even in prison they could speak the truth.

He told them that the beacon of light that had been ignited in this valley had been seen by the whole world—it was all he could ask for. The rest was out of his hands. Most people would vow to stomp out the light, and they would not stop until they believed they were successful. But a few would follow the light and step into the kingdom.

Then he fell silent.

And so did the crowd.

Someone whispered, "Thank you, thank you, Father," nearby. The gentle sound of sniffing could be heard here and there. But otherwise even the children had been trapped in Johnny's silence. No squabbling, no crying, just . . .

. . . silence. Beautiful, sweet silence.

Kat wanted to scream at the top of her lungs. Raise her fists and just scream because she felt like she might burst if she didn't.

Instead she stood there and let her fingers tingle.

And let the silence work deeper.

Then Johnny spoke.

"Who has believed our message, and to whom has the arm of the Lord been revealed?"

Kat knew these words penned by a prophet several thousand years ago! Johnny had poured over them with her like an excited child. He had a copy of the scrolls found near the Dead Sea dating back to the time before Christ. The book of Isaiah, chapter fifty-three.

She knew the words and had become as addicted to them as Johnny was.

Kat gripped both fists before her chest and raised up on her toes in her excitement. *Show them, Johnny. Show them the light!*

"He grew up before the world like a tender shoot out of dry ground." Johnny's voice was soft and low, so that she had to lean into the words. They should have been screamed.

But in his softness, Johnny was screaming. Not a single soul could hear this and not know: Johnny was indeed screaming.

"He had no beauty, nothing in his appearance that would make man desire him. He was despised and rejected and hated by men. A man of sorrows, acquainted with grief. They hid their faces from him. Who was this man?"

No one dared answer. It was Johnny's prerogative, Johnny's honor. His voice trembled with each word, as if by uttering them he sowed magic in the air.

The sound of weeping began to wax through the valley, softly, like the hushed sniffs of a mother remembering the long-past death of her son.

Johnny lifted one hand and spread his fingers. "He was pierced for our transgressions. He was crushed for the evil in our hearts. He was smitten and afflicted, and his brutal punishment brought us peace."

A single tear leaked down from behind his dark glasses. *Show them, Johnny. Show them!*

"Who was this man?"

Still not a soul dared speak. Not yet. Who could dare interrupt?

"He was led like a lamb to the slaughter, cut off from the land of the living. He bore the sin of many and his name was Jesus."

A roar erupted. From humming silence to ground-shaking thunder, these three thousand followers who'd entered the kingdom of light could hold back their agreement with the words of magic no longer.

They tilted their heads and opened their throats and filled the air with a cry that drew tears from Kat's eyes in rivers.

It was so dramatic, so over the top, so unearthly, yet so, so, so real. And Kat could hardly stand it.

"Show them!" she cried, eyes clenched, hardly aware that she was yelling aloud. "Show them. Show them, Johnny!" In this moment there was nothing she wanted so desperately as to see that light again.

"Show them, Johnny!"

The crowd's roar had peaked, and that last cry screamed above them all in its high pitch. *Show them, Johnny.*

He slowly turned his head and looked down at her. A tortured smile spread over his face. He continued to speak but kept his eyes on her.

"He taught that he was the only way, and that following him made for a light burden, open to all: the poor, the disadvantaged, the sick, the lepers, the widows, the lost and hurting and wounded. And he taught that the path was narrow, missed by most. For that teaching they hated him, and he warned any who dared follow him that they, too, would be hated."

Johnny took his eyes off Kat and scanned the people who stood in the lights of the surrounding porches and three overhead streetlights. The sun had vanished behind the western mountains, leaving behind a gray sky. The evening was cool, but Kat's skin tingled with heat.

Show them, Johnny.

"They will come for us because they hate us. Not because we are Christians or Muslims or Hindus, but because we would rather follow the teachings of Jesus and die than deny them and live."

Kat had been so fixated on Johnny that she hadn't seen the woman who approached the right of the stage, staring up at Johnny. It was the woman who'd spoken to Holly yesterday. The government's agent, Darcy Lange, who'd come wearing sunglasses like Johnny, despite the dark.

Had he seen her?

"But I'm not asking you to die," Johnny said. "I'm only asking you to follow the light that first rescued you from the darkness."

"Is this the same light that I followed?" Darcy's voice rang out for all to hear. She walked toward the stage as Johnny turned.

"When I was a child, was this the truth that the priests shoved down my throat, Johnny?"

She stepped up the two crates that led to the platform.

"Are all my nightmares and my cold sweats the result of this light from heaven that has miraculously come to save the lost?"

They've come, Kat thought.

"When all of this is over, will all your faithful disciples be left with the same fears that have haunted me for the last thirteen years?"

She faced the people and snatched her glasses from her face. Kat stared into her bright eyes.

"When they kill your daughters and sons who blindly followed you here, will you clap for joy and sing praises to the light?"

Kat wasn't sure what kind of power the woman possessed, but her voice sliced through her heart like a razor.

"Do you really want blood on your hands?" she cried.

The words might as well have been kicked from a mule. Kat caught her breath.

"You're fools! All of you, complete fools for believing all this nonsense about the sweet little baby Jesus!"

Kat wanted to scream again, this time in fear. How dare she say this? *Show her, Johnny. Show her!*

But Johnny only smiled.

"Hello, Darcy."

The woman spun back to him, jaw set.

"Welcome to the kingdom of light."

BILLY BOILED with hatred but he was no longer confused, and that alone was worth any price he might pay for the evil roiling through him.

He burst into the command center with Kelly at his side and eyed Kinnard, who still wore his glasses. "I need to speak to you."

Kinnard closed his phone. "Of course."

Billy glanced around. "Where's Darcy?"

"She's not with you?"

Billy had offended Darcy. The thought that he should discuss all of this with her before he pulled the trigger crossed his mind, but Kelly touched his elbow and he pulled back from the thought.

"This is Kelly. You'll recognize her from the photographs on the wall." He nodded at a corkboard that held a dozen pictures of the featured conspirators in Paradise. Hers was next to Johnny's and had a question mark under it.

"We have some information. Outside."

Kinnard exchanged glances with the others and followed them outside. "We're ordering the evacuation of Johnny in fifteen minutes," he said, closing the door behind him. "Does this—"

"Change of plans," Billy interrupted. A shaft of fear crashed through his mind and was gone. "We need to take them out."

Kinnard hesitated before speaking. "Take them out."

"Make an example of them. Before this becomes contagious. Meaning kill them. Drop a bomb down their throats. Take them out!"

He hadn't meant to hurl the words at Kinnard, but they came from a place of dark hatred that had fermented in his belly for a very long time.

"I'm not sure you have the authority—"

"You know very well that I have the authority to do whatever I think is reasonable to remedy this flagrant disregard for our nation's laws," Billy snapped. "We have inside information that confirms the town is planning an all-out assault on any force that enters the town. They will let us enter and then slaughter us. Knowing this, I'm ordering a preemptive strike on Paradise. I want you to bomb them. I want you to kill them all."

"Do you have any idea what kind of fallout we would be facing?"

"What did I tell you?" Kelly mumbled under her breath. She faced the mysterious CIA man who'd first saved Billy and Darcy from the killer in Pennsylvania. "Don't tell me the idea of cutting them down doesn't draw your blood to the surface. Their betrayal is unpardonable. One strike and this is all over. Just do it!"

Billy glanced from one to the other, surprised at the frankness of Kelly's demand, as if she were the true leader here.

But she was right. One strike would end it all, including Johnny's life.

Billy pressed. "Truth be told, I don't care one iota what you think we should do here, Kinnard. I want you to order the strike, and I want you to do it now. This is my responsibility, my call."

"The snipers are in place, we could take out Johnny."

"And create a full-scale revolt? Make a martyr out of a felon? Aren't you listening? They're armed to the teeth down there! The guns they dumped on the road were nothing but a lie. We need to end it. Now!"

For a few moments they stood in the night air, the woman born of Black and two men, deciding the fate of the world. At the least a very significant part of the world.

"You're sure?" Kinnard said

But the right corner of his mouth twitched, unsuccessfully betraying a grin of approval.

"Absolutely."

Kinnard dipped his head once. "Okay. Okay, then. I hope you know what you're doing. The bomber is fueled. We can get it airborne in minutes."

"Just do it."

Billy glanced around. Where was Darcy?

He needed Darcy.

CHAPTER THIRTY-EIGHT

"WELCOME TO the kingdom of light."

He was smiling, not a big grin plastered on his face, but a whisper of a smile that reached deep into Darcy's chest and filled her with rage.

The world was gathered and would peer in on this stage through the camera's eye. Enough military force to wipe out every living creature in this valley was gathered on the cliffs above them, waiting the order. Three thousand believers stood to her right, most probably willing to live or die for this so-called kingdom of light.

But all of them were truly at the mercy of two people now, facing each other on the stage. Johnny and Darcy. Two childhood acquaintances who'd grown up on opposite sides of the question that the whole world wanted answered, even if they long ago stopped asking.

Is it real?

Is there really another "kingdom" unseen by human eyes?

And what, please tell us, what does the here and now have to do with this ancient prophet named Jesus?

Darcy knew the answers. No. No. Nothing.

True, she acknowledged there was more to the way the world worked than what we can see with our eyes. Her own gift was proof enough. But reality, in its purest form, surely had nothing to do with a solitary rebel who'd been put to death two thousand years ago!

But Johnny . . . he stood there with that gimpy grin because he actually, truly, completely believed all that hooey.

She took a deep breath, stilling the fury building in her chest. "Johnny, please. You have to listen to me. They don't know I'm here."

"Why did you come, Darcy?"

She glanced at the people, expecting more participation from them. How had three thousand strangers fallen into lockstep so quickly? Well, she'd affected them with her one outburst, and she wasn't done with them yet, not by a long shot.

But Johnny first.

She looked into his glasses. "Maybe I shouldn't have come. Do you realize what's about to go down here? How many snipers have us in their sights at this very moment? They're going to use force if you so much as lift a finger, I thought you should know that."

"Force?" Johnny looked at the people. "My friends, this is Darcy Lange, a representative of the United States government, and she says they're going to use force."

"Please, I'm begging you, Johnny," Darcy said, keeping her eyes on him. "It doesn't have to be this way. You've taken this too far." Those who were looking at her eyes shifted uneasily under the power of her words.

Johnny swung around and faced her. "But we haven't taken it anywhere yet. This is only the beginning, surely you know that."

Her anger seeped out. She shoved a finger at the mountains. "The monastery was the beginning!" she cried, leaning into her words. "The beginning of a lie! We can end it here, tonight." She stomped one boot. "Give this up!"

"How can you ask us to deny the truth?"

"And just what is that truth, Johnny?"

"That Jesus is the Light of the World."

"Jesus? Only Jesus? Do you even know how foolish that sounds? You're spitting in the face of the world!"

She was still focused on Johnny, but her words reached into the crowd. A well-rounded woman standing at the front was shaking, bug-eyed eyes on Darcy. She looked too frightened to cry.

The whole western half of the crowd had been smothered by her accusation of foolishness and was already staggering under the weight of doubt her words had awakened in them.

Johnny looked out over the people again. "We are not here to itemize the rights or wrongs of Christianity or Islam or Buddhism or any religion. We are here because we believe the Light that came into the darkness is hated by that darkness. I believe Jesus is the Word made flesh. Despised and rejected by all but a few. He said you would call us fools."

Darcy leapt to the edge of the stage and faced them all. "It's a lie!" she screamed.

The effect was immediate. As if her words had physical power, they hit the nearest people like a gale. But it wasn't enough. They should be *falling* under the force of their doubt, Darcy thought.

"It is all a big mistake," she cried, "taught to you by your parents and their parents, all this nonsense about light! Think for yourselves! How dare you insult the American people by defying our laws and dying for a faith in what you can't prove!"

The round woman in the front was on her knees, eyes clenched tight, begging some unseen force to rescue her. Darcy's words reached all the way to the back of the dimly lit town square, filling it with the sound of whimpering and shifting feet.

Darcy pushed before anyone could form an argument against her.

"You're giving up your lives as zealots for a truth that is based on a lie!"

"No!"

The scream came from Darcy's left. A young, dark-skinned teenager with hair past her shoulders stood at the front, glaring at her.

She knew this girl from the Net reports. It was Katrina Kivi, the one who'd stopped the school riot in Boulder City, Nevada.

"No, that's not true!" the girl cried. "I was a witch full of hate until I saw the kingdom of light. It filled me with love, although I can say that loving you at this moment isn't easy. How dare you step on our stage and tell us that we are foolish!"

Darcy was at a loss. The girl stood firmly against the full weight of Darcy's words. She'd swayed all of Washington to embrace constitutional change but she couldn't sway the mind of one teenager?

"I was once a true believer too," she finally said. "I've earned the right to question."

"Then question," Johnny said from her left.

She watched Katrina Kivi's eyes shift to where he stood. They widened and the girl's mouth parted slightly.

Darcy turned. Johnny had removed his glasses and stared at her with bright blue eyes

"Show her, Johnny," Katrina said. "Show us all."

"I've heard your words, Darcy. I've listened to you explain the world and remain unconvinced. The question is, are you willing to look into my world and see the light?"

"There is no light but what your trickery shows," she said. "You are a trickster." But she felt inexorably drawn to see what all the fuss was about. Her breathing thickened at the mystery of it all.

"No, I won't use any illusion. I'll simply open your eyes. What you see is beyond my ability to control."

"Show her, Johnny." There was a desperation in Katrina's voice now. Darcy glanced over and saw that she was walking slowly toward them with her hands clasped in front of her. Tears wet her cheeks.

"Please, Johnny, show us."

"Why, Kat?" Johnny asked.

"Because I want to be reminded."

"You have eyes of faith."

"But you're here, and she's here, and we're all here. Isn't that why he gave you your eyes?"

Johnny gave her a slight nod and looked at Darcy.

"I've listened to you. Will you look at me?"

"I am looking at you."

BILLY PACED in the command center's lounge, ignoring Kelly, who stood with her arms crossed watching him. Looking into her eyes did nothing but fill him with more hate, and he already hated the hate seeping from his pores like a sour sweat.

He'd ordered the room closed to all but them and Kinnard, who was making the final arrangements now. The clock on the wall read five minutes past six o'clock.

They were looking for Darcy. She'd gone off sulking, and not having her with him at this time was making him sweat.

"Stop it, please," Kelly said.

Billy absently lifted his hand and trimmed the nail on his index finger with his teeth. "Stop what?"

"Pacing. You're making me think that you're full of second thoughts."

She lowered her arms and walked up to him. Placed her hand on his cheek and brushed his hair back.

"Are you?"

"How could I have second thoughts about killing Johnny?" he snapped. "He's ruined me!"

"Not Johnny. I know how much you hate him. I'm talking about the others."

The three thousand or so conspirators who'd joined Johnny in his stand against the law.

Billy turned away from her, fighting back a fresh wave of fury.

At Johnny.

At Paradise.

At the three thousand.

At Black.

At Kelly.

At himself.

Where was Darcy?

"They've made their own choice," he said. "Three thousand fewer bloggers to clog up the Net next week."

His eyes stung and he blinked away blurred vision.

Kelly turned his face back to hers. Her eyes watched his lips, then rose to his. "Accept it, Billy. This is what you were born to do. It's a great honor."

She kissed his lips where she'd bitten him and pulled back, fighting to control some unnamed emotion. "I would give anything to be you. To be flesh, real flesh. Human. You're the king of the world."

He felt a moment of pity for the beautiful woman who walked because he'd written Black into flesh. Black had written Kelly for the sole purpose of delivering Johnny to this night.

And all of it was because of him. Billy.

The door opened and Kinnard entered. He stopped at the sight of Kelly's hand on Billy's face, but she didn't remove it until he reached them.

"Well?" she demanded.

"In the air now. One air-fuel bomb. Over the target in fifteen minutes."

"Air fuel?" Billy asked. "What will that do?"

"It's twenty thousand pounds of high-explosive, designed to spread as it burns. It will detonate two hundred feet above the ground and has a blast radius of 1.2 kilometers. Basically? It will incinerate the whole town, including the buildings, the media, the cars—all of it will burn. We'll be able to say whatever we want about how this went down. There won't be any evidence to the contrary."

"Good," Kelly said.

Billy nodded. "Good."

KAT STOOD in front of the stage, looking up at Johnny and Darcy squaring off.

"I *am* looking at you," Darcy said, and Kat knew by her tone of voice that she was saying yes.

Her hands were trembling and her heart was racing because she wanted to see the light on the road to Damascus the way the apostle Paul had seen it.

"The problem, Johnny," Darcy said, placing both hands on her hips, "is that you just don't—"

But that's all she could say, because Johnny's eyes went black and she sucked at the air as if a huge boot had landed in her belly.

Johnny was showing Darcy herself.

Kat felt fear's familiar fingers lock on to her heart as she fell into the twin holes where Johnny's eyes had been. She ripped her stare away and threw her hand up to block the image. She'd been here before and the image had been much stronger then, but she couldn't bear to face it again, weak or not.

A terrible groan swelled behind her. She leaped to the stage and spun to face the crowd. Looks of horror had rounded their eyes in shock. Most stared at Johnny, unable to tear themselves from the striking sight of blackened eyes, from the very real, albeit forgiven, evil that haunted them all.

The light, they needed to see the light!

"Look away!" she cried, sweeping her hands to one side. "Don't look yet!"

They threw up their arms and buried their heads in their hands, but most were weeping already.

Kat whirled back and faced Johnny, whose eyes were fixed, coal black. She clenched her jaw against the terror that lapped at her mind and turned to the woman.

Darcy had fallen to her knees and allowed her arms to go limp as the darkness flowed into her. Her body shook with terrible sobs and her face was twisted in such anguish that Kat couldn't help but feel her pain.

Still, Johnny refused to remove his gaze. Darcy's eyes were held captive.

The woman's mouth went wide in a silent cry.

"Johnny?" Kat cried.

Still he would not let her go. Darcy clamped her jaws shut and bared her teeth as if trying to keep her head from shaking off.

Kat had stared into those eyes for only a couple of seconds and nearly died. Darcy had endured thirty seconds, and Kat wondered if it just might kill her.

"Johnny!"

But he kept it up. Deeper, harder. Her eyes began to roll back into her head. That she was reacting meant she'd opened herself to the truth, which was a good thing, but not if it ended her life!

"Stop it!" Kat jumped in front of Darcy, blocking her from Johnny's eyes. "You're going to kill her!"

He closed his eyes and opened them again. Blue.

For a moment he looked at her, dazed. She could hear Darcy breathing hard through a soft whimper behind her, the only sound on the night air.

Then Johnny blinked and his eyes became white, and Kat caught her breath.

"SIR, WE'VE located Darcy Lange."

Billy swiveled to the door and looked at the staffer who'd intruded. They were now less than two minutes from the strike and Darcy had finally come out of hiding. Lovely.

Kelly stepped up behind him and placed a supportive hand on his elbow. He had no idea what Darcy would think of Kelly, who wasn't really vying for his affection as much as returning to him. She presented no real threat to Darcy, not in a romantic way.

Darcy was flesh and blood. Kelly was flesh and words. She was here to help them take down the traitor who would destroy them all.

"Is she coming?" he asked.

"She's not on the base, sir."

"At the armory then, whatever. Why isn't she coming?" Heat flared up his neck.

"She's in Paradise, sir."

Billy's blood ran cold. "Paradise? She's in the town of Paradise?"

"That is our understanding, yes, sir."

There had to be a mistake.

"*The* Paradise?"

"A helicopter pilot just called in reporting that she forced him to fly her to Paradise almost an hour ago. He left her there and is on his way back now."

Billy was too stunned to speak.

"I knew she would betray you," Kelly said in a low voice. "It was the way she was looking at him that first day in the tent. She's—"

"No!" He shook her arm off and ran forward, then pulled up and paced back, gripping his hair. "No, no, that's not right, she would never do that."

The staffer watched them with big eyes.

"She's there, isn't she?" Kelly snapped.

"She isn't there for Johnny."

"Then why?"

Billy didn't know why. Nothing else made any sense. Darcy had crossed over to Johnny? No, this wasn't right.

"Should we call off the strike, sir?"

"No," Kelly whispered. "Johnny has to die."

DARCY DIDN'T have the thoughts, much less the words, to describe what had happened to her in those eternal thirty seconds, but she knew that everything she had known for the past ten years was in fact wrong.

Not just wrong. Dreadfully, horribly incorrect.

She'd looked at the world and seen dark gray, when all along it was a brilliant red.

She'd walked through life looking for nice, neat squares to protect her from her past when in reality there wasn't a straight line to be found.

Tonight she'd come face-to-face with the rawest kind of evil and this feeling, this terror . . . it had made a mockery of her worst nightmare.

Then she'd become perfectly aware that this evil resided in her. Was a part of her nature. Was a disease that she had contracted and protected like a deep pit might protect the fungus growing on its walls. She drowned in the black lake of her own soul.

She was drowning in that lake, unable to scream, when the water had turned red. And for a moment she thought she had died.

Now someone was standing in front of her, the young girl, Katrina Kivi, yelling out for Johnny to stop. It occurred to Darcy that she was trembling on her knees, not drowning in a lake.

The girl gasped and stepped away.

Johnny stood where she'd seen him last. But his eyes weren't black any longer; they were white.

And then the world erupted with white-hot light. The brightness rushed her, slammed into her chest, and knocked her back on her seat.

For the briefest of moments, she wondered if a massive explosive had been detonated right here on the stage. But she wasn't dead. Was she?

No. Two realizations crashed through her mind with equal force. The first was that she was shaking again, but this time with pleasure.

The second was that she was more alive than she had ever been. And at this moment she was seeing the kingdom of light.

Darcy began to weep.

CHAPTER THIRTY-NINE

HOW MUCH time passed was difficult to tell, because the minutes had either slowed or sped up and Darcy couldn't tell which.

It seemed as though the sum of all Darcy's awareness had been concentrated into a drug and administered to her intravenously. Every synapse, every nerve ending, every sense she possessed was stretched to the limit of its capacity.

There was light, yes, but this particular light wasn't just white beams floating around the town square. It was a warm charge of energy that she could breathe and feel on her skin. It was the complete absence of darkness here in Paradise, Colorado.

Darcy stood and turned slowly, gazing at the town square. Johnny faced the people, frozen in time, eyes blazing white. But it wasn't just his eyes, it was the whole town square, swimming in light. He wasn't the source of the brightness, he'd simply opened their eyes to what was already here—a prophet showing them the chariots of heaven.

Slow motion. Perfectly ethereal, perfectly real. And silent.

The people were moving, heads turning, tilting, eyes wide as they gazed in wonder at the change. But slow, very slow, at one tenth the normal speed of things.

An older gentleman on the front row had his arms spread wide, his head tilted back, and his mouth wide open in what could only be a scream of pure delight. A silent scream.

Next to him, a gray-haired woman dressed in the brightest yellow dress Darcy had ever seen stood with both hands over her mouth, looking up. Tears streamed from her wrinkled eyes that seemed to cry out on their own. *I knew it. What did I tell you? I knew it!*

Darcy looked over the three thousand. To a man, woman, and child they breathed the light, some jumping, some trembling, all gripped in this force that had slowed time and was filling their mouths, their throats, their bones with raw power and pleasure.

Joseph Houde, the newsman who'd first broken the story about Paradise, stood next to two other reporters apart from the crowd, filming, but they were anything but steady. One of them had dropped his camera and was on his knees, face in hands.

But of them all, young Katrina Kivi stood out. She was leaping two feet off the ground in slow motion, flinging her arms over her head and grabbing at the light. Silent words cried from her mouth, like a delighted child who was finally allowed on that ride, the big one that she'd stared at for so many years until she was tall enough to buckle in.

They were all swept up in one overpowering sentiment, Darcy thought: *It's here. It's really here. It's really, really here.*

And it was. So real and vibrant, so heavy with power that she wondered if this was heaven.

Darcy saw all of this at once, maybe in the span of a few seconds, maybe an hour. But there was no transition for her. She knew the moment that the light slammed into her that she'd been wrong about Johnny and the three thousand. About Jesus and the kingdom he'd insistently talked about over two thousand years ago.

And about preventing any human being from placing this light on the top of the tallest mountain for all the world to see.

Darcy wept.

For joy, for sorrow, for regret, for desire of whatever was now coursing through her veins.

And then the light collapsed into itself and vanished, as if someone had pulled the plug. Slow motion fell into real time and the silence was pulled away like a blanket.

Her own scream was the first to reach her ears, and she hadn't even been aware that she was screaming. Then Katrina Kivi's high-pitched cry of delight, several feet away. Then the whole crowd's, a roar of approval and cries, the sound of weeping and moaning, all rolled into one symphony of fascination and bliss.

It only took a few seconds for everyone to realize that it was gone. The only sound came from their weeping, and then even that softened.

They stared around in wonder, stunned by the change. Breathing hard.

Darcy ran her hand through the air, half expecting to hit something. A wisp of light trailed off her fingers and then even that was gone. She faced Johnny, who watched her, eyes now blue.

"None of that was me," he said.

She knew, but she couldn't manage an answer.

A smile curved his mouth. "Tell them, Darcy."

Tell them?

"Tell them what you know. Use your voice for them."

Then she knew, Johnny had his eyes; she had her voice.

She was facing Johnny with her side to the crowd, so she twisted to see them again. They were still shell-shocked, looking around. A murmur was growing.

Darcy looked at Johnny. "Tell them?"

He chuckled. "Tell them, sing to them, scream to them, do your thing, Darcy. I think they deserve it, don't you?"

She strode to the edge of the stage, captured by the idea. "Listen to me," she said, but her voice came out hoarse from all her screaming.

"Listen! Listen to her!" Katrina Kivi shouted.

They looked up at Darcy.

"I . . . I was . . ."

The floodgates of her soul broke open, and she could not hold back her emotion. She couldn't say *wrong* because her throat wasn't cooperating. Her heart was lodged firmly there.

She began to sob again. Staring through tears at the three thousand, sobbing and sobbing.

Darcy thrust two fingers into the air and spoke as clearly as she could. "The kingdom of heaven actually *is* among us." The words from the priests who'd raised her filled her mind for the first time in thirteen years. As did the opening from the Gospel of John, the apostle who gave his life for the words he penned.

"In the beginning was the Word, and the Word was with God, and the Word was God."

Any unbelieving soul could have heard the words from her and stared back dumbly, because her voice could only excite what already was hidden in a person's mind. But Paradise was not filled with unbelieving souls.

These were the three thousand who had crossed the country to stand for the truth they believed and now saw. And now the Word reached into their hearts and minds as it never had.

Katrina Kivi shoved her hands in the air. "Tell us, Darcy!" she screamed. "Tell us more!"

Darcy gained strength. "Through him all things were made; without him nothing was made that has been made. In him was life and that life was the light of men."

They began to cry out in agreement, white knuckles gripping the air high over their heads.

Darcy screamed the words.

"The light . . ." She grabbed some breath. "The light shines in the darkness, but . . ."

Their roar drowned out her words, but not their power. They bent their heads back like birds desperate for food, and they screamed at the black sky. The roar ran long, and even though she could hardly hear herself, Darcy hurled her words into it.

Because she couldn't wait for them. She was as impatient to speak as they were to hear. So she drilled them with her eyes and spoke the truth, knowing that they could hear with their hearts if not their ears.

"But the darkness has not understood it. He came to his own, but his own did not recognize him or receive him. Yet to all who received him, to those who believed in his name, he gave the right to become children of God."

She took a deep breath.

"The Word became flesh and made his dwelling among us. We have seen his glory, the glory of the One and the Only, who came from the Father, full of grace and truth."

She wanted to sing this. To cry it out with more than just words. The power that flowed from her mouth begged to be carried by music.

Trembling, Darcy began to sing the only words that came to mind, but she sang the song in a new melody, not the one the priests used to sing on occasion. A melody she'd heard on the radio once, sung by an artist called Agnew who had a deep, rich voice that had made her chest shake as her hand hovered over the dial.

The voice that sang the words now was hers, soft and light in a high, pure tone. But a thousand times more powerful than any voice that had ever sung the words before.

Amazing grace, how sweet the sound;
That saved a wretch like me.

The words, however thin, slammed into the audience as if God's breath were visiting Paradise and had come with the force of a hurricane. They were his words, but they were her story—and she could barely stand under the weight of their truth.

I once was lost, but now am found,
Was blind but now I see.

The song thundered from three thousand voices and shook the ground in Paradise.

"HOW LONG has she been on that stage?" Billy demanded, staring at the image Kinnard handed him as the National Guard helicopter homed in on the dark valley.

"Nearly an hour."

His hands were shaking, and despite Kelly's reassuring hand on his knee, he felt torn apart by the growing realization that Darcy had defected.

"I don't understand."

"And that's the problem," Kelly said. "Not that you don't understand, but that Johnny has this kind of power even over someone as strong as Darcy." She looked out the window. "He's a dangerous man."

Kinnard sat with arms crossed, stoic in this moment of crisis. "So that's it, then?" Billy said.

He dipped his head once. "So it seems."

"She's the one who demanded all of this," he snapped. "Begged me to follow her. Spoke of ruling the world, all that nonsense. Darcy changed the Constitution, for heaven's sake! Now she's joined the enemy?"

"She didn't start this," Kinnard said. "You did."

A chill washed down Billy's spine. Yes he did, when he wrote Black, although Kinnard was probably thinking about the decision to destroy Johnny.

"And she didn't change anything," Kinnard continued. "She just helped things along. It was always only a matter of time."

An air force sergeant leaned out of the cockpit. "Sir, where do you want me to drop it?"

"As close as you can."

"I can put it right on top of them if you want."

"Then put it on top of them!" Billy snapped.

The helicopter wound for the ground. Kelly's insistence that he take out Johnny personally rode up his throat like a black acid. Killing him outright in front of the three thousand would only result in the kind of upheaval that followed a martyr's death.

There was a kind of poetic justice to the plan Kelly had suggested.

What she couldn't know was that the hatred she'd dumped into him left Billy with more than this crawling desire to end the life of Johnny Drake once and for all.

It had also left him feeling the same about himself. And if it was true that Darcy had betrayed him, then more so. It had all started with him and it would all end with him.

But not before he ended Johnny.

CHAPTER FORTY

THE HELICOPTER seemed to come out of nowhere. Low from the north, thumping just above the trees that surrounded the town square.

Kat jerked her head skyward and shielded her eyes from gusts of wind. It was a green army chopper. Maybe the authorities had seen the change in Darcy and decided to think things over before enforcing their twenty-four-hour ultimatum.

But Darcy evidently didn't think so. She ran to the edge of the stage and cried out to the audience, "Leave!" Johnny was frozen in place, center stage, but Darcy ran to the right, waving the crowd away.

"Get out now, hide, back behind the buildings!"

They might not have followed the demands of any other person, but this was Darcy, and the crowd was running before she finished.

All but Steve, Claude, and Kat.

The helicopter hovered above the lawn, then began to sink, scattering the crowd into the corners of the town like windblown dust bunnies. The microphone on the platform toppled over, and one of the wooden chairs caught a gust and tumbled along the back of the stage before dropping from sight. The chopper settled on the lawn, smack-dab in the middle of Paradise, surrounded by boiling wisps of dust from the street.

Darcy's dress whipped around her calves, but she stood firm beside Johnny, hands now clenched into fists by her side. Kat jumped onto the stage and took a position beside them.

"Johnny?" Claude Bowers had his eyes on the helicopter's door, now swinging open.

"Keep everyone back, Claude. Go with him, Steve. Just keep them back, out of sight."

"You're sure you—"

"Go, Steve. Go now."

They both hurried off, yelling at onlookers who hung close, ordering them back, out of the way, inside.

Now only Kat and Darcy remained with Johnny, and that place of honor wasn't lost on her. Kat and Johnny.

Kelly stumbled out of the helicopter and sprawled face-first onto the lawn, followed immediately by the redheaded man who'd delivered the ultimatum. Billy Rediger. Wearing glasses. A taller man who also wore sunglasses strode around from the other side of the helicopter, looking like a Las Vegas hit man in his black sports jacket.

Billy scowled, grabbed the back of Kelly's collar, and jerked her to her feet. He lifted a gun and pressed it against her temple, drilling Kelly, then Johnny, with a dark glare.

The helicopter's blades roared and lifted the chopper into the night sky.

"Johnny!" Billy cried, frantic. "This is *your* doing, Johnny!"

Kelly had been quiet these last few days, staying clear of the limelight, helping out where needed without propping herself up as Johnny's trophy. And he'd seemed content to allow her to play that role. When Kat hadn't seen her near the stage at the outset of tonight's meeting, she'd thought nothing of it, assuming she was helping behind the scenes.

And judging by Johnny's wide blue eyes, he'd assumed the same.

The beating blades of the chopper faded. The wind settled.

"Get your hands off of her." Johnny's voice came low and with a bite that surprised Kat. He was often stern, but always gentle. But the man who stared at Billy now might cause any stranger to cross the street rather than meet him on the same sidewalk.

"Or what, Johnny? Or you'll kill me? With your bare hands? Wring my neck? I don't think so. I think this time you've ruined enough lives."

Kat stood with Johnny and Darcy, but the fact that she was the smallest, weakest voice in this particular gathering began to assert itself. She'd never feared much, but the bitterness on Billy's face qualified.

The helicopter was hovering in the distance, waiting.

"I think this time you'll come with me, away from the valley, where you and I can talk through this like reasonable men," Billy said. "If you refuse, I'll kill her."

A fresh cut marked Kelly's right cheek. She shut her eyes and bit a trembling lip. "Johnny, please."

Johnny seemed to be at a loss. He could kill Billy with the flip of a knife. With a pistol he could shoot the redhead right through his forehead before Billy had time to blink.

But Johnny had left his guns at home. He was now a man of peace.

"I'm sorry," Kelly cried. "I thought I could talk to them. I'm sorry, Johnny."

"No." Johnny walked to the platform's edge, palm extended to urge calm. "You did the right thing." He dropped to the ground and walked forward.

Darcy broke from Kat's side and ran to the front of the stage. "Stop, Johnny! What is wrong with you, Billy?"

"You are!" he screamed, shaking with rage. "You're what's wrong with me, Darcy." She thought he might start to cry. "I . . . I can't stop it now."

Kelly looked like a rag doll in Billy's grip. "Don't listen to him," she said, but she didn't sound convinced.

It was odd, Kat thought. Kelly had been Johnny's handler, not the kind who would show such weakness. She was in obvious pain. Johnny was staring at her, either so distraught that he didn't know what to do or confused.

Something wasn't right. The realization hit Kat squarely, and she shifted her right foot forward. Something about all of this was terribly wrong, but she couldn't put her finger on it.

"Johnny, be careful."

Billy looked up at Kat as if she were nothing but a nuisance, then glared at Johnny again.

"I'm going to call the helicopter back, and we're going to go now, all of us. Up to the plateau. And we'll end it there, once and for all."

"He's going to kill you, Johnny." Darcy dropped off the stage and strode forward. "Who put you up to this, Billy? What's gotten into you?"

"You did," he said.

She measured him with a skeptical eye. "Take your glasses off."

"I'll go," Johnny said, putting his hand out to back Darcy down.

But she stepped closer to him. "Take them off, Billy. You swore to love me. You swore to follow me, and I'm ordering you to take your glasses off now."

"No," the man in the jacket said, as if he were the final authority here. "I spoke to the attorney general before we left, and she made it clear that we can't leave this valley without Johnny. Not this time, Darcy."

"You heard Kinnard, Billy," she said. "He's using you. *We* have the power, not him or the bureaucrats back in Washington. But he thinks he can just step in and make the final call. He doesn't want you to remove your glasses because he's afraid I'll talk you out of this madness. And what about you, Kinnard? Why don't you ever show your cards to us? Are you afraid?"

A grin tempted the man's mouth, but he said nothing.

"Take them off, Billy."

Billy scowled. "You heard Kinnard. Johnny goes with us or Kelly dies. You can stay, but Johnny goes with us."

"No," Kinnard said again. "Darcy comes. She's now a liability."

"I said I'll go!" Johnny said, pushing past Darcy.

But Darcy wasn't ready to give in. "What is it, Billy?" she demanded, circling to her left. "What's not right here? What's wrong, Kelly?"

She was right, Kat thought again. Something wasn't right. Something about Kelly. What was missing?

"You don't need to cry, honey," Darcy said. "This is exactly what you need now, to throw your life on the line for the man who you once tortured—"

"No!" Johnny cried. "Call your helicopter, Billy. We'll settle this away from here. Call it in!"

Kinnard lifted his phone and spoke quietly into it.

Her glasses, Kat thought. Kelly's eyes were bare!

She spoke from behind them. "She isn't wearing glasses, Johnny."

This time she'd proven more than a nuisance to Billy. He turned his eyes up and stared, and his face immediately registered concern.

"Why isn't she responding?" Kat asked. There had to be an explanation.

"I've seen his eyes, Kat!" Kelly cried.

But in that cry Kat knew that something was very wrong with Kelly. There was no reason for her to defend herself, but she had.

"But have you seen mine?" Darcy demanded. "Why aren't you responding to my voice?"

"You think you own the world?" Billy cried.

But Darcy fixed on Kelly. "Fall to the ground and beg forgiveness for the horror you caused Johnny!"

Kelly's face remained stricken, but she did not react as Kat had seen others react to the voice. She didn't weep or sag at the accusation.

The helicopter started to approach.

"This is completely absurd!" Johnny snapped.

Kelly isn't who Johnny thinks she is, Kat thought. Her heart was pounding with the certainty of it, spinning back to the times she spent in Johnny's house. She more than anyone here had spent time with both of them, and all along she'd wondered why Kelly remained so distant, so mysterious.

If so, her jealousy had been partly justified.

Kat leaped off the platform, landed on light feet, and ran forward, eyes fixed on Kelly. She sprinted past Johnny right up to Billy, who held

Kelly like a puppet with one hand and had the gun pressed to her head with the other.

She was counting on the fact that she was young to save her, but as she neared Billy's crazed stance, she wondered if it would be enough.

"Johnny will help you, Billy. There's no threat here, he just needs to know the truth about Kelly so that he can go with you peacefully. They just want to know if you're being tricked by this man and Kelly and . . ."

She reached up, jerked his sunglasses from his face, and hurled them to one side.

"They just want to know the truth!"

The thumping of the helicopter grew.

"Tell me who she is, Billy," Darcy said, staring at his frenzied eyes. "You cannot lie to me. Tell me who she is now."

A look of terrible anguish gripped Billy's face and distorted it.

Kinnard turned his back and paced away, speaking softly into his phone again. The helicopter's descent stopped.

Tears ran down Darcy's face. "Are you betraying me, Billy?"

Kelly jerked away from Billy with a swing of her arm. She spun back and slapped his face. *Whack!*

"You pitiful worm, you can't even be *you* without messing it up!"

"Stop it!" Billy screamed, leveling the gun at her face. Flecks of spittle flew from his mouth and wet his lips. "Don't say that!"

"Go ahead, Billy, kill me. Crucify me. Put a bullet in my head." She breathed hard. "Be who you are!"

Johnny's face had gone white with shock.

"But you can't kill your own children, can you?" A crooked grin snaked over her mouth. "It would be like killing yourself."

"Kelly?" Johnny's voice was hardly more than a whisper. Kat wanted to stand up for him, to protect him. But the sickening turn terrified her as much as it did him.

Kelly looked over at Johnny. "You. I should have killed you in the pit." Then she faced the barrel of Billy's gun.

She reached up and took the weapon out of his hand as if he were a child. Spit to one side. Flipped the gun on end and lifted it into his face.

"I hate you, Billy."

Billy's shoulders began to shake. He lowered his arms and went limp.

"Should I kill him, Johnny? Should I put Black's author out of his misery?"

Johnny's mouth parted, but his throat was frozen.

"No," Darcy said. "We'll go. We'll go with you, please just let Billy go."

Kelly wasn't listening. "I really, really hate you, Billy."

The detonation sounded like a thunderclap, there on the lawn in Paradise. Kat flinched.

But Billy's head did not move, did not snap back, did not blow into a dozen pieces.

Kelly's, on the other hand, did.

Her chin jerked skyward, exposing her neck as the bullet slammed through her forehead. She collapsed in a heap with her head twisted at an odd angle and her lifeless eyes staring up at the night.

The round hole in her head started to smoke, and as Kat watched, still too stunned to move, Kelly's eyes turned as black as the deepest, darkest pit.

"No." Johnny sank to his knees, blue eyes leaking tears.

"Hello, ladies and gentlemen."

Kat jerked her head in Kinnard's direction. But Kinnard was nowhere to be seen.

In his place, twenty yards off, stood a man dressed in a black trench coat, two guns cocked up by his cheeks, grinning wickedly. A thin trail of smoke rose from one gun's barrel and coiled around the rim of a broad black hat.

"Welcome to Paradise," Marsuvees Black said.

CHAPTER FORTY-ONE

WHEN MARSUVEES Black spoke those so distant but familiar words, a sense of déjà vu swept through Darcy with enough force to knock her back a step.

"Welcome to Paradise."

With sudden clarity she knew the sum of it all.

However clever Black thought himself, he was proving now—by orchestrating the events over the last thirteen years, by forcing this showdown tonight in Paradise—that evil was utterly predictable.

His very presence proved that the evil spawned from the hearts of men did not walk into the sunset never to return for another go.

Billy had never rid himself of Black, so Black was back, facing him down in the same way, in the same place, wearing the same cocky-gunslinger grin.

But Darcy had also learned tonight that things would not end Black's way. Because the light did exist, and it was swimming around them with more power and brilliance than even Jonathan Frakes, vampire word-smith extraordinaire, could possibly conjure.

Nevertheless, Darcy felt powerless to stop the sharp fingers of fear that raked her spine as she stared at Kinnard, who'd become Black.

Billy hadn't yet turned. He sagged with his arms limp at his sides, eyes closed, tears silently sliding down his cheeks.

She wanted to hold him and tell him that this mess wasn't his fault, even though it was. She wanted to tell him that she was as guilty as he was, but that she'd seen the light and so could he.

And you are the key, Billy. The end of this story is all about you. You have to shine the light on this man of darkness that you breathed life into when you were a child.

Black strutted forward in the same black boots Billy had dressed him with thirteen years ago. Pleased with himself. He'd used the pages from a stolen Book of History to write himself as he saw fit, and to write more like himself into existence. For all Darcy knew, Agent Smith was one of Black's characters. He and Muness, who'd manipulated Billy, had been part of the larger plot to draw Billy and her to Washington.

Where they'd been guided by Kinnard.

Who was none other than Black himself.

It had all been perfectly set up, perfectly executed.

"Ain't it great?" he said, spinning two six-shooters in his hands. "Just like old times. We should make us a campfire. A big one like the last time. Have a little song and dance before we cook the goose."

Katrina Kivi had stepped aside and was staring at Black with huge eyes. Johnny was still on his knees, powerless in the wake of Kelly's betrayal. Both he and Billy had been reduced to shells of themselves.

Darcy could see the similarity between Black's grinning mug and Kinnard's, and how he'd worked his magic to change it. Like a wolf in sheep's clothing, the monks used to say.

"I know," he said, pacing around them slowly, guns now up by his ears. "You're wondering how deep it all goes. How much of it was actually my doing."

She refused to engage him with more than her eyes.

"How long I've walked the halls in Washington. How many people I hung from the neck until dead to make this all happen so smoothly. Why I didn't just have Kelly shove a needle through Johnny's eyes while he was asleep in his bed."

He took a deep breath and sighed long. "So many opportunities to put all three of you in the dirt."

Billy. It's all about Billy.

Darcy eased closer to Billy, whose eyes were still shut as if he couldn't bear to look at his own creation. This was why he'd been so terrified of coming back to Paradise.

She faced Black. "You could have killed us, but that wouldn't extinguish the light, would it? You can only make what's already dark darker. You need us to extinguish the light. You need him."

She'd asked it to test Black, and she knew by his slight hesitation that she was right. Billy was indeed the key.

"There is no light in him," Black said. "And for the record, speaking about the light is now illegal, thanks to you." He winked.

From the corner of her eye, Darcy saw that some of the three thousand had stepped out from their refuge and were watching. She recognized some who lived in the town. Steve and Paula.

Black still didn't seem to have any idea of the trap he'd walked into. He was too enamored with his own darkness to understand the power of the light, and up until an hour ago, she'd been in lockstep with him.

"You think you can really play all the way to the end?" Darcy said, moving closer, closer to Billy. "We were given the power to fight evil, which I now understand means to dispel the darkness."

"Is that so?" Black's eyes darkened to onyx. He exhaled hot air and it came out like charcoal smoke from a stovepipe. "Do I look like Billy's maker? I think not. I came from him, baby. So go on, dispel him. God knows he deserves it. My precious little sinner."

This was his play: to accuse Billy, who'd breathed life into him.

But there was more to that fact. It meant that Black was *dependent* on Billy. She didn't see how evil could exist without the humans who chose it.

Steve and Paula had been joined by dozens of others. Perhaps as many as a hundred, stepping out on all sides. The original citizens of Paradise were coming out to see Black again.

He glanced around and chuckled. "It's a happy, happy day."

"What do you hope to accomplish?"

"Not me, Darcy. Billy. Billy's going to kill Johnny the Baptist."

Katrina Kivi stepped in front of Johnny and faced Black, shaking but courageous. "I don't know who you think you are, but if you think anyone can just kill Johnny, you obviously don't know him."

Black grinned wide. "I know. I trained him. Do you want to die as well, little lady?"

She hesitated, then spoke in a very plain voice. "I don't think you're thinking straight."

They were coming out of the woodwork now, a couple of hundred at least, maybe three. Walking in from all sides in a large collapsing circle.

Johnny took one last look at Kelly, then stood and slowly turned his head, judging what he saw. Suddenly nervous.

"Step back, Katrina."

"Yes," Black said. "Move your skinny backside back, Kat, kitty cat. You don't want to get burned."

She did as she was told, stopping ten paces out, where the first of the circle now stood, watching. Paula, Claude, Steve, Katie—Darcy recognized them all from when she was a child, writing.

Black turned to the circle, arms spread with the six-shooters in each hand. "Thank you. Thank you all for coming. I had hoped for some, but this is too much. Have you all played nicely in my absence?"

"You shouldn't have come back," Paula said in a tone that could have frozen milk. "We have Johnny."

"But Johnny isn't who you need," Black said. "You need Billy, lover. He's the one who gave me life, you know that. And now I'm in his belly."

Darcy moved then, while Black had his back turned. She took the last two steps up to Billy, put her arms around his waist, and kissed him lightly on his lips. "I'm here, Billy," she whispered. "It's okay. I'm here, and Johnny's here, and we don't blame you. I love you more now than I did then, you hear me, Billy?"

"No, but I do," Black said. "How about a kiss for the inner child?"

Darcy ignored him. "Billy, he needs you. You're the one who feeds him and gives him life. I've seen the light and now I know it can wash away all that darkness he put inside of you. Take it, Billy. Let it fill you."

"Too late, peaches," Black chuckled. "You've just gotten reacquainted. I've been with him all along. You really think your pathetic kisses will do the trick?"

She kissed him again, deeply this time.

"Take the light, Billy."

She knew that there was nothing in her display of affection that did any more to heal him than rubbing mud in a blind man's eyes. But she wanted to comfort him and let him feel her love.

"I love you. I will always love you."

His eyes opened, and she spoke while she had his attention.

"Kill him," she whispered.

He swallowed.

"In the kingdom of light there is no darkness," she whispered under her breath so that he could feel the words as much as hear them. "I know that now."

"Step back . . ." No chuckle from Black this time.

Darcy spoke quickly. "He doesn't know it, because the darkness doesn't understand the light, but if you accept the light, he can't exist."

It was that simple. She'd spent countless hours fighting her nightmares and all along, victory was as simple as the Word, which was the Light.

"Yours wasn't the only word that became flesh, Billy. Another came and it was the Light."

He blinked.

"Step back!"

She did when she saw that Black had trained his gun on her. But she spoke loudly now, so that they could all hear her.

"Put an end to him, Billy. Once and for all, put this snake in the grave where he belongs!"

Billy's eyes turned to Black and he began to tremble again. His vocal cords sounded as if they might snap when he spoke, frantic. "Can I write him out like I wrote him in?"

"No more books!" Black said. "Gone. Good while they lasted, but gone."

"You don't need books of paper! You need the book that's in your heart! Write it!"

"Don't be a fool, boy!" Black snapped. "This is all so much nonsense. All this light-and-darkness brouhaha, please."

"She's right, Billy," Johnny said. "You can end this."

"He can end nothing," Black screamed, face red and twisted. "You think I'm stupid? This isn't just about our dandy little reunion here, it's about a whole world out there that hates your kind!"

"Because they hated him first," Johnny said.

"Don't throw that at me! I either take Johnny's head to them or they come in here with bazookas blazing like Billy ordered. I told them to give me fifteen minutes. They know that Darcy crossed over, and I've just informed them that Billy has as well. His last order to level this valley stands. From where I'm sitting, Billy can either kill Johnny like a reasonable little sinner, or he can let the whole valley go up in smoke."

Darcy's eyes darted to Billy's and she saw they were misted again. "Is that true?"

"Darcy . . ." He began to cry.

"No, shh, no more." She took his face in her hands and forced him to look at her. "Billy, I need you to listen to me. End Black's life."

"Kill me," Johnny said.

"No!" Darcy cried.

Johnny glanced down at Kelly, dead on the ground. Darcy couldn't imagine what kind of emotions must be tearing him up. He looked up.

"Take my life, it's the only way."

"Don't be ridiculous!"

Johnny eyes darted around at the circle of onlookers. But they remained silent—it wasn't their fight, not this time. The ultimate showdown had started with Billy, and it would end with him.

"There are three thousand people in this valley," Johnny cried. "I can't have their deaths on my hands! Kill me and he'll call it off."

But Darcy was ahead of him.

She spun to the three hundred. "Get out!" she screamed, turning to look at them all. "Into the mountains. Run! In that day, flee to the mountains! Run, run."

Her voice struck them like a battering ram and they ran, like mice for their holes when the lights go bright.

"Run!"

Darcy whirled back to Billy. "*Now*, Billy! Or he'll hunt us down."

Black was smiling, but a tremble had overtaken his fingers. "It's a big bomb," he said.

Johnny paced, wringing his fingers. "He's right, they'll never make it out!" He shook his head. "We don't have a choice, Darcy. This is my fate. It's my time." To Billy: "You have to kill me!"

But Billy was staring at Black, face wrinkled, breathing heavy now. Darcy couldn't tell if he was terrified or enraged. Either way, he was rooted to the ground like a tree rattled by the wind.

"No!"

The cry had come from Kat.

Tears brimmed her eyes. "I can't believe you're arguing over Johnny's life!" She marched up to Billy and stared at him, jaw set. "Now you listen to me. Three weeks ago Johnny showed me the light and it turned my world upside down. I don't know what happened when you were all kids to make this happen, but I don't care. It doesn't matter any more. What does matter is that if you can get rid of the black thing back there, you should!"

She breathed through her nostrils deliberately.

"And you can, just like they told you. Why are you still standing here? Finish him!"

Billy slowly shifted his gaze down to her. Where Darcy had failed to penetrate him using her gift, this one young woman was reaching him.

"Can I?" He sounded not even slightly confident.

"Yes!" she said. "I did!"

"Shut up, you little runt." The order from Black came out like a bitter growl. "Shut your little hole."

She spun to the man, fists by her side. "I've seen the opposite of you and now there's nothing you can do to me, so why should I shut up? Why should any of us shut up about the light?"

"Stand back, Kat," Johnny said, taking a step forward. "This isn't your—"

"It is my battle, Johnny. I won't stand by while some monster threatens the truth."

Johnny spoke quickly, sensing danger. "Of course, but you don't know what he's capable of. Stand back. This is mine!"

"He can't hurt me, Johnny," she said, looking at him. "Not really. That's why he wants me to shut up."

"Johnny's right." This from Billy, who seemed to have been awakened by Kat. He glanced at Black, whose jaw muscles worked slowly, crushing molars. His eyes darted back to Kat. "Please, this isn't your problem."

A small smile twisted her mouth. "It is now, Billy." And then, drilling him with a bright stare, "Kill Black."

Black's left hand flashed. His gun bucked in a big fist. *Boom!*

Kat flew backward a full ten feet and landed on her backside, bright stare and smile still on her face. But she was facing the dark sky now, and blood seeped into her white shirt over her heart.

It took three full seconds for Darcy to get her mind going. When she did, it told her that Black had just killed Katrina Kivi.

"No . . ." Johnny stood in a crouch, frozen by horror. His face was wrinkled in the awful realization that Kat was dead. "No . . ." He stumbled over to her and sank to his knees. "Noooooo . . ."

"I'll hunt you down and kill every last one of you," Black said in his gravelly voice.

"Do it, Billy," Darcy whispered, trembling with it all. "Kill him!"

Billy tore his stricken eyes from Kat's body and began to cry. He reminded Darcy of a man forced to kill one child to save the rest of the family. Was he so deceived? Even now?

But there was fire in his eyes. The look of rage was so sharp, so visceral, that Darcy shied back a step.

"Do it, Billy," she said, softly now. Then again: "Do it."

"Yes, Billy, do me. Please, Papa, do me in. Put a gun to my head and shoot me dead." Black grinned, but sweat had beaded his upper lip.

"Ahhhhhh!" Billy's mouth gaped, then clamped shut. He growled again through clenched teeth. His whole body was shaking badly, from his head to his knees. But he didn't move. Didn't embrace the light. Didn't finish Black.

"You abused me . . ." he breathed.

"Did I?"

Now in a cry of agony. "You violated me! You kissed me . . . You came in . . ."

Black's grin spread wide. "Yes. And you made me, baby. How about another one?"

With those words, Billy froze. Darcy had never seen the look of such anguish on a face before. She was tempted to run to him and tell him it was okay, he didn't have to do this now.

Johnny jumped to his feet. He leaned into his words, red-faced. "Kill him!"

Billy's body was coiled like a large spring about to break.

Darcy opened her mouth to stop him.

Billy wrenched his feet from the earth and rushed forward. Right at Black. Before the man whom Billy had spawned could react with more than a blink, Billy grabbed him by his hair with both hands, thrust his head forward, and slammed his mouth onto Black's.

He screamed, a blood-freezing shriek of fury and regret and torment.

Black's lips peeled back as if the force of the scream itself had pushed them off his teeth like a blast of wind. His mouth was open so that Billy's teeth appeared to have locked onto Black's pearly white enamel.

Screaming into his mouth.

And then the scream took shape. Light, beaming from the gaps between their teeth.

Darcy's throat had locked tight. Light was streaming from Billy into Black's mouth, carried by that scream. Which could only mean that Billy himself had embraced the light.

Black dropped the six-shooters in either hand and flung his arms up to break Billy's grip on his hair.

But Billy's grip was iron, and his rage only intensified as he raged against the evil that he himself had given breath to.

Still the light flowed, rushing into Black's mouth, blasting into his throat and his lungs and his belly.

Black began to flail his arms, frantically jerking and pulling to get away from the light. Like a rat desperate to pull away from the trap whose metal jaws had clamped on its head in the middle of the night.

Black was a bigger man by a head, but now that head was locked in Billy's vice, and his legs began to thrash. The light streamed out from the corners of Black's eyeballs first. Then his eyeballs were gone, replaced by cords of light that shot into the night sky. His fingernails cracked, spilling white. Then his skin, cracking to reveal the light that had ravaged the darkness beneath his flesh.

The blazing hot light burned Black to a crisp from the inside out, reducing him to ash that fell away in clumps, leaving only the man's head in Billy's hands.

Still he screamed into Black's gaping teeth.

The head—skull, hair, and flesh—imploded, became black powder, and drifted to the ground. Only Black's teeth stubbornly remained, as if trying to bite back at Billy's teeth in retribution.

Then the demon's clackers fell as well, and the scream died in Billy's throat.

The teeth landed in the pile of ash, one at a time, *plop-plop-plop-plop*. Like bullets. A muted drum roll that announced the end of Marsuvees Black.

He was finished.

Dead by Billy.

Dead by the light.

Darcy was sure that this time he was gone forever.

Billy opened his eyes and faced them all. Johnny looked slowly over the forms that lay around their feet. Kelly, his lover. Kat, this young disciple who'd given her life to save theirs. Surely the pain in his chest would tear any lesser man in two.

They stared at each other, all three of them, stunned by the light's display of power, broken by the price paid.

"The bomb," Darcy said.

Johnny moved fast, scooping up Katrina Kivi's body in both arms. "Run for the overlook."

Darcy could hear the roar of engines high above. For all they knew the bomb was already in the air . . .

"Run!" she cried.

And they ran.

CHAPTER FORTY-TWO

Day Twenty-Two

DARCY STOOD between two large pine trees at the cliff's edge staring down at what had been Paradise, Colorado, just last evening. The blast had gutted half of the town, smashing everything from the Episcopal church to Smither's Barbeque into blackened splinters. Most of the wreckage was still on fire, and the orchards were incinerated from the edge of the blast radius to the ridge line. The concussion from the detonation had stripped the trees above them.

And when they'd climbed high enough to clear the trees that blocked their vantage, the town was nothing but raging fires in the night.

Paradise was lost.

Johnny, Billy, and Darcy had spent the night in the cabin, where young Katrina's body still lay on an old bed covered by a blanket. Johnny had lain beside her and cried himself to sleep.

They woke early and worked their way down to this white cliff edged by stubborn pines overlooking the entire valley.

The burnt-out husks of several vehicles lay on their sides like tossed toy cars. Flames had swept through the houses that surrounded the main town before finally petering out near the trees. Some of the buildings still stood at the extremities of the town, and some walls had survived the blast, but nothing was worthy of more than a bulldozer.

Three large green army helicopters sat on the black lawn where Marsuvees Black had killed Kelly last night. Twenty or thirty troops were picking through the smoldering ruins, presumably looking for bodies.

It's a nightmare, Darcy thought. *I'm going to wake up now because this is all just a nightmare.*

"It's my doing," Billy said next to her.

She looked at him, reminded that this was not a nightmare. "No, Billy, it's our doing. Yours and mine."

"No," Johnny said. "Black did this. And you killed him, Billy."

They stared in silence for a long minute. They'd already decided what to do, but standing over the scene now, their plans felt pointless. What was done was done.

"Do you think anyone was hurt?" Billy asked.

Yes, of course, that was the question on all of their minds.

Darcy took out her cell phone. Flipped it open. "We'll know soon enough."

"The Net will ultimately say the government did what it had to do," Johnny said. "And the world will remember Paradise as a tragic but unavoidable step on the path to global harmony."

Darcy turned away from the valley. "All in the name of tolerance."

"When you enforce tolerance it's natural to be intolerant of those who stand against you," Johnny said. "Someone has to be intolerant of the Hitlers and Stalins of the world. I don't blame them for that. They're just doing what they think is right."

Darcy cringed at the words. *They* had been her and Billy, not some faceless government.

"So. Christians are now criminals . . ."

"It's not about a religion." Johnny looked at Darcy. "Is it?"

Despite an initial backlash against the National Tolerance Act from all the expected quarters, it was supported on the Net by a strong majority. And that was the Pandora's box Darcy and Billy had now opened.

She swallowed. "No. It's about Jesus, who had the audacity to stand on a hill and say, 'I am the Way, and no one will find their way into the kingdom without me, and without me you will be condemned to hell.' The majority of the world now believes that's hate speech."

Darcy hit the speed dial on her phone. "But he's love, not hate."

The phone rang twice before Annie Ruling answered.

"Darcy?" Annie sounded surprised.

"Hello, Annie."

"Hold on." Darcy could hear her tell someone that she needed to take this call, and then she was back.

"You're alive."

"More than you know," Darcy said. "You thought I was dead?"

"Well . . . we had our doubts. Where in the world have you been? Do you have any idea what kind of mess this has all become?"

"Actually I was hoping you could tell me."

"What do you know?"

"I know that Paradise was incinerated last night. What I don't know is if anyone was hurt in the blast."

"One dead that we know of. They were apparently warned. By you?"

"By Billy and me."

The phone felt heavy in Darcy's hand.

"So . . ."

"So," Darcy agreed.

"You're not telling me that the reports are accurate."

"If they're saying that Billy and I have seen the light and joined Johnny, then yes, the reports are accurate. We all survived the blast. Brian Kinnard—or should I say Marsuvees Black?—killed Katrina Kivi. We have her body with us."

Annie Ruling remained silent. Her world had just become rather more complicated. She had to choose her words carefully, Darcy knew. What

Johnny, Darcy, and Billy could do as a team was hardy thinkable. Clearly Annie didn't want them as enemies.

"And Kinnard?"

"He's dead," Darcy said.

"We haven't recovered a body."

"You won't. Is any word of the attack on the Net?"

"A few images, nothing except for some footage that appears to be the faithful whipped up into a frenzy. Some footage taken during the detonation, nothing that changes anything if that's what you're asking. The spin is all in our favor."

As they'd predicted.

"I was wrong, Annie. Just so you know, I was wrong."

"I don't think so, but it's moot at this point, isn't it?"

"We have a deal for you."

"I'm listening."

"You owe Billy and me a favor. You may not feel obligated to honor your promise to me, but I did deliver what you asked, and you do owe me."

"Go on."

"No one knows if Johnny, Billy, or I survived the attack. Let the world think we're dead. And don't come after us. It's better that way for now."

"For now?"

"Paradise," Johnny said, as a reminder.

She nodded at Johnny, who was watching her from behind his sunglasses. "Rebuild Paradise from the ground. Pay damages to the tune of a million dollars to each resident."

A pause. "And in exchange?"

"I'm not finished. Drop any case against anyone who participated in this debacle. The three thousand go home peacefully. If any lost their cars, buy them new ones."

"And?"

"And in exchange we will consider your obligation to us met, and we will agree not to undermine this administration or any of those on the council. You do realize that we could bring any individual down quite easily."

"Is that a threat?"

"No, just making sure you realize we aren't powerless. Does this work, or do I have to come out there and speak more frankly with you?"

Annie chuckled on the other end.

"I'll have to make some calls—"

"No, I want this agreed to now. You promised me far more."

"You step foot back in Washington and the deal is off."

"Agreed," Darcy said. "And Katrina Kivi's mother gets a federal stipend of five hundred thousand dollars to help with her daughter's funeral."

Annie was silent.

"Agreed?"

"Fine."

"I want to verify all of this."

"You're sure you want to do this, Darcy? We could have done so much together, you and I."

"We could have. But I'm seeing things differently today. It was fine working with you, Annie."

"And you, Darcy."

"I hope we don't cross paths again. It could be a problem."

"I understand."

"Good-bye, Annie." She hung up.

"So she agreed, I take it?" Billy asked.

Darcy took his hand in hers. He was the sinner but then so was she, and no less guilty than he. She would love him and cover a multitude of his sins, because she liked Billy very much.

No, she loved him.

Darcy squeezed his hand. "She agreed."

"How many do you think there are?" Billy asked, facing the burnt-out valley.

"How many of what?"

"Kinnards. Kellys. Makes you wonder if one of them has a 666 stamped on the crown of his head."

"There are three fewer than yesterday," Johnny said, turning with him.

They let the statement stand.

Darcy sighed. "Now what?"

"Now we run for the hills," Johnny said. "We run for the hills and we pray that the end will come quickly."

THE END

Then you will be handed over to be persecuted and put to death, and you will be hated by all people because of me.

At that time many will turn away from the faith and will betray and hate each other, and many false prophets will appear and deceive many people.

The love of most will grow cold, but he who stands firm to the end will be saved. And this good news of the kingdom of light will be declared in the whole world as a testimony to all.

And then the end will come.

MATTHEW 24:9–14

To dive deeper into how
the themes and issues in *Sinner*
are unfolding in our world today, visit
Teddekker.com and click on the
"Free Speech" link.

The Beginning and the End

GREEN

COMING SEPTEMBER 1, 2009

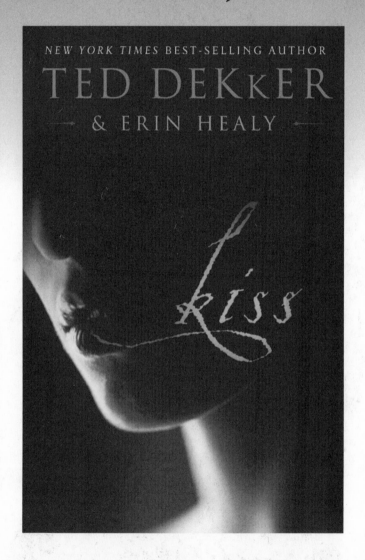

prologue

The view from my therapist's window is unremarkable. Four stories down, the parking lot blacktop ripples under waves of Texas's blazing summer heat. I stand here facing the view because it's easier to look at than the two men in the office behind me. There is dear Dr. Ayers, the wisest old soul I have ever met. He might be eighty, judging by that wrinkled cocoa skin and his head of hair whiter than cotton, but he's agile as a fifty-year-old. My beloved brother, Rudy, is also here. He has kept me tethered to my sanity in ways that should earn him sainthood.

Rudy comes to these sessions because he knows I need him to.

I come—have been coming for weeks now—because I am trying to put the past behind me.

But today I am here because tonight I will see my father for the first time in five months. My encounters with Landon are hard enough in the best of circumstances. They always end the same, with flaring tempers and harsh words and fresh wounds. But tonight, I must confront Landon. Not about my past, but about his future.

Yes, I call my father by his first name. The distance it creates between us helps to dull my pain.

"So your dilemma," Dr. Ayers says to my back, "is that you fear the consequences of confronting him could be worse than the consequences of staying silent."

I nod at the pane of glass. "Of course, I'd rather avoid everything. Even Rudy thinks I should wait until I know . . . more. But if I'm right, and I don't speak up now . . ." Why am I here? I have made a mountain out of a molehill and am wasting everyone's time. I should drop this. "Landon probably won't even listen to me. Not the way he listens to you, Rude."

"He listens to you too," Rudy says. Always looking for the positive spin.

The truth is, Landon does not listen to me. But Rudy, who is deputy campaign manager of Senator Landon McAllister's bid for the United States presidency, is following in the man's footsteps and so has his undivided attention. Also, Rudy doesn't look a thing like our mother, as I do. Mama was a Guatemalan beauty with a *café-au-lait* complexion. I have had her personality and her looks since the day my head of thick black hair came in. Even today, I wear my hair short and windblown, the way she did. I have her leggy height, her long stride, her laugh.

Against all odds, our father's recessive Irish genes won the genetic dispute over Rudy. As for me, I have always believed it is painful for my father to look at me.

"And I don't think she should gloss over this," Rudy says to the therapist. "I think Shauna should step very carefully. Avoid burning more bridges with Dad, if it can be helped. If she's right, God help us all."

I finally turn to look at my brother. "It's not my goal to burn anything, Rudy, even though I'll never have what you have with Landon." This truth pains me more than the truth of what I've learned. And what I've learned, partial though it may be, is monstrous.

The tension headache that has started at the top of my spine spreads its fingers over the back of my head. The sickness I feel right now might come from what I suspect, or it might be rooted in my certainty that he will reject me again tonight.

Yes, I'm pretty sure that I am nauseated by the prospect of another rejection.

I'll never forget the first time my father turned his back on me, though the second time was more painful, and though all the times since have clumped together in a unified throbbing heartache.

Rudy was the unwitting cause of Landon's first abandonment. My brother came into the world when I was seven, and our mother died nineteen minutes after his birth. I remember not being able to breathe when I heard she was gone. I honestly thought that I might die those first few hours, my mother and I both dead in the same day all because of this baby boy.

My father said it was God's fault, though he seemed to blame Mama's passing on me. I guess I was the more tangible target.

After Mama's doctor delivered the crushing news, my father turned away mumbling something about my uncle and carried Rudy out of the hospital without me. Uncle Trent found me two hours later, hiding behind a chair in the waiting room.

Truth not only hurts, it shames: at the time, I wished Rudy were dead. The day I stood at the head of Mama's casket, I wondered what would happen to Rudy if I covered his squalling face tight with that silky blue blanket. Wishing that the balance of the universe might require Mama to come back.

It took just one night for me to understand that Rudy's heart had been broken into more pieces than my own. The tears he cried for Mama came from some well that would not dry up. That night I fed him a bottle of warm milk and took him into my bed, promising to keep Mama's memory alive in this little boy who'd never met her.

I'm twenty-eight now, and I have long since realized that the wounds of rejection do not heal with time. They reopen at the lightest touch, as deep as the first time they were inflicted. The pain is as real as flash floods in the wet season here in Austin, overwhelming and unstoppable.

The pain, even when I can successfully numb it, has kept me at a distance from people and God. Now and then I consider the irony of this: how it came to be that my mother's God, who once seemed so real and comforting to me, managed to die when she did.

So many deaths in one night.

And here I am, expecting yet another tonight. The death of hope. For most of my life, hatred of my father and hope of gaining his affection have lived in stressful coexistence behind my ribs.

I'm crying and didn't even notice I had started.

Dr. Ayers's voice is gentle. "Do you believe your father is culpable in this matter you are investigating?"

The question behind the question stabs at the tender spot in me that longs for Landon's love. *Do you believe your father is guilty of anything more than hurting you? Do you care about truth or only about the past?*

Somehow I care about both. Is that possible?

"I believe he is capable. More than that . . ." I sniff. "I don't know yet. Very soon, though, I will. Very soon."

Dr. Ayers leans back in his leather chair and folds his wrinkled hands across his slender stomach.

"Tell me: what do you want this confrontation to do for you?"

Several possible answers rush me. I want to be wrong, in fact. I want Landon to tell me that none of what I suspect is true. I want my father to reassure me that I have nothing to worry about, that he is an upright man who would never do anything so foolish, so hurtful. Nothing like what he has done—

Rudy's eyes bore into the side of my head, and the truth of what I really want punches me in the stomach. I step to my chair and sit.

"I want to bring him down," I say before I think it through. "I want him to know what betrayal feels like. I want to get him back."

My tears turn into sobs. I can't help it. I can't stop.

Rudy places his hand on my knee. Not to urge me to stop bawling, but to remind me that he is by my side.

Hatred for my father did not become a part of my life until the second time he turned his back on me.

I was eleven. Patrice had been my stepmother for three days when she took over my upbringing, with Landon's permission. He claimed Rudy and she got me.

Her style of parenting, if it can be called that, involved locking me in closets and burning the scrapbooks my mother had made me and refusing to feed me for a day at a time. As I grew I quit trying to make sense of such behavior and simply became more defiant. She responded by graduating to more extreme measures. There was no hiding our animosity for each other.

I suspect I reminded her, too, of my mother.

When she turned brazen enough to beat and burn me, though, I broke down and told Landon. I showed him the triangular burns on the inside of my left arm, imprinted by Patrice's steam iron for my failure to pull my clean clothes out of the dryer before they wrinkled.

Landon handed me a tube of ointment and turned away, saying, "If you ever go to such lengths to lie about my wife again, I'll bandage those myself. And you won't like my touch."

My wife. He had always called Mama *my love.*

Dr. Ayers makes no attempt to calm me. He has said before that crying is the best balm. Eventually I fumble through my mind for the words to justify what I have said.

"If Landon pays for what he's done, I'll get closure."

"On what?" says Dr. Ayers.

"On my past."

He takes a few moments to respond. Rudy produces a tissue out of thin air and I try to compose myself.

"So you're saying that closing yourself off from your past is what you need in order to move on with your life."

There is more than an attempt at clarity in Dr. Ayers's tone—a challenge perhaps.

"Yes." I swipe at my nose with the tissue. "That's exactly what I'm saying. I want to put the past behind me."

"By inflicting on your father what he has inflicted on you. By betraying him, you said."

"No. By forcing him to remember me."

"Ah! I see. So when he remembers you, then you will have accomplished your goal and can forget your past."

His words fill me with confusion. The way he says it, I have this all wrong. But in my mind, my goal is—was—clear. Isn't that how it works? Deal with the past, get justice, make the pain go away?

"Something like that," I say.

Dr. Ayers nods as if he sees everything clearly now. He rises and comes around the desk, propping himself against the front of it and leaning toward me.

The doctor reaches out with an aging hand and touches my shoulder. "Would you mind if I gave you an alternative theory to consider?"

Honestly, I have no idea.

Dr. Ayers straightens. "It is possible that your plan will only root you more deeply in the pain of your past, not separate you from it."

My confusion mounts. "So how do you suggest I put my past behind me?"

"It is behind you, dear. And that's where it will be forever. You can't make it vanish—"

"But I want to. I believe I can."

"By creating more pain? The mathematics of that isn't logical."

"I can't just ignore it!"

"No, that's true."

"But you think I shouldn't confront Landon."

"Oh, I'm not making any judgment about what you should do, Shauna. I'm only talking about your motivations. What do you *really* want?"

"To *forget*. I want to forget every single, stinging moment that was inflicted on me by people who were supposed to *love* me. I want someone to take these memories away from me."

Dr. Ayers wags a finger in my direction, smiling. "I felt that way once."

I take a steadying breath.

"You know I used be a reverend before I began helping people here?" He gestures to the modest office. "Ministry of a different but no less valuable kind. Got thrown out of my pulpit by some folks who said they loved God but hated his black children. I spent a lot of years feeling the way you do now—that if I looked far and wide enough, I'd find a way to erase both the blight of my memory and the stink of people I held responsible for my pain."

He leans forward again, encroaching on my space. "But I discovered something better. Shauna, your history is no less important to your survival than your ability to breathe. In the end, you can only determine whether to saturate your memories with pain or with perspective. Forgetting is not an option. I tell you the truth now: Pain was not God's plan for this life. It is a reality, but it is not part of the plan."

I exhale. "God and I aren't exactly on speaking terms. Especially not about his plans for my life."

"Pain or perspective, Shauna. That's all that's within your control."

I drop my head into my hands, feeling more certain than ever that absolutely nothing is in my control.

In spite of Dr. Ayers's warning, I decided to talk to Landon tonight. Regardless of the outcome—closure for me or more pain for him—I hoped the truth would count for something.

Instead, when the moment came, I tripped all over my words. Landon's larger than life and had the upper hand from the outset. Instead of staying on topic, I took offense at something he said. I can hardly remember now, something about a man's world, and when I tried to set him straight he cut me to the floor with a few harsh words.

So here I am once again, driving fast through the night on a rain-slicked road away from yet another argument with Landon. And as he has so many times before, Rudy has come along to calm my explosive temper. He is smiling slightly at my ranting. Sometimes I think he finds me entertaining.

The hum of tires kissing asphalt through water soothes my anxious heart. "I don't know why I let him roll over me like that, Rude."

"You handled yourself just fine. I thought you showed remarkable restraint."

"But not enough."

"Okay, not enough." Truth does not make Rudy flinch. My car follows a downward slope onto a bridge, pointing me east into Austin.

"Underneath it all, Dad worries about you, you know."

I look at Rudy. No, no I didn't know. Just as Rudy doesn't know about my scars from Patrice's iron. I've told Dr. Ayers, but not Rudy. He and Patrice get along.

"What does he worry about?" The relative unsafety of my little car? The condition of my heart?

My heart is even more mangled than the skin under my arms.

So why have I never stopped wishing? Wishing that Landon would only—

"Watch out!"

Rudy's cry comes at the same moment that glaring lights from another vehicle blind me. It all happens so quickly that I don't have time to think about swerving or stopping.

A horn is blaring, and voices are screaming, and then the terrible sound of metal smashing into metal.

Daddy . . .

This is the last plea for help that fills my mind before the world ends.

He shifted his cell phone to the opposite ear and stared at the hospital entrance through the windshield of his car. The parking lot lights were still on, though dawn had broken the horizon behind him.

"She was in surgery six hours," he said. "Internal bleeding."

"Where is she *now?*"

"Private room."

"But still in a coma, correct?"

"Yes." Ironic that Shauna McAllister had dodged death only to end up in a coma. "I can get to her easy enough now. She'll be dead within the hour."

"No. Change of plans. Our hands are being forced. I'll explain later, but for now she stays alive."

"She's too big a risk to just—"

"What's her prognosis?"

"Too early to tell. She could be in a coma for a day or for a year."

"Or forever. Even if she comes out, she could have brain damage."

"Yes, that's possible."

"So she stays alive for now. She's not a threat as long as she's unconscious."

"And when she comes around?"

"With any luck, she'll forget everything."

"I don't do business with luck."

"You will today. Like I said, our hands are being forced in this. Her condition buys us time. I'll call Dr. Carver; he'll have options for us. If we have to change course, we do it later."

"What if she remembers?"

"If she remembers, she dies."

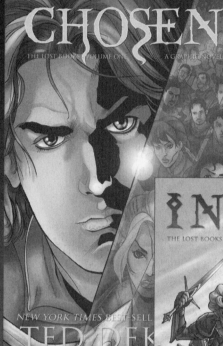

THE BOOKS OF

THE CIRCLE TRILOGY

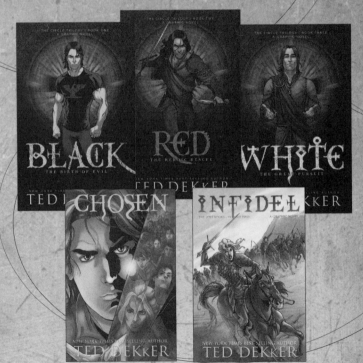

COMING NOVEMBER 2008

THE GRAPHIC NOVELS

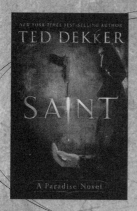 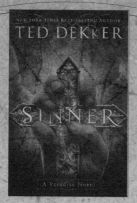 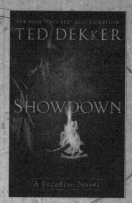